The Eternal series

Cinders & Rime

Ila Quinn

Dedication

"To my loving parents, wonderful siblings, and my supportive friends, this story was born from vivid dreams, strong emotions and a belief.
We can achieve whatever we set our mind to.
Always remember that."

Ila Quinn

"Life doesn't get easier as you get older. You just learn to manage it better."

Sir Volknor Costello – Cinders & Rime

Contents

CHAPTER ONE

In the beginning

One of Asira's earliest memories began when she was about five. She was a cute little girl with a button nose, green eyes to match her dad's and the same brunette hair as her mother. She had always been a daddy's girl. She had no choice. It had always been just her and her dad, Kai.

She was very inquisitive, especially for a five-year-old, and questioned every action and every decision her dad made, not out of rudeness but because she was curious and wanted to understand everything in the world. As a kid, Kai was just as inquisitive. Maybe that is why he was so good at his job.

A lot of the time when she was bored, she would fantasise about her mother. What she would look like now and what she would sound like. Asira lay across her dad's bed gazing fondly at a photo of her parents as children.

"She was quite beautiful. You look just like her."

"How long did you know mommy?"

"We were friends all our lives. She only lived a few houses down the road."

"What was she like?"

"Well, let me see…" Kai stepped back from his open wardrobe and sat on the edge of the bed. "She was caring and sweet. She was adventurous and so loud all the time. She never could sit still. She loved ice skating."

Immediately Asira's eyes lit up. "I want to learn ice skating. I'll be as good as mommy."

"Will you now? It's quite tough. It takes a lot of practice."

"What was her name?"

"Crystal."

Asira slipped off the bed and walked towards the photo of her mother. "What happened to mommy? Everyone in school has a mommy and daddy. I sometimes feel left out."

"Your mommy was… Asira, it's not a good story. I would rather not talk about it now." He stepped into the ensuite as a pounding headache quickly swept across his forehead.

"But dad, what do I tell people if they ask about mommy."

A familiar sick feeling crept up his oesophagus. Shivers ran up and down his arms, his spine. It had been a few years since he had felt this way. But Crystal's birthday was approaching, and he couldn't help but think about the events that had torn his family apart.

"Dad, what's wrong with your eyes?"

Gazing into the mirror he witnessed his eyes change colour. Beastly yellow irises were staring back at him. His stomach was twisting at the thought of losing control to the vile curse. It was starting all over again. The mere mention of the past sent a terrifying ripple through his body.

"How about a story?" He squinted and pushed Asira out of the bathroom. "Go find a book. It's getting close to bedtime."

Making a U-turn for the ensuite, Kai stood over the sink again. He took in slow, deep breaths. He couldn't lose control. Not now.

Not in front of Asira. She was only five years old… He reached for his mobile and hovered over Erika's number. What would she say? She wouldn't leave him alone. She would make herself comfortable and stay for several days until she was happy with his progress. He took in another slow, deep breath. Maybe the feeling would pass.

Asira ran back into the room and leapt onto the bed. "I want you to read the book Erika brought for me." She handed him the glossy book. "There are doggies on the cover."

Kai glanced at the book with contempt. "Are you sure this is the story you want? It's only silly myths from Velosia."

"But I want to read it. I want to know more about Velosia. Please!" She crawled on her knees across the bed.

"Okay but one story and then bed." What was Erika thinking buying this book? His nightmare started with this story.

"Dad? Your eyes are still yellow. What's wrong?"

"It's a spell. One story and then bed." His body was still shivering and Asira noticed this. She took the fleece blanket from the end of the bed and wrapped it around his shoulders and cuddled in close to him. Kai was praying internally that nothing bad would happen. He never wanted to show Asira the dark side of Velosia. He cleared his throat and opened the book to the first page. "In the beginning there was an island filled with beautiful flowers and mysterious creatures."

Asira was gazing intently at the beautiful illustrations.

"Four tribes, each represented by one of the four original elements, lived in harmony with nature. They worshipped many gods and carved many statues to honour them. The villages grew and grew and eventually there were hundreds of villages covering the island."

"Look!" Asira pointed to the images on the next page of a flame, a teardrop, a swirl and a jagged rock. "The elements – fire, water, wind and earth."

"As the villages grew, the resources shrank. People began to fight over water and crops. Then one day, a terrible war broke out between the villages. The war raged on for months tearing families apart and killing many people. One day a lonely young man wandered down to a nearby lake. He prayed to the gods for days and begged for their help. He was so desperate to end the suffering that he offered his own life as sacrifice. Then one night under the light of the moon, the mother of the gods appeared before the young man."

Asira gazed at the silver apparition on the following page with a flowing dress and graceful hair.

"The young man was granted incredible power. He cured the sick and injured. He made sure there was enough water and crops for all the villages. And as quickly as it started, the war suddenly ended."

The images were simply drawn but the colours were vibrant and dramatic. Kai was entranced by the imagery – a figure encased in a brilliant white glowing light and the villagers bowing down before him. This was the bitter-sweet part of his legacy. A valiant hero risked his life to save his fellow man. He had heard this story a thousand times growing up. But it was only in recent years that the story was causing such trauma for him.

He flicked to the next page and the imagery became more sinister. The young man was no longer surrounded by the brilliant white light but now was doubled over in agony. Thunder clouds raged overhead, eclipsing the moon light.

"Shortly after the fighting ended, the young man realised that the great power that was bestowed upon him was too mighty for one person. He prayed and pleaded for his suffering to end. Once again, the mother of the gods appeared before him. She gave the young man two options. He could die and go to heaven or he could live on as a guardian spirit of the forest. Afraid of the first option the young man chose to become a guardian spirit of the forest."

It had been years since he had read the storybook *Tales of Velosia*. It wasn't a part of Velosia he ever wished to share with Asira. He was only ever concerned with protecting her from all the bad in the world and if that meant keeping his past a secret, then so be it.

Kai stared intently at the next image. The page was divided by a thin inky black line with a full moon drawn in the centre. The forest was sketched to appear dark and eerie. A black wolf ran left through the forest while a white wolf ran in the opposite direction. "The young man's soul became split into two majestic beings and he became the protector of the forest." Kai closed the book.

"Is that it?"

'*Is that it?*' Her words repeated in his head. His whole adult life was spent running from this story and this was only the beginning of a cursed tale. Even now shivers still rippled across his skin. He just hoped his eyes returned to normal. "Yes, that's it for tonight. Time for bed, Asira."

"Aw, but Dad, can we have one more story?"

"No. Maybe some other time." Suddenly the doorbell rang. Who could be calling so late at night? "Get to bed, Asira." Kai shut the door behind him and ran to the mirror in the hall letting out a sigh of relief seeing his eyes were back to normal.

Asira peeked through the crack and watched as her dad cautiously opened the front door. Silently, she crept down the stairs after him.

"Master Draskule, strange to see you in England, of all places. What are you doing here?"

"Good evening, Kai. I do apologise for arriving at your home at such an ungodly hour. I hope I have not woken the little one, but I do need to talk to you about something important."

She could only hear the voice as the figure remained hidden. Her dad stepped back, allowing a cloaked figure to enter the house.

"Hello Asira. It is lovely to finally meet you." He glanced through the banister. The man's hair was dark and tightly cut like a soldier.

"Are you a wizard? You are wearing a cloak just like one," asked Asira.

He crossed his arms into the long draping sleeves and followed Kai into the sitting room. She leapt down the stairs and ran to behind her dad, gripping his pants tight.

"Asira, this is Master Draskule. He is an old friend from the army."

"Please Kai, I hope to keep this informal. We have known each other a long time."

"Of course, Draskule. Take a seat. Tell me, what have you come to talk about?" said Kai gesturing to the comfortable and worn couches.

"It's Lady Pearse. She was diagnosed with a rare type of cancer a few months back." Draskule said sitting down with a nod.

"Oh, I didn't know. I am sorry to hear that."

"She is getting treatment on Kalis Island, but she is refusing any other type of help." Draskule sat forward with his hands clasped together. "Because of her race, they expect her to live for years but it is hard to tell. It is slowly eating away at her."

"I don't understand what this has to do with me."

"Master Adams is concerned that with Lady Pearse unwell, this could lead to an imbalance with the vampire nation. He wants to secure a strong presence in The Council to provide some sort of security to the other nations. Master Adams has brought me on to The Council and has requested you also join."

"What? Me join The Council? I've never really been interested in politics." Kai leaned back in the chair with Asira still clinging onto him.

"He feels the presence of a strong warlock and a strong sorcerer who have defied all odds and survived the war would be a great addition to The Council, as well as a few other names."

"Who are these names?" Kai furrowed his eyes almost knowing what Draskule was about to say.

"He has also instructed Dame Airies, Sir Volknor, Sir Rowan, Master Erika Roberts and Sir Inferno to join but only the first two have accepted his offer."

"So, I'm a replacement for Inferno?"

"Far from it actually. Master Adams has ranked you as the top sorcerer in all of Velosia. He wants you to continue your training and become an ambassador of The Council and gain the trust of the royal families once again."

Kai leaned forward and lowered his head for a moment. "I don't know. I have so much to do here." He peeked through his arm at Asira's green eyes staring back at him.

"Master Adams understands your responsibilities and has said you can be as flexible as you want or have to be. Please think about it and come back to us by the end of the week." Draskule rose from the chair and crossed his arms into his sleeves. "We would be honoured to have you join us on The Council."

Kai escorted him to the front door while Asira curled into a pillow on the couch. After a few short minutes he returned and exhaled deeply as he leaned on the door frame.

"Who was that man?"

He glanced at his little girl. She was all he had in this world. He picked her up and wrapped her in his arms. "He is just an old friend with a new job offer."

"Are you going to take it?" she asked, burying her head into his shoulder.

"I don't know. I might. Why? Would you miss me if I went to work? I'd miss you, but nothing would change. I would still be here in the morning and at night. I would still bring you everywhere and collect you. I would still make you all your favourite meals. I would just be gone in the day instead of sitting around the house waiting for you to come home."

She glanced up from his shoulder. "Can I come to Velosia with you?"

"I suppose. I don't think we've said hello to mommy in a while. Would you like to go?"

"I can make cookies."

"That's a great idea. We can bake some cookies. She'd love them. Now let's get you to bed, little one."

CHAPTER TWO

The Little Sorceress

K ai stood in front of the mirror with a thermometer in his hand. He had been constantly checking his temperature all week. He had been carefully distracting Asira from asking any questions relating to his past or to her mother. What was he doing going for a job back in Velosia? He had summoned all his courage five years ago and escaped the war-stricken hellhole with his baby daughter. But the memories were still haunting him. He loved his daughter but every time he gazed upon her sweet face, he saw Crystal smiling back at him.

Asira spun in a circle and curtsied like a princess. "Okay Dad, I'm ready."

Kai crouched down beside her, a wooden staph materialising in his hand. "This is a spell that comes from the heart." He poked her chest. "It's a conjuring spell which will open up a portal to Velosia."

Her eyes opened wide in amazement as two large doors appeared before them. Various orange colours – mango, tangerine, marigold, amber, marmalade and sandstone colours – swirled like whipped cream. "Daddy, can you show me how to make this?"

"This is a difficult spell. When you are a lot older you will have no problem casting this portal."

She joyfully watched her footsteps create ripples through the honey, carrot and rustic colours.

His eyebrow rose as he glanced down at her with a warm smile. Even though she looked like her mother, there was nothing he would change. He loved his daughter with all his heart and would do anything to keep her safe and happy. "Every sorcerer has a unique colour to their soul and only some spells echo the colour of their soul. Orange just so happens to be the colour of my soul."

"What's the colour of my soul, Dad?"

"I don't know. We haven't figured that out yet."

Her eyes gazed fondly back at him. She may never have known her mother, but she knew she was lucky to have her dad. "Dad," her fingers pinched his hand, "do you think I'll become a great sorceress like you?"

Kai stopped and crouched down to her level. He did everything he could to keep her safe and happy, even if that meant upsetting himself slightly. "I know you will be a great sorceress. And do you know why? Because you have me helping you every step of the way, but you also have mommy watching over you wherever you go." She followed Kai's pointing finger tilting her head back and gazed at the continuous blend of colours. "Now, let's get this over with. When we get home, we have to write your name on all your new schoolbooks."

It had been a while since he had returned to Velosia. At one point, he had promised himself he would stay away no matter what, but the desire to see his beloved again was too great. They stepped through the portal into a long and wide hallway with green marble flooring and several white columns. Kai led the way to the end of the corridor and knocked firmly on the door.

A man in a black cloak swung opened the door with great enthusiasm. "Master Soniar, it is lovely to see you again!" He ardently shook Kai's hand.

"Master Adams, it is a pleasure to be here. Please meet my daughter, Asira."

"The little sorceress! It is an honour to meet such a fine young lady." Adams crouched slightly and shook her hand. "I made sure to bring a colouring book and some crayons and markers today. Feel free to use them."

"Hello sir," Asira curtsied, "it's lovely to meet you."

"Master Adams, it is an honour to be a part of The Council. Apologies about bringing Asira to this meeting."

"Nonsense Kai. She is more than welcome anytime. I know how difficult raising a child can be. We can arrange the contracts shortly. Now, let's run through some of your expected duties." Master Adams searched through his desk drawers for a few moments before pulling out a clipboard and a pen. "Your title will be Council Ambassador. This is the sole position. I don't plan on bringing in any more people. You will represent The Council, Velosia Mainland and the entire Velosian Kingdom. You will assist with anything that is needed within Council matters. You will gain the trust of Velosia's ruling families. Also, do try to have a little fun with the title."

"Thank you, sir. I will." Kai stood almost ceremonially with his arms crossed behind his back and his legs slightly apart.

"Also, I think congratulations are in order. I have officially dubbed you the strongest and most powerful sorcerer in all of Velosia. No one has challenged your title yet. I don't expect anyone to challenge it either."

"Thank you, sir, but would you not rather take the title yourself?" Kai quickly glanced at the little girl standing next to him.

"I am getting a bit old and have more things to worry about. Besides, I have seen you in battle. You are far stronger than I am. You deserve the title."

While Kai was busy, Asira glanced around the room quickly spotting Master Draskule in the far corner staring at her. She hesitantly walked over to the middle of the room to the single table with the colouring book.

"Hello young sorceress," Draskule crouched down to her level. "How are you today?"

She glanced up from the pages nodding slightly. "I'm good. How are you?"

"I am very well. What are you colouring?" He picked up a blue marker and began shading the sky.

"It's a boat."

"Asira, do you know any spells?"

She looked up at him before quickly glancing over her shoulder to her dad who was still preoccupied. "Yes, but my dad says I can only use spells when I'm training."

"I understand but don't worry, this is a safe place where you can use magic without getting in trouble. What magic can you use? I am a warlock and can only use dark magic, spells and incantations. But a sorcerer can use every type of magic."

"Oh, I know that. Dad has been teaching me loads of spells. He's a great sorcerer."

"That is very true. Your dad is a great sorcerer. That would mean you are a great sorceress. Can you show me a spell?"

"I'm not allowed. Dad says we can only use magic when we're training."

From the corner of his eye, Draskule watched as Kai and Master Adams strolled out of the room talking. "I promise you won't get in trouble. Watch this." Draskule's hand hovered over a jug of water. Asira watched carefully as ice crystals began to form and the water froze over.

A smirk crossed her face as she cupped the jug with both hands. The glass began to heat up, steam rose, and the ice quickly melted. At the same time the glass began to crack and almost simultaneously the cracks receded leaving the glass crystal clear again.

"Did you use fire to melt the ice without using a spell? That is hard to do for such a young girl."

Asira nodded. "Fire spells are easy. So are the other elements."

"Really, well that is impressive. What harder spells have you learned?"

"I'm learning about illusions now."

"Asira, have you ever read the storybook *Tales of Velosia*?"

"My dad is reading the book to me. It's kind of sad."

"Ah, you do know about the white and black wolves..."

"Asira," Kai peered into the room. "It's time to leave." She dropped the marker and ran to her dad's side. "Goodbye Master Draskule. Thank you again, Master Adams." Kai shook hands with Adams one last time. "Okay Asira, let's head home."

Draskule watched from the back of the room as Kai and Asira left. He examined the jug carefully and dipped his finger into the water. "The water is ice cold, and she left the jug in perfect condition."

"Draskule, great news! Kai has accepted the position." Master Adams closed the office door. "What's wrong? You look bewildered."

"I've trained many sorcerers and warlocks and a lot of them cannot perform two spells at once." Draskule responded with his eyes still locked on the jug.

"What do you mean?"

"I set up a little experiment. I figured the young sorceress would focus on her mother's speciality. That is why I froze the jug of water. Instead, she focused on another family trait and melted the ice."

"So, the fire element runs in the family," said Master Adams leaning back against the desk.

"Then the jug began to crack, and she repaired it without any incantations. This proves my theory." Draskule rose to his feet and pointed to the jug. "This proves what I've been saying for years."

"This proves nothing Draskule. All it proves is that Kai is an excellent teacher and has passed his skills onto his young daughter."

"Exactly! He has *passed* his powers to his daughter – his five-year-old daughter!"

"Nonsense Draskule. She is a child with talent that is all. She is a sorceress just like her dad and nothing more."

CHAPTER THREE

Magic Tricks

Thirteen years later

H er head lay resting on her crossed arms. She was a bit of a
daydreamer. Sometimes she couldn't help but think about
some far-off place filled with wild animals, beautiful plants and
trees, or a castle hidden in the forest. She would often get in trouble with her teachers for not paying attention but luckily this never affected her grades. She was an exemplary student. She flew
through her lessons with ease. She was incredibly gifted when it
came to her studies. She just never seemed interested in school.
She was more interested in fun, adventure, and far away architecture.

"What is the square root?" She was fiddling with her pencil
when a screeching noise assaulted her left ear. "Asira!" She glanced
up from her folded arms to her maths teacher Ms Carrie. "Asira,
what is the square root?"

"Erm..." her eyes quickly flickered from her teacher's cross face
to the white board. There was nothing on the board. This was
awful.

"Page sixty-five, question 10a." Ms Carrie walked away and turned her attention to the rest of the class.

Just then the school bell rang for the end of day. Asira jumped with delight as she made sure she was the first to leave class. Maths wasn't her best subject. It was the only subject she found difficult. But she was trying extra hard as her final year exams were around the corner. Daydreaming just couldn't be helped, especially when she had a boring teacher.

There was another reason she left maths class first. Once the final bells rang, the halls became swamped with a sea of grey uniforms. They were disastrous. There were hundreds of students squeezing past each other. At first glance everyone looked the same. Asira quickly dived for her locker and snatched whatever books she needed for study.

"Hey Asira," the locker to her right banged shut. Asira was clever enough to seize a corner locker at the beginning of the year and her best friend had the only locker next to hers. "Maths was a pain today." She stuffed her books into her bag and threw it over her shoulder.

"You'd think Ms Carrie would leave me alone, Amy."

"You were daydreaming again."

"Obviously. Maths is so boring. I just don't understand it. My daydreams are far more interesting. Only a few more weeks of this and we'll be done – no more boring maths class!"

"Yeah, very true! So, are you going to the fair next Saturday?"

"Yeah, as long as my dad doesn't have any other plans for me." Asira rolled her eyes. "What about you?"

"Of course I'm going. Who wouldn't? I think my cousin is going as well. You remember Stephen, right?"

"Yeah of course. Red head. Four eyes."

"I know his two friends are going as well. They are coming over a fair bit. I think they're staying with Stephen." Amy led the way from the lockers. "Do you want to go to Sweetz?"

Asira pulled a deck of cards from her coat pocket. "I wasn't going to, Amy." They walked through the corridor, down the stairs, and out through the back door.

"Aww please!" Amy put her hands together and gazed up at Asira with begging eyes.

"Yes, okay. Where's the harm?"

"No harm. Now let's go!" Amy cheerfully squealed as they stepped outside the school gate in unison.

Soon they were sitting by the window drinking double chocolate milkshakes with chocolate chips. "Hey, are you doing anything tonight? Do you want to catch a movie maybe?"

"I can't. I have a show tonight."

"Oh yeah! How is that coming along?"

"The shows are good. You should come along."

"Okay! I've nothing else to do tonight. What time and where?" Amy slurped the last scrapings from the bottom of her glass.

"The Four Seasons Hotel at eight tonight." Asira played with the change from her purse. One coin danced across her fingers. "Tickets are sixteen euro, but I'll leave a request for you and Stephen at the door."

***

"Guys come on! This place is packed out." Amy squeezed through the hotel lobby to reception clutching onto Stephen's wrist and pushing two males in front of her.

"I don't get why we have to pay when you and Stephen were able to get free tickets." The teen with black hair fixed the cap upon his soft head.

"Are you seriously complaining, Tim? Are you eight or eighteen?" Amy pouted behind them.

"Don't complain. Just pay the man." The blond teen shoved his hand at Tim.

"Here." Tim handed back the ticket to his blond friend. "Just shut up, Jack. Why am I paying for your ticket anyway?"

"Because I drove us here in my father's Bentley – a very precious car which you made me take. If anything happens to that car, I will be paying for it with my life." The doorman pulled back the curtain to the darkened room.

"Just get in there!" Amy shoved the two guys in front of her and the four hurried to a table.

"When did your friend become so interested in magic tricks?" Tim gawked at all the figures around him squinting at the torches passing by his face.

Amy pondered the question for a moment. "Well, erm... actually she has always been into magic, ever since we were little."

"Ladies and gentlemen! Will you please welcome back for a second appearance with us," the voice echoed from the speakers above. There was a drum roll and a spotlight centred on the stage. "Miss Asira Soniar!" In the spotlight, smoke rose from the stage floor and twisted like a whipped ice cream. The smoke melted away and a figure in a black robe appeared on the stage. The inside of the black cloak was lined with rich red velvet. The hood was draped over her face.

Two assistants appeared from the sides of the stage and carried out a small table and a jug of water. Asira swirled her hand around the jug before removing her hood. "For my first trick I need someone to name an animal. Any animal." There were a few suggestions shouted out from the crowd. "I heard a python. Do you want to see a python?"

"How can she make a python appear?" Stephen whispered loudly into Amy's ear.

"Ssshh!" Amy hissed.

Asira dipped her hand into the jug and swished it around a few times. "It's just an ordinary jug of water." But then her hand clenched as if she had grabbed something inside. She tugged her clenched fist from the jug dragging a large python's head from the narrow neck. She pulled and pulled as more of the large reptile was being dragged from the jug and the water began receding.

"Wow! How is she doing that?" Stephen jumped back in his seat.

Asira yanked out the last of the python's length, leaving the jug bone-dry. The large python wriggled its long bulky body around on the stage floor. "I would not advise anyone to try this at home." She smiled as she reached for the jug and turned it upside down.

"I see the way you're looking at her," Tim teased, elbowing Jack in the side.

"What?" Jack said in a hushed tone.

"You like her, don't you?"

"Shut up!" Amy yelped quickly.

"No water left inside the jug and... no more python." As she rubbed the reptile's skull, the skin broke. She rested the now still python across the stage and continued the invisible line with her finger breaking the scaly skin. There was a movement inside the python. "One, two, three!" Butterflies began bursting from the scaly creature. Butterflies of blended colours fluttered across the stage and around the room. Then they transformed into confetti, exploding from a height over the audience.

A little later on at the end of the show, Asira returned to the stage and bowed to applause from the entire room.

"Wow!" Tim punched his fists into the air. "That was totally incredible!"

"That was amazing, I must admit. How does she do it?" Stephen said from his seat next to Tim.

"You fancy her, Jack. I can see it written across your face," Tim teased, running backwards to hide behind Amy and dodging Jack's dangerous glares.

"A magician never reveals her tricks," Amy giggled in response.

"You mean, a *sorceress* never reveals her tricks," said Asira as she snuck up behind Amy.

"Ahh Asira, you were completely and totally incredible!" Amy jumped around and hugged her. "Asira, this is my cousin Stephen."

"Hello Stephen," Asira smiled.

"And these are Stephen's friends, Jack and Tim."

Asira smiled softly and waved. Tim glanced over at Jack blushing slightly and began winking at Jack profusely. Jack grunted and folded his arms.

Asira turned to Amy. "I'm always anxious after I finish a show."

"Don't worry! Asira, you were fabulous. It was completely amazing. The python, the butterflies, everything!"

"I'm glad you liked it."

"It was amazing!" Tim winked. At first appearance Tim seemed to be a joker and able to laugh at himself. Jack however looked as if he came from a proud aristocratic family, like his dad could have been a baron or a viscount.

"Thanks. Well Amy, I have to be heading home. My dad is coming to collect me. I'll see you tomorrow?"

"Yeah, no problem. I'll see you then." Amy waved goodbye.

"Bye guys!" Asira waved goodbye to the others and headed down the poorly lit street.

She walked along the path slowly, staying visible under the lights. Her phone was gripped tightly between her nervous fingers. There were a few cars nearby, empty and lifeless. Suddenly someone shoved her shoulder.

"Excuse me." A man of about six feet tall stood before her. He looked to be in his forties, though he did his best to keep out of the streetlights. From what she could see, he had stubble across his face and his skin looked grey.

She took a few steps back, clenching one fist, praying for her dad to appear.

"Are you lost?" He examined her closely, looking her up and down. "Do you need any help?"

"No, I'm fine." She took another step back and pivoted.

His fingers twitched with excitement. "Tick tock, first verse of the curse I cast to infect and endeavour to sever your perfect soul," the man mumbled in a low and ominous tone. "My young, corrupted puppet."

She glanced over her shoulder in fear. "Excuse..."

The heels of a silver car skidded abruptly in front of her. She jumped as it screeched to a halt and Kai hopped out. "Get in!" The car doors locked and revved loudly as they drove away. "Who was that?" Kai glanced back at her.

"I don't know. He said something strange. He looked like a drug dealer."

"Next time I'll be waiting for you. You just don't know who's out there anymore." He grabbed her hand but pulled back suddenly. "You're freezing!" He turned the heating up in the car. "It's not even cold out. Are you feeling okay?"

"I feel fine," she said. "I don't feel cold." She rubbed her hands together and sat on them in an attempt to warm up.

He glanced over at her. "So, how did it go?"

"It was incredible. I think I received the most applause tonight. Plus, Amy and her friends were there."

"Well, that's great news, Asira." The car drove through a quiet junction. The roads were empty. The traffics lights were all green. "What's up?"

"Hmm...?"

"I know you want to ask me something, Asira. You can't keep anything from me." He glanced around at her again. It was dark, pitch black if the streetlights were not on. It took them no time to leave the town and head to the coast.

"Well," she paused for a moment, "my final exams finish Thursday. And there is a fair on at the end of the month. I was wondering if I could go?"

He slowed the car bringing it back down to third gear and glanced across at her with a strong grin and chuckled. "Of course you can go. I wouldn't stop you. Who else is going?"

"Amy and her friends."

"Yes, go out and have fun, Asira." The car pulled into the drive and the electric gates closed behind them. "Now, I think a celebratory snack is in order to finish off a successful night."

"Awesome! I'll grab a pizza from the freezer." Asira hopped from the car and skipped into the house. She quickly made her way to the kitchen and preheated the oven. As she approached the utility room, she suddenly felt woozy. A pain struck her in the chest and a blue haze distorted her vision.

The lights on the car flashed and Kai locked the hall door calling to her, "Grab the bottle of cola from out the back as well. I'll set the table. You better hurry up and put the pizza in the oven."

Kai reached up to the top press and grabbed the plates. He set the table neatly and set up the pizza trays on the counter. He ran the tap for a moment until the water became lukewarm and washed his hands swiftly.

"Asira?" Kai found her curled on the ground of the utility room in the foetal position. He brushed the hair from her face. "Asira, can you hear me?" Her eyes flickered beneath her eyelids. He scooped her up in one fluid movement.

Carrying her back out through the kitchen he snatched his phone from the counter. Straight away he dialled the only person he trusted. "Erika, please can you come? It's Asira – she just collapsed." Kai made his way upstairs and laid her gently across the bed.

"Hello Andrew." Erika appeared from nowhere and quickly moved to Asira's bedside. "She does have a slight temperature."

"You arrived very quickly." Kai smiled having missed Erika's presence, but his attention quickly reverted to his daughter. "She was freezing not so long ago."

Erika glanced up at him from the corner of her eye before stroking Asira's hair. "I'm not sensing anything wrong with her." She placed a hand on her chest and then on her forehead. "Her heart and head seem healthy. But you're a sorcerer too. This should be a doddle. To be honest you're probably running her into the ground with all your training."

He had shown her some new techniques over the last few months. She was studying hard to pass her final exams. Her social life was still as busy as ever. "Maybe you're right."

"Why is it you only call me when she's sick? You never call me to just hang out anymore. I bet Asira doesn't even remember me anymore." She smirked. "Andrew, you worry far too much. Has she been ill lately?"

"No, she hasn't been sick. And would you please call me Kai. It's been a long while since I've heard that name."

"I've never liked those aliases. They were stupid then and they're stupid now. And what? No thank you? Buddy's not happy I had to leave all of a sudden."

"Thank you, Erika. I do really appreciate you coming. Buddy the cat?"

"Buddy the dog. He's a Bichon Frise. How long has it been now since you last phoned my number? Four, five years?" She glanced at the family photos hanging along the staircase. "I can't believe how much she resembles Crystal. Asira is very beautiful. You should be so proud, Andrew."

"I am very proud of her. She has grown up so much. And every day she looks more and more like her mother."

"Andrew, I'm so sorry. I really wished she'd had a chance to get to know her mother."

"I tell her stories."

"What? Stories of us as stupid kids?" Erika began to laugh. "Did you tell her about the time Crystal turned the town centre into an ice rink and you went head-first into the fountain? That one was my favourite!"

"Actually yes, I've told her that one," he chuckled.

"That's good. She needs to hear them. As do you. I bet you have Asira call you Master."

"Yes, but only when we're training."

"Oh, that is very old-school. I like it. I thought you would've been more liberal since you packed up and moved away from Velosia."

CHAPTER FOUR

Silence

A silver car screeched to a halt as a man jumped out from the driver's seat. "Get in!" The young female did as she was told and hopped into the car. The dark-haired man with a greyish hue to his skin watched from the shadows as the car pulled away abruptly and disappeared out of sight.

The sea foam fragrance wafted along the evening summer breeze. Even though many people were on their way to their beds, he stood in silence and watched as the evening light smudged the dark sky.

He honestly thought it would have been a lot harder to find the teen. He had little detail to go on. He was only told that she lived in a small coastal town of England and that she looked a lot like her mother.

That statement was never truer. This teen with brunette hair and a pale complexion, resembled her mother in every physical way. However, her emerald eyes reminded him of a young soldier he once knew.

He glanced down at his trembling fingers. It had been a while since he had exerted himself so much. The spell he had cast when he bumped into the teen was the first part of an ancient curse.

Once, a long time ago, this type of spell would not have caused him any affect or effort. A long time ago he was known as the greatest sorcerer in the land. He was unmatched in his skill and strength. That had all since changed.

He threw his hood up and stepped back into the light pulling out a mobile phone and dialling the only number in his contacts. "I found her. She was easy to track. You know this spell is hard to perform. I'm not sure how effective it's going to be, especially in my condition." He listened to the response. "I'll see you in a few days." The call then ended.

He took a glance over his shoulder following the scent of the ocean before making his way towards the town. A few cars passed by him. He took no notice. To anyone passing by he looked like a regular guy walking back from a late night at the beach.

He clenched his fists before shoving his hands back into his pockets. He realised he was out of energy. In order to leave the coastal English town, he would have to wait a few days. He needed time to regain his magical strength.

He spent all his energy cursing some strange girl, but he was also cursed, cursed by his own foolish desires. It was something he could not stop. It caused him much grief and frustration. It was something he couldn't let go off. It was something that would haunt him his entire mortal life.

He came to a stop outside a closed pub. A bed and breakfast sign hung over the entrance next door. Turning the key in the lock, he let himself in and made his way silently to the room he had rented.

He found it tough most days to step out into the world. His life had been hidden for eighteen years. He knew the best thing was to take a step back from the situation. He tried to disconnect himself emotionally from his life but sometimes when he was left alone with his memories, the silence became overwhelming.

Back in his golden days, he was respected by those above him and below him. He had risen through the ranks from a petty soldier to a top general. His success was so vivid he could almost reach out and touch the distant memory. He would have done anything to go back in time and live out the remainder of his days in respect and honour. Then like a beating heart being ripped from someone's chest, it had all ended. The warm images that filled his dreams crumbled before his eyes. The dreaded silence took over once again. His life was turned upside down and suddenly the world wasn't black and white. He fell from the path of life. He stumbled to find his way. The silence kept growing deeper and darker in his chest and tainted his mind. And the one person that could pull him from his downward spiral was gone into a different silence, one he wished he could follow. A silence that brought peace and took away pain.

CHAPTER FIVE

The Fair

The clock in the car read eight o'clock. He hoped he would have been home sooner, but time had just caught up with him. It had been a few days since Asira felt a little unwell and she was still lazing around the house feeling cold and under the weather. "Asira, I'm home. Sorry I took so long."

Erika raised her head over the couch. "Andrew, what took you so long?"

"I told you don't call me that."

"Calm down, she's asleep. I will call you Kai in front of her. Promise. Anyway, where were you?"

"I'm on the parent council at Asira's school and it was an evening meeting. How is she?" He poked at the duvet lump nestled into the corner and tugged slightly on the edge.

"We made spaghetti with meatballs for dinner and baked some cupcakes for dessert. There's some wrapped up in the kitchen for you. Then we sat down to watch some cringeworthy vampire movie she apparently loves. Though I don't know why, and she's been asleep for the last hour or so. I may have slipped a drop of whiskey into her tea. Trust me, it will do her the world of good."

"Well, let's get her to bed." Kai scooped Asira into his arms and made his way up the staircase.

"Is she not a bit heavy and too old to be cradled like a baby. At some point you will have to let go."

"If I let go now, she'll fall down the stairs." He let out an exhausted breath.

"She was so cute as a baby." Erika gazed fondly at the baby pictures hanging along the wall. "Oh look, she's in her school uniform." Asira was about five years old wearing a grey pinafore and carrying a small pink bag on her back.

In the third photo, Asira was leaning into Kai's embrace. She was only about ten years old and carrying around a stuffed tiger cub. They were at the zoo standing next to an elephant. Her hair was long. Her braids sat on her shoulders. The final photo at the top of the staircase was the most recent one taken. It was of Asira standing with her best friend Amy beneath a *Happy Eighteenth Birthday* banner with a ton of silver and gold balloons scattered around the floor. She was wearing a red dress with a flared skirt and black swirl designs.

"She's just run down. She's young and will bounce back. You really worry too much. You're just afraid of the worst." Erika glanced over at her old friend.

Kai laid Asira in bed and quietly closed the door behind them. "You've always been there for me, Erika. Thank you for everything. I couldn't have raised her as well as I did without your help and intervention."

"Andrew, I would never leave a friend in need."

"I've been thinking about us lately." Kai walked closely behind her down the stairs. "I was hoping we could pick up where we left off?"

"Andrew, I was thinking about us as well. Maybe we should take it slow." A red portal appeared before them. "I'll give you a call in a few days to check in on Asira."

Kai watched as she left his sights. The rippling wine, blush and merlot colours that were her portal, swished and swirled before fading into the air. It was all Erika. Though he could see her whenever he wanted, Kai missed Erika's affection greatly.

***

Asira sat in an uncomfortable cushioned chair which was worn down to the metal bars. She kept crossing her legs one way and then the other. Her only distraction was the boring magazine dated two months ago.

A little girl in a raincoat became a source of entertainment as she ran frantically around an older girl, screaming and giggling before leaping onto the chair next to Asira. She was wearing a pink raincoat with shiny red shoes and her hair was tied into pigtails.

"Mia! Sit still. Stop fiddling please. I am so sorry about this." The older girl with mousey blond hair cut neatly to her shoulders bowed apologetically. "Hello, my name is Cara." Her eyes were an aquamarine. She wore a pink skirt, a pink and white horizontal striped string top and a beige suede jacket.

"Hi, I'm Asira."

"I've never heard of that name before. May I ask what you are doing here? Mia, please sit down." Cara pulled the little girl onto her lap. "I am sorry if I am being terribly rude. We've been waiting here for hours and I guess Mia is just bored. You see, my older sister is having a baby." She poked the little girl playfully in the cheeks.

"Oh no, it's okay." Asira waved excitedly. "I'm just in for a check-up."

"Oh, I hope you are okay."

"I am, don't worry about it. My father just worries about me all the time."

"My father is like that as well. But if they don't worry about us, who will? Excuse us Asira, but I think it is time to go." Cara stood up and lifted the little girl into her arms. "We have to go visit mommy." She fixed the raincoat on the little girl before curtsying. "Goodbye Asira. It was lovely meeting you."

For Asira, time ticked by slowly. She waited patiently watching other patients enter and leave the premises. She unclenched her fist summoning a small copper coin and flicked it around her fingers. Her eyes lit up as soon as she saw Kai walking down the hall towards her. "I've been in that hospital for over two hours. It was a waste of my life." Asira skipped down the hospital steps and stood on the path soaking up the suns light.

"Just be grateful you're okay."

"Okay? Of course I'm okay. Why wouldn't I be? Dad, please can we go for a walk or explore. Whenever we are here, we never go anywhere."

"The city is under lockdown. I'm sorry but I guess we just have to head back."

"Under lockdown?" She stared, only just noticing the police cars parked along the path. "Why so?"

"There's royalty in the hospital."

"Dad, I'm bored. We never go anywhere. Please can we go somewhere exciting?"

"I don't know where you would like to go."

"Anywhere! I don't know this place at all. I've never seen Velosia in all the times I've been here."

"Right. Well then, I have to visit an old friend in one of the kingdoms. Would you care to join me as my apprentice?"

Her eyes lit up. "Yes please! Oh, this is so exciting! Where is it? Which kingdom?"

"We will be travelling to the Essence Kingdom. I've been requested to join the prince there."

"This is so exciting. I can't wait!"

"Calm your excitement, Asira. I'm going as the Council Ambassador."

"Of course, Dad. I'm totally cool, calm and collected."

***

"Just give me a call when you're ready to go home and don't wander off by yourself." Kai pulled the car over in a small car park.

"Yeah, no bother." Asira waved back as she hopped out of the car. "Thanks for driving me to the fair."

"Who are you meeting here?"

"Amy, her cousin Stephen and two more friends."

"Okay. Well, have fun, Asira."

"I will! Thanks!" She waved again before slamming the door.

"There you are, Asira!" Amy ran to the car park. "How are you?" She crouched down to the window. "Hello Kai. How have you been keeping? Don't worry, I won't leave Asira's side."

"Hi Amy, do say hello to your mother for me. Okay you guys, have fun." Kai waved one last time before driving away.

Asira glanced over her shoulder. "Hello." She waved excitedly at the three familiar faces.

"This is so exciting. I love these fairs!" Amy quickly pulled Asira towards the deafening crowds. "I'm so glad you were able to make it."

"I wouldn't miss it for the world. So, how's the car, Jack?" Asira nodded over to the silver vehicle.

"Not a scratch."

"Not a scratch." Tim mocked. "You're rich. You can afford a new car."

"That's the last time I give you a ride anywhere," Jack scoffed.

"I'm your best friend, Jack. You can't stay mad at me," smirked Tim.

"Boys and their cars." Amy rolled her eyes. "We have a mission, Asira," Amy whispered secretly.

"A mission?" Asira was suddenly yanked through the crowd and away from the guys.

"Yes, a mission. I really, really like Tim. My mission is a kiss before the end of the night."

"Amy, wait!" Tim ran up behind them.

"Ear's burning, Tim?" Amy giggled to herself.

"So, Asira I was wondering if you would come to my little sister's birthday party and perform some of your magic tricks for her and her friends. She is really big into magic at the moment, and I've told her great things about your show."

"Amy had mentioned that. I would be delighted to help you out. Just give me a time and date."

"Asira, over here!" Amy suddenly tugged her again to the left towards the enormous wheel of lights. Green, red and yellow lights twirled and flickered in a clockwise motion. "It's a Ferris Wheel. Tim, look! How exciting!"

Lights flickered in amazing and hypnotising colours. "I don't do well with heights, Amy." Tim swallowed a hard lump in his throat.

"Don't be such a baby." She released Asira's arm, running to Tim she pushed him into an open carriage. "You guys get the next one." Amy called out as the carriage started to move.

"Traitor." Asira smiled in disgust and jumped onto the next carriage. "Are you coming?" She patted the seat next to her as Jack and Stephen hopped in. "This is kind of cool." She poked her head out the window as it started to rotate.

"How did you do those tricks?" Stephen poked his head through the window next to her.

"I've already told you, a sorceress never reveals her tricks, Stephen."

"Oh please!" He pulled himself back in.

She glanced over her shoulder. "I'm sorry, Stephen."

"Remember Stephen, a sorceress never reveals her tricks," Jack singsonged.

Asira giggled. "Thank you, Jack." She glanced back out the window at the bright lights.

Jack silently moved seats with Stephen and stared out the window next to her. "It's a lot colder up here." He stared at the flickering lights before meeting her emerald green eyes.

"Can I tell you a secret?" Asira said quietly. "I'm a bit afraid of heights. I was never terrified. I can get up a ladder. But this is a bit high."

He stared at her fingers tightly gripping the door frame. "I've a secret that not many people know. I've never been too happy about the dark. Creepy, haunted stories always start at night. Burglars lurk in the dark. It's just an unsafe time of the day. I always have lights on. Even when I go to bed, I have some sort of light on."

"You don't seem the type to be afraid of anything."

"If you're afraid of heights, why did you get on the Ferris wheel?"

"I wanted to see the lights." She clenched her eyes shut and swallowed a lump in the back of her throat.

"Straight ahead are the bumper cars." He moved a little closer and reached for her hand. "Over there is my favourite ride." He pointed to a tall structure. The fixed seats rose slowly before crashing back down in a straight line. Asira continued to follow his pointing fingers to the flickering lights. "There's a shooting range over there."

The carriage abruptly jerked as the wheel began to rotate again. Jack lost his footing and fell forward. He hovered just over her face. His warm breath whispering across her cheek as he struggled to hold himself up with one arm. His other hand cushioned the back of her head, stopping it from banging against the carriage. His eyes were fixed on hers. His mouth dried up. His palms began sweating profusely. In that moment, his heart skipped a beat as his lips parted slightly.

"You're going to crush her!" Stephen hauled Jack back to his feet.

Asira glanced back out the window at the bright lights and watched as the carriage finally arrived back on the ground. Stephen was the first to flee the awkward tension. Jack leapt out next. As soon as Asira moved to step off the carriage, Jack held out his hand.

"Thank you, Jack." Her cheeks began to blush as she took his hand.

"Over here!" Amy waved excitedly from a food stall. Asira sighed with relief as she rushed to the security of her friend. Amy was hyped up on sugar, dancing on her tiptoes and speaking at high speed. "The fair was beautiful from that height." She took Asira by the hands and began twirling in circles.

"Geez Amy, I think you had way too much chocolate," Stephen sniggered.

From the corner of her eye, Asira glimpsed a unicorn teddy bear. "Amy, I want to win a teddy!"

"That's a great idea, Asira! Tim, win me a teddy bear please!" Amy tugged Tim over to one of the stands.

Asira rolled her eyes. "Every summer after exams, she gets hyped up on cotton candy and anything else covered in sugar."

"I've known Amy for years and I've never seen her this crazy," Stephen remarked.

"Well, I would know. I am her *best* friend," Asira giggled as she walked off towards the others.

"Asira," Jack hesitated as she turned to him with a smile. "I was wondering if..."

"ASIRA!" There was a yell from behind them.

Asira flicked her head and pivoted to see Amy waving a large teddy bear over her head in victory.

"COME LOOK AT WHAT TIM WON FOR ME!" Amy roared at the top of her lungs.

Asira giggled. "Excuse me, Jack."

As she wandered through the crowd, Jack was left with a lonely feeling. "I was just going to ask if you were single," he mumbled to himself.

They stayed at the fair long into the night.

Stephen glanced at his watch as he yawned loudly. "Well, I don't know about you guys but I'm getting tired." He stretched his arms high above his head and yawned again.

"You're such a party pooper, Stephen," Amy pouted as she cuddled her new teddy.

"No, I think Stephen's right. We've been here ages and it's getting really late," said Tim.

Amy rolled her eyes. "Girls."

Jack swallowed a dry patch in his throat. "Hey Asira, would you like a lift home?"

"Oh..." Asira thought for a second and saw Amy nodding excitedly as she stuffed the last of the cotton candy into her mouth. "Yes please, that would be perfect." She pulled out her phone and began texting.

Asira: *Getting a lift. See you in a few.*

Her dad replied almost immediately.

Dad: *Keep in touch.*

The orange lights of the silver Bentley flashed in the car park. Amy smirked back at Asira as she pushed Stephen and Tim into the back. Asira hopped into the front seat a little anxiously. She watched as Jack turned on the ignition and immediately turned up the heating. The doors locked automatically, and a voice came from the speakers. "Hello Jack. Would you like some music?"

Asira's jaw dropped. "Your car talks?"

"It's programmed in," he smiled as he hooked his phone to the speakers. An indie playlist began playing in the background.

"I LOVE THIS SONG!" Amy screamed at the top of her lungs and tried to unbuckle herself from the seat. "Jack, open the sunroof."

Jack flicked his head quickly. "Tim, pin her down and put her seatbelt back on."

"Geez Amy, you'd swear you'd been out drinking," Tim said, pushing her back in her seat and clipping her seatbelt down firmly. "What was in that cotton candy?"

Asira fiddled with her mobile between her fingers. She directed Jack along the coast road. She couldn't help but feel her cheeks blush and her stomach began knotting.

Jack glanced at her quickly and then for a second time gazing at her for a little longer. "You can change the music if you like."

Asira shook her head. "No, I like your playlist. You have good taste."

Before long they were parked in front of her house. The electric gates opened slowly. Asira inhaled deeply as she reached for her seatbelt. "Thanks for the ride home, Jack. I had a wonderful time. See you all again." She let out a shaky breath as she jumped from the car, glancing back in to say goodbye and rolling her eyes at Amy fast asleep on Tim's shoulder.

"I'll tell her you said goodbye," Tim smiled, a little annoyed.

Jack tightened his grip on the steering wheel. He could feel the tension clenching the muscles in his forearm. "Asira," he called and suddenly stopped. What was he doing? She appeared back by the passenger window. What was he going to say? He panicked. "It was lovely meeting you again."

She nodded. "Likewise. See you again." She gave a little wave as she walked away, and the electric gates shut behind her.

Jack watched for a moment as he very slowly reversed from the house. The breeze blew past her thin frame. She was coated in shadow and only highlighted by the porch light. His heart skipped a beat.

CHAPTER SIX

The Council

Kai led the way through an unfamiliar hallway. Guards in shiny silver armour, like knights of old, stood either side of the long corridor, which was lit by the sun streaming through the golden stained-glass windows. Asira tried to take as much information in as she could. The night before she tried to read up on the kingdom she was visiting.

She knew she was standing in the palace on Granite Isle, the capital of Essence Kingdom. From history books she learned that essences were a branch of fairies. Unlike fairies, they were born without wings. There were only a few races that had distinctive features like fairies, mermaids or angels. What set essences apart from everyone else, was their intense power.

Asira was pulled from her thoughts as large wooden doors opened before them. Kai smoothly bent down on one knee, and Asira swiftly followed his example.

"*Mi amigo!*" A sallow skinned man wearing tight black trousers and a loose white shirt rose from his throne. "I am delighted you were able to visit. I would not trust anyone else."

"It is my pleasure, Prince Manolito. I would like to introduce you to my young apprentice, Asira."

"You are her master, I see. It is my pleasure to meet you, *joven hechicera.*" The Prince slowly reached for her hand and kissed it softly, addressing her as young sorceress in his native tongue. "I can see you will grow strong. Master Soniar is a skilful sorcerer."

Kai cleared his throat. "Shall we depart, Prince Manolito?"

"Of course, Master Soniar." He clapped his hands. "Prepare the ships."

"I'm sorry but I think there is a quicker way to travel." Kai nodded across to Asira. "It would also help my young apprentice."

Prince Manolito nodded and led the way to the courtyard where twenty guards in silver armour waited alongside a large black carriage pulled by four black Andalusian horses.

"I would like to make an appearance. I want people to know that the ruler of the Essence Kingdom has arrived. Master Soniar, would it be possible to teleport us to the outskirts of the town?"

"Don't worry Prince Manolito. We can accommodate your wishes," Kai lowered his tone. "Asira, you do know where to go, don't you? All we want is to appear at the edge of town."

She nodded a little nervously. "Yeah sure."

"Remember," he whispered, "the key to this spell is focus."

Asira took a deep breath and remembered back to her training. Kai had told her months ago that her spiritual energy, her soul, was linked to casting spells. A strong will allowed a sorcerer to be the best they could be. She took in another deep breath and her emerald eyes became foggy as purple doors appeared before her.

"Is it done?" The prince strapped a long blade to his hip.

"Well done." Kai examined the portal. "Are you able to hold it?"

She turned and smiled back at him; her eyes were still fogged. "Yes, I've got a tight grip."

"Good job. Prince Manolito, the portal is ready for travel."

"Are you sure it is safe, Master Soniar? After all she is still an apprentice – your words and not mine, *mi amigo*."

"I've trained her myself, Prince Manolito. I have faith and pride in her as a Master and as a father."

"My apologies, to the daughter of the great master." The Prince waved a few of his guards through the portal while he jumped into his carriage.

"How's your vision?"

"I can still only see blotched colours." She clutched onto Kai's arm. "How come I'm still having difficulty with this spell?"

"Unfortunately, sometimes there can be a negative to more difficult spells. You just haven't mastered this one yet. But don't let that get you down. It takes some much more experienced sorcerers' years to perfect this spell, so to be perfectly honest, you are doing exceptionally well." Kai gazed at the mauve, lilac, and amethyst colours swirling around them.

"Dad," her fingers dug a little into his arm. "I was hoping to say this to you the other day but never found the right time. I suppose it's as good as ever. I feel like I need a challenge, just something more exciting for the summer. I want to take the masters' exam. I was speaking with Erika and…"

"So, this is Erika's idea?"

"No. It's all mine. She was telling me you received your title when you were really young, and I just want to be able to do more with magic."

"I knew I could never keep you away from Velosia. I'm glad you're interested in magic and if you're interested in partaking in the master's exam, I can train you for it."

"I'd love that. I was hoping to be as young as you were. It would like be keeping on a tradition."

"You think you can steal my title?" he raised an eyebrow.

"I'm pretty good at spells. You said so yourself. I want to become a master. I want to learn as much as I can. I really love this part of my life but sometimes I feel its second to my life at home."

"What do you mean?" he glanced at her from the corner of his eye.

"Well, I love living in England. I love my friends. But I feel like I'm hiding who I am from them, especially Amy. That's also why I love performing my illusions. It's exciting. I get to share who I am, and people love it."

"That world is not meant to have magic. You do have to be careful."

"I know. I do know but I just wish I had some friends here that I could talk to about even the most stupid questions magic related. I wish I could just explore this world some more."

Kai loosened his grip on her arm. "Okay Asira, you can close the portal now." He glanced back at the closing purple doors.

The fog faded from her eyes and the emerald colour filled her irises once again. "I'm fine." The guards lined up the horses on the path. Asira sighed. "You'd think this prince would give us a ride in his lavish carriage. It's going to take us ages to walk through the town."

Kai scoffed. "He's a bit of a womaniser and a strange character."

As they passed through old medieval gates, Asira focused on the high walls surrounding the large town. The bricks were mossy in parts and other blocks were covered in vines. Her eyes drifted to her dad. "What's the matter?"

His eyes were locked on the upcoming fountain. "You are right. I should show you more of Velosia."

"You never usually admit to being wrong."

"See that fountain? That's where your mother started her very own ice rink."

"What? No way! I remember you telling me that story when I was little. You said she was a pro at ice skating, but you kept falling over and she had to hold your hand all the time."

Kai pointed across to a row of terraced houses. "The middle one with the green door was where I lived. Six doors down, the last house with the yellow door, that was your mother's house."

"Oh wow! You lived in the centre of Cora Town. Why did you leave?"

"This place was a bombsite at the end of the war. It was just you and me against the world. I thought it would be better to have a fresh start somewhere peaceful."

Asira swallowed a lump in her throat. "Do mum's parents still live here?"

"No, they were killed along with many others. This place was ripped apart years ago. Look at it now – it looks like there was never a war to begin with."

"Dad, where are we going exactly?"

"We're heading to Topaz Castle. Though, we have to walk through Saffron Forest first."

The walk through the forest took over an hour. A sudden relief washed over her when they came across a stone wall and wrought iron gates. As they approached the gates, Asira could feel blisters forming on her heels. The horses clip-clopped around the fountain in the courtyard.

Asira's jaw dropped as the castle doors opened. Green marble decorated the floor. Beautiful large landscape paintings hung along the walls. Chandeliers were suspended from the ceiling. "Wow, this place is amazing! This is where you work?"

"Yes, this is the headquarters of The Council."

The Prince stopped at a door on the left of the long corridor. Two guards pushed opened the doors and stood on ceremony for the Prince. They entered into a huge grand room. A crowd of people were gathered around a large table.

"A grand entrance as always, Prince Manolito." A familiar man in a black cloak sat at the top of the table. He then nodded to Kai and pulled a seat out to his left.

"Thank you, Master Adams." Kai took the chair.

"Master Soniar. Asira. It is a pleasure to meet you again." Master Adams nodded towards them. "I do believe we have all arrived." He cleared his throat before starting. "Welcome back to the annual meeting of the nations. I'm glad to see some new faces."

Asira zoned out for some of the speech. She was more interested putting faces to the names she knew. If this was a meeting of The Council, then these were all the royals. There was Prince Manolito, who sat directly across from her dad. There was a woman next to him. She had wide yet elegant transparent wings. There was another woman a few seats down who had narrow dark purple wings. Beside her was a man wearing a big gold crown and a blue cloak clipped to his shoulders. There was a younger person beside him. She was wearing a tiara and then it dawned on her.

"Are you ready to mingle?"

Asira was dragged from her trance. "What?"

"We're taking an intermission break. It's time for us to mingle."

"Dad, you said your job was hard. Can you tell me who that girl is?" Asira whispered as she nodded towards the teen wearing the tiara.

"That is Princess Cara. She is the daughter of King Roland from the Maria Empire. She is in line to take his place when he passes."

"Wow! That is a lot of responsibility. Wait," she snatched his arm to stop him from walking away, "if he is a mermaid, then where is his tail?"

Kai laughed quietly. "Look at that history book I gave you."

"Master Soniar, it is very good to see you again." King Roland approached and shook hands immediately with Kai.

"King Roland, it is always a pleasure. This is my young apprentice and daughter, Asira."

"Asira, it is a pleasure to meet the offspring of such a great man. This is my youngest daughter, Princess Cara."

Asira curtsied. "Hello again, Your Highness."

"Hello Asira. It is splendid seeing you again. Father, Mia and I met Asira in the hospital. Would it be possible, Asira, if we could amble and chat together? To be truthfully honest, I do not know anyone here my own age."

"Yes, of course, Your Highness."

Cara immediately linked arms and whisked Asira away. "It is so good to see you again. How have you been?"

"I'm good, Your Highness. How are you?"

"Please Asira, stop saying that. Call me Cara. It is my name."

"Alright, if that suits you. I was a little uncomfortable saying it anyway."

"What brings you to The Council meeting? They are frightfully boring."

"Dad brought me along. Please tell me about all these people. I don't know any of them except for Prince Manolito."

"Oh him. Everyone knows about him. His father was meant to have been a very brave man. But Prince Manolito has yet to show his bravery. Oh, that woman over there." Cara pointed to the woman with dark purple wings approaching Prince Manolito. "That woman is Princess Sylvia. She is the ruling princess of the Renassies fairies. Her cousin is the other fairy over there." Just across the room Cara gestured to the tall woman with short blond hair and transparent wings. "Her name is Amelia, and she is the ruling princess of the Greek fairies. Both fairies are kind of hostile towards each other."

They continued their leisurely walk around the great hall whilst being discreet about whom they were talking about. "Who is that?" Asira stopped dead in her tracks. "That rugged, beautiful example of human flesh."

"He is quite far from human," Cara sniggered. "That is Aaron. His father is the leader of the Australian Sand Clan, the largest werewolf pack in both worlds."

"There are werewolves in Australia and I never even knew!" Asira quickly covered her mouth to subdue her excitement.

"There are four clans in the world. He is very beautiful, but I think he is engaged."

"Already? Isn't he a bit young?"

"Not really. All my sisters were married before they were twenty-five. My father is in the process of deciding my future husband. It has something to do with power as well. If Aaron marries someone of his own kind, his children will have the powers he has now. It's just the way things work."

"I wouldn't marry if I didn't love the person. It's horrible to think some stranger you barely know could be sleeping next to you for the rest of your life."

Cara shrugged. "Then you would not be strangers for long."

CHAPTER SEVEN

The Birthday

"Asira, where are you??" A voice screeched down the phone at her.

"I'm on my way, Amy. I'm so sorry. I'm caught in traffic. You will have to stall for a few more minutes. Tim's house is not exactly next door."

"Okay. Well, you better be here before they serve the cake." The phone went dead.

A nerve twitched in the side of her head and she sighed, releasing the tension. "I'm very late. We won't be moving for ages. Our path is blocked somewhere a mile up the road and that's all we know. We can't even see the accident – if there is one at all! I'm going to have to teleport."

"What? No, you're not. You don't even know where you are going." Kai gripped the steering wheel. "Teleporting is a little more difficult than portals. You just vanish and you don't always step out onto solid ground."

"Dad, please!" She pleaded with her hands clasped together. "I'll give you a text when I get there. It can't be too hard."

"Well, what's the incantation?" He glanced over at her with a serious stare as she turned away in a huff. "Incantations are tough

and trickier to perform. You need to get the words exactly right."
He let out a big sigh. "The incantation is *Amer-ula tec-ika raela*.
Concentrate and please be careful."

"I will." She took a deep breath. "*Amer-ula tec-ika raela*." Her
eyes were taken over by a white glaze.

In the blink of an eye, Asira had vanished from his side. His
fingers had become sweaty, clenching the steering wheel. He knew
he was an overprotective father. He couldn't help it. And he knew
he couldn't hold onto her forever.

Asira blinked and found herself standing on a beautiful quiet road
lined with quaint bungalows. One house in particular had ten cars
parked outside it. She walked closer to see a bunch of colourful
balloons floating on the gate. "I made it." She took a breath of
relief and immediately began to text him.

*Asira: You had no faith. But I made it in one piece a few doors
down.*

She hurriedly knocked. Tim answered the door, but it was Amy
who squealed. "Asira! What took you so long?"

"I was stuck in awful traffic. But I'm ready to entertain."

"Great," Tim said in a relieved tone but then worry broke
through his voice. "Where's your bag?"

"My what?"

"Your bag of tricks?!"

"Oh, don't worry about that. I don't need a bag of tricks. I'll
use what you have in the house. Take that worried look off your
face, Tim." She stepped into the house and ran into the sitting
room with Amy. "Hello everyone. I'm sorry I'm so late. Where's
the birthday girl?"

"That's me!" A little girl with brunette pigtails bounced into the
air jumping around the sitting room with enthusiasm.

"That's my little sister, Nikki." Tim was a little embarrassed by his sister's excited attitude. "Calm down, Nikki. You're going to throw up your lunch. Okay everyone, sit down. Time for a magic trick." Nikki jumped onto the couches with her friends.

"For my first trick," Asira glanced around the sitting room, "what's that under the pillow?"

Nikki gazed curiously under the pillow and flung it into the air. "Oh, it's a rabbit!" she screamed thrilled. "Do another trick!"

"How old are you?" Asira bent down to her level.

"I'm seven."

"Okay, you have one rabbit in your arms. How many more rabbits do you need to reach seven?"

Nikki counted on her fingers. "Six...."

"Take a look in the garden." Asira winked at her. Nikki's eyes lit up and she ran outside with her fifteen friends. Everyone suddenly screamed with excitement.

Tim's mother ran into the sitting room. "There are rabbits in the garden!"

"How did you do that?" Tim turned on his heels with his jaw to the floor. "We're in an estate and have a walled garden."

"I've told you before, Tim. I shall not give up my tricks of the trade so easily."

"Well, I am impressed. Let's head outside. The kids haven't touched the bouncy castle all day. Stephen and Jack have been bouncing on it since noon," Tim said leading the way.

Amy pulled Asira through the house as they followed Tim out to the back garden. They tried not to step on the rabbits as they made their way towards the bouncy castle. "You two are such children!" Amy rolled her eyes. However, Asira ignored her eye roll and immediately proceeded to leap onto the rubbery fortress. "Asira! You are not helping my point."

"Oh, chill out, Amy!" She leapt from wall to wall. "I bet I can bounce higher than you."

"We'll see about that!" Jack began chasing her.

"He is so different around her," Tim crossed his arms and relaxed. "It's nice to see he is finally over her."

"He never spoke about his old girlfriend. What happened?" Amy asked turning towards Tim.

"Jack is really a hopeless romantic. He will devote himself to any girl. He just chose poorly I suppose. That bitch of an ex broke his heart and then stomped on it."

"That bad, huh?"

"Worse. He was locked up in his house for ages. It took me weeks to pry him from his bedroom."

Asira jumped excitedly leaping across either side of the castle. Her mistake was trying to run. She tripped over her feet and fell against the wall. Jack then tripped over her leg. He stretched out his arms just in time. He found himself staring down at her quivering lips. He could feel her warm gasping breath against his own. His heart thudded against his rib cage as their eyes locked.

"Jack, your weight will crush her!" Tim bellowed from the mouth of the bouncing castle.

"Yeah, I'm sorry." He rose slowly and pulled Asira to her feet. "You didn't hurt yourself, did you?"

"No, I'm okay. Are you okay?" Her fingers nervously pinched his and realising they were still holding hands she quickly pulled her hand back. "Sorry."

"They're cutting the cake," Tim bellowed again.

"Yes, okay," Asira anxiously brushed her hair behind her ear and hurried over to Amy's side.

They walked over to the table and waited for Nikki to blow the candles out.

"That was weird," Amy whispered to Asira.

They went through the motion of wishing Nikki a happy birthday and eating cake.

"So, what are you going to do?"

"What?" She glanced up from the ground.

"Have you been listening to me, Asira?"

"Of course I have. What are you on about?" She sat beside Amy on the back doorstep.

"Jack and your moment on the bouncing castle – there was something there."

"I don't know what to say, Amy."

"Ah come on, Asira!"

"Hold up, my phone's vibrating." Asira pulled her phone from her jeans pocket "Hello?" Amy slumped over her knees. "Hello Dad. Yes, I'll be there in a minute." She hung up. "Dad's outside waiting in the car. I better go. I'll see you soon."

"Keep your phone close. I'll be texting you tonight," Amy said to her.

She tried her best to ignore Amy's comment, but the truth was she had felt a moment. Her stomach somersaulted at the thought. Her cheeks flared up again. She hopped into the car, but she did not speak to Kai until they got onto the main road.

He cleared his throat. "So, we have been invited to join Lady Pearse in Kalis Mansion next Friday night. She is hosting a dinner party. She is an old acquaintance of mine."

"Oh, that sounds lovely! I'll have to buy a new dress."

"She has a son around your age as well. It will be nice for you two to meet and hopefully, get along."

"Get along? Is this diplomacy?" Asira giggled to herself. "Kalis Mansion? That's on Kalis Island? Who is she?"

"That's the thing," the car pulled away at the lights. "She is Lady of the Kalis Republic, formerly known as the Mortem Empire."

"*Mortem...* Latin... That means death. Vampires?"

"Yes, now you don't have to go if you don't want to."

"Oh no, if I am invited, I will go with you. It will be... interesting. Fun... It will be fun."

Vampires! She thought about the many fantasy novels she and Amy had read together over the years. Her mind was tossed into a whole new world. She read both the horror by Bram Stoker and the romantic novels. But most of the romantic stories were based on a naïve girl falling in love with an irresistible pale-faced man who for some strange reason found the moping young adult enticing. The love stories were her favourite though – it was the love of a stranger, strong and irresistible. It was the raw passion that attracted her to those novels. The alluring sensation, knowing he would do anything to be with the woman he loved, to protect her and to keep her safe in his arms. That was the love she dreamt of, tender and fiery at the same time.

Her phone vibrated.

Amy: *Jack's been talking about you.*

Asira re-read the text.

Amy: *He has been asking me if you are single. Are you interested? What should I say?*

Asira: *You can tell him I'm single ;-) but don't make it sound like I'm desperate.*

A shy smile crossed her lips as she sank back into her seat.

CHAPTER EIGHT

Kalis Mansion

Amy: *What dress did you get in the end? I'm very jealous that you're going to some fancy dinner party.*

Asira: *The same dress we saw in the window in the boutique the other day. The mint green and white dress with the black skirt.*

Asira attached a picture of the dress to the message.

Amy: *GORGEOUS!*

Asira: *I know ;-)*

Amy: *So? Have you thought about it?*

Asira: *Thought about what?*

Amy: *Jack! He has been texting Tim and Tim has been bugging me about it. Personally, I think it's cute. Jack is also very rich, as you know. So, what do you think? Are you going to go out with him?*

Asira: *Go out with him? He hasn't even talked to me!*

Amy: *Can I give him your number?*

Asira: *Sure, go on. I've to get ready. Text you later.*

Amy: *You better! Ttyl*

Asira took a deep breath before putting her phone down again. She was almost ready anyway. She'd had her shower and curled her hair. All that was left to do was slip into the dress.

"Asira, are you almost ready?" Kai called from the bottom of the stairs.

She opened her bedroom door. "Yes, just putting on my high heels." She slipped her dress on and reached for the zip on the back. "Blasted zip! Zip, pull up." She turned with her back to the mirror and glanced over her shoulder. She flicked her wrist and watched the zip rise slowly by itself. "That is why you need magic."

"Asira, are you ready?" Kai called again.

She stumbled out of her bedroom, stuffing the phone into her handbag and her feet into her shoes. "Okay Dad, I'm totally ready now." She held onto the banister and carefully walked down the stairs.

"You look a little tired. You're not wearing yourself out with those spells?"

Asira rolled her eyes. "Dad, this dress cost me a small fortune."

"Sorry. You do look stunning, Asira."

"Why thank you, Master Soniar. You also look quite dashing." She wrapped her hand around his arm. "I'm so excited! I've never been to a ball before."

Kai waved his hand and an orange portal opened before them. The orange rippled under her high heels. "Your portals are like a sea of happiness," said Asira smiling.

"Ha! That's a new one. I suppose the colour is uplifting. I was worried that you would be frightened off because of the vampires but I think that made you even more inquisitive." The portal opened up at the steps of a manor home. The doormen opened the heavy mahogany doors. "Asira, welcome to Kalis Mansion."

"WOW!" Her jaw dropped as she made her way into the hall. Large family paintings hung on the walls. Lights hung over the paintings and curtains draped the edges. "This place is incredible!" They were escorted down a red carpet to the ballroom where Asira found herself quickly overwhelmed by the hypnotising colours.

Kai kept her close, still holding onto her arm. "There are a few dignitaries from other kingdoms here, but this place is mostly filled with vampires. Lady Pearse hosts this ball every year in honour of the Goddess of the Seasons, Stagioni." Chatting couples stood by the food tables while colourful dresses and black suits whisked past them to the beat of the orchestral band. "Lady Pearse, how are you feeling today?" Kai bowed in front of an older woman and kissed her hand softly.

Asira gawked in astonishment before pinning her lips shut.

"Oh, Master Soniar, please," the woman blushed at the affection. "You have made the night even more splendid. I am so glad you were able to come." The young man next to her cleared his throat loudly. "Master Soniar, you already know my son, Anton." She gestured to her right.

Anton stood tall with striking good looks. His hair was neatly combed, and he wore a slim-fitting tuxedo.

"Lady Pearse, Anton, I would like to introduce you to my young apprentice and my daughter, Asira Soniar."

"Ah Master Soniar, so this is your daughter. She is so very stunning." Lady Pearse snatched Asira's arms pulling her close. "Your skin is so soft. You have been hiding this beautiful treasure away from us. It is a pleasure to finally have you grace our nation."

"Mother, please! You are frightening her."

"Apologies, my dear, Master Soniar."

"Catherine," Kai smiled "I know this is a formal ball but please call me Kai."

Lady Pearse's eyes lit up. "Well then, Kai, I must show you this landscape I bought the other week. It cost me a few hundred thousand, but it was for a good cause." And she quickly whisked Kai from Asira's side.

"Your father has been good to my mother over the years," Anton said as he stood a little awkwardly with his arms behind his back.

"Oh, that's good to hear. I wasn't aware my father and your mother had a relationship."

"Purely friendship." He cleared his throat. "So Asira, you're a sorceress like your father?"

"That's correct and you are a..."

"Vampire. Does that make you nervous?" He watched her body language carefully. She stood straight and she held her purse in front of her with both hands.

"Why would I be nervous? You're just another person."

"That's good to hear because I was wondering if you would care to dance?"

"Oh no, I... I don't dance." She stepped back waving both hands hesitantly. "I would much rather watch."

"Nonsense. Everyone can dance." Quickly taking her by the arm, Anton led her onto the dance floor. His fingers clutched her hand, his arm enclosed her waist drawing them a little closer together. He whispered, "I've got you. I promise." With the beat of the music Anton took a step to the left and then to the right while Asira watched her footing carefully. "Look at me. You will only confuse yourself," he said softly raising her chin.

"Your eyes, they're red."

"More of a maroon actually. Your eyes are beautiful. Green is an unusual colour to see here."

"I've never seen red eyes before."

"Red eyes are nothing special in the Kalis Republic."

The orchestra continued to play in the background as she was whisked around the room. She was entranced in the flow of the passing colours around her.

"See," his voice was so smooth, "I told you, everyone can dance."

"I'm only following your lead."

His skin was soft to the touch. With each twirl he pulled her in a little closer. His arm wrapped a little tighter around her waist. Their palms were pressed firmly against one another. With each moment that passed, her stomach began to knot, and her throat began to dry. She found herself lost in his eyes. The moment was so familiar, and she soon realised how vulnerable her heart actually was.

"Asira?"

She watched his eyes ever so carefully. "Yes, Anton."

"Everything feels so right. My heart feels ready to burst."

"Maybe you have indigestion."

He smiled at her amusing thought. "No, that's not what I mean." He glanced down at his feet feeling anxious. "I mean I want to be with you. I... I think..." They came to a sudden halt as everyone in the room began to clap before the next instrumental piece began. "Follow me." Taking her by the hand he led her out to the balcony where the breeze cooled her face.

"I hope it's not too cold. The weather generally doesn't bother us. It's quite hot during the day but at the night the temperatures can drop quite dramatically."

"No, the air is fresh. It was too stuffy inside." She leaned on the balcony.

He stood to her right. His heart thudded against his chest in rapid successions. "Asira," his lips became dry. "Do you know anything about vampires?"

She turned and leaned back into the balcony frame. "You may think I am very ignorant but no, I don't know anything about real vampires. I've read and watched a ton of movies back at home. But they don't represent the people of the Kalis Republic."

"I've never travelled to the human world. I wouldn't know much about how we are represented there."

"I can take you some time, but I don't think you would be impressed. It is a lot of gore or sappy romantic films. Though to be honest they are my favourite."

"I like to compare vampires to mute swans. I'm not sure if you have those creatures where you come from, but they essentially have one mate for life. They instinctively devote themselves to each other. They are soul mates."

"I know what a mute swan is, and this is starting to sound like a cheesy film."

Moving closer he brushed her hair back and his warm breath grazed her neck. "Are you afraid of me?"

"Anton, what are you doing?" she murmured as she felt her heart skip a beat.

His fingers brushed against her waist before yanking her closer. "I asked if you were afraid of me." His warm breath skimmed her lips. "I need to know now." His voice was quiet but urgent. "Asira?"

"No, I'm not afraid." Her gasping breath said differently. She found her head tilting upward to meet his. Once again, her eyes were locked onto glowing red.

"ANTON!" Lady Pearse suddenly snatched his wrist. "I hope you didn't hurt her."

"Asira, are you okay?" Kai rushed over and examined her blushing cheeks.

"I'm fine, Dad. I just need a cool drink." She pushed past them and quickly rushed back into the ballroom.

"What did you do, Anton?" Lady Pearse furrowed her brow as her son looked away. Then her voice levelled out. "Oh, I see. Kai, maybe we should get a drink now. Dinner will be served shortly."

Anton was left to his own thoughts, gazing out at the stars. His chest was warm as his heart continued to beat profusely. His palms were sweaty. He could still feel her fingers gripping his, her skin pressed against his and her apprehensive eyes dazzling in the candlelight.

CHAPTER NINE

School Request

Asira had returned to Topaz Castle with Kai a few days later. Kai hadn't said much, just that something happened in Australia that frightened him. Immediately, she could feel cold tension envelop the room. Master Adams sat at the top of the table waiting for silence. King Roland was also there with his daughter Princess Cara, who had eagerly found a seat by Asira's side.

Asira recalled some of the faces from the last meeting. Five seats down from Anton was Chief Connelly. He was tall and sturdy like a brick wall. He was also the leader of the largest werewolf pack.

"I don't understand why we're here. Dad never specified," Asira whispered into Cara's ear.

"Apparently there were some unfriendly and articulate words said between the werewolf race and some vampires from the Kalis Republic. This will undoubtedly cause the unsettled ground to crumble a slight bit."

"What are you talking about?"

Cara stared back at Asira with a '*are you that clueless?*' look before moving in a little closer. "There have been wars on and off in Velosia for many, many years. This is the most peaceful time ever in recent history and it is all thanks to The Council, according to my father."

"Cara," Asira interrupted, poking her shoulder, "who is that guy there?"

"Which one?"

"Who is that blond man sitting beside my dad? He looks very hassled and frazzled."

"I do not know who he is. Wave back to Anton. I think he is trying to get your attention." Cara elbowed her.

Asira caught the stare of maroon-red eyes from across the table and she smiled. Both Asira and Anton had been texting every day since their encounter at Kalis Mansion. To Anton's surprise it had been Asira who had initiated the communication the very next day.

Asira quickly glanced at the other faces around the table. Prince Manolito was sitting next to Lady Pearse. Princess Sylvia and Princess Amelia were also at the table but at opposite ends. Her gaze finally fell onto another young man. "Cara, who is that guy staring at me?"

Whispering Cara turned toward Asira. "Remember that is Aaron, the son of Chief Connelly. But why is he staring at you like that?"

Master Adams opened a brown envelope and slipped on his reading glasses. "Now, I am at the end of my tether. Both races just seem to be natural enemies. In this day and age, I would think each and every race would mature just a *little* bit. Two men were killed in Australia." He threw two graphic photos on the table. There were two bodies, half covered by white sheets soaked in blood. "The first victim was a werewolf. Both his arms were snapped in half. Puncture holes were found on the man's neck. The second victim was a vampire. He had bite marks along his right arm and his left arm was ripped clean from his shoulder." He threw another photo on the table. A house had been burnt to ashes. The roof had collapsed and crumbled into the shell of the building. "There are several people in hospital. One of which is a human bystander." He glanced down at the images and then back around at the room. "I was able to get one of my men in briefly to cover up the incident. I am totally outraged and disgusted. There is no reason to pick fights anymore. You live in completely separate territories. I don't know why the vampires were in Australia, but they were clearly in werewolf territory."

"Clearly is an understatement," Aaron snarled under his breath.

Master Adams raised an eyebrow. "You will hold *your* tongue in the presence of The Council. I am issuing a report and sending some of my people out to survey locations. I do *not* want another attack like this ever again." He waved his hand in dismissal. Everyone stood up from the table and began walking away.

Kai stepped aside with the blond gentleman with the spiky hair. Asira decided to stick close to Cara. She observed the tension in the room as Anton and Lady Pearse moved to the far end of the room, away from Chief Connelly and Aaron.

"Cara, I can feel so much hatred in this room." Asira glanced around one last time before locking eyes with the young werewolf.

"Asira?"

She turned on her heel. "Hello Anton. How are you?"

He sighed. "Tired. We heard about this two nights ago and since then I haven't gotten a proper night's sleep."

"I don't see why one of such divine magic is conversing with bloodsuckers," snarled a voice from behind.

Asira examined him carefully. He had sandy coloured hair and hazel eyes. He was tall, but not as tall as Anton and he was about the same age as well.

"My name is Asira Soniar. I am a sorceress. Who are you?"

"My name's Aaron Connelly. I'm the son of the Chief, the leader of the Sand Clan."

"You're a werewolf," Asira glanced at him again from head to toe. "So, are werewolves the same in reality as they are in the movies?"

"I come from a long line of pure werewolves. Have you never seen one?"

She shook her head. "No, I've never actually seen a werewolf in person."

A deep growl echoed from Aaron's chest. "What are you staring at?" He locked eyes with Anton. "Are you using the sorceress as a shield?" He snarled again under his breath.

"I'm sorry, what do you mean?" Asira clenched her fists. "You are being obnoxious. How dare you speak to my friend like that. Who do you think you are? Can you even hear yourself?"

"Me?" Aaron snapped his fangs. "You are so hot-headed. This is not your fight, sorceress."

"Did you just come over here to start a fight?" Asira began to roll up her sleeves.

"Is there a problem?" Kai, the blond man and Aaron's father approached them. Aaron quickly turned, unfolded his arms and lowered his head in his father's presence.

"No Dad, everything is fine here." Asira brushed down her sleeves.

"I'm glad," Kai glared at Aaron and Anton individually. "I believe it's time to go home. Aaron, I will be bringing you home first. I will then be back for you, Anton." Kai gave Asira a nod before swiftly exiting the room with Aaron and Chief Connelly.

"Asira?"

She turned to the deep voice and saw a man in a black cloak towering over her.

"It is a pleasure to see you again after all these years."

"I'm sorry," her voice became timid as a dark aura radiated from him, "but have we met?"

"My apologies, young sorceress. It has been a while since we last met. You probably don't remember me. My name is Master Draskule. I am the resident warlock of The Council. I have known your father for years."

"No, I don't remember you. But it's lovely to meet a friend of my dad's." Asira unconsciously took a step back.

"Draskule. Asira." She turned again. This time she saw the man with blond spiky hair approach. "You don't mind if I steal the young sorceress away, Draskule? Good." He promptly escorted her to the opposite side of the room. "I suppose you wouldn't remember me either. I think I only saw you when you were a very small baby. My name is Sir Volknor Costello. I am an old family friend." He turned with a warm smile. "Hello Princess, Anton. I've been told to keep an eye on all of you but especially you, Asira. Your father's orders."

"I don't know why he worries so much."

"You're a very outspoken young lady, that's why. I'm surprised you were so quiet, Anton. Trying to be diplomatic?"

"If you have nothing nice to say, do not say anything at all, sir. If you would please excuse me, I must go see to my mother." He walked away quickly.

"Diplomacy is a key aspect when you reach such a high status. Life doesn't get easier as you get older. You just learn to manage it better. Lady Pearse raised Anton well. Aaron needs a little more training but he's a good kid. Follow me. I will introduce you to two more friends of your father's." He led them across to the buffet table. "This is Dame Airies Kennedy and Sir Myron Morgan."

"Well, well, well, who do we have here?" Airies sprung to her heels, almost spilling her drink, and shook their hands vigorously.

"You'll scare her off, Airies," said Volknor rubbing the back of his head, laughing.

"You are such a spoilsport, Volknor," she pouted.

"Asira, are you ready to go home?" Kai appeared beside her. "I've brought Anton home already."

"Yes, I'm ready." She turned back to Cara. "I will text you later." She turned again to the adults. "It was very nice meeting you again, Sir Volknor. Dame Kennedy, Sir Morgan."

***

That night Asira lay awake in bed. She had been catching up on her Velosian history, trying to understand the animosity between the werewolf race and the vampires when her phone vibrated on the covers next to her.

Amy: *This Saturday do you want to meet me in town? Tim and Jack are coming.*

Asira stared at her phone for a few minutes. So much had happened over the last few days that she had forgotten all about Jack.

Asira: *Yeah sure. Sounds fun.*

Amy: *Great! I've been telling Jack how amazing you are ;-)*

How would Asira tell her best friend that she met someone else at the ball? That he was completely different from any boy she had ever met before? That she had the same warm feeling in her chest that she had experienced with Jack?

Asira: *Where are we going?*

Amy: *I was thinking bowling. Sound fun?*

Asira: *Sounds great.*

***

Asira stood in front of the mirror trying to match a top to her jeans. "Which colour?" She looked back and forth between her wardrobe and drawers. "This skirt and this top look cute." She gazed in the mirror again and sighed. "My hair is in bits."

"Asira?"

She ran onto the landing and peeked over the banisters.

"We have a guest. Would you mind coming downstairs?"

"Okay but I have to head out to meet Amy in an hour or so." She walked back into her bedroom swiftly brushing her hair. She took one last look in the mirror before skipping down the stairs and into the sitting room. "Oh, hello Sir Volknor."

"Hello Asira. Lovely seeing you again."

"Asira, would you mind making us some tea please?" Kai cleared his throat.

"Okay no problem." In the kitchen, flicking the switch to boil the kettle, she grabbed a tray and some biscuits. In the background, she could hear Kai and Volknor talking quietly. "All ready." She hurried back into the sitting room. "It's a little quiet in here. Is everything okay?"

Volknor glanced across at Kai before speaking, "Asira, The Council have been arranging for several months to open a school in Velosia. It was delayed temporarily but Master Adams has finally signed off on it. It was actually Draskule that has been persuading Adams to sign off on it for the last number of months. This has been Adams' biggest project for the last few years. I suppose he just wanted to get it right. This would in no way interfere with your regular schooling."

"A school?" She sat down in the armchair.

"Yes, it will be a school for Velosians."

She began pouring the tea. "What has this to do with me?"

"You have heard first-hand the trouble still bubbling between the races. Master Adams and The Council agree that one school in which to teach the younger generations together would be beneficial to everyone. It would be a great opportunity for the younger generations to learn from one another and to begin putting their ancestors' hatred behind them. He has invited at least one of every race to the school, to see how everyone will get on. It took a lot to convince the royal families to let family members attend." Volknor picked up his cup and stirred in some sugar. "I'm not going to lie – it will be tough. We are not sure what everyone's reaction will be. We have a fair idea that the werewolf children and the vampire will not see eye to eye. The fairies might cause a bit of trouble. But we are optimistic."

"Is it a school for elite students?" Asira asked.

"No, it will not be a school for elite students," Volknor responded.

"What are the subjects?"

"You will be studying general subjects, but it will focus on the history of Velosia, biology of the races and your powers."

Asira glanced over to Kai excitedly. "Powers? You mean, we get to study magic?"

"Yes, you will gain great knowledge regarding techniques and learn what everyone else can do," Volknor smiled knowing immediately he had won her over. "This is a very political move and as Kai knows, I hate dealing with politics. I have been asked to teach at the school. And the question was asked by Master Adams personally whether you would join our new Academy as the first sorceress?"

"It would be a great opportunity to develop your skills during the summer months," Kai added. "No harm meeting people your own age that have similar powers."

"Oh this is so amazing. I can't believe I will actually be going to a school to learn magic."

"It would only be for the summer months. This is only a pilot," Kai continued.

Volknor sat back against the couch. "The open day is next week. Then you will find out more." He stretched and grabbed three more chocolate biscuits. "I think you will enjoy it."

CHAPTER TEN

Bowling

As Asira jumped from the car she patted down her black velvet skirt and fixed her pink blouse, while fluffing her hair out. "Goodbye Dad."

The window rolled down. "Stay in contact. Let me know if you are getting a lift. And remember to have fun."

"You worry too much. I'll text you later on. Thanks. Bye!" She waved again as she started walking towards the entrance. Disco music blared loudly across the speakers as soon as the automatic doors opened. The reception was packed with groups of kids screaming and chasing one another. Nervous, she scanned the busy area in a desperate search.

"Asira, over here," Amy skipped around the crowds quickly snatching her by the arm and leading her over to the bowling lanes. "You look pretty cute this evening." She winked at her and giggled.

"It's a date, isn't it?" Asira skidded to a halt behind her as Amy shoved a pair of bowling shoes into her arms. "Thank you." She quickly sat in the only available seat next to Jack. "Hey," she smiled nervously, "have you guys been here long?"

"Hey. No, we only got the lane about ten minutes ago." He sat uncomfortably back against the hard plastic seats.

"Oh good! I was afraid I was running really late." Asira jumped to her feet testing the fit of her bowling shoes.

"I'll take the first go. We are in teams of two," Tim nodded to Jack and Asira and then to Amy. Gripping the orange bowling ball with both hands he took two steps onto the lane, swung his arm and released his grip. They watched the heavy ball glide down the shiny floorboards, drift left, knocking into the pins and leaving only two standing.

"Well done, Tim!" Amy bounced up and down clapping her hands wildly.

"Your turn, Jack," Tim said smugly.

Jack picked up a green bowling ball and firmly gripped it with two fingers. Taking two steps he crouched, swung his arm low and released. The ball slid straight and struck the pins. He turned on his heels. "And that's..."

"A strike!" Asira hopped to her feet excitedly.

A large smile stretched across Jack's face and a warm feeling filled his chest. "In your face, Tim!" He turned to Asira, double high-fiving her.

"That was incredible. I can't believe you were able to get a strike on the first go."

"Would you like a drink, maybe some food?" asked Jack blushing, his hands clenching at his side nervously.

"Eh... yeah, a cola and nachos would be nice," Asira replied shyly. "I'll come with you."

"Cotton candy for me! Thanks, Jack." Amy slapped his back before slouching back in the uncomfortable plastic seats. Amy and Tim watched curiously as Jack and Asira laughed together as they walked over to the food counter.

"I thought you said she wasn't competitive?" Tim sat slumped over his knees. "Jack is bad enough. His ego doesn't need a cheer-leading squad. You said she would calm him down, Amy," Tim complained.

She shrugged just as bamboozled. "I didn't know she liked to bowl. But when we were kids, she was pretty amazing at Mario Kart." Amy stared blankly over at her friend who stood next to the tall blond. "They would make a cute couple."

"Do you think they'll end up together?"

A huge grin stretched across her face. "How about *Jacira*. Jack and Asira."

"I hope you all like nachos." Asira carried the cheesy plate back to the table while Jack carried the cola cans.

"My turn, I guess." Amy took her place at the lane. The ball was heavy, and she struggled with the swing. The pink ball dragged right, knocking only five pins.

The evening progressed smoothly. Asira and Jack were in the lead by a few points. Amy was lounging back in the seats with her legs curled in against her chest. A cotton candy cone rested between her knees. Tim was at the lane concentrating and aiming at the last three pins. Asira was sitting across from her. Both girls were caught up in a giggling fit as they shared the pink cotton candy.

Jack made his way to the lane while Tim flopped down next to Amy. He let out a sigh. "Here," he snatched a chunk of the fluffy sugary treat.

"Well," Amy said once she finally caught her breath, "what do you think of Jack?"

"He's lovely." Asira stuffed her face with a lump of pink fluff.

"Would you date him?"

Asira laughed as her cheeks blushed brightly. "He hasn't even asked me out." She buried her face behind her hair as Jack returned.

Amy returned to her giggling fit. "Oh, my turn!" She stumbled to her feet and ran to the lane. "Watch this, Asira. I will show you how professionals play."

Asira scrambled to her feet and she leaned forward to pick up a blue bowling ball. All of a sudden, her breath shortened. The world felt like it was in slow motion. Sounds were muffled. Her vision momentarily blurred, blue specks floated across her iris.

"Strike! Oh wow! I got a strike!" Amy screamed at the top of her lungs. She shook Asira by the shoulders before running over to Tim excitedly.

Being shaken from her trance, Asira dug her fingers into the three holes in the bowling ball. She took a slow breath and chose to ignore her dizzy moment. She aimed the ball and released it. It rolled, knocking over nine of the ten pins.

"And that's game." Tim called in defeat. He gazed up at the screen with a sour face. "Jack and Asira win."

"Woohoo!" Asira bounded to her feet and took Jack by the arms swinging him around.

He stopped suddenly turning to Tim with a pointing finger. "Only the best win!"

Tim stuck out his tongue in response.

"Oh Tim, lose with some grace." Amy punched him lightly in the arm. She glanced down at her phone. "I actually have to go home now."

"What? Amy, it's only eight o'clock," Tim groaned.

"I know but daddy's orders." She rolled her eyes and lowered her tone. "As long as you live under my roof you will live by my rules." She let out a harsh giggle.

Jack pulled out his keys from his jeans pocket. "No problem. I have to be getting back anyway."

Asira once again found herself in the passenger seat of the silver Bentley listening to the indie playlist. Amy was happily sitting in the back, trying her best to cosy up to Tim. Without a single direction or guidance, Jack began driving towards the coast road and out towards Asira's home.

"Oh Asira, what were you saying about school?" Amy poked her head between the seats.

Asira turned around. "Erm... well..." she began "I will be attending a summer school starting next week."

"What?" Tim yelped.

A feeling of dread began in Jack's stomach.

"Yeah, I know. It is an extra curriculum study thing. Dad said it would be good for me." She played with a strand of her hair. She hated lying to her friends, especially Amy.

"So, you're abandoning me for the summer?" Amy crossed her arms in disgust and flopped back into the soft leather.

"Aww Amy! Please don't be like that. It is a prestigious school and I'm really looking forward to it." She pleaded for forgiveness.

"Amy, you're not going to be heartless?" Tim hid his sly grin under a scowling face.

"Of course, I'm not heartless," Amy pouted looking away from everyone. "I'm happy for you, Asira." She turned back to her friend and gripped the head rest. "You will have to text me every day and you're not allowed to forget me."

Asira laughed. "Of course, I will. I could never forget my best friend."

"How long is the summer school?" were Jack's first words for the entire car ride.

Asira thought for a second. "All of July and August. Then I will be back for college."

The car slowed, indicated and eased up to the electric gates.

"I had a lovely time, Jack. Thank you." She turned to Amy and Tim. "Bye guys."

"See you and enjoy your summer school." Tim pointed his finger like a gun and flicked his wrist.

Amy jumped between the seats. "I'll call you tomorrow!"

As Asira closed the car door, Jack sank back in his cream leather seat. His heart had skipped a beat once again. She gazed back and waved, smiling softly. He watched as she walked down her driveway. The car's headlights lit her path. The gates gradually closed in front of them, and he peeked through the bars.

"Will you stop drooling and put the car into gear. She will think you are creeping on her," Tim said with a sarcastic grin.

A nerve twitched in Jack's temple, but he bit his bottom lip as he put the car into reverse, backed onto the country road and drove off.

CHAPTER ELEVEN

Velosian Academy

"Topaz Castle is the prized jewel of the Velosian Kingdom. It is the home to Council Chambers. It is the ancient capital to the Elfish Empire." Master Adams gazed at the young crowd from the steps of the castle. "The history of The Council is long and rich with loyalty and royalty. When the royal family perished, The Council continued to protect and serve. Growing to prominence during the unsettling times in Velosia and acting as the mediators between the divided nations and kingdoms. Today The Council is made up of many leaders."

Asira glanced to her left and then to her right. She began counting all the teenagers that were gathered, starting with the ones that stood out. There were at least two fairies and two angels. She knew there was at least one mermaid and one vampire. She subtly tried to stand on her tiptoes and glance over the looming guards. It was then she wondered how many of these new students were direct descendants of a throne.

"Sixteen people – sixteen young individuals, leaders-in-training – stand before us. This is the start of what I hope will become a very prosperous and rewarding school," Master Adams spoke firmly. "Topaz Castle will be your home and school for the next few weeks. Your lessons will involve the rich history of Velosia's past. You will also study who you are as an individual and what it means to be of your ilk. I personally welcome you all to Topaz Castle and to the Velosian Academy."

"This is remarkable!" Cara stood next to Asira. Five guards in Atlantean armour surrounded her. The armour comprised of a four-foot trident which was fixed neatly on their backs and three-quarter length skin-tight black leggings with an orange streak down either side. Each guard wore an orange beaded bracelet and matching shell necklace. Orange straps crossed their bare chest in a 'X'.

"Atlantean armour is quite unusual. It is barer than I would have imagined."

"How else would we travel?" Cara immediately pointed to the orange colouring. "All my personal guards have the orange colour. It is so people know Princess Cara is around."

"That's cute."

"We are more dressed than some people," Cara gestured across to two barely dressed women. They wore silver plaited breast plates, knee and elbow pads, and a brown feathery mini skirt. Large white wings curled behind their backs and each woman held a serrated spear. "Those are female soldiers from the Bonum Kingdom."

"I don't see the point of armour if you are not covered completely."

"Asira, you are so naïve. That is traditional armour from the Bonum Kingdom. Oh look, there's Father and Mother!" Cara waved excitedly over the crowd.

King Roland was seated among a group of adults at the foot of Topaz Castle. He wore his usual gold crown beaded with jewels and a long blue cloak falling from his shoulders. A woman in a slimmer gold crown wearing an aquamarine dress sat at his side.

Her hair was braided and fell to her knees. Ten guards stood on ceremony behind them and thirty more stood no more than thirty feet away.

Prince Manolito sat next to them. He had as many guards standing in a similar fashion. He was accompanied by an older woman with a beautiful dark complexion and ebony black hair. She wore an excessive number of pearls around her neck, her wrists and on her ears.

Lady Pearse sat between Princess Sylvia of the Renassies fairies and Princess Amelia of the Greek fairies. Next to Princess Amelia was an angel and next to her was Chief Connelly. There were a few more people who Asira did not recognise but assumed these were the parents of the other teenagers.

"I hope you didn't miss me too much."

"Anton!" Asira turned into his arms. "I heard you were attending."

"I wasn't going to, but then I heard you were coming." A sly smile touched his face and then his smile faded.

"I smell something vile." Four people appeared from the crowd, three girls and Aaron. "Uh Aaron, I can't believe they allowed a vampire to join the academy." One of the girls had her hand wrapped firmly around Aaron's arm. She was half-caste with flawless skin. Her hair was dyed platinum blond and tied in a high ponytail.

"Let's go, Angelica," said a brunette with dark sallow skin, as she pulled on her arm.

"No matter where we go, we'll still smell him," Angelica sniggered as she passed, locking eyes with Anton.

Anton quickly took Asira's wrist and gently pulled her closer. Leaning his chin on her shoulder he closed his eyes. "I'm just going to rest here. I hope that's okay?"

"I have assigned five incredible men and women to teach you while you attend the academy. While studying here you will address them all as *Master*." Master Adams took a step to the side. "Let me introduce you to Master Soniar, Master Costello, Master Kennedy, Master Roberts and Master Draskule. Master Costello, Master Kennedy and Master Roberts will be your main teachers and mentors while Master Soniar and Master Draskule will deal with other matters and teach occasionally. As of today, you are students of the Velosian Academy. These are your mentors. This is your academy."

"I'm so nervous!" Asira squealed.

"Why, Asira?" Cara grasped her arm and gazed at her from her reflective fish-like eyes.

"Well, to be honest, I've never really used my magic in front of anyone except Dad, and the occasional illusions for audiences. And I suppose I've never hung out with other races before."

"Do not worry about it, Asira. Honestly. It will all be fine once we settle into our rooms."

The crowd began moving towards the castle and very quickly Asira found herself next in line.

"Here you are, Ms. Soniar," Master Airies said and handed over a key. "I hope you like your new bedroom."

"Thank you, Master Airies," Asira examined the regular looking key. She had hoped for an ancient medieval style to fit the theme of the castle.

"Which room are you in?" Cara pushed past her guards and clung to Asira's shoulder.

"I'm in room twenty-three. How many rooms are there?"

"I am in room twenty-seven. I am just down the hall." Cara squealed with joy. "This is the most excitement I've had in a long time. Anton, which room are you in?"

"Room fifteen," he replied as they made their way up the centre staircase and down the corridor. "This is my room." Anton stopped just behind them. "I'll see you at dinner later." He gave a little nod before closing the door to his room.

"I hope he's okay," said Asira as she took a second glance down the hall. "Do you want me to walk with you to your bedroom, Cara?"

"Not at all, Asira. It is only a few doors down. Besides, I have my entourage. I will catch up with you before dinner." Cara gave a little wave and was escorted down the hall.

Asira held the key tight between her fingers. She heard the clinks and clanks within the lock and swiftly opened the door. One step over the threshold and her jaw dropped. The room had been decorated with purple walls. Her suitcases were lined up, waiting.

She leapt onto the four-poster bed with its curtains draping each side. She sank into cotton sheets as soft as marshmallow. There were thin black knitted curtains pulled back across the window and even thicker curtains draped beautifully against the wall.

The room was massive, just what you would expect to find in a castle. There was a vanity table with a large mirror against the opposite wall to the bed. She stepped into the ensuite, and found it was as big as the bedroom and painted a wine-red colour. There was a bath and also a shower in the corner. "This place is so posh!"

Hair care products, shower creams and towels sat in a perfect line along the tiled sink. A white fluffy dressing gown hung on the wall next to the shower. Pristine white slippers sat neatly under the free-standing bath.

A bowl of mint sweets sat next to a card. '*Asira, enjoy the sweets. Dinner is at 8. Dad.*'

After her shower, she began unpacking. She laid all her accessories along the vanity table. From her suitcase she pulled out thin black tights, a purple dress decorated with thin turquoise loops at the bottom, and a high waisted leather jacket.

Kai always taught her to never use magic for unnecessary things. Whenever she went on trips, she always brought her hair straightener and curler. He always said possessions define a person's personality. So, she did what she always did, she curled her hair into cute loose curls.

Taking one last glance in the mirror, she sprayed her neck in perfume before stepping out into the hall. She walked straight into someone and fell back against the door, sliding to the floor landing on her bum. "I'm so sorry." She glanced up, rubbing the back of her head.

A hand stretched out in front of her. "Are you okay?"

"Aaron, thank you." She was pulled to her feet and immediately straightened her dress and dusted her tights. "I'm sorry again. I just wasn't looking where I was going."

"Don't worry about it. I'm sorry too."

"I better head." She inched back along the wall nervously and scooted down the hall in the opposite direction. She hurried to another door and knocked twice. "Cara, are you ready?"

"Yes, I am ready." Cara swung opened the door and slipped on her heels.

"Where are the guards?" asked Asira peering into the bedroom.

"Unladylike as it may sound, I screamed down the phone at father. It was unbecoming of a student to have guards follow me around. He agreed and they went home." She stopped at the top of the stairs briefly to pin up her hair. "Did you see if any of the other guards left?"

"I haven't seen a thing." As soon as they moved away from the stairs the smell of cooked food wafted through the corridors. "I'm starving. Your dress is gorgeous, Cara. Where did you get it?"

"I had the royal Atlantean dressmaker prepare several outfits before leaving home." Cara twirled in the jasmine dress.

They strolled into the dining room. Everyone else had already arrived. The table was about eighteen foot long and at either end it stretched at a right-angle for another eight feet. It was large enough to seat all the students and mentors. Kai was seated at one end with the other mentors and Master Adams. Asira followed Cara to the other end where Anton was already waiting.

"Hey, are you okay?" Anton whispered to Asira.

"Yes, why wouldn't I be?"

"I just want to make sure. This is a strange new place."

"That's true. This place is strange. I'm not used to the different faces and the fact we can use magic," Asira snorted a giggle under her breath, "but I'm really excited."

"Are they bothering you?"

"Who? Aaron? No, not at all." Asira glanced down briefly. Aaron was three seats away and glancing across occasionally at Anton from the corner of his eye.

"Good, me either." Anton picked up his glass and poked at the ice cubes with the straw.

"If they annoy you, let me know. I'll protect you." Asira glanced up at him with a smirk. "One time my friend Amy was bullied by these kids in school. She was so stunned that someone tried to bully her that she couldn't defend herself. As soon as I found out, well, I gave out to them. I threw rocks at them as they cycled around us on their tricycles."

Anton choked on his ice. "Tricycles?" He let out a snort. "How old were you?"

"We were about five. Don't tell my dad but I used a little magic to stop the bullies."

"Oh really? What did you do?"

Asira played with her necklace. "I set their tyres on fire. But they were okay. I swear."

He took her hand. "Asira, I..."

"This is our first meal as a school," Master Adams began. "As you are aware, this school was set up to teach the young generations of Velosians that the ways of our fathers and our grandfathers are not our ways. We can live in harmony with each other. We can prove past wars wrong and alter the course of history. Now, please, enjoy your meal." Several waiters and waitresses gathered around the table with plates.

"This is so fancy." Asira gazed at the fine silverware. "I can actually see my reflection."

"As a princess, we are taught from birth about etiquette. I will teach you everything I know, Asira. So do not feel left behind," Cara smiled.

"Thanks, Cara. Were you brought up like a princess as well, Anton?" She nudged his arm. "You seem lost in thought. Are you okay?"

"Just a little uneasy," Anton said.

"I don't know much about the racial dispute and I'm not going to pretend I really understand it all. But I see similar disagreements and fights back home, and I empathise. I wouldn't worry too much. You have me here. And as long as I am around, I won't let anyone hurt you." She smiled back, hoping to see him cheer up. "What always helps turning a frown upside down is stuffing your face." She stretched across the table and snatched a plate of spring rolls. "These are vegetable and very crunchy. Eat up!"

"Asira, this fork is for salads," Cara picked up the fine silverware. "And this fork is for the main course," She pushed another fork in her face.

"Cara, I see no difference."

"Asira, this is a smaller fork, and it is for salads. This larger fork is for main courses."

"That's stupid. A fork is a fork."

Cara mumbled on in the background while Asira gazed around at all the strange faces. There were so many names she would have to learn. Every race was represented at this table. She could name every race but that made no difference. The fifteen teenagers surrounding her, eating the same food and breathing the same air, were just acting like regular teenagers.

She had always wanted to explore more of Velosia, and this was her chance. She had always wanted to learn about all of the species living in this realm. She wanted to make new friends. But most importantly, she wanted to learn more about herself. She wanted to learn where she came from and what she could do.

CHAPTER TWELVE

Class Introduction

A sira: *Hey, sorry for the two-day late text. How are you?*
Asira was lying on her bed. To tame her frizzy locks, she had them pinned back loosely. While at the academy, she had decided to stick with smart casual clothing. She would not wear tracksuit bottoms unless instructed to do so. And although she would be doing a lot of physical activities as well as classroom activities, today she had decided to wear black jeans, her purple cardigan, and a white blouse with white runners.

Amy: *It's been three days. What have you been doing?*

Asira: *I've been settling into the academy. There have been loads of introductions with the teachers and students.*

Amy: *I've been so annoyed. Tim is completely ignorant to my feelings.*

Asira: *What? No way? Is he just being stupid?*

Amy: *I will just have to be more obvious tomorrow.*

Asira: *What's happening tomorrow?*

Amy: *Jack is taking us out on his boat. I wish you were able to come. It's going to be so cool.*

Asira: *I wish I was coming too, Amy. It sounds so cool!*

Amy: *Jack seemed genuinely disappointed when you said you couldn't come. Swimsuit weather! Lols!*

Asira: *Do you think?*

Asira gazed at the message a second time.

Amy: *Yeah. I will brag about you tomorrow ;-) When are you home?*

Asira: *Not sure. I have to go but best of luck tomorrow xx*

Amy: *TTYL :-)*

Asira took a deep breath, slipping her phone into her jeans pocket before hurrying outside to the courtyard with the other students.

Cara whispered, "Are you okay?"

"I should be going out with friends tomorrow, but I can't because I'm here."

"Ahh, they will understand. You are at the Velosian Academy."

Asira shook her head. "They don't know. They're human."

"You are full of surprises! Do you know what we are doing today?"

"I think dad said we were training." She looked up the steps at where Kai was standing.

"Good afternoon, students." Erika stepped down from the castle with her arms spread wide. She was of average height, skinny, with jet black hair tied tight into a high ponytail. "As part of your curriculum, one of your classes will be skills-building. It will be based on assessing and building your skills. The best way to do this is through combat."

Asira heard loud whispers from the far right. Angelica was leaning into Mandy and momentarily locked eyes with Asira. "I don't know what the sorceress is thinking befriending a vampire."

"Let's start with making some space." Erika stepped through the crowd pushing the students out into a circle. "We need two contenders, who would like to go first?" Everyone stood silently as the uncertainty began to develop. "Well, don't be shy." Erika walked around the crowd.

"I don't like the look of this," Asira said with a glance at Anton. "I just have a bad feeling."

There was a whispered argument to her far right. She glanced over to Angelica again who was murmuring loudly to Aaron. Then she pushed the sandy haired male through the crowd. "Aaron will go!" Angelica announced. "We will have to show everyone how strong we are by sending our best out."

Aaron took a step cautiously into the circle and clenched his fists.

Everyone waited a few minutes for another person to step forward.

Cara finally broke the silence with a murmur to Asira. "That's Thomas." She said pointing to a young man around twenty years of age with jet black hair and golden eyes, who had stepped forward. He was sallow skinned and wore jeans with a light blue skintight jumper. "He is the nephew of Prince Manolito."

"What is he?" Asira asked, studying the man.

"He is an essence."

"He does kind of look like Prince Manolito," Asira whispered back.

"Now you are allowed to tease and play. Stay within the circle. Just do not hurt each other. All we want is to see what your skills are." Erika stepped back into the crowd.

"You can do it, Aaron!" Angelica screeched excitedly. Asira admired her chocolate complexion and her platinum dyed blond hair. Her eyes were a beautiful light blue. She wore large gold hoop earrings, blue leggings and a long cream top.

"Go Aaron!" Mandy was the sixteen-year-old and was screaming the loudest. She had dark brown hair braided and held in a high ponytail. Her eyes were brown. Her skin tone was deeply tanned. She wore denim shorts and a string t-shirt with white runners.

"Yes, show them what a werewolf can do," a teenage girl of seventeen years of age called out. Her hair was white and cut in a pixie bob. Her eyes were a frosty blue. She had stud earrings and wore tight dark jeans and a grey t-shirt.

"Britanie, this is so exciting!" Mandy squealed in delight next to the white-haired teen.

Thomas glanced over Aaron's shoulder at the cheering squad. "So, which werewolf are you then?"

"Show him, Aaron!" Angelica yelled eagerly.

Anton crossed his arms and stood up straight. He could smell the tension in the air and gazed somewhat protectively down at Asira.

Aaron snarled. His fangs ripped through his expanding jaw. Fur rippled across his skin that matched his sandy hair colour. He leapt onto all fours. His skeleton altered in a matter of seconds. Then he howled towards the sky, quickly stomping his front paw, the dust from the ground momentarily hovered.

"So, you are the werewolf from the sand clan?"

Asira gasped in astonishment as shivers crawled along her skin. "Wow! I have never seen anything like this before."

Anton glared down from the corner of his eye and furrowed his brow.

"Guess what I am?" Gold sparkled between Thomas' fingers and thick gold dust swayed around his hand like a brandy glass.

Aaron snarled and leapt forward into a dash. He jumped on top of Thomas knocking him onto his back. He chomped his jaws inches from Thomas' ear and drooled along his cheek.

In a moment, the gold dust jolted from Thomas' hand and tangled in Aaron's fur. The dust knotted like Japanese knotweed and began to strangle him.

"Oh no!" Asira cried out throwing her hands across her gaping mouth. "Is no one going to stop him?"

"Thomas, stop this," Kai came down the steps.

"Master Kai, just a moment. I want to see where this goes," Draskule stretched his arm out like a barricade.

Aaron rolled around on his back and wheezed, desperately struggling to breathe.

Anton unfolded his arms, ready to move in when Asira pushed her way through the crowd. Aaron's body changed shape. The fur fell from his skin as he crawled on his hands and knees struggling for air before collapsing onto his face. His canine fangs were piercing his lower lips. He pulled and tore at the gold dust around his neck as his oesophagus began to crunch.

Asira stomped hard on the gold threads and the golden dust just evaporated away.

Aaron wheezed and gasped for air while the blood rushed back to his face. He gazed up at her with watery eyes, trying frantically to catch his breath.

"Aaron!" Angelica ran to his side knocking into Asira's shoulder. Her knees trembled. "Are you okay?"

"That went a little far, don't you think?" Asira glared back at Thomas. "You weren't meant to hurt anyone."

"I'm sorry. I don't know what came over me. It is hard sometimes to control the dust." Thomas glowered at his own hand.

"Asira," Draskule bellowed "you are next." She stared across the circle. "Your opposition is the young witch."

Asira gazed around and saw a timid girl in a black velvet skirt and a bright yellow top step out from the crowd. She had long blond hair tied in a loose ponytail and pulled a long, thin wand from her sleeve. "Master Draskule, I will not fight."

"I would have been disciplined for speaking back to my mentor like that."

"That is enough," Kai called out. "We will take it from here, Master Draskule."

Volknor turned his back to the students and stood immediately in front of the warlock. "Draskule, that form of teaching is decades old and look what it has brought us."

Kai moved in front of Draskule. Taking a breath and gazing at the somewhat traumatised teens, he said, "We will start your studies with a history lesson."

Asira let out a sigh of relief. "A history lesson sounds lovely."

"Asira, you were so brave, and you saved Aaron." Cara ran into her arms.

"It was nothing. Cara, this is all I've ever wanted. Studying and living here in Velosia. It's like a missing part of me I am only discovering."

"Asira, these history lessons will be good for your studies. The other students are one step ahead of you," Kai said with a cheeky grin as he walked by.

The students followed Kai and Volknor down into the forest behind the castle where the fresh water of the River Agápe ran. The grass was green, and the trees were oak.

Cara slipped off her runners dipping her feet into the chilly water. "Ah, this feels so good!" A shimmering reflection formed under the surface and her feet fused together to form a tail.

"Mermaids are attracted to the water," said Volknor as he knelt down beside the river's edge. "Just like werewolves, mermaids go through an incredible transformation. The scales grow out from the skin and encase the lower half of the body essentially fusing the legs and feet together."

"The Maria Empire is the only place in Velosia that has kept its empire for the last number of centuries. Mermaids are social creatures. Even though they live in the seas and oceans, they have to come to land for certain things. Mermaids are born on land and must be taught to swim like we are taught to walk," Kai continued.

"Can anyone, besides Cara, tell me the names of the gods that are worshipped by the mer-folk?" Volknor looked around at the students.

"The gods they worship are the land and sea," Katie replied sitting on the grass with her legs crossed.

"That's correct Katie but what are their names?" Kai asked again.

"Our gods are Moana and Terra," Cara replied swinging her tail in and out of the water.

"Correct," Kai stated. "And that is the point of this school. You are going to learn about all the races and kingdoms. There will be no more fires."

"What do you mean?" Katie asked curling her wings loosely behind her back.

"War." Kai spoke with a dark tongue. "War is the devil's spawn which should never have been born."

Volknor yawned and stretched his arms back behind his head. "History will be a big part of this curriculum. So too will the skills-building class. The rest of the time will be divided equally to discuss the different races."

***

The day had been long. It was eight o'clock and the students had retired early to their dorms. Asira had not realised that the day had taken such a lot out of her. Her fresh bath towels were sitting outside her ensuite. For the last fifteen minutes she had been lying across her bed kicking her feet off the edge. She had been texting back and forth with Amy, who was filling her in on all the sales and the new lifeguard down by the seaside.

Amy: *I don't think I can make myself any more obvious! I have invited him to do different things with me. We have gone shopping, to the cinema and to the cafe for food.*

Asira could feel Amy's frustration.

Asira: *Have you actually told him how you feel?*

Amy: *No but...I shouldn't have to. He should have picked up on it by now... right?*

Asira: *I think Tim is ignorant to feelings. Maybe you have to be direct.*

Amy: *But that's not a girl's job...*

Asira: *Maybe tomorrow he will see sense – sailing means swimming. Have fun!*

There was a sudden knock on the door.

"Dad? What's going on?"

"Can I come in?"

"Yes, of course." She closed the door behind him.

"I just wanted to see how you were settling in. I know it has only been a few days." He gazed around the room. "Well, I see all your stuff made it." He chuckled at the sight of her hair straightener on the countertop, a pack of hairclips which had somehow exploded across the table and several packets of chocolate biscuits lined up across her vanity table. Her empty suitcases were leaning against the wardrobe. The bathroom door was open with her dressing gown hanging from it. "Comfortable?"

"This place is incredible. We have to start living in a castle!" She moved to her chair and picked up a few tops she had thrown there and began hanging them in the wardrobe. "But there was something I wanted to ask you."

He glanced at her from the corner of his eye. He knew what she was going to say.

"What was that earlier today? The whole fight scene with Thomas and Aaron? Master Draskule wanted a fight. I know you said I would get a chance to use more spells but Dad, that was..."

Kai took in a deep breath. "Aaron getting injured was not anyone's intention. Believe me. Draskule is a brilliant warlock. He has saved me numerous times." He sat down on the edge of the bed.

"Then what was that about? I was afraid for Aaron."

"Don't lose sleep over it. Erika went through Draskule for a shortcut afterwards."

"Dad, it's a real shame it didn't work out between the two of you. I think you two would make the cutest couple."

"As the time went by, we just drifted apart. We stayed in contact but sometimes the things we want never really work out the way we plan." Kai thought back to when he was young. "When you were a baby, I was a stupid young fellow. Erika was my rock. Fate threw us together. She is an incredible sorceress."

"It sounds like you still like her."

"Nonsense. Now I better head out."

"Dad, I was actually wondering when we would be able to go home. Amy won't stop asking me."

"I think it will be another week or two. There is a lot of stuff to get through first."

She nodded slowly in agreement. "Okay, I was just hoping to meet up with her and the others." She flopped back on the bed.

Kai gazed around the room noticing an open packet of pain-killers. "How have you been feeling, Asira?"

She rubbed her tired eyes. "I've been getting headaches now and again. I wasn't sure if it was tiredness, stress or dehydration."

"Okay, I will let you get back to bed. Rest up and if you need anything just ring my phone."

"I will and thanks, Dad."

"Good night, Asira."

CHAPTER THIRTEEN

First Class

"So Asira, you have never lived in Velosia. Is that correct?" Cara held a hardback copy and flowery pencil case close to her chest. Asira had noticed something different about her the last few days. The little freedom she had been given was allowing Cara to express herself a little more. She was wearing more colours and more casual clothes. She walked closer to Asira than when her guards were present. But she remained diplomatic and caring. She was aware at all times that she was a representative of the Maria Empire.

"Yes, I've lived my entire life in England and only travelled occasionally with dad."

"How do you find actually living here so far?"

"Well, we're only here four days, so let's see. The first two days were not very exciting. There were a lot of guards hanging around the place. I couldn't find dad anywhere. I basically hung out in my bedroom watching rom-coms. To be honest, I'm glad all the guards have gone home."

"Really? Why so?"

"Well, I don't see why there would be any issues. We have three sorcerers, a warlock and the SNs as teachers. Dad was saying

Master Roberts and Master Draskule also put a protective spell around the grounds so no one can enter or leave without permission." Asira pulled the purple sleeve of her cardigan over her hand.

"I am not familiar with the term SN. What does it mean?" Cara asked.

"From what Dad has told me, SN just means supernatural. They are individuals who are born into a race with no physical attribute but have an elemental power, like a fairy being born without wings but can control fire. Volknor and Airies are both SNs, skilled in a particular element. Anton, how are you finding it? I know it might not be pleasant with Aaron and his cheerleaders."

"It's actually been a little more pleasant than I had anticipated. I get to hang out with you and Cara and have made some new friends."

"Aww, Anton that is so sweet." Cara elbowed her in the ribs. "Isn't that right, Asira? He is so sweet."

"Though I hope today doesn't turn out like yesterday. Poor Aaron looked so embarrassed after his interaction with Thomas. I wasn't even aware an essence had that sort of power," Asira pushed some fallen locks behind her ear.

"I've always been taught that if you are facing an essence, you never turn your back on them and try to avoid a fight at all costs," Anton said.

"Aaron could have been killed but they both looked mortified."

"Are you concerned for Aaron?" Anton glanced down at her.

"It wasn't fair on either of them to be pitted against one another. Anyway, Aaron doesn't seem like a bad guy. He seems more influenced by Angelica then his own mind."

Asira, Cara and Anton joined the rest of the class at the end of the corridor where they had gathered outside a room which was specifically designed and outfitted as a traditional classroom.

"It's nine o'clock. Why are we waiting outside?" Asira leaned down next to Bobby and peeked through the ajar door. "What is it?"

"Master Volknor is trying to draw a dog on the white board," he sniggered in a whisper. As he turned, she caught a glimpse at his distinctive chestnut eyes but more unique was the ring of gold around his pupils.

"Your eyes, they're…"

"Beautiful, I know," Bobby immediately cut her off, leaning against the wall with a cocky smirk. "It's a family trait. I get these eyes from my mother you know, who is a world-famous zoo whisperer."

"Don't mind this *coileáinín beag*," Eoin spoke with a charming accent. He was tall, standing an inch or two over Bobby.

"*Coileáinín beag?*" Asira glanced up at his regular blue eyes and for a change there was something serene about the normality of his appearance and presence.

"It means 'little pup' in Irish, which is what Bobby is." Eoin glanced through the gap in the door. "Anyway, I think Master Volknor is trying to draw a werewolf."

Bobby glanced again. "He is awful at this."

Asira rolled her eyes. "Well, maybe he's not great at drawing but I don't see you doing any better."

"Oh, so we have a feisty little sorceress among us," Eoin snorted in amusement.

"For your information, I actually know what I'm talking about. I'm a bit of an artist. I design comic books," Bobby said holding a sketch pad under his arm.

"More like mangas," Eoin leaned back against the wall pulling the sketch pad from his grasp.

"Hey man!" Bobby let out a yelp of frustration as a nerve jerked on his forehead.

"I'm impressed. I've always preferred mangas over comics anyway," Asira stated before stepping into the classroom and taking a seat in the second row by the window. "Good morning Master Volknor."

Volknor turned from the board and clapped his hands. "Good morning students!"

Asira gazed at all the strange students entering the room trying to put names to faces. It wasn't until everyone sat down that she noticed the immediate divide in the class.

The seating arrangement was set out in four rows with four seats in a row. From left to right in the front row there was Bobby, Thomas, Fabia and Chloe. In the second row there was Asira, Cara and Aaron followed by Angelica. The third row consisted of Peter, Blake, Britanie and Mandy. And in the final row were Eoin, Anton, Zayne and Katie.

Volknor picked up the marker. "I see social convention already dictates where we all sit. Pen and paper, these are your classes during this short term." He cleared his throat and pointed to the far left of the white board. "We will be studying all about the races starting with *Werewolves – Anatomy & the Clans*. Then we will be moving onto *Witches & Sorcerers – A Magical Difference*, followed by *Elves & Leprechauns – An Understanding of the Earth, Greek Fairies, Renassies Fairies & Essences – Power Balance, Hexites – Primal Beings, Vampires – Myths VS Reality, Mermaids – The Maria Empire, Angels – Grace & Virtue*. And finally, we will of course be studying the vast history of Velosia, as well as re-introducing you to the skills-building classes."

Asira scribbled down the titles of the classes. Beside her, she noticed Cara taking extra pride in her notes as she switched between blue, black and red pens. She glanced to the back of the class catching Anton's eye. He was already smirking over at her.

"We are going to start with the werewolves." Volknor pointed to the crude black outline on the board.

Mandy giggled out loud. "We are going to nail this class!"

"We can't really be taught anything that we don't already know," Angelica was smug, crossing her arms and leaning back in her seat.

"Werewolves have an incredible metamorphic ability to change their appearance and imitate an actual wolf. Once in this form, they are unrecognisable against any other wolf. They have the usual features – ears, fur, fangs, four paws. The transformation is unique as it involves a complete skeletal reconstruction. The bones of the werewolf alter shape to complete the transformation."

Asira gazed across the room. It seemed Aaron was keeping himself distant. His arms were folded, and he was slouched across the desk.

"You probably think yesterday damaged your pride," Volknor empathised gazing down the classroom. "But get over yourself. Come up here Aaron."

Aaron tensed at his desk. He was hesitant, slowly edging off the seat before walking to the top of the class.

"I'm not trying to embarrass you so don't look so frightened," Volknor said with a cheeky grin before turning back to the class. "I know you all saw Aaron's transformation yesterday, but it happened so quickly that you actually missed out on the beauty of the transformation." He pulled Aaron's arms out straight like a ruler. "I would say Aaron is of average height, about five foot ten. He is a good build with strong shoulders. He has blue eyes and sandy hair."

"What are you doing?" Aaron grumbled under his breath.

"These features are key to identifying who your werewolf is. Aaron, can you please transform?"

"What?" He put his arms back by his side. "You want me to transform into a werewolf?"

"Yes please and transform slowly. This is all part of the lesson."

"Well, you will want to stand back. I'm not sure you really know how different we are from regular wolves."

Aaron shook out his shoulders, closing his eyes to concentrate. Transforming was easy. He had been transforming into a werewolf since he was three or four years of age. But in the Australian outback it was survival of the fittest. Transforming as quickly as possible was basic and transforming while running was a survival technique. It became instinct.

With one slow breath a fang began to overlap his bottom lip and a deep growl grumbled from the back of his throat. His sandy hair fell across his face as his ears pointed outwards. His shoulders and hips began to crack and alter in an awkward manner. His frame lowered as four muscular paws gripped the wooden floor. He snarled as he shook his head and shoulders into the final position.

"That was breath-taking!" Asira whispered loudly as she leaned across her desk.

Volknor crouched onto his hunkers and grabbed the hairy snout. "Look at those fangs and notice how the eyes have remained the same colour and that his fur is the same colour as his hair." He continued poking Aaron's jaw with the marker until he grumbled deep from his throat. "There is no big difference between Aaron now and a wild wolf."

Angelica sat back. "He did it," she whispered in disbelief.

"Wow Aaron, that was amazing!" Mandy jumped to her feet.

Volknor gazed down the class. "Interesting. You've never transformed slowly before? This is interesting. Well done, Aaron. If that was your first time transforming at such a slow speed, I'm impressed," Volknor clapped excitedly. "Well class, this is an Australian Sand Clan Werewolf."

Mandy jumped to her feet. "My turn! I have much nicer fur than Aaron. Do you want me to transform slowly? Or super-fast?" She snatched Britanie and Angelica's hands and dragged them to the top of the class with her.

"Obviously, the werewolves are not native to Earth," Volknor spoke to the class. "The clans adopted the earthly names after their migration. The werewolf race is minimal in comparison to what it was one hundred years ago, but the species is thriving and continues to grow at a steady pace." He turned back to Mandy. "Please transform normally."

Mandy's dark chocolate brunette hair eclipsed her dark sallow skin. Her brown eyes glimmered as her bones cracked and changed shape. She lowered herself to the ground and snarled as her snout formed last. Britanie crouched on all fours. Her shoulders and hips shifted. Claws scratched the ground. White fur graced her pale complexion. Angelica's long platinum hair began wrapping along her back, changing colour. Black fur exploded across her hot chocolate skin tone. She jumped to four paws with her glaring blue eyes.

"Interesting. Dyed hair doesn't matter when you transform. Your natural hair colour depicts your fur." Volknor rubbed his hand through his hair. "The four werewolf races as of today – the Australian Sand Clan," he pointed to Aaron. "The African Savannah Clan," he gestured to Angelica at the far end. "The Antarctica Snow Clan," he pointed to Britanie and finally he pointed towards Mandy, "The Amazon Forest Clan."

"Sir," Asira raised her hand just over her head. "I really think earth wolves are much smaller. They are only about two feet tall. Aaron looks the height of a lion."

"Maybe I don't know wolves as well as I thought," Volknor pulled a measuring tape from the desk drawer. "You may be right."

He measured the wolves individually from shoulder to paw. "Aaron you are four foot five inches. Britanie is three foot and two inches. Angelica is the second tallest at three foot eight inches and Mandy you are three foot and six inches." He turned to a notebook on his desk and scribbled down the sizes. "Impressive. You learn something new every day."

"Sir," Fabia raised her arm into the air.

"What is it?" He glanced up from the measuring tape.

"When are we having another skills-building class?"

"Did you enjoy the last one? It was kind of a flop."

"But sir, it will be interesting to see each other's powers and skills. I've never really used my power against anyone competitively," said Eoin sitting back in the wooden seat. "When does anyone get a chance like this?"

Volknor thought to himself for a moment. "Okay, I will make sure the next skills-building class is done properly."

CHAPTER FOURTEEN

The Sorceress

"When will they be taking us outside to train?" Bobby sank back into the wooden seat as he scribbled a doodle of a puppy inside his notebook.

"I know I would love to see what everyone can do." Eoin flicked a pen between his fingers. "Asira, what tricks can you do?"

"Tricks? Well, I used to perform illusions back at home."

"Illusions?! Can you do one for us now?"

"Eoin, you get too excited. You're like a big child sometimes." Peter sat in between Asira and Eoin. He was so much shier than the other boys. His voice was timid. He always wore a black and grey woolly camo hat pulled right over his ears, baggy jeans and a green hooded jumper. He was pale and was much shorter than Eoin or Bobby.

"Peter, this is the most exciting thing to ever happen to me. Back at home magic is a thing of make-believe. No one would believe that I have met an actual sorceress." Eoin let out a yelp of excitement.

"I totally understand, Eoin. No one at home would believe me either. Sure, all my friends are regular people. They don't believe in magic," Asira added.

"See! No one here understands the excitement of being at a magical school. It's like a novel."

"You've probably never even seen a human before," Eoin said to Anton.

"Well, how different are they from you? Besides making plants grow."

Eoin furrowed his brow. "Good point, I suppose. Well, Asira, have you seen a vampire, fairy or mermaid before now?"

"Anton is my first vampire, Cara is my first mermaid, for definite."

"Zayne," Katie stretched one wing to the right of the room as she rested her head against her crossed arms. "When do you think we will be able to go home for a visit? Do you think Mummy misses us?"

"Of course she misses us." Zayne leaned back in the wooden seat and curled his wings behind the metal frame. "What I miss are open spaces."

"Do you miss the heat from South Africa?" Britanie spoke softly amusing herself with the beaded bracelet on her wrist.

"Yes," Angelica extended her arms into the air. "I do miss the heat and the good weather. But I love the luxury here. The bed is beautiful. The sheets are cotton. The bath is superb. I don't have a bath at home. I'm in heaven here."

"Well, this place is lovely, but I miss the forest," Mandy said slumped over the desk.

"Where are you from?" Britanie asked in the same soft-spoken tone.

"I live in the heart of the Amazon forest."

"That power, what is it called?" Fabia turned towards Thomas. She was wearing a mellow yellow summery dress.

"An essence power is called the core. It comes from our soul. With it, we can see a person's aura and sense their emotion."

"That is incredible. I've never seen anything like it. The power – it was like golden threads and fairy dust." Fabia swung her legs through the rung of the chair. "It's beautiful."

Thomas smirked. "It really is beautiful but it's hard to control. That is why my uncle suggested it was a good idea for me to attend this place. If I ever want to become a leader, I have to be able to control my emotions. That is the only way to control my power."

"You will get it. It may not be today but some day you will have a grasp of that power," Fabia smiled.

"What about you? You're a witch?" Thomas asked. "You don't look like a witch."

"Everyone stereotypes a witch. You expect to see a witch in a long black cloak, a black dress, a broomstick between her legs, and a book of spells in one hand, a mini cauldron in the other." She shook her head vigorously. "Nope, I love bright warm colours. I love going to the beach and painting. I am definitely not a witch from spooky fairy tales." She giggled. "Chloe, what do you do?"

"Hmm..." Chloe was sitting to Fabia's right. Her wings were transparent and wide, so she was leaning forward, keeping away from the back of the chair. "What do you mean?"

"What is your power?" Fabia reiterated.

"Well, I can use the power of light and sense emotions. That's about it."

"Light? How do you use light? I don't get it." A puzzled look settled on Fabia's face.

Chloe opened the palm of her hand and a white light coated her skin. "It's handy for seeing in the dark, and I suppose for distractions, I can use it like a flash grenade. And umm..." She thought to herself for a moment. "If I really focus on the light, I can make it physical as well. It could be used as a weapon..." From over Fabia's shoulder she could see Blake gazing across at the light shimmering on her palm.

"Blake?" Fabia turned swiftly, frightening him into a little jump.

"Yes?" he gripped the edge of his seat.

"What power can you use?"

"Oh power, yes…" he held out his hand as a black and purple light formed on his palm. "I can also sense the emotions of individuals and use the dark energy to create different things like force fields."

"Your powers are like polar opposites but parallel as well. It is sooo cool!" Fabia squealed as she hopped onto her knees.

Chloe closed her palm over and turned back into her seat.

"What's wrong?" Fabia watched, confused as both fairies turned away from one another. "What did I say?"

Thomas stretched his head over to her desk. "Don't worry too much. Fairies have been sort of enemies for years. I would be surprised if they even talked to me."

"You? What did you do?" Fabia sat back into her seat a little saddened.

"I am an essence. We are related to the fairies. None of the species really talk."

"That's very upsetting. Mummy would be very cross at me if I was ignoring people in class, especially if they didn't do anything to me."

"Welcome to the class *Vampires – Myths VS Reality*," said Volknor stepping into the room closing the door behind him. "There are many books on Earth that revolve around vampires. The books are fiction, and the facts are not facts at all. Don't expect anything to be accurate." He gazed around the class. The mood was sort of poignant. He clapped his hands together. "Together, we are going to pull fact from fiction in this class." He wrote *Vampire* on the board, circling it and started drawing a spider diagram. He jotted down the word *blood*. "All vampires drink blood. They do eat and drink other things. Blood is just their main diet. Vampires cannot go without blood for long."

"Wait, wait, wait!" Bobby said loudly swinging to Anton's direction. "You drink blood every day?"

"On a regular basis," Anton replied in a matter-of-fact tone.

"That is bad ass!" Bobby thumped both fists into the desk. "Can I try some?"

Anton raised an eyebrow curiously.

Asira covered her mouth in disgust. "Is it human?" Her stomach began to turn sour. Bobby's face suddenly went pale.

"No," Anton replied bluntly, "it is animal. Mainly cow."

A smile crossed Volknor's face. They were learning. He wrote another word on the board *immortal*. "No vampire is immortal. No one in Velosia is." He wrote *fire*. "Not all vampires can manipulate fire."

Anton turned his hand in a clockwise motion as a small flame danced and flickered along his fingers.

"Not all vampires can manipulate fire, but Anton can," Volknor restated what he had previously said. *Stake* was written clockwise on the board. "Because they are mortal, a wooden stake through the chest can kill a vampire – as it would kill anyone. Garlic does not harm a vampire either. They have reflections. They are just people."

At those words Angelica slumped back into her seat. She was doodling a picture of fangs and next to it she wrote *Vampire? Werewolf?* 'They are just people,' she thought as she focused on the scribbles. Her eyes then locked onto the word *mortal* written on the board.

"Vampires have venom in their system. If they bite and intend to, they can turn people into vampires. Though, it is frowned upon in society, especially by The Kalis Republic. Turned vampires are a little mentally unstable."

"Sir," Fabia raised her hand "what do you mean by that?"

"Well, maybe my wording wasn't quite right." He tapped the marker against his forehead for a moment. "What I mean is when a person is bitten, they go through an enormous change. Their body has to quickly learn to cope with the venom and the brain sometimes cannot keep up with the change. Their emotions can be more volatile than when they were human."

"Sir," Eoin raised his arm slightly, "I think it would be a good idea if we could see a vampire in action. That is, if it's alright with you, sir?"

'Sly, Eoin,' Asira thought to herself, glancing around and catching Anton smiling at her immediately.

"Well, I suppose we could combine the skills-building classes with some facts. Wait here." Volknor stepped outside.

"Well done," Anton high-fived Eoin promptly.

"Yes, well done, Eoin. This is great. We can finally go outside." Bobby threw his arms into the air excitedly and leaned back into his chair.

"Please, we haven't even had a proper class yet. How can you hate it that much?" Angelica crossed her arms and stared across to the white board.

"If we go outside, does that mean we can have a race?" Katie stretched across to Zayne's desk poking him in the upper arm.

"Not a bad idea. I need to stretch my wings," Zayne lazily straightened his shoulders.

"Oh! I want to race!" Mandy jumped from her seat bouncing on the balls of her feet as Volknor entered the room again.

He blankly stared at Mandy for a moment. "Okay class, let's go outside."

Mandy laughed nervously before taking Britanie by the arm.

"If this is another skills-building class, I wonder what's going to happen?" Asira questioned as she followed behind Cara.

"I am not too sure," Cara responded. "The other teachers were not impressed with how it went the other day." They stepped out onto the steps on the castle where Erika was already waiting.

"Nervous?" Anton whispered into Asira's ear.

"We were going to leave the skills-building classes for the afternoons but Volknor has said you were all eager to stretch your legs." Erika paced up and down the stone path. "I know you were learning about vampires in your last class, but I thought we would start by giving you a proper introduction to this skills-building class. The purpose of this class is to learn, experiment and develop your powers and abilities in a safe environment. As young leaders, you will have to command groups and subjects but in order to do that, you will have to know yourself inside and out. As a king or queen there is no room for error. It may seem redundant now but think about it. A good leader will need to know how far they can push themselves. And to be honest, what leader cannot control his or her power?"

"Erika is right." Volknor was standing between the students. "There is not a chief, king or queen in command right now that does not know the full extent of their own power. They know exactly what they can do and how far they can push themselves. I know we are living in peaceful times now, but at some point in the future, that could change. You will have to know how to defend yourself and anyone close to you."

"Asira and Eoin, you guys are first." Erika stood straight and kept her arms down by her side. "One thing we were taught very quickly in the war was how to identify a person by their power. What they were able to do. This can either be their trait in terms of physical ability or their element in terms of supernatural ability."

Fabia raised her hand. "Does that mean because Anton can use fire that he has an elemental ability and because Zayne can fly that he has a trait ability."

"Correct. Of course, people can have two of these. For instance..." She looked around at the students. "Cara is a mermaid. That is her trait. But she can also manipulate water. That is her element. As part of this class, we would like each student to develop a signature move. It would be like their particular fighting style."

Asira watched the movements and stance of both Erika and Volknor carefully. Their posture, composure and even their attitudes were somewhat military like. This is something she had always noticed about her dad as well.

"Asira, as a young sorceress in training, has your master ever tried to develop a particular spell with you?"

Asira nodded immediately.

A sly grin crossed Erika's face. "I'm very interested in seeing what you can do, Asira." Erika swung back on her heels and turned her attention to the rest of the class. "In a few moments Master Volknor will demonstrate the skill that defines him."

"Oooh!" Eoin exclaimed loudly. "Now I understand."

"This class will be about fitness and guidance. You will be able to train freely with your powers. We will have one-on-one with peers and teachers. We will have group matches as well. It will be a controlled and safe environment." She glanced around at the young faces.

A lump formed in Asira's throat as her lips dried. She had never fought before. Kai had never taken her to karate classes as a kid nor did he teach her to defend herself from any circumstance. She learned to cast spells and was good at it. She wasn't even built for fighting. Her arms were too scrawny.

An almost evil smile crossed Erika's lips. "You may begin in your own time."

Asira and Eoin looked at each other for a moment before their attention was simultaneously drawn to Volknor sauntering down the steps, stretching his arms over his head, and cracking his jaw open. "It's been a while since I've been able to stretch like this." He shook his hands vigorously. Yellow electricity sparked between his fingers. It charged around his palm in a marvellous blue blur and quickly coated his hand in flickers.

"As you may be aware," Erika began to narrate as she ran to stand next to the class by the castle steps. "Volknor is a SN of lightning." As she spoke, the electricity oozing from his skin seeped onto the stone pavement. The blue electricity danced along the ground and in a fluid motion, became a serpent. Its head jolted forward hissing aggressively. "This is Volknor's signature move. It is a very difficult spell based on a particular element. This one is based on the transitional element of lightning and is known as the Aviul serpent."

"The Aviul," Asira murmured under her breath.

Erika took a step back. "A sorceress has many elements at her disposal. Eoin, as a leprechaun you have a unique advantage in open territory."

The electrical serpent charged forward with incredible speed slithering across the ground.

"Draskule, what are you doing here?" Erika glanced to her left.

"This is rather exciting. So instead of pitting them against one another, you have chosen a more brutal option?"

Erika furrowed her brow. "This is in no way brutal. They can be experimental without hurting each other. Volknor can restrain himself. He has good control."

"Good. I can help. Those with single powers are easy to train. However, the young sorceress can do far greater things than parlour tricks. How do you expect to test her?"

"I am a sorceress as well. I know the best way to test her skills." She crossed her arms in irritation. "Though, I did overhear her say she performed illusions for audiences back home."

"Illusions?" Draskule scoffed. "That is parlour trickery. Has Kai taught her nothing?"

"I have taught her plenty, Draskule." Kai stepped down next to them. "I'm glad you were able to join us. Will you be staying long?"

"Only a few minutes. I have some important Council matters to attend to shortly."

"If you cannot attack you must defend!" Erika yelled across to them.

With one arm and without hesitation, Eoin hooked Asira's waist pulling her into his chest. He held up his other arm vertically, as if to block the charging serpent. Instead, vines and roots grew from the depths of the ground and created a thick wall between them. The serpent charged headfirst into the wall and the blue sparks dispersed in every direction.

"Leprechauns have the incredible ability to most accurately read the land around them and manipulate plant life," Erika continued to narrate to the class.

Asira glanced back over her shoulder. Eoin's arm was still wrapped firmly around her waist. His head was facing the wall. Her breath had been knocked out of her, so it took her a few seconds to compose herself. "Thank you," she began softly "that was so swift."

"That was incredible, Eoin!" Bobby cheered from the castle.

"Asira," Eoin finally looked around at her. His grip loosened. "Do you have any plans? I think a long-range attack would work well. It means we can still hide behind the wall."

She sank into a heap. "I... I don't know if I can fight. I've never done any sort of physical combat training before. I've only ever trained with dad and outside of that, my illusions are pretty good."

Eoin knelt down next to her. "You are a sorceress. There is no way a sorceress can't defend herself. I know you can use your training here. You just have to believe in what you're doing. My plants will not be great at attacking but I can keep up the defence. I've got your back. I promise."

With those words of encouragement, she closed her eyes. She thought back to the endless late nights she had spent with her dad trying to perfect techniques and trying to learn spells. She swallowed the lump in her throat and inhaled a deep breath.

Eoin peeked around the vines watching as the blue electricity began to build up a charge in front of Volknor again. "Now would be a good time to come up with something, Asira."

She pushed the few pebbles to one side and pressed her hand flat against the stone pavement. The ground beneath began to pulsate like a gentle heartbeat, quivering and then cracking. She rose to her feet keeping her arm outstretched. The cracked ground and dirt levitated and formed before her. The broken earth transformed into a long and slender stony body. Two horns were curled backwards on the narrow head.

"What is that?" Eoin asked poking the rocky tail swinging next to his face.

She stared back at the slender head of the creature. "This is my Avio," Asira answered softly as if not wanting to frighten it. Just like the electric serpent, the Avio did not have any pupils. Its eyes were a carving of the ground. It looked soulless but there was something distinctively beautiful about it. She swung her arm to the right and the rocky serpent followed her direction, darting swiftly around the vine wall.

"It's so fast," Eoin remarked lowering the wall.

"The strange thing about the Avio serpent is it's incredibly agile and nimble."

"Is it a spell?"

"It's an old and tricky spell that not many people know." Asira's eyes were locked dead ahead. She watched as Volknor twitched his fingers ever so subtly essentially controlling the Aviul like a puppet. The blue electric serpent hissed aggressively as it darted forward. Asira swayed her hand to the right and the Avio serpent copied her motion.

Although Asira hated to admit it but there was no way she was going to defeat Volknor. She had spent years trying to cast the spell and create the serpents from their elements. She had not quite mastered the spell, but she was able to control it without losing her sight. This was because she had been working with the spell for almost six years, a lot longer than the portal spell. But Volknor had been using his powers for over forty years. He was a skilfully trained soldier.

The Aviul dodged the stony serpent and charged directly for Asira. Eoin snapped his fingers, and a grassy wall blocked the electric serpent again. Blue electricity sparked everywhere but the serpent quickly reformed. Asira pushed herself in front of Eoin and threw her arms outwards. The Avio serpent rammed right through the electric serpent, causing the blue electricity to spark wildly and the stone to crumble.

"That was amazing!" Erika was clapping passionately as she ran onto the courtyard.

Finally able to catch her breath, Asira collapsed to her knees. "That was the scariest thing I've ever done." She threw her head back as Eoin leaned over her, blocking the sunlight.

"Really? The scariest?" He held his arm out and pulled her to her feet. "That was incredible. I knew you could do it."

Asira blushed brightly. "You technically saved me first."

"But we wouldn't have been able to stop Volknor if you hadn't thought of a plan."

"There really was no plan. The Avio is just the spell I was most comfortable with."

"Either way it was very impressive."

Erika stepped between them. "I cannot believe Kai taught you those serpent spells." She crossed her arms, a little jealous. "He wouldn't even teach me that and I spent years listening to him moan and groan."

"How did Volknor come to learn it?" Asira glanced across over at his blatantly carefree face.

"His master taught him," Erika said quietly. "Volknor," she turned on her heel.

Volknor strolled towards them. "I wonder if I kept going, would you have been able to regenerate the Avio?"

Asira shook her head. "It takes a lot out of me. I would have been able to recreate the spell after a few minutes."

"Master Volknor, sir!" Mandy leapt from the steps. "Can we have a race now, please?"

"I would love a chance to stretch my wings," Zayne's wings uncurled.

"Please sir!" Mandy leapt into the air leaning on Britanie's shoulders. "I want to race! Please can we race?"

"I'd love to get some sun on my back." Britanie stretched her shoulders, hunched from Mandy leaning so hard on them.

"It's settled then," Erika stepped over to the castle. "It will be a race against the sky and the earth."

Katie and Zayne high-fived each other as they walked onto the courtyard spreading their swan-like wings as wide as they could.

Mandy and Britanie followed behind growling, fur promptly unfolding across their skin, their bones cracking and shifting into place.

"It's not every day that angels race against werewolves," Eoin smiled taking a step closer to the castle. He glanced across at Asira for a second before returning his gaze to the starting point. "This will be quite something. Any bets, Asira?"

"I've never seen either of them race before," she said watching in amazement.

"On your marks," Erika began. The wolves crouched and growled competitively. Katie and Zayne crouched on their hunkers curling their wings back and then spreading them out again in a graceful bow. "Get set," the stony path of the courtyard was their racetrack. "Go!" The wolves dashed off immediately. Katie and Zayne ran, flapped their wings in chorus before taking flight.

They flapped and flapped until they were high enough in the air to dive and gain speed. The angels swooped overhead, instantly catching up with the speedy wolves. Their wings were white, blending well with the clouds above, and if they were high enough, they would just look like a bird soaring through the blue sky. The wolves were swift and strong. Their powerful leg muscles allowed for rapid and nimble movement. They adapted to blend with their hunting ground.

They were coming up to the forest entrance. It was neck and neck. Then Katie and Zayne swooped in a fraction of a second before the wolves. Mandy tumbled into herself and bounded to her feet. "That was amazing! I can't wait to tell mom and dad about this!"

Britanie plopped onto her tail and fell back against a tree. "Truly... one for the records!"

"It was fun," Katie added, dangling upside down from a tree. Her wings drooped behind her head.

Zayne was sitting upright on the branch next to her. With an eagle's grace, he glided down to the ground and held out a hand to Britanie. "You are indeed fast and lissom. I'm impressed. We must do this again sometime."

Britanie was shy and it echoed in her personality. She pulled a strand of hair over her eye and turned to Mandy for comfort.

CHAPTER FIFTEEN

Bluebird

"Leave them to mingle and they will open up to each other." Myron crossed through the bar of the pub into a back room and entered his private garden where he began watering his Venus Flytrap with great care. "What did I tell you, tensions will fall once the new generation of kings are brought together to learn about one another. It was a lack of respect and tolerance that fuelled the war."

Volknor and Kai were standing against the outer wall gazing out at the beautiful hidden paradise. Plants of many varieties had thrived within this garden for many years.

"What do you think?" Volknor gestured.

"Well," Kai rubbed this hand through his hair. "They've shown great promise. There was a bit of tension between the werewolves and Anton for the first few days, but things seemed to have eased a bit. I haven't taken classes with them yet. Though what I hear from Asira is that class relations are promising."

"Things were aggravated by Angelica more so than anything else. She was so bitter and resentful towards Anton. And I don't think he had personally done anything wrong. I think it was just animosity towards vampires." Volknor stretched for a chocolate biscuit from the tin.

"We were always expecting some conflict," Airies added reaching for the pot of tea.

"She hasn't really done anything more than give back talk and snippy comments," Volknor continued, "but this is only the end of the first week. However, I have noticed a huge improvement in the class interactions. The fairies are still sitting away from each other but since yesterday they have been chatting freely to one another. I think they were just apprehensive and too nervous to break the ice."

"The first week was critical to judge the social interactions," Kai said. "We've had classes back-to-back. The students rise early and finish late. They don't have time to think negatively. In order to complete assignments, they have to work in groups or in pairs. They have been forced to interact with one another and I don't think there have been any objections."

"That's true. They haven't had any time to think. By dinnertime they are too exhausted to even think of reasons to hate each other. The class are really warming up to one another. And any pent-up frustration is released during the skills-building exercises," Erika added taking a sip of tea.

"Well, it really sounds like you have a good class to work with." Myron sat down next to Erika.

Airies suddenly squealed with excitement. "Did anyone notice how much Asira looks like her mother."

"She really does!" Erika turned to Kai. "Andrew, she has Crystal's hair and bone structure, but she definitely has your eyes and stubbornness."

"On the contrary, Crystal could be very stubborn," Volknor butted in.

"Oh, she definitely has your eyes, Andrew," Airies nodded in agreement.

"Does she know about Crystal?" Volknor asked.

"I've told her some stories," Kai replied.

"I'm sure it wasn't easy raising her all by yourself?" Airies sympathised.

"But he did it!" Erika uttered proudly. "You were dead right to leave Velosia. It gave you and Asira a better chance at life. It was the fresh start you needed."

"But she always wanted to learn as much as she could about this place. Once she has her mind set on something, it's hard to persuade her otherwise."

"That's a good thing, Andrew. She wanted to learn about her past. She wanted to see where you grew up. She wanted to learn as much as she could about her family. That is the curiosity of a sorceress," said Erika sipping from her hot mug again.

"Do you ever regret leaving?" Volknor asked not looking away.

"No, I don't regret leaving. I couldn't have stayed." Kai took a small breath. "Leaving allowed me to focus one hundred percent on Asira."

"If you think about it," Erika began, "you never really left Velosia."

"What do you mean?" Airies enquired.

"Well, you have shown Asira parts of Velosia. You do come back every now and again. You have taught her magic and you told her stories of your home and of the war. And now, Asira is attending school here. Velosia was always in your blood. I wouldn't be surprised if you died here."

***

Mandy and Britanie, Katie and Zayne had spent from midday racing one another around the courtyard. The day had been glorious and once morning classes ended, the students had taken some time to unwind.

Left to their own devices and with dusk approaching, the group of sixteen students wandered carefree into the surrounding forest, not too far away from the castle. They set up a campfire which Anton had kindly ignited.

"When you light an ember, do you even think about it or how do you go about it?" Asira asked Anton as they stood over the fire.

"Are you able to control fire?"

"Well yes, I'm actually quite good at it. But I was just wondering if it's the same feeling."

"What does fire feel like to you?"

Asira gazed at the crackling wood. "Some people think fire is frightening but to me fire is warm. It's comforting. It's reassuring."

Anton took her hand, his index finger gliding gently around her palm and a small ember was born. "Fire feels the exact same to me." Her cheeks blushed as she looked from her hand to his glistening maroon eyes. "It's the same warm feeling I get when I'm around you."

"Do you guys tell scary stories around campfires?" Mandy asked wrapping her arms around her knees. "Back home we would camp out under the stars, tell scary stories and melt marshmallows on a stick."

"We did the same," Aaron said leaning back on his right arm.

Angelica was curled into his waist. "We would usually sit on the open savannah with a fire in the background. The blanket of stars was our night light."

"I think melting marshmallows over an open fire is a common practice no matter where you're from," Asira smiled thinking fondly of the movie nights she had with Amy as they stayed up for hours stuffing their face with junk food.

"I think it is more of an earthly tradition," Eoin remarked as he glanced around at the bewildered faces.

"What's a marshmallow?" Katie asked as she pushed her wings behind her.

"What?? You've never had a marshmallow before?" Asira immediately jumped to her feet.

"Wait! Where are you going?" Anton snatched her wrist.

"I'll be back in a moment. I promise." She quickly made her exit as large purple doors closed behind her.

"Did Asira leave us?" Cara stared blankly to where her friend had vanished. "How do we tell the teachers she has disappeared?"

"I'm sure she's coming back." Anton jumped to his feet and anxiously waited.

Three long minutes passed before the purple portal reappeared and Asira stepped through with a bag. "Sorry, finding the skewers took a little longer than expected."

"Where did you go?" Anton walked over to her. "I was worried. I didn't think you could teleport out of here. I thought this area was protected?"

"Dad gave me permission to leave ages ago. Why, were you worried? I brought marshmallows." Asira handed out the bags of marshmallows and napkins. "So," she stuffed a marshmallow onto a skewer and handed it to Anton. "All you do is roast the marshmallow over the fire until it becomes sticky and melted."

"This is the best dessert ever!" Eoin cheered roasting three sticks simultaneously.

"Thank you." Anton held onto her hand for a few seconds before pulling the marshmallow away with his teeth. "It's very sugary."

"Asira, you said you were an illusionist before. Can you do a trick for us?" Eoin asked staring at the melting marshmallows.

"I love magic tricks," said Bobby, crouched over his knees gazing at a cute little hedgehog sheltered between his feet.

"I don't know," Asira twisted the stick over the open flame.

"Don't be embarrassed," Peter spoke with a slight quiver in his voice. He was trying to feed the hedgehog a leaf.

"Look who's talking, Peter," said Chloe fluttering her wide transparent wings for a moment. Her hair was soft and golden, plaited and tied with a red ribbon.

"She's right," Blake responded as he glanced over the dancing flames at the Greek fairy. "None of us have anything to be ashamed of."

Chloe blushed and glanced back down to her feet and immediately played with her plait.

"This is going to sound stupid," Asira began, "but besides your wings, what is the difference between the Greek and Renassies fairies?"

"Well," Blake cleared his throat directing his gaze at Asira, "I am a Renassies fairy and Chloe is a Greek fairy. The fairies just deviated down different paths a long, long time ago. While Chloe can focus light magic, I can use dark magic. I suppose," he gazed back across the open fire, "there are no real differences between the fairies."

"Back at home children are told stories of vampires, fairies and mermaids but these are just mythical creatures. They're told to put kids to sleep." Asira blew onto the roasted skewer.

"Makes sense that the other world doesn't know anything about Velosia," Fabia remarked. "They probably couldn't fathom the exponential forces here."

"So Asira, can you do a trick for us now?" Katie sat shoulder to shoulder with her brother. Her long white-blond hair and turquoise blue eyes were the total opposite to Zayne's short jet-black hair and green eyes, but both had a powdery complexion.

"Yes. Asira, show us a trick." Thomas also had jet black hair, but his eyes were a golden colour.

Fabia excitedly shook Thomas' arm. "Yes, show us a magic trick. Pretty please!"

"Well, okay." Asira took a deep breath, cupping her hands on top of one another. "My dad has always said that illusions were a manipulation of the mind. Real magic is a manipulation of the environment. Those untrained will not be able to tell it apart." As she opened her hands a small bluebird chirped, stretching its wings before flying to the treetops.

"Was that an illusion?" Fabia stared at her intently.

"No, that is the real thing. Only a trained eye can spot the difference."

"You created life?" Fabia flopped back to the ground in amazement.

"A bluebird! Wow," Eoin's whisper was breathy as he gazed in her direction. "Asira, how? How did you do that? I hope you realise I'll be calling you Bluebird from now on."

Asira blushed brightly. "It took practice, but I can only really conjure up generic, simple forms. That bluebird will probably live a happy long life and procreate but it will never be like what nature intended. There will always be something missing."

Anton leaned forward and stared across at Eoin. "Eoin, what can you do?"

Eoin stared back and furrowed his brow irritably. "Master Roberts aptly described what a leprechaun is." He rubbed his hand through the dry forest floor and blue flowers immediately sprouted. "I manipulate plant life. I can hear that the forest is happy. I can tell the trees are really old."

"Wow Eoin, that is incredible." Asira gazed at the blossoming flowers.

"Hey guys, the stars are out," Britanie spoke in a soft voice.

Anton gazed fondly at Asira as she tilted her head back to stare up at the sky.

"They're like diamonds," she said in a low tone.

"Where we're from, the stars are the souls of those who've passed away. That is how they can keep an eye on us from above," Zayne said as he continued to stare up through the gaps in the trees.

"I never get to see the stars. They are just out of my reach." Cara lay on the ground next to Fabia.

"They're the eyes of our ancestors. If you see a new star, then a person close to you has died," Chloe added as she decided to lie on the grass too.

"Does anyone have any stories?" Fabia said now propping herself against Thomas' shoulder, unaware that her knees were pressing against his jeans.

"Like funny stories?" Mandy sat in front of the fire with her legs crossed. Britanie was next to her, resting her head on Mandy's shoulder.

"One time the pack was out hunting," Aaron began. "There is not much cover in the desert. We came across a few kangaroos along a cliffside. I was hunched behind a bush with my cousin Blue. This was his first or second hunt ever. He was only fourteen, I think. Our job was to separate the weak from the rest of the group. Well, Blue thought he was a big man and decided to take on a male kangaroo, head on." Aaron stopped to try and catch his breath from laughing so hard. "He was flung across the ground and struggled to transform back into a werewolf. When he did get back to his feet, it took him ages to catch up with the rest of the pack." He laughed so hard he stopped after every three or four words to catch his breath. "The kangaroo kicked him so hard he was thrown into the air and bruised three ribs."

"That was more horrific than funny," Fabia's smile turned upside down.

Bobby roared out laughing alongside Eoin. "That is the funniest thing I've heard in ages. He…" Bobby broke down in a giddy fit. "He was flung in the air!"

"Yeah!" Aaron continued, "I watched as this fur ball was flung fifteen feet into the air by a kangaroo! His legs were flailing everywhere."

Angelica shifted slightly and threw several sticks onto the fire.

"Here, let me help," Anton thrust his arm forward extending his fingers out. The dying embers reignited burning brighter than before and Angelica nodded gratefully.

"Oh, I know, let us all say one thing about what we like. I will begin. I am addicted to chocolate ice cream. I think it is the best thing about the land." Cara licked her lips just thinking about it.

"Okay, erm…" Peter murmured, "I have a pet llama called Heidi."

"Aw! I love llamas. They're so cute," Fabia screeched with excitement.

"I love alpacas. It's the one thing I won't eat," Mandy said leaning her tired head against Britanie this time.

Britanie glanced up from the fire. "I'm a ballerina."

"What? No way!" Asira blurted out. "That is incredible."

Britanie hid behind Mandy slightly.

"What to tell you guys that is any way interesting about me." Asira thought for a moment. "I love action movies, romantic novels and my favourite food is pasta. Oh, and my favourite dessert is mint ice cream."

Anton smiled next to her. "Well, I am a bit of a coffee addict."

Aaron smirked from across the campfire. "I am a bit of a marksman."

"You have a gun? Are you a sniper?" Peter enquired timidly.

"Don't be silly. There is no way he is a sniper," Thomas scoffed.

"Well, I have used a gun before," Aaron said. "I suppose you've never used a gun?"

"Why would a werewolf need a gun? You have claws and teeth," Eoin sniggered.

"That's enough boys." Katie stretched her wings behind her. She glanced to her brother. "Zayne and I are marksmen as well. We use bow and arrows. Often we go out to hunt wild deer and rabbits."

"Rabbit is my favourite meal," Britanie said licking her lips.

"Oh no!" Blake turned his head feeling queasy. "I much prefer fish."

"Salmon?" Chloe asked bluntly.

As Blake nodded slowly, a bright smile lit her face. "Salmon's my favourite too."

A cool breeze swept through the forest and without realising it, Asira shivered.

"Here," Eoin pulled off his jacket and wrapped it around her shoulders.

"Thank you, Eoin." The jacket was a bit baggy, but it was warm and cosy.

Anton leapt to his feet. "It's very late. Maybe we should head in for the night. Master Volknor and Master Kai will be wondering where we wandered off to." Anton's hand hovered over the dancing flames and without giving anyone a chance to object, he smothered the fire.

The group of students walked back along the forest path. Chloe was in the lead. Her arm outstretched as she emitted a bright light from her palm.

Blake was walking along next to her. "Does it feel warm?" He examined the light emanating from her skin.

"It's a strange feeling. It's kind of tingly, I suppose. What does the darkness feel like?"

Blake clenched his fingers back and forth and a black light encased his hand. "Sometimes it tingles. But most of the time, I can't even feel it. I suppose it is similar to your light element."

"The forest looks so scary in the dark." Angelica was clinging tightly to Aaron's arm. They were at the back of the group and the furthest away from Chloe and her light.

"I will gladly shine some light." Anton was walking just in front of them and with a click of his fingers, several little flames appeared above his shoulders and arms. They flickered in the breeze, but it was just enough light to ease Angelica's anxiety.

Angelica clutched Aaron's sleeve a little tighter. Her stomach felt queasy as an unsettling knot twisted in her gut as she thought, 'He seems so nice.'

As they reached the edge of the forest, Asira slipped off the jacket. "Here you go, Eoin. Thank you for lending me your jacket." She stepped back next to Anton, cupping her hand around a floating ember and playing with it between her fingers. "I hope you don't mind me taking this one. I'm a little clumsy in the dark."

Anton moved a little closer to her until his shoulder was grazing hers. "Not at all. Are you still cold?"

Asira shook her head. "The little flame is keeping me warm now."

Volknor stood on the steps of the castle. "Did everyone enjoy the free evening?"

Fabia yawned as she walked by. "It was so much fun, sir."

"Well, that's good to hear." He counted the heads as they walked by. "I have a trip planned for us tomorrow. Sleep well. It will involve a lot of walking." He waited for the students to ascend the stairs before closing the door. He felt proud that the students came back tired, happy, and together. It was something he was not expecting after the first week.

***

Asira peeked out her bedroom door and glanced down the quiet halls. A few candles were lit on the tables outside her bedroom. These candles were lit every night as a source of light. They never went out and they never melted. She stepped out into the hallway wearing her favourite purple dress, tights and cardigan. Then her stomach grumbled loudly into the silence.

She hurried down the stairs as quickly and as quietly as she could. She had been out so late last night that she hadn't gotten to eat dinner and her monstrous empty belly finally got the better of her.

She poked her head into the dining room. Someone was already sitting at the top of the table. A newspaper was covering their face. Slowly she crept into the dining room.

"You're up early."

Asira stopped dead in her tracks and turned to the figure at the table.

"It's only gone seven. Couldn't sleep?" said Eoin.

She laughed nervously. "We were out for such a long time last night I actually forgot all about dinner. My stomach woke me up this morning. Why are you awake, Eoin?"

"I just didn't sleep well."

Asira pulled out a chair and grabbed a bowl and cereal from the centre of the table. "Want to talk about it?"

"Bluebird, have you..."

"I thought you were messing when you said you would be calling me Bluebird," she laughed, glancing up from the milk.

"I was dead serious. You made an impression on me, Bluebird."

"Tell me about yourself. Where did you grow up? You have an Irish accent. What part of Ireland are you from?"

"Well, my family have been living in the south-east for years. I live in a small village outside of Enniscorthy."

"I'm afraid I have never been to Ireland. What's it like?"

"I think you would really like it. Dublin is very built up, but the south is still very rural. It is easy to get lost on a long twisting back road. Almost every luscious field has cattle or sheep. It's just such a serene ambiance. My parents live in a large house surrounded by fields. The only way to get to a shop is by car. The pace of life is just so different. People are nicer than in the cities. The shops are always busy, but they are never packed. The pubs are lively. There are so many castles and historical sites."

"It sounds wonderful. I'd love to see it sometime."

"I'd love to take you, Bluebird." Eoin's cheeks flushed a slight bit as he gazed at her smile. "Asira…"

"Good morning students of Velosia!" Mandy burst through the dining room doors and jogged to the table. "Yum! What's for breakfast?"

Britanie quietly followed behind her, closing the door and sitting down at the table.

"The sun shone through the curtains and I just couldn't stay in bed. We are also going on a fieldtrip today!" Mandy pumped her fists wildly into the air.

"Where are we going?" Britanie poured tea from the pot already on the table.

Eoin leaned back into the chair and let out an exhausted breath. "God only knows."

"Your necklace is quite beautiful, Mandy." Asira squinted at the silver.

"Why thank you, Asira. It was a gift from my clan. The acorn means continuous life and the silver chain – well, it is just a silver chain."

Britanie pulled a necklace out from her jumper. "In my village, the bone represents life."

"Britanie, what bone is that and where did you get it?" Mandy asked nervously.

"It is a bit of leg bone from an arctic fox. It was the first thing I ever killed on a hunt."

"Tea guys?" Mandy bounded to her feet. "Asira, would you like some?" She glanced up. "Asira?"

Eoin gazed from his newspaper. "Bluebird?" Asira was staring into the milk in her bowl. Her eyes were a little fuzzy and her head was a little dizzy. "Bluebird?" Eoin half rose from his chair when Asira suddenly gazed up at his face. "Are you okay? Your cheeks look a little flushed."

"Sorry. I... I just don't feel too well."

"Do you want to go lie down? I can take you upstairs." He pulled out his chair but stopped as soon as Asira rose from her seat.

"No. No, it's okay really. Please excuse me." Asira pushed out her chair and hurried from the dining room.

"Good morning, Asira." Peter passed her on the stairs. He was still wearing a woolly hat pulled down over his ears.

"Morning, Peter."

"Not even this morning's beautiful sun compares to the beauty of the sorceress standing before me." Zayne stood at the top of the staircase. "Are you feeling alright? You look a little pale."

"No, I'm actually feeling a bit better. Thank you though." She passed Zayne on the top step and continued down the hall.

"Good morning, Asira."

She stopped just outside her bedroom. "Anton, good morning."

"You look a little pale. Are you feeling okay?"

"I was just feeling a little dizzy at breakfast but I'm okay now."

"Still hungry?" He held out his arm.

"I could eat some more." She quickly linked arms with him. "How did you sleep?"

"Last night I was awake for a little bit, tossing and turning."

"That's funny. Eoin said the exact same thing."

Anton furrowed his brow in disgust. "Maybe it's the heat."

"The castle can be awfully warm at night."

Anton sniffed the air. "Is that a new perfume?"

Asira giggled. "My best friend bought me this one for my birthday. It's called strawberry queen. It's one of my favourites."

CHAPTER SIXTEEN

Bonum Kingdom

"Do you remember the first time you walked through these halls?" Airies gracefully skipped with every step.

"The first time I walked these halls was the first day I stepped foot in Velosia after the death of my father."

She pouted. "You just have to put a negative spin on everything, don't you?" As she spun on her heel, she moved across in front of Volknor. "Do you remember the first time we met?" She seductively traced her fingers along his forearm. "Do you remember the first time you laid eyes on me?" She stretched up on her tiptoes. Her warm breath skimming the edge of his ear.

"Of course I remember the first day we met." He rubbed his hands from her shoulders, down along her arms pulling her closer to him. "You were wearing a black leather skirt, dark blue leggings and a pair of white runners. Your hair was tied up in a high ponytail and you had a full fringe. You were also wearing your favourite red blouse. And later that day it rained, and I noticed you weren't wearing a bra."

The heat rushed to her face and her cheeks turned bright pink. "That was very detailed." Her fingers danced along his chest and grabbed him by the collar as she pulled him in for a kiss.

He pushed her back after a moment. "Maybe we should start this field trip."

Airies let out a sigh and pirouetted gracefully from his gentle hold. "I suppose we can't be late." She took his hand and together, they walked down the corridor. With a flick of her wrists the dining room doors swung open. "Good morning all!" Airies strolled in ahead of Volknor, who sauntered ten seconds behind. "And what a beautiful morning it is. I hope you are all ready for your fieldtrip this morning. We leave in an hour and a half." She was so elegant. Every movement was almost like a dance.

"Where are we going?" Zayne sat at the end of the table next to Thomas and Katie.

Aires spun on her tiptoes. "That is a surprise!" she smiled before skipped out of the dining hall. Volknor unfolded his arms, sighed and sauntered behind her without a word.

***

"I hate waiting. We've been waiting outside for ages. I'm getting bored."

"You have to learn to be more patient, Angelica." Aaron's arm was wrapped around her shoulders.

"I can't help what I dislike," she replied as he leaned in, kissing her forehead.

Cara elbowed Asira rolling her eyes in disgust.

"Let's predict where we're going." Bobby was crouched on his hunkers at the end of the castle steps trying to encourage a ladybug onto his finger.

"Should be easy for a witch or sorceress?" said Blake, who was sitting beside Bobby and was trying to catch a spider.

"Well?" Bobby stood up holding the ladybug.

"Bobby, I may be a sorceress, but I am not a fortune-teller," Asira remarked.

"My cousin is a fortune-teller but it's not as easy as it sounds. We cannot just look into the future. My cousin says that when you look into the future you just see a blur of images and it's hard to find the right one. There are too many possibilities," said Fabia.

"Stand up. It is time to leave," said Airies as she and Volknor walked past everyone. Her footing was so light, she barely touched the steps.

"Where are we going?" Katie jumped to her feet.

"What a good question! It is now time to reveal the field trip. Asira, are you able to open portals?"

"I, eh… Yes, I am."

"Would you be able to open a portal to the Bonum Kingdom?"

"Erm… Yes, I think I can," she replied hesitantly.

"Bonum Kingdom?" Bobby watched as the ladybug flew off his finger.

Asira walked to Airies' side. "I've never been before. Where do you want to go exactly?"

"Oh, just outside of the city. I think a little walk will help you all appreciate the beauty of the Bonum Kingdom."

Asira nodded slightly as she took a deep breath. She had never been to the Bonum Kingdom, so opening a portal was a little trickier. She had to try and visualise the spiritual energy of the people and it actually helped having angels standing in front of her. As she opened her eyes, a white fog eclipsed her vision. Large and heavy purple doors materialised before her and the swirling mass of colours twisted and blended together. Asira's vision blurred immediately. She watched nervously as the hazy figures walked by her. She stretched her arm out desperately for someone to hold onto.

Suddenly a hand fell on her shoulder. "Kai asked me to watch over you. He says you have a hard time seeing sometimes."

She let out a loud sigh of relief. "Thank you. I was afraid everyone had left."

"Don't worry, I can guide you."

She could make out a blue torso and a yellow head. It was comforting to have someone next to her but still she wasn't as confident as she hoped. She took one small step and stopped. Her fingers gripped his upper arm so tightly that he flinched.

"Don't worry, I have you. Promise." He spoke softly trying his best to reassure her.

Asira swallowed a lump in her throat. Her every step was carefully calculated. As they stepped across the threshold, she could feel the light of the portal tickle her skin. The colours swirled like a cascading ocean and in a matter of seconds it was all over.

"We're here," Volknor whispered into her ear. Asira shut her eyes tight, and the portal immediately closed. Her vision came back with each blink and the figures became undistorted.

"Welcome one and all to the Bonum Kingdom!" Airies arms were spread wide. She stood on a cliff edge gazing at the villages carved into the face of the mountains.

"We are so close to the clouds," Cara gasped in delight.

"Now," Airies turned to the group, "the altitude might get a bit much for some of you. If you feel lightheaded or sick, just let us know."

The cliff path they walked was narrow and stony. Airies was light-footed. She was made to bounce about the steep mountain sides. Almost like a goat, she was born for this terrain. In the far distance they could hear mountain sheep and farmers calling out to one another, but they could see no farms or fields.

Asira walked close to Katie. They had only just arrived, and Katie was already so giddy and jumpy. "Asira, the Bonum Kingdom is the best place to be in the world. I hope you love it." She tugged on her arm before running to the edge of the cliff and without hesitation leapt straight off the edge.

"Katie!" Asira gasped in horror.

"What happened?" Mandy squealed from the back of the group.

"I think you've forgotten that Katie and I are angels. She's fine," Zayne pulled Asira gently to the edge. "Can you see her?" He was leaning right over the edge, balancing on the tips of his toes.

She glanced over the edge and all of a sudden, the world became distorted again. She could feel her brain pound against her skull almost screaming at her to run away. She tried to pull away, but she was unable to move. "No, thank you. I believe you."

He bent down to look into her face. "You're not afraid of heights, are you? Why don't you just peek over the edge?"

"I'm a little afraid of heights."

With small baby steps, Zayne tried to coach her to the lip of the mountain. "Look," he pointed, "there she is."

Asira peeked. Katie was soaring alongside the mountain.

"Let's take away that fear."

"No! Wait. Stop!"

He dragged her by the arms, pulling her closer to his chest as he secured his arms around her waist and carted her off the edge. "Don't struggle. I have you." His arms were locked firmly around her waist. Her nose was pressed into his chest and she could hear the beat of his wings and feel the small currents of air swishing past her face. "This is how we teach our young to fly. There is absolutely nothing to be afraid of. It's okay to open your eyes."

She glanced up. "I hate you, Zayne," she said, her fingers digging into his shirt.

His wings were graceful like a swan. Each flap was effortless. It was second nature. To Katie and Zayne, it was like walking. "You don't mean that." His eyes were fixed on hers and she was finally able to appreciate Zayne for who he was. "You can look around. I won't let you fall. I promise, Asira."

Her breaths were slow and deep. Her heart was thudding against her rib cage. "I believe you." With all her strength, she raised her head. Katie swooped around them in a graceful dive while to her right, both Chloe and Blake zoomed around each other along the cliff face. "I really don't feel well. Can you please put me down?"

Zayne delicately caressed her head and rested it back against his chest. For a few short seconds she could hear the beating of his heart, strong but calm rhythmic patterns. "Flying is just not for everyone. You can open your eyes. I'm standing on the ground. I promise."

"Asira?" Anton caught her just as her legs gave way to the fear.

"She'll be fine, Anton."

"Next time when she says no, she means no." Anton held Asira on her feet.

Asira glanced over her shoulder and watched Zayne smile back at her before diving backwards off the cliff.

"How are you feeling? You look green."

"I feel like I am going to get sick." Her stomach was still doing somersaults.

"He shouldn't have taken you out like that. You were obviously uncomfortable. Do you want to hop onto my back?"

"No, I think I can walk." She fixed her arm across her waist praying she would not throw up.

They continued up the steep mountain path for another hour. The villages they had seen at the beginning of their journey had faded into the distance. Katie and Zayne continued to soar through the clouds while Chloe and Blake occasionally walked to rest their wings.

"You couldn't have teleported us any further away," Angelica snorted glaring back at Asira. Mandy and Britanie were in their werewolf forms walking alongside Angelica and Aaron.

"I've never been here before. You're really lucky you didn't walk off the cliff," Asira retorted.

"Okay everyone, stop here." Airies stood still at a sharp cliff edge.

"Are we stuck here?" Thomas asked wiping the sweat from his forehead.

"We are so close to the clouds." Fabia's fingers passed through the misty substance. Thomas watched carefully as Fabia edged across the path. In the blink of an eye, he had reached out and snatched her by the elbow pulling her away from the sheer drop. "Thank you, Thomas." She gazed down nervously at the valley below.

Airies pushed her arms out straight and a gust of wind blew the clouds in the same direction and a wooden rope bridge became visible. Mandy and Britanie stepped back behind Angelica whimpering.

Bobby crouched down on his hunkers. "I'm not afraid of heights but I'm still not going on that. It looks unstable."

"Don't be ridiculous." Airies twisted her hand, and another gust of wind blew across the mountain pushing the students along.

"Hold on! I'm not going anywhere!" Bobby clutched the wooden posts as he was abruptly driven by an invisible force to his feet. "Hey stop this! I am not going anywhere!"

"Walk the bridge, Bobby." Chloe fluttered past.

"Don't be such a pain." Blake flurried by on the opposite side.

Anton's arm gripped Asira's waist a little more, wanting to make sure she knew he had her and that she was safe as long as she was with him. Mandy and Britanie followed closely behind Bobby and Eoin. Their ears flat against their heads as they mumbled a cry each. Angelica and Aaron walked behind the two werewolves.

Peter shoved his hands into his jumper pocket. "Bobby, I thought you were fearless."

Airies kept the clouds at bay as both she and Volknor were at the back of the group. "Do you remember your first time in the Bonum Kingdom?" Airies flicked her head back.

"You do love to reminisce." Volknor looked over her and straight ahead at the class walking single file across the rope bridge. "The first time I was here was back in 1980, maybe 1981. We came here to introduce ourselves to Queen Shire."

"Back then we were still courting." She skipped along the wooden planks.

"Back then you were a tough cookie."

"Are we at the capital?!" Cara called excitedly out as she finally stepped onto solid ground.

Asira stood next to her. "Is this Venus?"

Only visible once they had passed the cloud-covered bridge, on top of the mountain was Venus – the capital of the Bonum Kingdom, decorated with Roman styled homes and columns. Some of the houses were submerged beneath rock with only the doors visible to the naked eye. The most exquisite structure was the beautiful Roman style palace, centred in the midst of the city.

"Okay guys," Airies turned to the group, "we were only allowed to come here by invitation of Queen Shire. She has a soft spot for my family. I want everyone to be on their best behaviour. This is the school's first official visit."

Volknor continued, "This is not just an educational tour. You are representatives of your own races and homes but also of the Velosian Academy. You wouldn't have joined if it didn't mean something to you. This is a diplomatic mission. Be on your best behaviour."

The students quietly followed Volknor and Airies through a monumental arch standing two hundred feet tall and made of solid stone. Latin writings were engraved into the pillars along with stone vines and grapes. On either side of the entrance were other pathways, much smaller than the one they passed though.

Many buildings were constructed of huge granite columns reaching more than seventy feet in height. There was one incredible building which Airies had pointed out as the largest library in the Bonum Kingdom. The front was graced with a nine-step portico. The facade of the building retained its amazing carvings which only added to the grandeur of the structure.

Airies said scholars from all races flocked to the great library for ancient scriptures which had been bartered and bought over the centuries. She said sorcerers and witches were particularly fond of the spells which were preserved there.

In the background were several three-storey aqueducts made of massive, precisely cut and well-fitted six-tonne blocks. The structure itself measured over one thousand feet in height. Airies pointed proudly, declaring it was the water source for the entire city. There were many small fountains dotted around the streets connecting to smaller stone tributaries of the aqueduct.

Asira took a step back and gazed in awe as she noticed the aqueduct structure circling the city. Then in a swift motion she was whisked back to Anton's side. "Stay close," he murmured.

She looked at him blankly for a second before realising they were attracting stares from the locals. Although many angels were working and getting on with their daily lives, there were a few who stopped to stare at the group of misfit strangers walking their streets. At the centre of the city, there were lots of food stalls which opened into a circular market bazaar, behind which was the royal palace. The palace stood as extraordinary as the rest of the architecture. It was the largest building by far, beautifully built of grey granite with white marble columns, capped with a triangular granite roof.

Volknor neatly shuffled the students into pairs before following Airies' lead through the marble and granite structure. Ten guards escorted them to the throne room, wearing nothing more than a steel skirt and white toga with a large bow on their back and a quiver of arrows strapped to their hips.

Volknor slyly took her hand. "Don't be nervous," he whispered softly.

"I can't help it. The last time we were here together it..."

He squeezed her hand firmly to shush and reassure her.

Asira gazed around. Every entrance, every corridor left, right and centre, was heavily guarded by sentries. There were a few suited in full silver armour wearing a metal skirt, silver knee pads and a metal chest plate.

The throne room doors opened.

"Your Majesty," Airies took slow steps into the room and immediately bowed in an elegant manner. Volknor, Zayne and Katie followed her lead. Steadily, starting with Cara, Anton and Peter, the rest of the students began to kneel on one knee. "Your Highness, I present to you the pupils of the Velosian Academy."

The queen in all her grace, rose from her white marble throne. Her wings visibly grander than those of other angels, sprung from behind. Her hair was a white-blond colour resting at her waistline and her eyes were a sapphire blue, deep like the ocean. She wore a long royal blue dress. The sleeves were draped and hung from her wrists. Her skin had a flawless powdery glow. She was the perfect example of an angel and the definition of perfection.

"Dame Airies Kennedy," her voice echoed with grace and authority, "I am pleased you have decided to grace my kingdom with your young students."

"I am honoured you accepted our request, Your Highness." Airies raised her head from the bow.

"I could not refuse a request from one of my own." As she stepped down from her throne, two guards in white togas followed closely behind. "What may I expect from your young students?"

Airies did not hesitate in responding with her previously rehearsed lines. "The beginning of an understanding among the races, species and nations of this world."

The queen gazed across at all the faces. "Dame Airies, I see you have two of my own." She gazed fondly at Katie and Zayne. "You also have two fairies." Her tone was surprised.

"Your Highness," Airies took one step to the side, "I present before you every species in our realm. Fabia Lux is the youngest witch and member of the prestigious Lux family from the Rune region of Velosia Mainland. Asira Soniar is the only daughter and apprentice sorceress to Master Kai Soniar, who is Council Ambassador. Peter Arbor is the eldest son of one of the remaining elf nobility lines in the Hy region of Velosia Mainland. Eoin Quinn lives on Earth and is one of the last ancient Irish leprechaun bloodlines left. Anton Pearse is the only child of Lady Catherine Pearse from the Kalis Republic. As well as being a vampire, he has the ability to manipulate fire. Bobby Ferox is the third son of the hexites lead family in the Fera region of Velosia Mainland. Taking after his father and brothers, he has the ability to speak to and understand any creature. Chloe Aetós is the niece of Princess Amelia Aetós of the Greek fairies from the Luce Caelo Kingdom. She is the only member of her immediate family to manipulate light energy. Blake Selinofoto is the nephew of Princess Sylvia Selinofoto of the Renassies fairies of the Dusk Kingdom. He has inherited the same trait as Princess Sylvia whereby he can manipulate dark energy. Katie and Zayne Crosby are brother and sister from the well-known angel family residing here in Venus. Our four resident werewolves are Aaron Connelly the son of Chief of the Sand Clan, Angelica Orie daughter of the African Savannah Clan, Britanie North daughter of the Antarctica Snow Clan, and Mandy Williams daughter of the Amazon Forest Clan. Thomas Aurum is an essence and nephew of Prince Manolito from the Essence Kingdom. And finally, we have Mermaid Princess Cara Griffith of Atlantis."

Queen Shire gazed at the young crowd of people as she circled around them. "You have an exquisite mix of students." Her eyes finally fixed on Asira. "Young sorceress?"

Asira stared back at the graceful being before her. "Yes, Your Highness?"

"Daughter of the great Kai Soniar, you are so blessed." The back of her hand softly grazed Asira's cheek. "Sorcerers are greatly honoured and respected. I can sense you have your father's spirit. The same aura flows around you too. Master Soniar has always had a special gift. People have always been drawn to him. It is almost inhuman, like a godly trait he possesses. Magic seems to be a dying skill. I don't see many sorcerers nowadays. Our library used to be bustling with great men and women from across the globe. Once a year we hold a festival to celebrate the god dedicated to knowledge, Alden the Wise. I would be honoured if you and your father would join us."

"I would be honoured, Your Highness." Asira bowed.

Queen Shire turned gracefully and without another word to Asira, gazed across at Airies and Volknor. "Dame Airies, Sir Volknor, I would like your students to explore our great city a little further but before you do, I assume one of the items on your itinerary is the Haven Jewel?"

Airies nodded immediately. "Yes," she nervously cleared her throat, "it is, Your Majesty."

"Excellent." She turned to her guards. "Open the treasury."

The guards escorted everyone down the brightly lit, heavily guarded hallway. Two guards opened thick steel doors which were designed in such a way to mirror dark wood. Old treasure chests lined the walls. Silver and gold chalices sat next to elegant silverware.

"This is the first chamber of the treasury."

Queen Shire approached a black column table centred in the middle of the room.

Asira stared curiously around the room and whispered to Anton. "Those candles are enchanted by magic. They will never go out and they will never burn anything."

"That is correct, young sorceress." Queen Shire peered back over her shoulder. "Your father gifted me with those candles many years ago."

The queen turned back to the students holding a circular jewellery box. Inside was a crystal, blue and silvery white in colour.

"This is the Haven Jewel." Queen Shire held out the large gemstone with both hands, protectively. "Like the other gemstones, the Haven Jewel is said to be the life force of the wind and air. Our ancestors always believed that the Haven Jewel gathered lost souls keeping them safe from the darkness."

"It is more beautiful than I remember." Airies was dazzled by the sight of the beautiful gem.

"How many other gemstones are there?" Asira asked.

"Well, presently, there are only five. The rest are lost and only Velosia knows where they are." Queen Shire returned the jewellery box to the column stand. "I do believe there are supposed to be twelve gemstones altogether. There is a tale that guardians used to protect these powerful items before a terrible tragedy befell them and the gemstones became scattered to the four corners of the world." She then ushered the group out of the treasury. "Dame Airies, I have always spoken fondly of you, even in the aftermath. I am glad you returned home. On your next visit, we will arrange festive events. I am fond of your students as well. They are very well-mannered."

Airies felt a tug on her heart strings. She did her best to hold back the tears as she bowed. "Of course, Your Highness, and thank you so much for your hospitality."

CHAPTER SEVENTEEN

Infected Portal

The day had gone by so quickly. The students had spent the remainder of their time touring the ancient city. Airies and Volknor had shown them the aqueducts up close. Airies went into every detail about the architecture and how the war hadn't really touched the city resulting in the preservation of the prehistoric records.

Mandy whispered to Asira in passing. "How come I never knew Master Airies and Master Volknor were a *thing*?" She gestured to both Airies and Volknor holding hands. "They are like love-struck teenagers."

They had explored the markets thoroughly. They had tried on different outfits. Thomas had bravely tried on a native toga and metal skirt. "Oh Thomas, what were you thinking?" Bobby let out a loud laugh.

"Dude, just put your pants back on." Eoin threw his head back in laughter and embarrassment.

Katie sat on a bench methodically braiding Fabia and Mandy's hair. "Hey Angelica, do you want a braid next?" Katie called over glancing up from the back of Mandy's head. Angelica swished her hand through her hair and walked away in a different direction with Britanie close to her side. "Do you think she heard me?" Katie leaned down to Mandy.

"I don't know," Mandy shrugged not really caring.

Asira turned to find Cara swooning over a fountain. The cherub statues were fixed in the centre of the basin. Water poured from the tips of the arrows and tiny togas were decoratively wrapped around the stone figures.

"Cara, why don't you take a dip?" Asira sat along the edge of the fountain next to her.

Cara was swishing her hand through the fresh and clear body of water. Her fingers glistened in the light. Green scales covered her hand like a fingerless glove. She sighed. "I am representing the Velosian Academy and the Maria Empire. I must restrain myself."

"Excuse me." Three little girls of about seven years of age appeared behind them. Their wings were soft and no more than seven foot wide. One of the girls with brunette pigtails spoke nervously. "Are you Princess Cara of the mermaids?" She held up a magazine.

Asira glimpsed at the magazine noticing Cara in her mermaid form on the front cover.

Cara nodded and smiled. "I am Princess Cara. How can I help you?" she said with a sweet and bubbly voice.

"Could you please sign my magazine?" The little girl handed Cara a black marker and the magazine. "We love you. Mermaids are just so cool!"

"Yes, mermaids are the best!" One of the other girls called out excitedly. The third girl nodded shyly.

"I would be honoured." Cara signed her name *Princess Cara Griffith xx* and handed the magazine back. "Here you go." The girls took the magazine, bowed and hurried over to their parents screaming in pure delight.

"Aww Cara, that was so sweet. That definitely cheered you up."

She shook her hand dry watching the scales vanish and smiled brightly. "It definitely did cheer me up."

"Cara!" Blake and Anton approached the fountain. "Airies and Volknor bought cake and are dishing it out."

Cara leapt to her feet. "Show me where the cake is!" She hastily followed Blake towards the market.

Asira giggled as she walked with Anton behind them. "I have a feeling Cara is going to eat all the cake."

He chuckled. "Well, Mandy and Thomas have already had a huge chunk each."

They were walking closely beside each other, elbow to elbow.

Asira's cheeks blushed a little at the touch of his skin. Suddenly she felt her head pounding. She rubbed her left temple, stopping in her tracks.

"Are you feeling okay?" Anton stopped next to her.

"I just feel a bit dizzy."

"Are you still feeling air sick?" His hand hovered over her arm cautiously.

"No, no, that passed a while ago. I don't know what it is."

"Do you want me to get Volknor or Airies? Do you want to sit down?"

Asira shook her head. "No, I'm good now." She stared up at him with a half-smile.

He stared back unconvincingly. "Are you sure?"

"Hey Asira!" Cara ran through the market skidding to a stop. "I snatched you a slice of chocolate cake before Eoin got too greedy. Everyone else has had one."

"Thank you, Cara." She took the plate of cake from her.

"Cara, do that trick again!" Bobby ran halfway tossing a bottle of water in his hands back and forth.

"I forgot how much I love it here!" nearby Airies sat back on the bench with her eyes closed and her head tilted back.

"It is a lovely place." Volknor took a small bite of the cake. "But I prefer the detached stone house we live in."

She peeked at him from the corner of her eye grinning. "You're afraid I will want to move back." Volknor shrugged his shoulders and continued to eat the cake. She jumped to her feet, took the plate from his hands and sat front ways across his lap, loosely wrapping her arms around his neck. She was at eye level with him. Her lips barely grazing his. "I love our detached stone house too much."

His hands were firmly locked around her waist in case she jumped from his grip. "I love you too much." His lips pressed hard against hers and he pulled her waist a little closer.

"I love you too much, you electric idiot." She pulled away slowly gently biting down on his bottom lip as she did. "How about we plan a trip after the school term? I have a nice little idea."

"Oh yes?" he asked smiling back at her. "What is it?"

"How about we take a tour around Italy? I would love to see where you come from."

His hands moved up along her waist as he pulled her in again for a kiss. "How long would you like to go for?"

"For as long as it takes."

"Are you feeling any better?" Anton turned to Asira noticing she had barely eaten anything all day.

She shrugged. "I'll be much better after some rest."

"Okay guys," Airies leapt to her feet with Volknor standing directly behind her. "Unfortunately, it's time to head back. Asira, could you please open a portal back to the castle."

Asira nodded. "Anton, why does the day have to end when the sun sets?" Just ahead of them the sun was like a fiery ball with beautiful colours of orange and pink painted across the sky.

She closed her eyes. Her arms tingling as the portal opened once again. The blurred colours walked by her one by one. To her left stood a blond figure.

"Asira?" Volknor stood next to her.

"Hmm?"

"What colour is your portal?"

"What?" She squinted seeing only a purple mass. "Purple."

"Yes, that's what I thought. It's just that there are blue lines appearing in it now." Like veins, the blue began infecting the purple colours.

"I've never actually seen my portal before. I..." She squinted still unable to see any change. "That's strange. I don't know what to say."

"Do you have a grip on the portal?" Volknor asked a little uneasy.

She nodded. "Yes, the portal is resting in the courtyard of Velosian Academy. Everyone's already safely passed through." She said confidently.

"Alright, good. We should be off then." He took her arm in his. As they stepped through, he could feel the swish of magic brush past his face, he could feel the energy and intense power the deeper he travelled.

CHAPTER EIGHTEEN

Dating

Asira gripped Volknor's arm tightly as they stepped through the portal onto solid ground. She instinctively knew they had arrived at Topaz Castle so closed the portal behind them.

"How are you feeling?"

She glanced up at Volknor who was staring down at her with trepidation. "Good."

They had returned to the castle around half past seven in the evening. Although it was still bright outside, everyone quickly retired to their dorms. The adventure to another kingdom, the long mountain hike and the tour around the city had exhausted everyone.

Though Asira was shattered, she was unable to fall asleep. She had been contemplating whether to take a shower or a bath for quite some time but feared that if she risked taking a bath, she may end up falling asleep in it. She reached for her phone. It had been nearly an hour since she had bombarded Amy's phone with missed calls and texts and her patience was growing thin.

There was a gentle tap on the door. Sitting up she listened, thinking it was a mistake but then she heard another tap this time a little louder. She slowly rose from her bed to open the door.

"Anton, what are you doing here?"

"Do you trust me?"

"What? What do you mean?" She poked her head around the corner and gazed up and down the hall. "We'll get in trouble being out this late," she whispered loudly.

He held out his hand. "Do you trust me?"

"I don't think this is a matter of trust. What are you planning?" She glanced down, hesitant at first. If this was a novel, the protagonist would take his hand and never look back. She would put all her faith in the strong figure before he would whisk her off on a romantic journey of self-discovery. Lost in her train of thought, she found herself timidly taking his hand. He swiftly led her through the hall, tiptoeing down the stairs and out through a service door in the kitchen.

Still holding her hand, he turned to gaze into her eyes. A cool breeze whisked across the opened grounds. "You were right, Asira."

"Right? Right about what?"

"The day doesn't have to end when the sun sets." He took a few paces away from her. "Come with me." He stretched his hand out again. "Do you trust me?"

"That's hard to say." She swallowed a fear in her throat. "Vampires generally try to suck the blood of an unsuspecting teen in all the movies I've seen."

"Then you'll be fine because you seem very suspicious."

"Sorry." Asira glanced back at the castle but hesitantly took his hand again.

He led her through a narrow dirt path in a remote section of the forest. It was going on midnight. The sky was a strange blend of dark navy and black and a few stars twinkled brightly in the night sky.

"Anton, where are we going?" Suddenly there was a break in the forest, and she found herself gazing beyond a clearing. "Where are we?" She peered over the cliff edge into a body of water, but Anton swiftly jerked her back.

"Be careful. I know you don't like heights." He kept a firm grip on her hand. "This is the Velosian Sea, known for its raw power."

Asira remained where she was, a few feet from the edge and gazed across at the vastness. "This place, it's beautiful, Anton, but why did you bring me here?" She gazed around at his nervous smile.

"Asira..." her name slipped his lips. His fist was clenched, and he quickly stared out to the still body of blue. "I...I..."

"I thought I would really miss home," she interrupted his nervous stammer. "I thought I wouldn't make friends. I thought I would be really homesick." Her eyes met his again. "But you have made me feel so at home here. Everyone has made me feel like I belong. I don't have to hide who I am around you. For that, I'm thankful to you and everyone..."

In less than a millisecond, Anton had taken hold of her shoulders. She blushed as his lips pressed against hers, parting ever so slightly. It took a second or two longer, but she finally relaxed in his warm and gentle grip.

His arm slipped around her waist, embracing her for longer than a moment. "Asira," he cleared his tense throat and his voice quivered, "I really like you."

"I really like you too, Anton."

He nervously chuckled. "Your cheeks are so red."

She turned away from him, covering her face. "I'm just blushing."

He pulled her hands away from her face. "I can see that. There is no need to hide."

"You're embarrassing me, Anton! And you are too warm!" She laughed pushing him away.

He shook his hands energetically, trying to disperse the heat. "Sorry about that. Sometimes I don't realise how warm my body heats up. Is it cold outside?"

"A bit," Asira admitted.

He wrapped his arm around her shoulders and in the blink of an eye, she was face to face with him again. "I suppose my next question is..." his lips dried. "Would you be my girlfriend?"

Her whole head went red. "I would really like that."

He leaned in again, pressed his lips against hers and embraced the feel of her hands as she clutched tightly onto his waist. It was a moment he never wanted to forget. It was like a firework had sparked and ignited inside his chest leaving nothing but a purple fiery ember. His arms tightened, drawing her closer.

She consciously pulled away, relishing in the tingle he had left on her lips. "Anton, I'm not familiar with vampire customs or culture. When vampires date, is it like humans dating?"

He blankly stared at her. "I don't really understand the question."

"Well, do vampires have a different idea when dating? What is a typical dating structure for a vampire?"

"Structure? Oh," he replied slipping into silence, contemplating. "Dating is usually a one-off thing." He thought carefully for a moment on how to phrase this, realising Asira was giving him a questioning look. "Vampires tend to have one partner, sometimes two, at different times obviously. We are not a polyamorous species. What I mean is vampires tend to have one soul mate. That is why my mother never remarried after my father passed away."

Asira's eyes glazed over. "Aw! That is so sweet and sad at the same time."

"I wouldn't call it sad. It's just how we're built. We're very protective and family orientated."

"That is very interesting to know." She pursed her lips and stared at him curiously. "If vampires choose one soul mate, are you saying I'm yours? Because that is a lot of pressure and to be honest, humans rarely do things that way." Asira felt her arm unconsciously slip away from him.

"No, I'm not saying that at all. Asira, I... I... what I'm trying to say..." he began to anxiously stammer. "I really like you and I would really like to date you. We can take this really slow and have it like a human relationship if you prefer. But I want to try."

Her eyes glazed over again in awe and nodded in agreement. "I would really like that." She reached for his hand and their fingers intertwined. "Okay so another question, how do you know you have found your soul mate?"

"It's meant to feel different for everyone. My mother said when she met my father, they were both just teenagers. They had met in school and were in different classes, but they had one random run in with each other. She remembers they made eye contact for three full minutes and that is how she knew they were meant to be."

Asira reached for her sleeve and rubbed her eyes and nose. "Anton, that is so cute." She sniffled.

"Why are you crying? That wasn't even a sad story," he remarked with a chuckle.

"Doesn't matter. It was so cute."

He tightened his hand around hers. "So how do humans know they have found their soul mate?"

"Humans don't really think of it like that. They fall in and out of love all the time. Dad used to tell me stories of how he met my mother. She was apparently the only woman my dad has ever loved. He says there will never be anyone else. They were childhood sweethearts and best friends. She was stubborn, spontaneous, adventurous and wild. Whereas my dad was stubborn, more cautious and played it safe."

"Well, you definitely have the stubborn gene."

She pouted. "I think I am very reasonable." A sudden dizziness drifted over her and she stumbled on her own feet.

"Hey?" He tugged her arm pulling her into his grip. "Are you okay? What's wrong? You were feeling dizzy today at the Bonum Kingdom as well." He moved his head to look directly into her weary eyes. "Asira?" He gripped her shoulders. "Hey Asira, focus. Can you hear me?"

"I just need a good night's sleep. I think the portal casting took a bit more out of me than expected."

Relief came over Anton and he loosened his grip on her shoulders. "You had me really worried. I definitely think you need a good night's sleep." His arm was securely wrapped around her waist as he led her back to her bedroom. He was hesitant to let go and before she could walk away, his lips were pressing firmly against hers. "Sleep well, Asira."

"Good night, Anton." She closed the door, leaning against the frame as her heart was beating fiercely. She ran to her mobile, hoping to reach Amy but before she could press dial, her heavy head hit the pillow.

***

"Asira, are you awake?" Cara called knocking on the door three times and then another five times. "I'm heading down for breakfast and was wondering would you join me?"

"Good morning, Cara." Asira rushed to the door. "I just need to put on fresh clothes." She shut the door for no more than three minutes. In that time, she had managed to put on clean jeans with a bright pink top and spray herself in perfume. "Thanks for waiting." She locked the door behind her. "How did you sleep?"

Cara was a real princess. She never slouched. She never complained. There was always a smile on her face. "I slept well. The waterbed in my room is so comfortable. It is like being at home in the palace, sometimes."

"You have a waterbed?" Asira mused. "Excuse me for a moment." She rang Amy's number, but a robotic female voice answered claiming that the number was not in service.

"Is everything okay?"

"I just can't seem to get through to my friend at home for the last few days."

"Oh, I am sure everything is okay."

"Good morning, Asira and Cara." Fabia bounced towards them as they entered the dining room. "Did you hear we are having the skills-building class for the entire day?"

"Oh yes!" Cara squealed. "Remember Master Roberts had mentioned it the last time. She wants us to train and develop a signature move." Cara screeched with excitement. "I think that is so amusing. It is like something from a comic book."

"I really can't wait to see what I can learn. There are so many spells I would like to perfect. Like the portals." Asira grabbed some toast from the centre of the table.

"Yes true, Cara," Fabia began, "we're going to be paired and put into teams later this morning."

***

Myron glanced at his watch. "It's seven thirty. You've been here all night. When are you going back to school?" He teased as he sat down to drink a cappuccino.

Airies was sitting across from him applying her makeup. "Thank you for dinner last night, Myron. You really are the best chef around."

Volknor lay across some benches with his eyes shut tight and mumbled a response.

"How are your students getting on now?" Myron lay back and slammed his foot into the chair next to Volknor, laughing as he did.

Volknor leapt from his lazy position and grumbled under his breath, "Ass!"

Airies darted a glare in his direction.

"The kids are great. They're getting on really well with each other," Volknor said snatching a biscuit from the centre of the table.

"Would you listen to him?" Airies butted in. "The children are doing exceptionally well. They're getting on better than we could have ever imagined."

"That is actually true. They are very curious kids," Volknor added.

"We thought we would have a much bigger problem with the werewolves and the vampire but there has really only been some snotty, childish comments at the start. There has not been a peep from the fairies. They seem to be a lot more tolerant than these upstarts you hear about in the news," Airies added as she fixed her mascara. "It is actually really cute. Volknor is like a proud father."

Myron laughed. "I always knew you had a soft spot for kids." He reached for another biscuit from the tin. "So, any plans to start your own family?"

Volknor choked on his tea and nervously glanced over at Airies from the corner of his eye. She was smiling back at him. "Are you feeling alright there, Volknor?" she teased and giggled.

CHAPTER NINETEEN

Team Building

Volknor, Erika and Airies stood out in a field adjacent to the castle. Volknor glanced down at his watch. It was ten thirty in the morning. He yawned as loudly as he could. He had been up a total of six hours already.

"Didn't get enough sleep obviously," Erika remarked audaciously.

He rubbed his hand through his upright blond hair. He was used to her cheeky remarks. "I've always had trouble sleeping." The students lined up in front of them. Erika straightened as if to announce something but was immediately cut off by Volknor. "We have a total of sixteen students. We will be dividing the class into four teams of four." Volknor folded his arms behind his back. "This is a teambuilding exercise, so listen up."

Erika pulled a scrunched-up sheet from her back pocket. "Cara, Britanie, Katie and Bobby."

"Fabia, Mandy, Blake and Thomas." Airies peered over at the sheet.

Erika cleared her throat. "Anton, Zayne, Angelica and Peter."

Volknor didn't even glance at the sheet Erika tried to pass him. "Asira, Aaron, Eoin and Chloe."

"Remember, this class is to help you understand your powers in a safe environment." Erika scrunched the paper back into her pocket.

"Don't forget to have fun," Volknor added.

"Into your groups!" Erika declared loudly. "Start moving people." She walked around and began to separate the students into their groups. "Zayne's group you will be training with Airies. Thomas' group you will be with me."

Volknor turned to the last two groups. "Asira's group and Bobby's group, you guys are with me."

Katie glanced back at Zayne as he walked away moving across to the other side of the field. Airies skipped freely. She picked up incredible speed. Unexpectedly, she leapt onto her hands and started cartwheeling down the field. She finally landed in a crouched position.

"I have one vampire with a fire element, an angel, a werewolf and an elf with the ability to manipulate vegetation." Airies rose to her feet. "Your job is to take this from me," she said and pulled a blue diamond-shaped keyring from her pocket. "Feel free to use your powers in any way you see fit. Try your best to coordinate your actions with one another."

Erika walked with her group to the opposite end of the field.

"We have divided the groups to get the best mix of students." She took a pink heart-shaped keyring from her back pocket. "Your task is to take this keyring from my possession. Your aim is to coordinate your approach. Remember your strengths and weaknesses. In this group you have a witch, a werewolf, a fairy and an essence."

Volknor remained in the centre of the field. He gazed around at the eight students.

"This was meant to work with teams of four. However, Master Kai was called away at the last minute in his role as Council Ambassador." He removed a yellow star-shaped keyring from his pocket. "I do not want you to think of yourselves as two separate groups. I want you all to work together, coordinate your attack and seize this." He dangled the keyring in front of them. "You may use your powers. Don't be afraid to hurt me. But do not hurt or impede anyone else. Remember the skills you possess, but also what your comrades have to offer. In this group there is a mermaid, two werewolves, a fairy, an angel, a hexite, a leprechaun and a sorceress."

"So, we just have to work together to snatch that keyring?" Bobby asked.

"That is correct," Volknor said shoving the keyring into his pocket. "While we are doing this, I will teach you some useful tips." He stretched his arms out horizontally. Yellow electricity began sparking around his jacket. He clenched his fist and the electricity instantaneously shifted to his hand. "It is important to be able to control how much power to exert and how to use it. You have to control your power one hundred percent."

He opened his palm and the electricity flickered with golden sparks and then concentrated into a blue ball.

"You have to balance the energy. You must focus your mind and let the energy pass through your body. You have to control the speed that it builds and how much you exert."

Like fluid, the blue electricity began to seep from his hand.

Airies threw her arms into the air and forced the students onto their knees with what felt like a tonne-weight of pressure pushed down on them. Anton and Peter dove to the ground. Vines grew up trying to take as much force as possible. Angelica hunkered down. Her bones shifted, black fur coated her skin and claws dug into the earth. Zayne spread his wings and using it like a parachute allowed the current to pull him up to the sky.

"I don't see how we can stand if the wind is this strong?" Anton's right arm covered his face. Although the vines created by Peter were taking the full brunt, it was almost impossible to stand.

"We'll just have to come up with a plan." Peter kept one hand on his head pinning his hat down.

Erika turned her back to the students. "I will give you guys a chance to take this." She threw the keyring a few feet in front of her.

Blake looked across at Thomas. "Do you have a plan?" he murmured. Thomas shook his hand.

"You guys know I am a sorceress. You should be coming up with a tactical plan." She flicked her head over her left shoulder and gave a wicked smile. "You should be afraid."

A shiver ran down Fabia's spine. She reached for her sleeve and pulled out her wand.

"What are you going to do?" Mandy asked standing to Fabia's right.

"How about the three of us distract Master Roberts and Blake can go in and snatch the keyring." Fabia pointed in the direction of the pink heart which was lying in the green grass.

"That sounds like a plan." Mandy's frame lowered as her bones began to shift and crack. Her brown fur eclipsed her skin, snarling as she stretched her limbs.

Gold dust lightly coated Thomas' hand and Mandy glanced up nervously. "Right," he cleared his head. "Mandy and Fabia, you take the left. I will go right with Blake. Blake, you can then slip over to grab the keyring."

"Are you okay?" Fabia indicated his glowing hand.

He hummed. "All good."

The oozing electricity sparked wildly stretching across the ground and promptly morphed into the electric serpent. Asira took a better look at the creature. It had a seven-foot-long slithery body with two large fangs. Its body was completely composed of electricity, similar to her Avio serpent which was composed of ground and dirt.

It lay its body against the ground and began to slither, charging like a bullet. Aaron managed to leap out of the way. As he landed on his hunkers, his bones shifted, and the crackling sound had the hairs on the back of Asira's neck standing up. His body transformed in a matter of seconds as the sandy fur exploded across his skin.

"The Aviul serpent is nimble. You have to be quicker than it." Volknor gracefully manipulated the movements of the serpent as he twitched his fingers. The serpent hissed, abruptly skidding to a halt changing direction.

Chloe fluttered high to avoid the sparking electricity.

Eoin snatched Asira by the waist. His opposite arm sprung up immediately and in the same breath the vine wall shot up from the ground. The electric serpent skidded to another halt slamming its lengthy body against the wall.

Cara moved closer trying to keep behind the confines of the shelter Eoin provided. Bobby clutched his fists realising he had no skills beyond his ability to speak to and control animals and to his disappointment there were no animals nearby. Britanie crouched on her hunkers as her white hair coated her skin. Katie bounced into the air next to Chloe.

"Any plans?" Eoin called out as he raised his head and lowered his arms.

Asira brushed her top down. "That is twice now you saved me." She giggled nervously.

"Well Bluebird, how about another stone serpent?" he smiled back.

Asira nodded in response. She knew that was the best course of action was her Avio serpent against Volknor's Aviul serpent. The best way to nullify electricity was with ground. She steadied her breathing and focused.

"It's on its way back!" Katie yelled.

Asira's head jerked up and suddenly the monstrous blue serpent lurked above her. Her heart stopped. *'Shit!'* she screamed internally.

There were two distinct howls in the background and from the corner of her eye she caught the sight of Aaron and Britanie. Sand and dirt particles rose from the grass and hovered in front of her. The sand seeped in between the spaces of the electricity. Volknor tugged the invisible strings and the serpent slithered backwards trying desperately to shake the dirt from its crevasses.

Eoin moved next to Asira ready to grab her at any second. "The serpent?"

"Right." She nodded firmly pressing her hand against the grass. The ground beneath her quivered and the earth began to break apart reforming in front of her as a long and slender serpent with two horns curled to the back of its head. She swung her arm out to the left and the serpent darted in a semi-circle moving the Aviul serpent's attention away from the students.

Katie landed softly next to Bobby. "You good?" She understood his given cheerlessness and frightened face. "You need to get a weapon," she grinned.

"How are we going to get the keyring?" Bobby asked.

Chloe fluttered down next to Bobby. "Our best bet is to immobilise Master Volknor." Chloe pointed upwards. Snow was drifting down from a clear sky and only within a small area.

"It's snowing?" Katie curled her wings back and held out her hands.

Chloe then pointed across to Britanie. The white werewolf was crouched grumbling quietly as Aaron stood guard in front of her.

The Avio serpent backed the Aviul closer to Volknor. He gritted his teeth and smiled. 'Fair play,' he thought to himself and then glanced up to the sky watching silently as the snow drifted down and stuck to the ground. "What? Why is it snowing?" His eyes examined the area and scanned every student. Asira was busy controlling the serpent. Then his eyes locked onto the barely visible white werewolf. 'Aaron is guarding her,' he smirked.

The electric serpent dissolved into the air.

"It's gotten blooming cold." Bobby rubbed his bare arms up and down. "She's good." The cascading snow became a small flurry.

Asira lowered her arm and the Avio serpent halted suddenly. "What is he doing?" She glanced around at Eoin who shrugged.

Blue electricity violently sparked around Volknor's lower arms and hands. Clenching both fists together, he smashed his hands into the grass sending the electricity riotously in their direction. "Look out!" Eoin roared as he charged forward, snatching Asira and rolling out of the way. The Avio serpent took a mind of its own and curled its long stony tail around them taking the brunt of the blow. Cara, Bobby, Aaron and Britanie charged for the safety of the vine wall while Katie and Chloe quickly made their way back into the sky.

Cara cupped her hands as she scooped up some snow allowing it to melt. "Bobby, I have a plan." Cara peered around the vine wall. "Snow is just a different form of water." Bobby popped his head around the corner and watched as the snow gradually melted.

Eoin sat up to gaze at the inside of the stony enclosure. "You all good?" He glanced down at the purple lump curled up in his arms. "Asira? What's wrong? Are you hurt?"

"I have a pounding headache." She clasped her head.

Anton lifted his head and straightened his arm. Flames spiralled from his elbow and shot out in Airies' direction. Zayne flapped his wings trying to make his way to the ground. Angelica was struggling to steady herself.

Peter glanced over at Zayne. A vine shot up, grabbed his ankle and pulled him to the ground. Another vine loosely wrapped around Angelica's waist keeping her tethered in one place.

"How can we get any closer?"

Volknor glanced down at the soaked grass around him. *'Clever'.* He glanced across at Cara smirking from her half concealed hiding place. Suddenly he jumped feeling a hand in his pocket. Chloe was standing directly behind him. She hurriedly sprung back into the air, her wings fluttering as quickly as possible and threw the keyring across to Katie who was already in the sky. Volknor raised his arms in defeat. "You guys win. You distracted me with the frontal attack and then I noticed the melted snow and I was unable to use my powers."

Eoin pried Asira's hands from her face. "Bluebird, are you okay?" She nodded. "I'm feeling better." She squinted.

"No, you need to see a doctor. You haven't been well for a few days." As the stone serpent began slithering away it also began to crumble. Eoin stood up, helping Asira to her feet.

"Hey Asira," Cara called from the vine wall, "we won!"

Asira glanced around at Cara and Bobby and then stared up at Katie waving the yellow star keyring in the air victoriously. "I can't believe we won." She started walking away when Eoin grabbed her wrist.

"Hey Bluebird, are you sure you're feeling okay? How's your head?"

"Eoin, I just need to take a painkiller. I promise I'm okay now. Thanks." She smiled softly before walking over towards Cara and high-fiving Bobby.

"How did it go, Zayne?" Katie swooped down halfway to meet the other group.

He held his head down. "It was tough. She finally just said it was over."

"Aw Zayne, I'm so sorry." Katie threw her arms around her brother pulling him into a sympathetic hug. She glanced over his shoulder. "Master Robert's is still training the others. Do you want to go watch?"

"Yeah, sure." Zayne followed Katie to the last group.

Gold dust sprinkled from Thomas' hand and shifted through the air towards Erika. A mini black twister shot from the end of Fabia's wand. It absorbed the gold dust and carried it across the field.

Erika punched her fist through the black twister, absorbing the gold dust and shattering Fabia's spell. The gold dust coated her hands and she played with it between her fingers. "I have spent a lot of time around essences." She glanced up at Thomas' shocked face. "I quickly learned a way to help contain the power." The gold dust spluttered and formed into several tiny gold embers. "My signature move allows me to steal someone's power and use it as my own." She gestured to the gold hovering around her in a protective circle.

"Wow! That is amazing," Asira said walking up next to Katie with Anton following closely behind.

"That is actually incredible." Bobby stopped near them.

Eoin walked with Bobby and gazed across at Asira, quickly earning a glare from Anton. He straightened up and shoved his hands in his pockets ignoring the obnoxious glare.

Blake fluttered down to the ground. Mandy transformed and came to stand next to him.

"You tried to distract me. Mandy ran in one direction and Blake went in the other. Thomas and Fabia, you were good at tag teaming. It was very impressive. And to tell you the truth, it is hard to impress me." She gently stretched out her left arm and the gold embers twisted around her ever so elegantly. "You had a good handle on your power today Thomas. Well done." The gold embers moved through the air, circling around Blake, Mandy, Fabia and finally Thomas. Thomas held out his hand, feeling the warm glow tickle his skin before it dispersed into nothing.

"That was a good warm up exercise." Airies shook her limbs and stretched her arms to the sky. "Do you feel a little more relaxed? I know I do." She jumped onto her toes.

"I hope this has helped you all to grow a little bit with one another." Erika walked across the grass and picked up the pink heart keyring.

"I still have mine." Airies reached into her pocket and pulled out the blue diamond keyring.

"I lost mine." Volknor rubbed the back of his head in defeat. "There was just too many of them to keep an eye on everyone."

Erika rolled her eyes. "You've gotten too soft in your old age."

CHAPTER TWENTY

The Fever

The skills-building class continued for the rest of the day. The students were divided into groups. Erika decided to take some time with Fabia, Asira and Thomas. She tried to explain the similarity between the powers they possessed.

"You see, the way your powers work, although different elements are involved, they are strongly connected to your soul. It is the way you are able to manifest your elements and control them, this is what makes your powers similar."

"Master Roberts, I understand that for a sorceress our will determines how strong our spells are," Asira began, "but a sorceress has the ability to use every element in order to cast spells. How is that the same as Fabia using the dark element or Thomas using his core element?"

"You just answered it. It is down to your will. What makes Fabia different from Blake is the way she exerts and controls her power. She has the ability to always improve upon her powers. She is able to cast certain spells, similar to you. Blake is born with the ability to use the dark element but because he is not a witch, he cannot manipulate the darkness in the same way Fabia can. Thomas has a unique ability in that he actually uses his soul energy. He has an unlimited supply of energy at his disposal. That is what makes the core so unstable and hard to control. But a sorceress," Erika opened her clenched fist to reveal a blooming rose, "can do much more. We have the ability to manipulate all the elements and in turn, influence the environment around us."

Asira nodded. "Okay, I think I am starting to understand."

"Master Roberts, I think my expertise can help." Draskule appeared behind Asira, sending a chilling shiver down her spine.

"Master Draskule, if you would like to assist in teaching Fabia, Blake and Asira in the dark element."

"I noticed something during the lesson earlier," Volknor said approaching Bobby. "This will go for some others too. We will have to get you a weapon. Something discreet. I think it will be worth your while having a short dagger, something you can conceal in your shoe or trouser leg."

"I was actually thinking the same. But I'm not great at using them."

"Don't worry, I can show you some hand-to-hand combat skills."

"Really, Master Volknor? That would be amazing! Thank you." Bobby jumped from his seat.

Airies bounced up and down on the tips of her toes. "As angels, you really just have your speed and height, but you will also have to learn how to defend yourself. I'm going to teach you some hand-to-hand combat." She leapt onto her palms and kicked her feet outwards. Zayne dodged just in time. "Chloe, you and Blake both have immobilising elements. We need to work on using these."

"How would the elements be immobilising?" Chloe asked.

"It's all about control. You must learn to emit and control the light."

"The darkness or shadow element is the quintessence of a witch and a warlock. Has Master Kai taught you anything, Asira?" asked Draskule.

"Yes, sir. I am fluent in all the elements."

"Good, would you be capable of demonstrating something for us?"

"Like what, sir?"

"Fight me. I'll make it easy you can choose anyone of your classmates to fight alongside you."

Asira was hesitant. "Sir, I don't really want to..."

"Nonsense, I assume you want to go for your master's exam someday. In order to pass, you must be equipped to handle all the elements. Generally, you train with more than one master. It's a good idea to get a different perspective. Follow me outside."

Asira was hesitant as she followed Draskule outside to the courtyard. Anton stood shoulder to shoulder with her, glued to her side.

"Be gentle with the students, Draskule," Volknor said, sitting on the steps.

Airies sat behind him and murmured, "I don't like this. I just get a bad feeling."

"He's a teacher. He has every right to assess the students," Volknor said a little tensely. "But I agree. I'm not a fan of this at all."

"Have you chosen who will fight with you?" Draskule made his way down the courtyard and turned. "You have chosen Anton. Very well." He loosened the sleeves of his cloak. "Deception is a major tactic a lot of people overlook. The aim of today's lesson is to leave a scratch on my skin. You can use any tactic, any spell, or any element. You can even try hand-to-hand combat."

She gazed up at Anton tensely as Draskule yanked black chains from his sleeves dropping them to the ground with a clunk. Asira pressed her hand to the ground and as the stone began to break apart, a chain bolted from the ground snatching her wrist and dragging her across the dirt.

"Asira!" Eoin leapt forward only to be stopped by Volknor. "We just can't sit here. He's hurting her."

"He's a teacher at this school and you will not disrespect him by interfering," Volknor said sternly, his eyes locked on the battle before him.

Asira finally managed to slip her wrist from the chain and rolled. She stumbled to her feet and quickly materialised the stony serpent. Another chain bolted in her direction. This time swirling embers separated her from the warlock.

"Asira, are you okay?" Anton gently examined her bruising skin. "He was a bit rough."

"I don't know what he wants, Anton. I don't think we'll be able to put a scratch on him."

A purple-coloured smog crept around their feet. "I can't move." Anton struggled to break his feet free.

"I've got a plan but it's going to get cold very fast." White glazed her eyes and her vision blurred. She grabbed onto Anton's shoulders as a sudden gust of icy wind blew across the courtyard. "Don't let go." Anton wrenched Asira into his arms and held on. The wind blew the leaves off the trees, picking up any light stones and dirt from the courtyard. Anton's flames whipped up around them in a protective swirl, knocking away any debris.

"What's going on?" Airies covered her eyes and fell back against the step.

Volknor tried to stand. "That wind is frigid."

Eoin stared out at the courtyard. The purple smog was retreating and Draskule was shielding his face from the oncoming debris.

"Is this Asira's power?" Bobby rubbed his arms frantically. "God, it's so cold!"

Asira's fingers dug a little tighter when the wind ceased, the flames died down, and the debris fell back to earth. Anton loosened his grip, but her knees immediately buckled. "Asira, are you okay?"

"I'm just feeling a little dizzy."

Volknor did not hesitate when he noticed Asira hunched over in pain. He leapt from the steps. "What's wrong?"

"She's dizzy and has a pain in her chest," Anton replied, fearful and anxious.

"Asira," Volknor brushed her cheek, "have you ever felt this way before?"

She mumbled, "No."

"Right, we'll get you inside." Volknor moved in front of Anton and scooped her up in one swoop and briskly walked back to the castle. "Airies, call the doctor. We'll get her checked out."

"What's wrong with her?" Eoin apprehensively followed behind Volknor.

"I'm okay. I just need to call Amy," Asira mumbled as she twitched in his arms. "I need to check on Amy."

"She's burning up. I think she has a fever." Eoin spoke quickly, obviously flustered as he tried to keep up with Volknor's brisk pace.

"Eoin," Anton stood back from him, "it may be best if we stay out of this. The teachers are able to handle this. We will just be in the way."

"But a fever is serious. What if she needs us? Are you not concerned? What happened to her?"

"She won't need us right now. She's delirious. Listen to her."

***

"How is she?" Anton knocked as he entered her bedroom.

Kai rose from his seat. "I've had the doctors check her over and they see nothing wrong, just that she's run herself ragged, that's all. She just needs a few days of rest. Would you mind sitting with her for a few minutes."

"Of course." He stepped further into the room just as Kai left.

Asira was lying tucked under her duvet with a damp cloth over her forehead. Painkillers and a glass of water sat on the locker next to her bed. Her mobile phone was charging next to her lamp and the curtains were half pulled to keep the light off her face.

There was a tap on the door. "How is she?" Eoin stood by the entrance. "Is she..."

"She only had a fever. Kai said she will be fine after a few days of rest."

"That's good." Eoin stepped into the room, nosily examining the different bits and bobs across her vanity table. "She has the same perfume as my sister."

"Don't touch anything. Respect her room and privacy."

"What's your problem with me? Or do you just hate everyone?"

"Asira and I are dating. I want you to back off."

Like a ton of bricks, Eoin's stomach turned sour. "Asira is still my friend. I will not be frightened away."

"Where's Amy?" Asira wriggled under her sheets, her eyes fluttering in the daylight.

"Good morning, sleepy head!" Eoin darted to her bedside.

"Asira, how are you feeling?" Anton grasped her hand.

"Amy, where's Amy?"

"Who's Amy?" Eoin whispered.

"I don't know," Anton replied. "Her breathing is still shallow."

"Knock, knock. Can we come in?" Katie, Fabia and Chloe stood by the opened door. "We want to check in to see how Asira is doing." Katie tiptoed into the room.

"How is she?" Fabia walked over beside Eoin.

"She's going to be fine." Anton patted Asira's hand affectionately.

"Oh, are you guys dating now?" Chloe cooed as she fluttered her wings excitedly. "That is so cute. You must be so concerned for her, Anton?"

Eoin's stomach churned with disgust. His fingers dug into the edge of the bed before turning and hastily leaving the room.

"What's wrong with him?" Katie moved around the bed to freshen the wet cloth. "She's still pretty warm. The poor thing totally wore herself out."

CHAPTER TWENTY-ONE

Amy

"I still can't believe it's been a whole month already!" Asira shoved her phone into her pocket.

"Are you excited to go home?" Cara fixed the straps of the backpack on her shoulders.

"I'm so excited! I've some old friends to visit. What about you, Anton? Excited to see your mother?"

"Well yes, but I can't wait to meet up with you again in a few days." He kissed her cheek.

Asira blushed playfully punching him in the shoulder. "Stop! My dad is over there."

"I'm not embarrassed," Anton sniggered glancing over in Kai's direction, who was preoccupied with the other students.

"Okay you lovebirds, I have to go. My parents are waiting by the coast for me." Cara pried their arms apart. "I will see you in three days!" She hugged Asira before turning to Anton and hugging him too.

"See you, Cara." Asira waved goodbye.

"Are you sure you're feeling alright? Two days ago, you were in bed and delusional."

"Anton, I feel so much better. I should be heading too. Dad is waiting for me."

He reached in one last time kissing her softly on the lips. "Stay safe."

"You too, Anton." She moved back from his arms and towards the steps of Topaz Castle where Kai waited awkwardly. An orange portal appeared before them and she turned one last time to wave goodbye before stepping across the orange gateway and into her sitting room. The clocks in the house struck six in the evening. "I missed this place." She reached for her mobile. "I'll call a pizza. Do you want anything else?"

"Some garlic bread and sweet potato fries would be lovely. Oh, and a bottle of fizzy orange."

"Perfect!" She sauntered off into another room.

Kai strolled around the house, spraying each room with a lavender scent. He had missed his home, but he hadn't realised how much he had missed Velosia. Though he never really left and continued to work with The Council, it was different with Asira living there. For the first time in a long time, he felt reassured that Velosia was a safe place for Asira to grow and learn. He was able to reconnect with some old friends but more importantly, Asira was able to start new friendships with people her own age who were familiar with her background, something he felt she was deprived of living in England.

***

The next day Kai parked right outside a dormer bungalow in a neat cul-de-sac estate, waiting while Asira walked fearlessly to the door. It had been a month since she had spoken to her best friend. She was so excited for them to spend the next few days together staying up all night watching movies and stuffing her face with chocolate. She was also eager to tell her all about Anton. She knocked on the door and waited patiently.

"Asira, what..." The short woman with brunette locks gazed sorrowfully at her.

"Hello Mrs Devlin!" Asira waved a pink teddy bear in the air. "I'm sorry I haven't been around a lot. I'm sure Amy has told you I'm taking private classes in preparation for college." She glanced over Mrs Devlin's shoulder and smiled. "Is Amy here? I haven't been able to get through to her. I think her phone may be broken. Is she out with Tim or Stephen?" Asira peered over her shoulder again and gazed down the hall of the house. "I'm dying to hear any gossip. She was telling me all about her crush on Tim before I left."

Unexpectedly, Mrs Devlin burst into tears.

A sudden sick feeling sank deep into her stomach. "Where's Amy?"

"Asira, I'm so sorry."

"Sorry? Sorry for what? What's wrong Mrs Devlin?"

"I swear I tried ringing you several times." Her voice cracked under the pressure.

Mrs Devlin began to explain the dire situation.

Kai stepped out of the car watching. "Asira, what's the matter?" Without another word, he instinctively knew what had happened. He led Asira and Mrs Devlin into the house. They found themselves in the sitting room staring at a shrine on the mantle. "Mary, I am so sorry for your loss."

Mrs Devlin wiped her tears and the running mascara. "I was just telling, Asira." She reached for the box of tissues and blew her nose loudly. "It was awful, Kai. Amy was out on a boat with three of her friends when it sank. They found pieces of the wreckage, but they haven't been able to find any survivors. I tried calling by your house. I wanted to tell you sooner."

"When did this happen?" Kai glanced at the candles and photos decorating the mantle. The recent photo of Asira and Amy arm in arm walking along the beach together only made the unsettling news even more real and harrowing.

"It's been nearly a month. She was so excited that morning. Stephen slept over the night before. She was telling me all about your date with Jack at the bowling alley. Jack came with Tim and picked them up early that morning. They came in for tea before leaving. Jack was telling me all about his dad's boat and that he was a sailor. He was showing me the awards he had won. I was nervous of them going out sailing. I shouldn't have let them go. The only thing they found intact was Jack's Bentley by the harbour."

Hearing the story again was like a dagger to the chest. Asira crumbled, leaning forward over her knees clutching the teddy bear tight. *Amy was on the boat. The boat had sunk. Amy was gone. Jack was gone. They were all gone.'* Those words repeated in her head.

"Mary, if there is anything we can do, please do not hesitate to contact me." Kai reached for her hand supportively.

"Thank you, Kai," she said blowing her nose once again. "I just haven't been able to sleep since the whole thing. She was my baby," she whimpered into her tissue.

"I have an old recipe that helps me sleep. I will come by later and leave you some. Just add some drops to your tea before going to bed. Once you hit the pillow, you will be out cold." Kai glanced down at Asira. "I think we will be on our way. We will be gone again by Sunday evening but as soon as we return, we'll come back to visit."

***

For the rest of the day, Asira remained curled under a duvet on the couch in the sitting room watching classic animated films, something herself and Amy had done together on a regular basis. It was a tradition. Every few weeks they would gather in either house to stuff their face with chocolate.

"Asira, I think this will come in useful for your training. It is a training staph."

"A staph?" She sniffled taking the short wooden pole from Kai and examining the purple and green scarves around the neck.

"A staph is a conduit. It will help concentrate and create a focal point for some more difficult spells. Erika was telling me you were learning some new spells and were still having a bit of trouble with others."

"Dad, it's beautiful. Thank you!"

"It should be easier to create those portals. When you want to put the staph away but access it again whenever you need it, there is a handy trick." Kai held either end of the wooden staph and as he pushed his hands closer together the staph began to disappear. "It just goes into a void until you recall it. Give it a go, put your hands together, think of the staph and then pull your hands apart. It's all about manipulating reality."

She clapped her hands together. Her mind was elsewhere, and her thoughts were jumbled. She pulled her hands apart, but nothing happened.

He crouched down to her level, gripping both hands. "I know it's tough right now, but sometimes we have to learn to distance ourselves from reality. Close your eyes. Take deep breaths." His voice was soothing. "Concentrate on the sound of my voice." Together they separated their hands and as Asira began to focus on the staph, she felt a tingle between her palms. She peeked and saw the wooden staph reappearing, bit by bit until she snatched it mid-air. "Right, let's go. Open a portal." A bouquet of white lilies appeared in Kai's open palm. "You know where to go."

She pushed back the folds of her cocoon, tissues falling to the floor and wiped her cheeks dry. She closed her eyes taking a deep breath through her nose. Focusing all her thoughts on the destination, she could feel the tingle run through her veins, like a spark of energy. Instead of dispersing mid-air, the power became trapped in the staph and purple doors appeared before them.

"Great." Kai smiled but taking a second glance, he looked at the edges, noticing blue threads tainting the purple hue.

"I can't believe this." She tapped the purple edges. "It's so weird. I can actually see the portal." She took a second glance, caressing the blue fibres. "Volknor mentioned that my portal was turning blue. Was there any blue in my portal before?"

He shook his head. "No, which is strange. Portals appear in the colour of your soul. Blue has never appeared before. Anyway, a lot of sorcerers' and sorceresses use objects to help focus their power and energy. As a lot of witches and warlocks use wands to focus their powers." Kai took the lead through the portal. "Portals are really hard to conjure and not a lot of people can do this. So for a young sorceress, you are doing extremely well."

For the first time, Asira could see the power she wielded in the beautiful swirling purple shades. Her fingers rippled through the wall of colour, like flowing water. They stepped through the other end. Asira gripped the staph just a little and the portal closed instantly. In a matter of seconds, they had crossed from Earth to Velosia. Headstones decorated the landscape. A few mature oak trees covered the grounds, and an iron fence surrounded the borders. There were a few people ambling around in silence.

Kai stopped in front of one particular headstone. "Your mother was a very brave woman and every day you remind me of her." The headstone was simple, curved at the top with just some writing. He placed the lilies down. "I sometimes tell her how well your studies are going and what you've been up to." He bit his tongue. "She would have been so proud to see you use your powers and just be yourself. I made sure to teach you what I know. I never thought it was right to stop you. No one ever stopped me. No one certainly ever stopped your mother."

Asira knelt down beside him. "You never really talk about her. It's nice when you do."

"It was tough losing Crystal. I didn't know a life without her. But you must learn to not let grief take over. Does that make sense?" He glanced up at her teary eyes. "Amy would want you to be happy."

***

It had only been a few hours since she had returned to Topaz Castle and Asira had already locked herself in her room. Not everyone had returned from home yet, so the castle was quiet. She hugged her pillow close to her chest, tears stained her bed sheets. Her phone lay six inches from her face and she had been staring at it for twenty minutes straight.

"Asira?" There was a knock on the door. She didn't flinch. She lay completely still. Her gaze was still locked on her silent phone. "Hey Asira, it's me, Cara. Look," she cleared her throat, "Master Kai... Your dad explained what has happened." There was another knock. "Asira, I am so sorry. I know you are hurting. Can I please come in?"

She rose from her bed, shuffling across the room to open the door. She pulled her sleeve over her hand and lazily wiped her cheeks.

"Asira," Cara hesitated, "how are you doing?"

She let out a cry as tears streamed down her face. "I can't believe she's gone." She sniffled loudly throwing herself into Cara's arms. "She was my best friend."

"Oh, Asira!" Cara embraced Asira as she sobbed, pushing her back a few steps into the room and closing the door behind them. "I can cheer you up." She sat Asira on the bed and crouched in front of her. "Smiling is my specialty." Cara quickly glanced around the room noticing an open packet of painkillers. "I have been so worried. Are you still getting those headaches?" She waited for an answer. Asira nodded. "I know we do not know each other long but I think you are my best friend. I want to help you." Cara suddenly jumped to her feet. "How about we get some ice cream?"

Asira sat up, dropped the pillow and smiled. "I would love mint chocolate ice cream."

"Chocolate is my favourite!" Cara grinned stretching her arm out. "Just remember, Asira, you are not alone, no matter what happens."

***

Kai strolled down the corridors of the castle. As he approached the dining room, he heard giggling from inside. He peaked around the corner. Cara and Asira were perched on the table eating ice cream from a large tub.

Asira sniffled. "We often went to this little cafe after school." She scooped a massive spoonful of mint ice cream. "We always ordered the same thing, a chocolate chip milkshake. Amy had a really sweet tooth." She shovelled the ice cream into her mouth. "We've known each other since we were little tots in play school.

Dad used to take us shopping with him. We would always sneak biscuits into the trolley." She wiped the tears from her cheeks again.

Kai gazed softly at his daughter.

"We would stay up til all hours watching movies and talking. That is why I thought it was strange, she never text me back. I thought she was mad at me. I should have known better. I should have trusted my instincts."

Kai moved back and stood in the hall for a moment. His little girl had never had to face death before. In the background he could hear her sniffle and sob. His daughter was grieving. She was hurting and he didn't know how to help her.

***

The rain was thudding against the windows. The sky was black. The wind was hollering. It was another day in class. Asira sat next to the window completely distracted. She began another session of daydreaming, twiddling her pen between her fingers. Her thoughts ran away with her and drifted to fond memories of Amy and the time they had spent together.

Volknor continued in the background about history. She glanced up occasionally from the window. The word *Velosia* was written across the board along with the names *Argentum Empire, Maria Empire, Mortem Empire, Arena Kingdom, Bonum Kingdom* and *Luce Caelo Empire* in a spider diagram.

After class Asira picked up her books and headed back towards the dorm corridors.

"Hey, Bluebird!"

She peered over her shoulder, turning on the staircase.

Eoin stood at the end of the stairs with a stupid look on his face. "Eh..." he rubbed the back of his head. "I heard what happened and I just wanted to say I'm sorry, Bluebird."

Asira softly smiled. "Thanks, Eoin. That means a lot."

"Considering we are finished class for the day, do you want to just chill?"

"Any suggestions?"

"Eh, well, we could..."

"I have an idea!" Asira pulled the staph from mid-air and conjured a purple portal behind her and again the colour blue began to contaminate the portal. She tilted her head. "Are you coming?"

He jogged up the steps with a stupid grin on his face but as they stepped through the swaying colours, he noticed her pale, sickly complexion. Eoin looked around at the bins and held his nose. "Where are we?" He followed her out onto the street and gazed at the heavy flow of vehicles and pedestrians passing by.

"England." She stood outside a cafe. "Sweetz Cafe." Asira swallowed a lump in her throat. "This is where Amy and I went all the time. I've wanted to come back here but honestly, I've been too afraid." She took in a deep breath before walking in. "You will really love the milkshakes. They're the best." She approached the counter and ordered before stepping across to a window table.

"Bluebird, can I ask you a question?" Eoin watched as she took out two painkillers and swallowed them whole. "Are you sick?"

She glanced across with a troubled stare and shook her head. "Nope, I just have this headache."

The waitress walked over handing them two tall narrow glasses. Eoin took a sip. "Oh wow! This is actually amazing."

"I told you it was good. We would come here two or three times a week."

"We definitely have to learn how to make these back at school." He stirred the bits at the end before chugging back what was left in the glass.

Asira gazed into her half empty glass. "She never knew what I really was. She never knew I was a sorceress. She knew I was into performing magic tricks, but I technically lied to my best friend. I never told her, and now I can never tell her." Tears dribbled down her cheeks. "I'm so sorry. I thought I cried it all out of me already."

"Bluebird," Eoin put down the glass, "you never have to apologise to me. What you're going through is really tough. I don't like seeing you cry. Just remember you're not alone."

Asira nodded. "Sure. Thank you, Eoin."

"Anytime, Bluebird."

***

For the rest of the week, Asira found the classes a little tougher than normal. They had a skills-building class where they focused on tactical training and casting spells with Erika. She took particular interest in Asira, Fabia and Thomas. Maybe because she was used to working with witches and essences and that Asira was just like her. Erika was a taxing teacher. Her classes were strenuous and arduous. But they were interesting, like her. She was a very private person, and they did not know much about her background. She mostly shared her classes with Volknor or Kai. In tactical classes, she and Kai had shown the class how to identify and utilise various weapons and tools. Asira wasn't sure why this was exactly needed but she was curious about the appeal.

Airies was a quirky teacher. As well as her designated classes, she taught them elegance and diplomacy, in preparation of meeting with different royals and dignitaries. Like Volknor, Airies was an SN, a supernatural. She was born into the Angels but was born without wings. Her classes were not as exciting as the tactical training, but as the class were already involved in diplomacy, it was a must-know subject.

Later in the week, they had a history class with Volknor. He delved a little deeper into the cause and effects of the Great War.

"The war only ended about eighteen years ago after much bloodshed and violence." Volknor led the students away from the castle, down a stony path ceremonially lined with cherry blossom trees. At the end of the path, they came to a white picket fence. Beyond the fence were twelve immense arches sitting upon a sheer cliff. The arches stood in a circle with a thin stony path leading from each arch to the centre where a five-foot column stood. "These are the Great Arches, created centuries ago by the first Council and are carved from solid stone." He stepped into the centre and stood by the column. "Each arch represents an element."

"Are they portals?" Asira asked.

He nodded. "Many people believe they are portals, but no one has ever seen them in use. The power to use them has been lost for a long, long time." Volknor pointed to the top of an arch with a fire emblem engraved. "Each arch has a carving at the very top to indicate which gemstone it represents."

"So that would make that one water," said Fabia pointing to a teardrop symbol on one arch. "And that lightning," she said pointing at a lightning bolt on another.

"In less than two years, it will be the twentieth anniversary of the ending of the Great War. The Council have agreed to host a special event in Cora town. Each kingdom will honour the event with a tribute. Master Adams has asked specifically for the first students of Velosian Academy to take part in the event. I know it is some time away, but it would help with the school if you all attended."

"Is this the Revenant Anniversary?" Cara enquired.

Volknor nodded. "That's correct. There have been no details confirmed as yet, but I thought it would be nice to tell you. It has huge historical significance for the world and the school."

"So, the purpose of the Revenant Anniversary would be to honour those who have fallen?" Katie curled back her wings smoothly.

"That's right. As time goes on, people tend to move on with their lives and forget about the past. Hatred can build back up and wars can always be restarted. The aim of this anniversary is to remember those who have fallen – soldiers and civilians, and to bring home the terrible outcomes of the war to ensure something like this will never happen again."

CHAPTER TWENTY-TWO

Cursed

It had been a little over a week since Asira had returned to the Topaz Castle. She was finding it hard to fall asleep. Most nights after everyone had gone to bed, she left her room and took a stroll around the castle to clear her head. She walked through the halls in her pyjamas. The castle wasn't as creepy as she'd first thought. The halls were always lit with decorative candles.

She flicked the switch to illuminate the kitchen before rummaging through the fridge and drawers, grabbing what she could to make a sandwich. Out the corner of her eye she thought she saw something move. She glanced over her shoulder but there was no one there. She kept her eyes on the door for a few more seconds before returning to the task at hand, buttering the bread and throwing some ham, cheese, and tomatoes between the two slices.

"It wasn't obvious before, but it oozes when you're afraid." A tall man with dark hair and a greyish complexion stood in the corner of the kitchen. "At first, I wasn't sure if I had the right person, but now I can sense it. You have the same power as your father."

"Who... who are you?" Asira dropped the knife as she turned her back against the cupboards.

"We met briefly. By the seaside," said the man, charging from the other side of the room to slam Asira's face into the countertop.

A stabbing pain gripped her spine.

She was thrown forward again, pushing the plate to the floor. She felt a cracking on the inside, something breaking inside her body. She tried to scream but couldn't find her voice. Her fingers dug into the countertop. She was pulled from behind. The pain was ravaging her. She was gasping for air, desperately trying to scream.

Then she was tossed to the floor like a rag doll. The figure had vanished. She was left in silence. She could barely breathe. Clutching her throat, she dragged herself across the kitchen floor. "Dad!" she staggered to her feet, screaming. "DAD!" She managed before the pain in her back overwhelmed her.

***

Volknor was leaning against the white board. His hair was ruffled, his shirt was sticking out of his jeans. Airies was slumped lazily on the desk wearing a long dressing gown, bare legs and pink fluffy slippers. Erika had her hair tied in a high messy ponytail and was wearing yellow stripped pyjamas. She glanced over at the students sitting at their desks in their pyjamas before glancing at her watch and reading seven in the morning.

"Do you think anyone here would have done something so vile?" Erika said with her back to the class.

"They are just kids." Airies moved her heavy head to glance back at the sleepy students.

"I don't think one of our students would intentionally do something so evil. But we have to investigate this before it gets any further up the ranks." Volknor gazed at the writing on the board.

It was the work from the other day when they were discussing the history of Velosia. "It's hard to believe someone could hospitalise their classmate."

"Master Roberts, why did you pull us all out of bed? I didn't think class started until ten today," said Angelica, slumped over her desk in her tiger striped pyjamas and white fluffy slippers and an eye mask resting on her forehead.

"Where's Asira?" Anton asked folding his arms across his black t-shirt.

Volknor turned around taking several deep breaths. He straightened his spine and puffed out his chest. "At three o'clock this morning Asira was rushed to hospital. She was found in the kitchen with extensive injuries."

"Oh my! Is she okay?" Cara gasped in horror.

"Where is she?" Anton jumped from his seat and marched to the top of the class.

Volknor put one hand out. "Sit down." His voice was stern.

"Who would do this?" Katie looked sick.

"Asira is getting the best attention. Did anyone see or hear anything last night?" Volknor asked crossing his arms again.

"No, I didn't sense anything out of the ordinary last night." Anton looked away in defeat. He had failed to protect her.

"Can we go see her?" Aaron asked, sitting at the back of the class with the other werewolf children.

"Are you accusing one of us?!" Eoin had his fist clenched on the desk.

"Calm down, Eoin. No one said anything about accusing anyone," Erika said steadily.

"I know it was difficult for everyone to be in the same room together at first. The opening day of Velosian Academy was not a shining moment. But since then, a lot of us – we have grown, and

I couldn't imagine anyone of our class hurting anyone else in this place. Especially Asira. I..." Eoin's words trailed off. "We all love Asira."

Anton glared at him from the corner of his eye.

"Eoin's right. I know sometimes it doesn't seem like we all get on. But we wouldn't like to see anything happen to anyone here," said Angelica, her hand clasped in Aaron's.

"At first it was a mad idea, I almost didn't sign up, but I've never regretted joining this academy." Bobby was sitting at the front of the class wearing stripy shorts and a baggy t-shirt.

"We are not monsters," Thomas added sitting at the front of the class next to Bobby.

Volknor glanced at Airies and Erika. "We will get an update on Asira's condition later today. In the meantime, go and get dressed and then come back down for breakfast. We're going to start class a little early."

***

"Asira..."

Her eyes fluttered with the sound of a familiar voice. Though at first her senses were all distorted, the voice came through muffled, and the light was far too bright. Her lungs throbbed with each breath. Her arms twitched with pain and her eyes were drawn to the IV drip stand. Her head tilted to the left and she stared at the green lines of her heart monitor and listened to the beeping.

"Asira..." the voice was clearer this time. She gazed down to the end of the bed. Kai was standing in a frozen running position as if he were ready to catch her any second. "I can't believe you're awake." He knelt down next to her. "You gave me such a fright. The doctor said when you arrived in, your blood pressure was dangerously low. You were here no more than ten minutes and they had to resuscitate you. I thought I was going to lose you last night."

Her head felt fuzzy. "Dad…" and her voice was hoarse.

"What happened last night? Asira, stay awake and look at me."

She blinked and squinted as the light stung her eyes. "Dad?" She glanced up at him again.

"What happened in the kitchen last night, Asira?"

"I hurt everywhere." Her voice was groggy. "I have a headache."

"Asira, we found you at the kitchen door unconscious. The doctor found bruising on your back and lungs." His voice grew cold and more agitated. "Volknor and the other teachers are questioning all the students. Do you remember anything?"

She swallowed a hard lump in her throat. "I…" she tried to think back to last night. Though her memory seemed hazy. "I heard a voice. It was a man's voice." Her throat stung from the dryness. "I…" Then she remembered a shadow pushing her against the counter and forcing her down. "I was pushed. There was a cracking sound."

"Did you see this man?"

She closed her eyes tight. "No…it was just a shadow."

"Did you hear or see anything else strange?"

She shut her eyes again trying to think through the pain in her back. "Dad," tears started to well. "Why do I hurt so much? What's happening? I can't breathe!"

Kai rang the bell for the nurse. "It's going to be okay." He pressed the bell again and again. "It is going to be okay. Just stay calm."

A nurse rushed into the room pushing Kai out of the way. He stepped back watching from the end of the bed. The sight of his daughter lying in the hospital was too much. It only took a few moments for the nurse to calm her down.

Two knocks broke the silence. "I'm sorry, Kai," Volknor opened the door slightly, peeking in. "He was very persuasive. Lady Pearse was down the phone to Master Adams giving him hell." He gazed across the bed before standing back.

Anton stepped in and bowed. "Master Soniar, I came to see Asira." He held a bunch of white lilies.

In a strange daze, Kai nodded and stepped out of the room, letting Anton in.

"How is she?" Volknor moved back into the corridor and watched as Kai took a few steps over to him and fell against the wall.

He was silent for the first few minutes, trying to comprehend what was happening. Who had attacked his daughter? Why would anyone want to attack her? "The doctors," his tone was grief-stricken and angry, "say she has intensive bruising on her ribs, spine and lungs."

"What?!" Volknor leaned back against the wall in incredulity. "Who would do such an appalling thing?"

"Someone is attacking my family. Patrick was the last person to harm us."

"Kai, Patrick has been dead almost twenty years. He had no followers to my knowledge. No one would be copying him. I don't even understand how this would happen. The palace is protected." It abruptly dawned on him. "Only someone inside the castle could have harmed her."

"We can narrow this down pretty quickly. She has no external injuries. In order for such intense internal bruising, someone would have to reach inside her. I could only imagine a sorcerer or a witch having this sort of power."

"That only leaves a handful of people – Erika, Adams, Draskule and Fabia. You can't accuse the kid or Erika."

"I've seen what Fabia can do. I don't think she is capable of hurting a fly. But I can't rule anyone else out at the moment, Volknor."

Anton stood at the end of the bed. His hair was ruffled. He was wearing an old t-shirt for bed under his coat. "I remember you saying these were your favourite." He placed the lilies on the locker next to her and stood formally. His stomach knotted at the sight of the IV drip and the sound of the heart monitor. "I... I'm so sorry I didn't hear anything strange." He leaned over her bed shutting his eyes tight trying his best to stop the tears from rolling down his face. "I didn't smell or hear anything. I'm a useless vampire and an even worse boyfriend." He edged himself up on the bed and wrapped his arms securely around her. As he lay there, his head still resting against her hair, he whispered, "I will never let anyone harm you again. I promise you on my life!"

CHAPTER TWENTY-THREE

Dinner

"Asira's coming home today. We have to show her how much we missed her," proclaimed Angelica standing on a chair in the dining room and waving a wooden spoon in the air.

"How are we going to do that?" Blake wore a black t-shirt with a square white skull. Just like Chloe's tops, this one had long slits down the back to allow the fairy wings to move without restriction.

"Some people think this school is not going to work. I could hear people talk when I returned home. They think we're too different. They think that the fairies will argue over stupid things and that the werewolves and vampires will rip each other's heads off. Personally, I'm far too elegant for that type of behaviour. I want to prove everyone wrong. We have already proven we can be together, learn together and play together."

"What do you suggest we do, Angelica?" Bobby asked sitting like a cowboy on a chair next to Peter and Eoin.

"What Angelica is saying is if we continue to do our best and work hard, we can prove our families and kingdoms wrong and show them vampires, werewolves, fairies – all of us can live and work together," said Aaron uncrossing his arms to help Angelica off the chair.

"I agree." Peter rose from his chair.

"That means taking your hat off, Peter." Thomas elbowed him in the side.

"For tonight, I think we should make Asira a feast! We should all make dishes from our homeland," Angelica continued waving the wooden spoon in the air.

"Oh, that sounds fabulous! I could make my mummy's eye and newt skewers!" Fabia bounced grabbing Thomas and swinging him around. "You would love my mummy's pumpkin bread and broomstick pastries." She had the energy and spirit of a sixteen-year-old, a young teenager with no worries in life.

"Zayne, we could make the King's dish!" Katie called over to him and then turned to Chloe. "It's heavenly, it's a feast of fresh vegetables and fruit and a pig and calf on a spit cooked slowly for hours. It is really delicious."

"It's a bit barbaric but sounds delicious." Chloe's face was a little shocked at the thought of a calf on a spit. "I think Blake and I will decline on the calf offer. In our culture, calves and cows are sacred. But if you like pork you should try our pork ramen. We cook it with scallions, goose eggs and ramen noodles. It's just bursting with flavour!"

"That's actually how we make it as well," Blake spoke excitedly. "I suppose we're not that different."

"I guess not." Chloe smiled at the dark winged fairy. "Have you ever made Zanzilla bread?"

"My mother makes it every Sunday. It's a family tradition," Blake replied.

"Guys!" Volknor sauntered into the room. "Kai phoned a few minutes ago. Asira will be home around six this evening."

"That just gives us a little longer to plan," Angelica began to mumble to herself.

"Time for what? What are you planning?"

"Master Volknor, we've all been talking. We want to make a dinner tonight for Asira, to welcome her home. We all want to make some dishes from our kingdoms and prove that we can work as a team," answered Angelica.

"You all came up with this?" Volknor stared across at Angelica.

"We did, sir," Aaron nodded over to Volknor.

"Well, I think that's a great idea. I look forward to trying some of your cuisine," Volknor said and left the dining room, closing the door behind him. He walked up the hall to where Airies and Erika were waiting. "They are all going to cook meals from their kingdoms tonight to welcome Asira home."

"What did you say to them?" Erika asked walking alongside Airies.

"Nothing, they came up with this idea themselves. And it's Angelica who seems to be taking the lead. She didn't look like the diplomatic type," Volknor responded as he held the door open.

"I said it before, this generation will surprise you." Airies skipped through and glided down the steps from the castle. "When is Asira returning home?"

"Kai is bringing her back about six this evening." Volknor took the lead around the school.

"No one could have broken into the school. Draskule and I created the security spell around the castle grounds. I have examined every inch of the castle. I've seen no tear or rip in the spell, not even a pin prick. Master Adams is keeping everything quiet, no one outside the castle knows about last night. Even Asira's doctor has been sworn to secrecy. I just don't understand who would have been able to do something like this. This type of spell doesn't even exist in common, modern or historical books. I had to look into ancient scripture, and I don't even know if it is the right curse I found!"

"Kai was saying she has intense bruising along her back," Volknor said stopping just ahead of them. Chills travelled his spine. "Erika, I want you to doublecheck the protection spell on this castle and its grounds. But you are to tell nobody."

"That can be done, Volknor. I'll prep one later and it will encase the current spell."

"No one is to know. If too many people know then word gets out and whoever did this will be one step ahead of us."

"Do you think whoever this is, is trying to sabotage the peace between the nations?" Airies skipping was a mere saunter beside him now.

"Volknor, who do you think has done this?" Erika asked.

"I don't know," he replied to them both in a sombre voice.

***

Britanie sat on the steps of the Velosian Academy next to Mandy in her werewolf form. Her fur was coarse but an exquisite dark brown. Britanie was captivated, running her fingers through the rich coat. The breeze was cool, and the sun was still quite bright.

A change on the breeze disturbed their languor. "Something smells odd." The sound of a car echoed in the distance. "Do you hear that, Mandy?" The werewolf beside her turned and barked. "We better tell Angelica."

Mandy tumbled into the dining room, landing on her jean clad bottom. "She's on the way!"

"She's coming!" Chloe glided across the dining room with the plates and bounced into the kitchen. "Angelica, she's on the way! Is everything ready?"

"Come people! You will not know a woman's wrath until you see me if these dishes are not out and ready for Asira in the next two minutes!"

Thomas glanced fearfully at Blake and Chloe. All three had the ability to see and feel the emotion of a person. The three of them stood staring at Angelica and watched as the usually narrow pink aura was now burning like hot pink flames.

"Wow, did Gordon Ramsey have a sex change?" Chloe whispered to Thomas. But she caught Angelica's demonic glare and intuitively floated backwards out through the kitchen doors.

***

A black car pulled up outside Velosian Academy. Kai had called a taxi from the hospital. He wasn't allowing Asira to walk through any portals while she was so weak. He opened the car door trying to help Asira out.

"I'm well able to walk on my own." She slipped her arm from his gentle grip.

"Welcome back, Asira." She glanced up to see Volknor waiting at the top of the stairs.

"Hello Master Volknor." As she reached the final step, Volknor opened the castle door.

"You and Anton should probably go through to the dining room and get something to eat."

"I'm actually starving." She glanced around at Kai. Her voice was still a little groggy.

"Go ahead, Asira. I'll catch up in a few moments." Kai waited until she was out of sight. "The wiccan doctor gave her powerful painkillers. Her body will be numb for a while. She's going to be exhausted as soon as they wear off."

"We haven't been able to find out anything. Erika is still working away." Volknor stepped into the castle.

"What do the students know?"

"They only know that Asira was attacked. We haven't gone into detail. How was it done? I've never heard of anyone breaking someone's soul."

Asira was using Anton as support, holding onto his arm. She walked slowly and steadily down the corridors. "I didn't eat anything in the hospital. The food there is gross. I would love a big bowl of pasta and maybe some chocolate cake."

"Pasta is a strange human food. I've never tried it."

"It's quite easy to cook. If they have any, I will show you. You need a special type of sauce as well. You can also bake it, but I don't have time for that. I want to eat it now!" She suddenly stopped as her eyes began to blur slightly.

"Are you okay?"

"Just a little dizzy." Her fingers dug into his arm.

"Do you need to sit down?" He draped his arm around her waist ready to catch her.

"No, I'm okay. The doctor gave me a really strong painkiller. I can't feel a thing."

"Does that include emotions?" he chuckled as he opened the dining room door. Suddenly a mix of sensual aromas whacked them in the face.

"Asira!" Cara ran at top speed into her arms, almost knocking her to the ground. "Welcome back. We were so worried. You probably have not eaten all day. The hospital food is never any good."

Asira shook her head. "No, not a thing. Cara, I didn't think you would worry about me…"

"We were all worried about you, Asira," she spoke sombrely. "The teachers said you were attacked! How is that even possible? What were you doing?"

"We really did miss you, Bluebird." Eoin stood the tallest amongst his classmates. His worried smile said more than words could.

"Eoin, I didn't think any of you would worry that much. We don't really know each other that long," she mumbled through her sniffles. "I didn't think you would miss me that much."

"Why would you say that?" Eoin had to restrain himself from reaching out and taking her into his arms. "Bluebird, you are our friend!" But he knew full well that Anton was watching him closely.

"Asira, why are you crying?" Dismay filled Cara's face. "Are you hurting?"

"Because," she sobbed, "you are all my friends too!" She threw her arms around Cara.

"This is lovely, but I have been sniffing this food for ages, and I'm starving!" Angelica pushed past Cara. "Welcome back, Asira. We're all glad you're home." She reached across and hugged Asira before nodding ever so slightly to Anton. "I will give you a makeup tutorial later. Your complexion is looking paler than usual."

Asira chuckled back at her. "I'm glad to be home!"

Chloe and Blake carried out a large pot between them. "Does anyone want pork ramen?"

"What's this dish?" Blake pointed over to the plate Zayne was holding.

"This is called the King's dish," Zayne replied.

"It's a simpler version," Katie added with a smile to Blake and Chloe. "This just has pork and vegetables on a skewer."

Asira's mouth watered as she watched Angelica scoop up a large plate of pasta. "I see you staring at this. Here. I knew this was your favourite. I've never cooked it before, so I hope it's good."

"Thank you, Angelica." Asira took the plate with both hands almost dropped it with the weight. "Here, Anton, try some." She picked up a loaded fork and Anton took a bite. "Good, right?"

"It's delicious." He licked his lips before taking another forkful.

Bobby stuffed his face with whatever was in front of him. "These brownies are amazing!" He swallowed a large spoon of ice cream next. "And Cara your seafoam ice cream is incredible!"

"Bobby, slow down or you'll choke!" Blake laughed.

"Here you go, Thomas." Fabia handed him a plate of brownies. "I made these myself. I hope you like them."

Thomas smiled taking one. "Thank you, Fabia. They smell yummy."

***

"I think it's best if Asira stays here."

"Kai, are you sure? From what you and Erika have said, it doesn't sound like she will have much time..." before Volknor could finish his sentence Kai cut him off.

"It would do her no good to sit in a lonely house by herself. Is there any news?"

"Erika found a scant black magic trail leading to the kitchen. She hasn't been able to find the origin of the trail. She doesn't know who created it. We have already explained the situation to Master Adams. He has refused to send the students home just yet. He wants to see if we can contain whatever is going on. I don't see how we can keep these kids here. We don't know who attacked Asira and we don't know if it will happen again."

"It's not right, I agree. But whoever has done this is either part of The Council or was close to us during the war. Regardless of whether it's an outsider, someone in the castle had to let them in."

"You said it yourself, we can narrow this down. Only a sorcerer can perform this sort of spell." Volknor leaned back into the chair. "We don't know many sorcerers. That only leaves Erika or Master Adams. Can we really accuse them?" He leaned forward, this time clasping his hands. "Can we really afford not to accuse them?"

"I don't understand the aim of this. I didn't understand the aim of it back then either." Kai covered his face for a moment. "I don't know what to do. Where is Master Draskule?"

"Why do you need him?"

"He's a warlock. He might have some idea. He might be able to trace the dark magic Erika found."

"Kai, I've never liked that guy. He's just too quiet."

"Draskule was a good soldier. I served with him for some time."

"You said we can't trust anyone."

"Volknor, I don't know what to do. I can't lose her. She is all I have left."

He gripped Kai's shoulder. "Don't lose yourself. You have to stay level-headed and strong."

***

"Thank you for walking me to my room." Asira tried to keep her hand steady as she attempted to put the key in the door.

"Here," Anton guided her hand and pushed the door open.

"Anton?"

"Hmm..."

She glanced over her shoulder. "Can you stay for a while?"

"I wasn't actually planning to leave you alone tonight." He closed the door behind them. "I'm under strict orders to keep you in my sights at all times."

She popped her shoes off before crawling into bed. Anton slipped in next to her, pulling Asira onto his chest. One arm was wrapped around her body, while his fingers grazed her soft dark hair.

"The painkillers are wearing off."

"Hmm..." He glanced down at her.

"The doctor said I would feel shattered once they wore off."

"Good, maybe now you will get a good night's sleep. Let me know if you're too warm."

"Anton?"

He glanced down at her again.

"Please say this was all a dream and I'll wake up in the morning and we'll be in a boring history class again?"

His muscles tensed and locked around her. "I promise I will do my best to keep you safe and comfortable."

CHAPTER TWENTY-FOUR

Shard

B lue veins infected a purple shard no bigger than a man's hand. "That is what a soul looks like?" Draskule examined the shard on the table.

"That is what a broken soul looks like." Patrick pointed to the ragged edges. "The purple is the colour of Asira's soul. The blue will be the colour of her doppelgänger."

"Explain to me again why we had to wait so long to take this from a teenager?" Draskule mumbled impatiently.

Patrick examined the shard fondly. "The longer you leave the cracked soul together, the more the new individual remembers and understands. Otherwise, it's like trying to mould a baby's brain inside an adult's body. It can get rather messy and upsetting."

"How does this work? I wasn't around when you first performed this curse."

Patrick picked up the shard and examined it in the light. "I have been saving all my energy to bring this one to life. Some doppelgängers come out as the opposite gender. It's hard to tell."

"What will this do to the girl?"

"Asira?" Patrick turned to Draskule with a questioning look. "I didn't think you cared?"

"I don't care. I am curious. I am a researcher after all. Asking questions is my job."

"She'll grow weaker and sicker until her heart fails. Doppelgängers and their original counterparts never live too long. In a matter of minutes, this person should be walking, talking and casting spells as if she were Asira."

Patrick sliced his thumb along the edge of the shard and allowed the blood to drip down onto the face of it. The blue veins began pulsating before spreading and consuming the purple colour.

Then Patrick began chanting once again in a low and ominous tone as his fingers twitched with excitement. "Tick tock, second verse of the curse I release the shard from the scarred soul." A blue light shone from the shard, overwhelming the room.

Frantically Draskule rubbed his eyes, trying desperately to regain his vision. "My word..." His jaw dropped as he watched in astonishment at a nude teenage girl curled up on the table.

Patrick took off his leather jacket and laid it across her. "Hello there."

The teenager stared blankly at him. It took a few seconds for a dark green colour to fill in her irises and her cheeks began flushing with colour. Patrick gazed curiously at the teen. She was a perfect doppelgänger. She was the image of Asira, from her head and all the way down to her toes.

"My name is Patrick. It is a pleasure to meet you." She sat up, the jacket slipping from her shoulders. Patrick quickly covered her back up. She stretched out her arm, extending her fingers, watching carefully as she did so before poking his cheek. Patrick found the naïve girl amusing. "I think we should get you some clothes and food before anything else." He encouraged her off the table as he secured the jacket around her shoulders.

Draskule watched quietly as Patrick left the room, closing the door behind them. He sat back into the black leather recliner. "Hmm... I love it when a plan comes together."

Patrick escorted the teenager to a room at the end of the hall. His cheeks flared red in embarrassment, and he turned his head away from her. "We have to get you some clothes." He started searching through the wardrobe and pulled out several outfits. "I wasn't sure if you were going to be a boy or a girl, so I picked up loads of different sets." He held out two outfits in particular.

On the first hanger dangled a pair of dark grey jeans with a red shirt. On the second hanger hung a blue dress and a leather jacket with fur around the collar. She examined both but quickly became interested in the blue dress.

"I thought blue might be your favourite colour." He turned his back to her again. "Hurry up and get dressed so I can start cooking something to eat."

CHAPTER TWENTY-FIVE

Doppelgänger

"Asira…"

The voice echoed through the halls.

"Asira…"

The haunting female voice resonated under the door and around the bed.

Asira jumped, awoken from her sleep. The room was dark. The moon's light barely lit the windowsill. Anton was sound asleep next to her. He looked so peaceful. His hair was tossed, and his arms were wrapped loosely around her waist.

She pulled herself free from his comforting hold to sit quietly at the edge of the bed. She now felt the effects of the attack from the night before. Her arms felt weak and heavy, her hands were still a little shaky and there was this aching across her chest and back. As she walked across to the ensuite she had noticed her balance was also a little wobbly. She leaned on the sink trying to steady the fright building up inside. The cold water came as a relief when she splashed her face.

"Asira…" the lingering voice whispered in her right ear. The hairs on the back of her neck rose. She glanced into the mirror and there was a blue silhouette standing behind her. "Asira, I see you." The voice was clear and familiar.

"Who... who are you?!" Asira turned around pressing her back to the sink.

"Well, silly," the blue silhouette raised her head and pushed the long brunette hair from her face, "I'm you!"

Goosebumps crawled along her skin and she fell against the sink. "ANTON!"

Flames danced around the woman in blue, but she vanished as quickly as she had appeared.

"Asira!" He ran into the bathroom where she was curled under the sink. "Are you okay? Who was she?"

"She...she was me." Asira was shaking in his grip.

"Come on. We're leaving." He pulled her to her feet. Slipping on their shoes on the way to the door.

"Where are we going?" Asira was gasping for breath.

"We're going to find Kai and Volknor." He clutched her shoulder as they picked up pace. His other hand began banging on the bedroom doors of his classmates.

"Hey, Anton, what's the story banging on my door at this hour?" Aaron stepped out into the hall wearing only his boxers. He immediately picked up a strange scent and without hesitation ran to the other doors to wake everyone up.

"Aaron," Angelica stepped from the same bedroom, her night dress hanging from her shoulders. "What's going on?"

Asira stumbled several times as they hurried down the stairs and each time Anton quickly picked her back up. A door at the end of the corridor opened and Volknor walked out yawning loudly before catching Anton and Asira from the corner of his eye.

"Hmm... What's going on? What's happened?"

"Asira?" Kai ran from the office. "What happened? You're shaking!"

"There is something in this castle. She attacked us in Asira's bedroom," Anton explained frantic panic in his voice.

"She?" Kai glanced down the hall. "Volknor, get everyone up. Something's coming."

"Dad, I can feel her presence," Asira said glancing around the corridor.

"Asira," a voice echoed down the length of the halls. "Oh, Asira!" It vibrated off the walls. "I see you."

"She's taunting me." Her fingers dug into Kai's arm. "Make her stop."

"Oh Asira!" The voice became louder. "Come play with me." The frightening sound sang in all directions.

"Out the back door!" Volknor bellowed pushing Kai and Asira down the hall.

"Peek-a-boo!" A young female in blue appeared before them. She pushed the brunette hair from her face to reveal a pale complexion and deep green eyes.

"Asira!" Kai uttered in astonishment.

"No silly! Father, it's me Saria!" An eerie smile spread across her face.

Flames shot passed Kai's head and in a blink of an eye, Saria had vanished. "We need to get out of here!" Embers were burning from Anton's palm. "Get out!"

They ran out the back door and around to the front of the castle. The night sky was full of clouds and eclipsed the moon's light.

"What in the hell are those things?" Volknor halted in his tracks.

"They are called Scarabs. I know they're not much to look at and they're really scary, but they are my bodyguards." Saria weaved in between the brawny soldiers dressed in black cloaks. Their heads were bald, their mouths were stitched shut and their complexion was a disturbing grey. "I don't like the idea of being Asira's doppelgänger. What makes her the original one? Hmm? I am a far greater sorceress."

"What's happening?" Asira let out a cry and she clutched desperately onto Kai's arm.

"Oh, dear sister, you know what I am. I know you can feel it too. I am you. The other half, or should I say the missing quarter of your soul. So, if you don't mind, please hand her over."

"You will have to get through us first." Lightning charged around Volknor's hand. "And to tell the truth, no one has ever passed me."

"I don't want to hurt anyone. Unfortunately, I need her." Saria grimaced.

Asira's knees buckled, and she fell back in Anton's arms. "Dad…" her whisper was almost silent. Her gut was knotted. Her insides were twisted in a loop. Her brain was doing summersaults.

A crashing sound grabbed everyone's attention. Glass shattered and flew across the courtyard. Above them a black figure was kicked from the top storey window. Airies was flying through the air. Her legs pushed against the Scarab and forced it directly down. The figure crashed against the earth creating a crater. Airies landed elegantly on the Scarab before dusting her short silky nightdress down.

"Airies!"

She glanced behind her. "Volknor!" and twirled elegantly to his side. "I need to get back upstairs. There are at least five more up there with the students.

"I will call them back if you hand her over." Saria pulled a staph from mid-air. It was black with a crystal stud on top.

"AAAAAHHH!" Screams bellowed from within the castle and howls hollered.

"That's it!" Lightning darted from Volknor's hand. It formed into the Aviul serpent and darted for Saria.

Anton threw his arm forward, halting the Scarabs with towering flames.

Airies bounded forward and jumped back through the shattered window. "Guys!" she shouted expecting to find troubled teens but instead she found five black figures flopped over one another and her students standing around them.

"Well Master Airies, what are these?" Bobby kicked one in the head.

"Are they dead?" Airies responded in shock.

"I don't think you could even say they were alive. We thought we broke their bones and they just cracked them back in place." Aaron stood in the centre of the group. Angelica was shivering in his arms.

"Master Airies!" Fabia tugged on her arm. "One of those things tried to grab me and Peter fought him off, but he's injured." In the corner of the room, Peter was curled up on the floor holding his arm in place.

"Peter, what happened?" Airies tried to examine his arm but he let out a yelp.

"One of those monsters snapped his arm with its bare hands." Eoin was crouched down next to Peter and was trying to comfort him the best he could. "We need to take him to the hospital."

He glanced up at Eoin and Airies with tears running down his face. It was obvious that he was trying to put on a brave face. "I'm really trying not to cry but it hurts so much." He wiped the tears with his other hand. His broken arm was now resting limply against his knee.

"Cry as much as you want. This is bad. I can't cover it up. But it can be fixed." Airies stood and looked around at the frightened faces. "Guys, we are strong. Chins up!" Her smile was so elegant and encouraging. "Zayne, only because you have strong wings, can you please carry Peter?"

"I can walk." Peter struggled to rise to his feet but the searing pain from his arm quickly immobilised him.

"Trust me, it's better if you don't. We need to take him downstairs to Volknor and the others. There are more of those things outside." She glanced around the room and thought. "We need to break down this wall."

The towering wall of fire and smoke had created a barrier. Volknor kept his grip on the lightning serpent as it stood guard.

"Asira, don't be afraid of her. Then she wins. Get up! Be strong!" Kai clutched her hand and pulled her back to her feet. "If you're afraid, she will get stronger."

"What?! Is this some freaky curse?" Anton yelled.

"It's an ancient curse," Kai pulled the staph from mid-air and handed it to her. "The key to this curse is fear. If you're afraid, it will take your fear as their strength. That is probably something Saria doesn't know."

"How do you know this?" Anton asked as he propped Asira to her feet.

"You don't become a great sorcerer without learning a few ancient spells."

A bright golden light and an explosion came from the castle. The broken window was blown out and the rubble landed a few short feet from Volknor. Zayne flew from the castle carrying Peter in his arms and Katie followed with Cara dangling from her hands. Between them, Blake and Chloe carried Aaron. Katie, Blake and Chloe returned to the gaping hole in the castle and helped the rest of the students escape the castle.

Zayne landed next to Volknor. "He needs to get to the hospital. One of those monsters snapped his arm in half." He flicked his eyes over his shoulder at the wall of fire.

The flames began to smoulder and die down. "I have had enough. I must return with my other half," Saria bellowed. "I will take her by force."

Four distinct howls hollered to the left. White, sandy, black and dark brown fur stood next to each other. Their fangs bared, snarling aggressively.

"STAND DOWN!" Volknor yelled at the top of his voice.

The Scarabs were now visible behind the dying flames and jumped from behind the dense smoke. Eoin raised his arm in a defensive position. The grass twirled and ravelled into a thick shield of vines protecting him from one of the assailants.

Two more Scarabs leapt forward but before they were able to get close to the students, Kai stepped in between them. Crossing his arms stone Xs rose from the earth creating a blockade and the lightning serpent snatched the two Scarabs burning them to cinders.

"Aaah!" Saria swung her black staph at Asira's back.

"Get away from her!" Anton punched his fists forward. Flames shot from his knuckles and singed the ends of Saria's hair as she jumped back and hid behind a Scarab. "Those monsters are protecting her!" Anton yelled at the top of his voice.

"They are protecting her?" Airies glanced over to Saria cowering behind a Scarab. She kicked her leg out and a gust of wind pushed all the Scarabs back.

"Saria, you are a sorceress. You were meant to be more capable than this." A black figure walked from the castle. He was gripping the black hair of a woman and tossed her down the steps.

"Erika!" Kai turned in horror.

"This was not meant to go like this. I had other plans. But Erika was too nosey."

Erika tried to rise to her hands and knees, but a foot stomped down on her back. Her face was bloodied and bruised. "Many moons ago I found out about an overwhelming power." A blade shot from his long sleeve and pierced her back. She screeched in agony and coughed up blood but in seconds her screeching had stopped, and her forehead was slammed against the ground.

The lightning serpent and Volknor stood like a barricade in front of Airies and the students. "Get them out of here! Get to a safe distance."

"But Volknor!" she yelled back.

"AIRIES!" Volknor bellowed. The Aviul serpent moved with incredible speed, ramming its entirety into the cloaked figure. Though not seeming to budge the man from his position, the electricity did knock off his hood. "Draskule?" The serpent stopped in its tracks. "I don't understand. What's going on?"

"Volknor," Draskule rubbed his hand through his hair. "You were not meant to find out this way."

"Did you take her from me?" Kai pulled a long, serrated blade from mid-air.

"What way were we meant to find out then?" Volknor glanced over his shoulders, Airies and the students had run less than thirty feet. The Scarabs were still guarding Saria. And Kai had a fire burning in his eyes.

"Did you kill Crystal?" A soft orange light coated the base of the blade.

"Kai, don't do it." Volknor turned to Asira watching in terror. Anton was still next to her. They were isolated from everyone, between the Scarabs and Draskule. "Why Draskule? What are you doing?"

"A curse is a painful burden you can never get rid of." Draskule's voice resonated. "Curses hurt everyone you care about. I remember you saying recently that Patrick Gervais had no followers. But you were wrong."

The grass tangled and knotted around Draskule's legs. Erika raised her head and grinned through the pain. "Run, Andrew." Her words were a mere whisper, but Kai heard every syllable. "Demons must burn!" The grass burst into flames and engulfed Erika and Draskule completely.

The electric serpent slithered to Airies guarding her and the students once again.

The Scarabs silently escorted Saria into the shadows.

"You are going nowhere!" Kai stretched his arm forward and an orange clock face appeared before him. The hands spun around stopping on the Roman numeral for twelve. "*Claudum Monstrum!*" Kai roared the Latin spell meaning 'halt monster'. The agony became frozen on Erika's face. A pain he was far too familiar with.

"Your spell won't hold me!" roared Draskule gripping his burning face as he charged forward, pulling a sword from his long sleeve and clashed blades with Kai. Metal screeched, just like on the battlefield eighteen years ago.

"You fought alongside me." Kai swung his blade again and again, slicing away at Draskule's cloak.

Draskule pulled off his cloak and gripped his sword with both hands. His skin had blistered and melted from the intense flames. "For damaging my face, Erika's death is on your hands."

"You fought alongside us! We were brothers-in-arms," Kai said through gritted teeth. "You saved me on the battlefield. How can you betray us now?" A harsh gust of icy wind blew across the courtyard scorching Draskule's skin.

"You're letting your emotions consume you again."

"Did you kill her?" Kai's grip tightened around the hilt.

"You want to blame everyone but yourself. You can't get over the fact you couldn't save her, and now you won't be able to save Asira either. You may be one of the greatest sorcerers I have ever known, but you let your emotions control you." Draskule took a few steps back and disappeared into the shadows.

Volknor glared across at his defeated friend as the sword dropped from his hands. "Andrew, pull yourself together. It has been eighteen years."

"And it's starting all over again. He just killed Erika!"

Volknor glanced over at the seared body of their friend.

"He killed Crystal. And he is killing my daughter."

"Then we must put a stop to it once and for all." Volknor nodded sympathetically.

Asira fell into Kai's arms burying her head into his chest. "I'm sorry you had to see any of that," he spoke softly.

"Lads and lassies, that is the power of a sorcerer," Airies said with zest, while wiping the sweat from her forehead and modestly trying to pull her nightdress to her knees.

CHAPTER TWENTY-SIX

Concern

Patrick sat back in silence, resting into the black leather recliner. A book was balanced on his lap. A marker was sticking out from between the pages. It was the first time he had let his creation out of his sight. He seemed calm, but on the inside, he was panicking. She was too new to this world and already Draskule was corrupting her.

He thought about following them. But it was too risky. What if he was seen? Besides, he had spent all his magic on bringing her into this world and trying to teach her some of the basics. Which to his surprise, she had picked up rather quickly. He assumed she retained any knowledge of the training received by the other half of her soul, almost like muscle memory. But it also meant he had no leverage to keep her with him. Draskule needed her for his plan. It was the whole point of creating a doppelgänger.

Almost like a sixth sense, he sat up and glanced around the dark room. There were no windows. A standing lamp in the far corner was the only light source. There were a few books scattered across the floor and table. A desk chair was pushed neatly against the wall.

Then a blue portal appeared in the middle of the room. Saria twirled straight into Patrick's waiting arms and for a moment he noticed the purple threads infusing the swirling blue of her portal spell. Two Scarabs stepped out and stood like guards by the wall. She sprung to her feet, a Cheshire cat smile across her face. "Hello Patrick!"

"Are you hurt?" His hands hesitated over her shoulders before he pulled her in for an inspection.

She shook her head. "Nope, I'm fine. Dad was scary though. Asira wasn't happy to see me either." She pouted. "They were all trying to hurt me."

"Where is Draskule?"

She stared up at him. "Draskule is injured. An older sorceress got him."

"What?" He stared at her as another black portal appeared in the room.

Draskule stepped out. His head was charred and blistered. His skin looked like it had melted. His hair was burnt to the roots.

"What the f..." Patrick stopped mid-sentence. "Draskule, what happened?"

"Master Erika Roberts is what happened." He fell back into the office chair by the wall.

"Are you in pain?"

Draskule pulled a small lilac sachet from his pocket and tossed it across the concrete floor. "I took a heap of this stuff before I approached Master Roberts."

"Geez Draskule, did you sniff all of this?" Patrick picked up the empty sachet. "There was enough in here to knock out a horse. What prompted you to take so much Pixie Dust?"

Saria turned her head trying desperately not to gag at Draskule's repulsive face.

"I knew if I were to get injured, I wouldn't feel a thing." Draskule slumped into the chair.

"If you are going to be out for a while, let me take it from here. I'll proceed with the next stage. You can step in again after that." Patrick turned back to Saria, taking her by the arm and led her out to the hallway.

Saria rocked back and forth on her heels. She watched as Patrick took a moment to himself. His forehead pressed against the cold wall. Suddenly he slammed his fist into the concrete prison. Blood ran between his knuckles. Saria jumped back and stood quietly.

"Draskule is such a fool." He clenched his fists watching the blood slide along his fingers. "Are you hurt? Did he lay a finger on you? Did anyone hurt you?"

Saria shook her head. "No, Patrick, I'm not hurt. I promise."

He let out a sigh of relief. "That's good." And smiled gently back at her. "I've been worried about you ever since you left with him. I don't like it. He never has a contingency plan. Now look at him. He could have been killed. I still need him."

"You never did get to explain the plan to me. Why do we need Master Draskule? From what I can see, you are a sorcerer, I am a sorceress, and we can do whatever we want." The black staph appeared in her hands and she leaned on it for support as she jumped onto her tiptoes.

"Draskule controls the Scarabs. We need them to collect the gemstones. Don't worry, I won't let anything happen to you. You are my little prodigy."

CHAPTER TWENTY-SEVEN

Beast

Peter sat as still as he could while a nurse put his arm in a sling. "The bone is broken. I think you might need an internal fix." Her elfish ears twitched as she gave a gentle smile. "I wouldn't worry too much. Our doctor is one of the best."

Peter swallowed a hard lump in his throat and dug his fingers into his trousers. There was a dull ache in his shoulder and when he twitched his shoulder, he could feel a stinging sensation ripple from the epicentre.

"It's going to be okay, Peter." Fabia reached for his hand. "Wiccan doctors are incredible. Believe me."

"This is disgraceful!" Angelica yelled suddenly, realising her entire body was quivering in fear.

"Angelica?" Aaron wrapped his arm around her waist trying to hush her.

"I'm terrified, Aaron. What is happening?" Even Angelica's voice was trembling.

"Everyone is frightened," Aaron hushed her again.

The dining room doors swung open as Kai stepped through with Volknor rushing into the room after him with his arms in the air. "Draskule has proven to be a threat! He is just like Patrick.

He pretended to be our friend. For years he pretended." His blond hair was spiked as usual, though it looked like he had just rolled out of bed. Dark circles sat under his eyes. "He tricked us all. How can we trust anyone? And you thought Erika could have been up to something. It was under our noses all this time. It was that dirty deceiving warlock!"

"Volknor, stop this nonsense! Don't start talking like a paranoid idiot." Airies chased after them pulling on his sleeve. She looked just as distraught and tired. Tear stains were visible on her cheeks and her mascara was smudged.

"But why, Airies? Why? We put our fate in Patrick and Draskule, and both of them have deceived and betrayed us."

"A warlock cannot perform that type of curse." Kai turned in the middle of the room to face Volknor. "It's too complicated. It takes too many elements to achieve. It would take a sorcerer, and a sorcerer only to perform this spell. I wasn't wrong to suggest Erika because she was a sorceress. I was wrong to suggest her because she was our friend and a trusted ally." Kai looked worse for wear as dark circles were noticeable under his eyes too, his hair was tousled, and his shirt collar was rumpled.

"I thought Master Draskule was one of the good guys?" Fabia perched herself on the table next to Peter.

"Who is Patrick?" Britanie pushed her hair past her worried frosty blue eyes.

Volknor turned to Britanie. "Do none of you listen in class!" Volknor's head fell into his hands and sighed.

"You didn't teach them about Patrick, did you?! I thought that was something we would leave behind us?" Airies snarled and smacked the back of Volknor's head.

He rubbed his head moaning to himself for a minute. "There was no need to get vicious. I only told them what was in the textbooks." He turned back to the students. "General Patrick Gervais was our commander, our Master during the war. He took SNs in and trained them. Patrick was a sorcerer. He was devious and he was a spectacular intellectual."

Kai interrupted. "He was an exceptional sorcerer and prided himself on his skill."

Volknor continued. "No one could beat him in any sort of strategy game. We didn't know it at the time, but he was planning a coup d'état. By the end of the war, we realised he was crazy. But by then it was too late. He turned on The Council and slaughtered the members where they stood. He tried to make his SNs believe The Council had turned on them." Volknor watched from the corner of his eye as Airies whispered to the nurse and then stepped outside with her. "We don't know what Draskule is up to." He turned his attentions back to Kai. "I suspect he was working with Patrick from the start."

Kai glanced around the room his eyes meeting with Asira's. "No, we don't know what he wants."

"We have to find a way to defend the school."

"I don't think that would help." Kai leaned against the table.

Airies re-entered the dining room with the doctor following behind. She had lost the spring in her step. "Erika is wrapped up." She tried to stem the flowing tears.

"We still don't know what Draskule is up to." Volknor watched Airies movements carefully as she made her way across the room to his side.

"We cannot hide the fact that Erika is dead. It would not be fair to her after all she has been through." As Kai continued to talk with Volknor, he was still watching Asira from the corner of his eye.

"What do we tell people?" Airies asked sniffling into a white handkerchief.

"We need to speak with Master Adams." Kai began walking from the dining room. Volknor and Airies turned on their heels following quickly behind him.

"Dad?" called Asira leaving Anton's side and following them into the hall. "Wait up. Dad, what's going on?"

Airies and Volknor glanced over to Kai as he stopped dead in his tracks.

"I don't understand. What's happening?"

"That makes two of us Asira," Kai said and began walking away again.

"Wait, stop!" Asira ran in front of him stretching her arms out. "Just tell me what is happening? Is this linked to your time in the war? I just don't understand."

"Asira, I don't have time for this." He took a step but was halted immediately by the stern stare of her emerald eyes. In that moment, all he could see was Crystal staring back at him just as she did all those many years ago when she was mad.

"I need to know. Am I..." she swallowed her sentence as fear began taking over.

He was frightened too. He was afraid of losing Asira. "Erika's dead." He examined every feature on her face, from her tired eyes to her jaded skin. "There are too many variables to explain right now." His voice had become cold and dark. He had to try and distance himself from his emotions. That meant he had to try and distance himself from her. "Go back inside." He took his chance and pushed by her.

A chill shivered down her spine and echoed across her limbs. "Dad!"

He stopped in his tracks one last time.

"What are you not telling me? You can't leave me here alone. Tell me what is happening to me!" she yelled after him as he marched from sight.

"Hey, so what's the plan?" Anton took her hand intertwining their fingers and pulled her into a warm embrace. "You're shivering."

Asira pulled her sleeve over her hand wiping the tears from her eyes. "I don't understand what's going on. I've never seen my dad like this, ever. He is always so placid. But there was this dark tension. He's frightened. They're all frightened."

"Can you blame him? Can you blame any of them? Last night was really terrifying." Chloe shuddered at the thought of the creepy black zombies.

"I know." Asira glanced down at the floor momentarily. "I don't understand what's happening. But I know they're all hiding something from us." She leaned on the wooden staph for support.

"Do you think they're really hiding something from us?" Aaron asked glancing around the room.

"Adults always hide things from us. They don't think we'll understand or it's their way of protecting us," Fabia said swinging her legs under the table.

"Airies was annoyed with Volknor for mentioning the name of their general, Patrick Gervais," Thomas added. "Whatever Draskule is doing, it sounds like it links back to their time in the war."

"How does it make sense? I don't understand what you are trying to say," Cara said.

"Cara, you told me before that the kingdoms have always been quite sensitive. Maybe Draskule wants to damage the peace? That would be a common villain thing to do, right?" Asira leaned forward rethinking her idea.

"That is a very Hollywood way of thinking," Eoin smirked from across the room.

Aaron gave a little curious smile. "Are we going to be like spies or explorers and solve a mystery?"

"I suggest we demand answers and confront my dad, Volknor and Airies. We're in just as deep as they are – or I am at least." Asira glanced up at her friends. "I know for a fact that we're not that terrible at history. We've passed all our exams. I didn't grow up in Velosia, but Dad has told me stories. I've read books. I know for a fact that Patrick Gervais slaughtered The Council in cold blood. That is not new to us."

"And then kings became Council members. It actually helped to unite Velosia," Cara said, propping herself against the table next to Fabia and Peter.

"I did hear a group of SNs helped end the war," Zayne said glancing at Katie. "That is why Airies was knighted by Queen Shire."

"I just know they are hiding something. I have a bad feeling in the pit of my stomach." Asira thought for a moment. "Something happened with Patrick that they're keeping secret."

"Do you think they're going to send us home?" Blake stated in horror.

"Oh my! They are going to send us home!" exclaimed Cara.

"So what if they send us home? It's too dangerous here at the moment anyway. The castle was attacked. This place was a fortress. It had a protective spell placed on it. Monsters were able to get through and break Peter's arm," Eoin raised his voice but quickly caught sight of Asira trembling. She was as white as a ghost.

"Eoin, what if Saria returns for Asira? And this time finishes her off," Aaron suggested his arms locked across his chest.

Asira gazed at Anton petrified and a cold shiver ran across her spine. "I don't want to put anyone here in danger."

Anton snatched her into a comforting hug. "I'm not leaving this castle and if they try to send me home, I will fight."

"I'm staying too," Aaron squeezed Angelica's fingers. "There is no way I'm leaving a friend unprotected."

Eoin glanced around. A bleak tension had settled upon the group. "I suppose we've no choice. I can't leave a friend behind." He exhaled deeply before smiling. "We would never leave your side, Bluebird."

"How can we fight?" Mandy stood hunched next to Angelica and Britanie. "I've hunted with my clan, but I've never fought for my life before." She pinched the necklace around her neck. "Master Roberts was a trained sorceress and soldier. She still died." The room went silent.

Angelica swallowed a lump in her throat. Her stomach was in knots. She was like a princess at home. She never went out hunting. She lived in luxury with her mother. She went for manicures and pedicures. She went out for dinner to posh restaurants with friends. She was not built for strenuous activities. But she knew how stubborn Aaron was. Once he set his mind on something, it was difficult to change it. "If we can't fight for our friends, then who can we fight for?" She looked up with a slightly worried smile. She took Mandy's hand. "If we fight, we fight together."

"Are we really going to do this?" Britanie also took Mandy's hand.

Peter pulled off his hat and clutched Fabia's hand a little tighter. "Time to show our true colours."

"Wait! So, we are fighting?" Bobby glanced up at Eoin. "Are we voting on this or just...?"

"If anyone wants to go home, I suggest leaving now," stated Eoin gazing down at everyone.

Aaron pulled Angelica closer, kissed her forehead and whispered, "Thank you!"

"If we run away now, we would be mocked as cowards," said Britanie pushing her hair away from her eyes. "I guess we could do it. We did stand our ground against the Scarabs last night."

"I don't think they'll send us home," Zayne added. "I don't know if they've even told the other council members yet."

***

"How are you holding up?" Volknor pressed his arm against Airies.

"I just can't believe this is happening again."

"I won't hold back. Too many have died over this stupid war!" Kai brushed passed them in a steady angry pace.

"What is Draskule's motive?" Volknor walked a little faster to catch up to him.

"Who cares? He is going to die by my blade." Kai swung his arms out and the doors to Council Chambers swung open. Master Adams rose from his seat in the back. "Adams!"

"Master Soniar, keep your voice down."

Volknor and Airies stopped on the staircase while Kai approached Master Adams slamming his fist to the desk. "Did you know?"

"Did I know what, Master Soniar?"

"Did you know Draskule was plotting with Patrick?"

"Andrew!" Volknor shouted for Kai to calm down.

"Do you think he could turn?" Airies whispered up to Volknor.

"No, Master Soniar, I did not know that. Why are we discussing the war when we have more pressing matters to attend to?"

"You were the only council member to survive the slaughter. Did you have some sort of agreement? Did you have an alliance with Patrick?"

Volknor took a step back. *'Another betrayal'*. He thought to himself gritting his teeth and clenching his fists. "Where were you last night, Master Adams?"

"In light of the current situation, I am taking severe regulatory actions, effective immediately," Master Adams announced.

"Patrick killed my love. Draskule is killing my daughter! And he has created abominations. They are roaming Velosia as we speak. Have you even warned the other kingdoms? If we don't stop him now, there will be another slaughter and this time it will be on your head! Not ours!"

It was evident that Master Adams was uneasy and fearful. "Master Soniar, please calm yourself. I am going to take full control of the situation."

"How can you take control of a situation you never had any say in?"

Blue electricity charged abruptly from Volknor's palm and tangled around his elbow.

"Volknor? What are you doing?" Airies stepped to the side.

"Airies, prepare to defend. I don't like this feeling I have in the base of my gut," he whispered.

"Master Soniar, as Head of Council I am ordering you to stand down. Leave Draskule to me."

"I don't believe you. Draskule was under your nose all this time. He was your right-hand-man. No one stands so calmly at their *throne* while a monster wreaks havoc across a school they worked so hard to build. What is your motive? What has he promised you?"

Master Adams rose from his seat steadily.

A sudden cold icy breath escaped Kai's lips. "Do you choose to remain silent?" A demonic smile curled on his face.

***

Aaron and Anton glanced at each other. Their heads quickly turned to the dining room doors and they simultaneously sniffed the air. Angelica, Britanie and Mandy were next to twitch with anxiousness.

"What's going on?" Asira glanced around confused at the change in her friends' demeanour.

"There is another werewolf present," Mandy said softly.

There was an abrupt bang. The dining room doors shook, ice seeped along the threshold and through the cracks. Asira held her staph close to her chest as Anton pulled her close. The dining room doors opened violently as electricity sparked around the door frame and the Aviul serpent slithered down the hall.

"What is that?" Peter stretched across the table gawping out the window.

"I didn't know werewolves could be monstrous like in the stories," Asira gasped in terror.

"We can't." Angelica stood in horror. Her knees buckled with fear.

"What the hell is going on?" Anton ran to the hall and crouched. "Someone's bleeding profusely." He followed the trail outside to the castle steps. "There is so much blood. How can anyone walk after losing so much?" His eyes followed the trail to the courtyard.

The electric serpent spun around the large black beast. Master Adams ran in horror across the courtyard occasionally tripping over his feet. He was finally knocked to the ground by the swipe of a massive paw. The beast had pinned Adams to the ground and in one flawless swoop crunched down on his left arm and ripped the already injured arm clean off.

"Andrew! STOP!" Volknor pulled the imaginary strings and the serpent quickly bashed into the beast.

Adams scrambled to his feet but was quickly knocked back to the ground by Airies. "You coward. Stay put." Adams eyes widened in terror as the blood pumped from his shoulder and suddenly his body stopped flinching.

"We have him." Volknor ran to his electric serpent placing his hands high over his head. "Stop this. We have him. Andrew, I am begging you to calm down!"

Aaron's bones shifted as he stood tall next to Asira. "It can't be..." His voice was quivering in disbelief. "That thing smells like Master Kai."

Asira's eyes widened. There must have been some mistake. That beast couldn't be her dad. That was preposterous. It must be an illusion. She gazed in horror. Volknor was standing in front of the beast trying his best to calm it down. Her eyes scanned the courtyard. She could only see Volknor and Airies.

She was sick to her stomach. Her gut was knotted with the image of the beast severing the arm clean off repeating in her head. Without a second thought, she ran leaping from the castle steps, clutching her staph to her side. Anton reached out to grab her sleeve but missed by a fraction of a second. The beast followed Volknor's alarmed stare. She cried at the top of her voice, "Dad!"

Asira was jerked to a sudden halt. Anton swiftly locked his arms around her body. She glanced up at his fuming face as she fruitlessly tried to wiggle free. He could feel her heart thudding hard against her ribs.

"Oh, daddy dearest, is that really you?" Saria appeared from nowhere swinging her own staph in the air. "Hello twin," she waved across. "What's wrong, Daddy?" She bent down to the hunched monster and circled around him.

Anton gritted his teeth, his fangs overlapping prominently. He gripped onto Asira a little tighter as Scarabs emerged from the shadows.

"Your job was to keep things normal," Draskule said appearing through a black portal next to Adams deceased body.

Airies kicked her leg into the air but Draskule ducked. His hood slipped off. Scars ravaged his face and melted skin.

"At least Erika was able to do some damage."

Airies swung her leg again but a Scarab grabbed her by the hair and tossed her ferociously against the ground.

"Draskule, you are an awful coward!" she screeched struggling in the grip of the Scarab.

Saria ambled away from Kai. "Daddy is awfully scary. I didn't know he could turn into a monster. I kind of like it." She glanced back over her shoulder. Like a Cheshire cat, a smile spread across her face.

"If I had known sooner that you were the beast, I would not have attacked Crystal," Draskule said kicking Adams in the head. "Idiot. He had one task and that was to keep you all here and calm."

Aaron threw his head back and howled into the sky. Three more howls bellowed from the castle steps.

"Asira, we are both going to die without one another. Come with me, and I assure you we will both live," Saria said stretching her hand out.

A large deep growl projected from behind her. An icy breath froze her scalp and drool ran down along her ear.

Saria screamed in disgust. "Blood or not, I need Asira, Daddy!" She swung her black staph and the black Scarabs pounded forward.

The beast snarled and ripped its fangs clean through a torso. Large claws dug into another one.

More Scarabs appeared around the steps of the Topaz Castle. Both Eoin and Peter swiftly created a defensive wall of vines.

Airies threw her legs forward and pulled herself free from the Scarab's grip.

Gold dust flowed from Thomas' hand and wrapped tightly around a neck of the zombies like wire. Fabia backed up against Thomas. She drew her wand and flicked her wrist. A black tornado spun from the tip, snatching a Scarab and tossing it aside.

"There are too many!" Katie and Zayne dragged a Scarab between them into the air and dropped it from a height.

Volknor stared around the courtyard. There were too many Scarabs to count. His students were not prepared to fight. They trained to learn their abilities, but they were not training for battle. He reached into his pocket and pulled out a key. 'This is a last resort, an escape route,' he thought as he closed his eyes.

The electric serpent disintegrated. In a matter of seconds large black clouds rolled in overhead. Thunder roared and lightning crashed in the sky. Volknor held his fist into the air the moment lightning bolted from the sky. It struck the key with intense force. In a sudden white flash, everything grew silent. The scenery changed. A dry, arid background quickly eclipsed the castle courtyard.

"Airies," Volknor yelled at the top of his voice, "count the students!" He tipped forward as his balance shifted but caught himself with a stomp of his foot. The energy of the lightning remained in his system, sparking in bright blue flickers.

Airies turned to each individual. "Bobby, Mandy, Cara, Britanie, Thomas..." and finally turning back to Volknor. "We have everyone."

Volknor exhaled in relief and slipped the key back into his pocket. He closed his eyes and concentrated on trying to expel the excess energy while shaking his limbs loose.

The beast grumbled and groaned before falling to his knees shrinking in size as the black fur moulted from his flesh. Asira was shaking but continued to struggle fruitlessly from Anton's grip but to no avail. Anton had her locked within his arms.

Volknor turned to the house behind them. It was a traditional Spanish villa, painted white with red roof tiles and a balcony at the front, sitting at the edge of a pine forest. The air was humid. The evening heat was far greater than that in the Velosian Kingdom. Knowing nobody would have followed them this far, he approached the door and knocked a few times. Not waiting for an answer, he raised his leg and swiftly kicked it open. "No one is home. Right, let's go in." He prompted Katie, Zayne, Thomas and the rest of the students to walk into the house. "Airies, you should settle their nerves a bit."

"Can you settle mine first." She jumped into his arms hugging him tightly, kissing his lips before heading into the house herself.

Volknor turned back to Kai who was doubled over on the ground. His muscles were clenched, and black ink ran through his veins. "I can't believe I did that..."

"Andrew?"

"I hate this feeling. I feel disgusting." He clutched his arms digging his nails into his skin. "My chest is on fire." He snarled bending back to reveal his prominent fangs.

Volknor hesitantly and slowly placed his hand on Kai's shoulder. "So much for keeping the past in the past." But he jumped back when Kai flinched. "Look, get up. We have to go inside."

They stepped as quietly as possible into the house making their way to the stairs. Airies had the sitting room door almost closed. It gave them some discretion and privacy as he helped Kai up the stairs. "You and your brother really have a tendency to make my life more and more difficult."

"Master Airies," Eoin broke the silence in the sitting room. "Whose house is this?"

"This house belongs to a ghost." Airies examined one old picture in particular, a familiar sight of her comrades standing together.

CHAPTER TWENTY-EIGHT

Inferno

Volknor sat in a chair by the door. The electricity was still tingling under his skin and was flickering through his limbs.

"Why are you sitting that far away from me?"

Volknor gazed up from his hands. "The last time you lost control was when Crystal's life was at stake."

"You're afraid? Still?"

He leaned back into the chair. "I'm not afraid. I'm just concerned. I suppose Asira never knew about your little transformation?"

Kai sat back on the bed his palms were still raw. "I let the anger take over. I let the monster out." He was so ashamed of himself. He had controlled the monster for so many years and learned to lock it away.

"I thought you had a handle on your emotions?" Volknor leaned back crossing his arms behind his head and stretching his back.

"It got easier after a few years and I forgot about it. I lived a very peaceful life." He thought about his daughter, how frightened she had looked, shaking in fear. She had called out for him. She knew he was the monster and she still called out for him. But when he had turned to face her, she was quaking in fear.

"Well, she knows now, along with the rest of the school." Volknor's arms twitched. The excess energy was still causing him great irritation. He clenched his fist again and tried to shake out the remaining electricity.

"I hate myself, Volknor. How will I ever be able to make this up to her?"

"Andrew, this is who you are. There is nothing to make up. She will either accept you or she won't. You have been through much worse. You have seen much worse. Asira is a brave and understanding young lady, just like her mother. I don't think you have anything to worry about."

"I've lied to her."

"Everyone lies now and again. I wouldn't worry about that either."

"Thank you."

"Thanks for what?" Volknor raised an eyebrow. "I'm only speaking my mind."

"For taking us away from the castle."

"Well, I knew Draskule wouldn't be able to find us here."

Kai glanced over to him. "It's a good thing that electricity doesn't bother you." He was gazing at the odd burst of power that flickered around Volknor's limbs every now and again.

"It still stings like a bitch. It's just too much power. That's why I don't like teleporting myself." He leaned forward in the chair. "Do you think Inferno will show up? Do you think he'll be mad we're in his house?"

"Mad? I think a smidgen." A figure appeared in the doorway. His hair was a wine red and tossed as if he had just rolled out of bed. "What are you doing in my house?"

"Inferno!" Volknor jumped from his seat and scratched the back of his head. "It's been a while."

"You are producing an awful amount of electricity, Sparky. What happened?"

The electricity still flickered in his eyes and itched under his skin. "We had to make a quick escape."

"You know that key is a last resort."

Volknor nodded in understanding. "I know. And it was a last resort."

"What happened to him?" He nodded towards the bed.

"I was wondering when you were going to show up, Inferno." Kai gazed back at the man with a sly grin.

"You are trespassing in my house." He unfolded his arms and approached the bed, examining Kai's skin carefully. "You turned?" His fingers grazed the outline of his black veins.

"Inferno, or do you prefer James?" Volknor gave a light chuckle before his tone became serious once again. "We were attacked at Velosian Academy."

"Attacked? Attacked by who? Who would attack a school?" James turned back around.

"So, you do care," Volknor laughed quietly.

"Andrew, what happened? Why did you turn?" His fingers grazed Kai's arm again as he gazed uneasily at him. "Andrew?"

Airies hastily ran up the stairs, stopping briefly to stare at a familiar face. "Inferno..." Her attention swiftly shifted back to Volknor. "Come downstairs and look at the news."

"Master Volknor! They have attacked everywhere!" Cara ran into the hall, meeting them at the bottom of the stairs.

"Zayne, they have attacked the Bonum Kingdom!" Katie squealed in terror.

"What are those things?" James barged into the sitting room.

"Those are Scarabs. Those things attacked us only a short while ago," Volknor responded in a dark tone.

"Volknor, they are in the capital!" Airies held her mouth in horror.

A news reporter appeared on the screen flapping her elegant feather wings close to the palace. "As you can see, monsters have rampaged through Venus." The camera was unsteady as the reporter tried to get closer. "We are not sure what they are yet. And we are not sure of their purpose." The camera zoomed in on the palace. A figure in blue skipped through the flames. She was accompanied by a group of brawny men in black cloaks and as she skipped, she flicked her head over her shoulder for a fraction of a second, but her face was clear as day.

James watched in revulsion. He turned swiftly, snatched Volknor's collar and shoved him against the wall, knocking a picture off a nail and the fireplace behind them erupted into flames.

"James!" Airies gasped.

"What are you doing?" Aaron snarled baring his fangs.

"What is my niece doing in Venus? Tell me!"

Blue lightning sparked around Volknor's hair, face and fists. "Your niece is not in Venus."

Airies struggled to break them apart. "Let him go! Asira is right here!"

"I will explain. I promise," Volknor said calmly. James' grip tightened around Volknor's collar before he reluctantly released it. "You haven't changed, James."

"She has a right to know." The fire crackled in the background as James' fists were still tightly clenched.

"How do you know Kai hasn't already told her?"

"Because I wouldn't have told her if she was mine."

"A right to know what?" Asira looked around the quiet room. "Why is everyone keeping secrets?"

"You just couldn't keep your trap shut! You always had to cause trouble. You and Andrew are the same. You are as stubborn as each other and don't think things through." Volknor drilled his finger into the side of his temple. "You're going to give me a heart attack someday." He took another deep breath. "Everything is so complicated." He gazed around at his students. "This is James, aka Inferno. He was the SN captain of fire and was a member of our squad back during the Great War," Volknor continued. Then he turned to James, "Draskule attacked us. He and Master Adams were working with Patrick from the start. Clever of them, however they worked it out, but no one knew. We only found out today when we confronted him."

"They were working with Patrick? Where is Adams now?"

"Dead," Volknor said sombrely. "Rather viciously."

Asira leapt from Anton's arms and pushed past everyone. She charged up the stairs and dashed into the bedroom where Kai was resting and slammed the door shut. "What is happening?!" she bellowed. "Get up and tell me everything! Stop keeping secrets!"

Kai gazed at her scared, confused, and troubled face. "Asira, I..."

"No more lies! No more hiding anything. I need to know. I have an uncle?" She began sobbing and breathing deeply. Her thin body was shaking. A pain gripped her rib cage and she collapsed into his arms. "My chest hurts..." She sobbed. "Dad, I'm so scared!"

All he could do was hold her close. He was so anxious and frightened that she would disown him for his terrible actions and lies that he remained silent.

"I want to understand but I don't know where to begin." Her head sat comfortably along the curve of his neck. She sniffled taking in shallow breaths.

He took a moment to appreciate the warmth of her body. She was his world. He had raised her. It was just the two of them for years. "I... I never expected history to repeat itself." She did look like her mother and that never bothered him. It meant that Crystal was never really gone as long as Asira was around. But now, now that history was repeating itself, so many thoughts and emotions rushed through his head. "I have let you down. I'm meant to protect you from evil and I let you down. I'm so sorry."

***

"So why are there four werewolves and only one vampire?" James sat back in the armchair with a glass of whiskey in one hand and the bottle on the table next to him.

"Velosian Academy is teaching tolerance. It is proving that many types of species can cohabit in the same space. These kids support each other and work hard together," Volknor responded without looking up from the maps he was examining.

"Times have changed." James sipped from the glass. "Back in my day, which was not too long ago, vampires and werewolves ripped each other apart."

"What do you want to go by?" Volknor asked his eyes still glued on the maps. "Inferno or James?"

"Why are you going by Volknor? It is a bit redundant at this stage?" James filled up his glass.

"History, meaning, remembrance." Volknor glanced up from the corner of his eye.

"I prefer James. Though if we are fighting another war, then call me Inferno."

Cara wondered over to the edge of the room and sat on the floor next to Anton. "What is going to happen to us now, Master Volknor?" She rubbed her arms and shivered but not from the cold.

"Princess of the Maria Empire." James stared across at Cara. "How many royals do you have at this academy?"

"I don't understand what's happening?" Thomas asked sitting on the arm of the couch.

"What are you?" James pointed across to Thomas.

He glared back for a second before responding. "I am an essence."

"What are we doing about Venus?" Zayne held Katie in his arms. "Our friends and family are down there."

"Hold on!" Volknor turned from the maps. "We can't do anything until we find out what Draskule is up to."

"What do we know?" Blake asked resting on the back of the couch with Chloe.

"What has this to do with Asira? Why is there a duplicate of her?" Chloe moved across the couch, closer to Blake. "Master Volknor, we are all really frightened. We didn't grow up in a war. We don't know what's happening."

Volknor took a moment to try form a sentence in his head. He wanted to say something that brought some reassurance to the group of teenagers before him. He wanted to be able to say anything to bring hope to this dire situation. He couldn't find the words. He had been the unspoken leader of the SNs when he was younger. But somehow back then it seemed easier. They were already at war. Right now, he was a teacher thrown into a disastrous and confusing situation.

Eoin turned the volume up on the television. The angel news reporter fluttered in front of the camera. "We have some more alarming news, according to reports, several more kingdoms have spotted the assailants near their borders." She put her finger against her earpiece as her eyes sunk back into her head. "Breaking news..." Her words came out slowly as her lips barely parted. "It has just come in that... Queen Shire has been killed protecting the Haven Jewel."

Airies dropped to her knees. "Queen Shire..."

Katie slipped from Zayne's grip. Her wings drooped over her shoulders. The tears filled her eyes and she let out a sorrowful moan. "Queen Shire..." Zayne bent down on one knee next to Katie facing the television.

James slugged back his whiskey. "I guess we have another war on our hands."

Volknor's heart sank as he mouthed the word, "Crap." He pulled the whiskey bottle from James' grip and gazed at the percentage before pouring out a glass for himself and swigging it back. "Patrick wanted power. What does Draskule want?" He took another whiff from the bottle.

James shook his head. "At the start, Patrick wanted the ability to stop the war. He wanted the power to bring the nations under one roof. That was his aim. He believed in The Council at first. He thought they were doing good things. This is why he led the war under their rule. He believed uniting the nations under The Council was the right way to go. It turned out that Council were only interested in their own selfish desires as all mortals are." He took another drink. "If Draskule was working with Patrick back then, he might have the same ambitions, but the nations are technically under one roof now. The war has ended. I think Draskule has a different agenda." He finally placed his glass tumbler on the table.

Fabia raised her hand. "I'm confused. Was Patrick the good guy or the bad guy?"

"It's never that simple," Volknor muttered. "Patrick had a mad idea to collect the jewels and use their power as leverage to stop the war. He brought this idea to The Council and they immediately shut it down. He soon realised that The Council were not interested in listening to their top general. It was a ludicrous idea to begin with, but they had knocked down all his ideas over the years and that was just the breaking point."

"Patrick was also very high at the time," James added.

"High?" Fabia questioned. "On power?"

Cara interrupted. "Anger?"

"Pixie dust," James said bluntly. "Pixie dust is a drug that was passed from soldier to soldier during the war. It was illegal but everyone had it. It made you feel invincible and euphoric for short periods of time. But Patrick had been taking it since his twenties."

"What has any of this to do with Asira?" Anton was still sitting on the floor.

"Well," Volknor began, "Patrick had told us of this incredible power. It was stronger than anything else you could imagine. Patrick theorised that if he was able to control the power, then he would be able to stop the war. We later found out, by accident, that..."

James rose from his seat. "Maybe we should wait for Asira and Andrew."

***

"Where do I begin?" Kai sat at the edge of the bed and gestured to his hands "It just happened one day. Since then, it has only happened when I become really mad and sort of lose control of my emotions. I can transform myself, but emotions seem to be a trigger."

How was she dealing with this sort of information? Yes, she was a sorceress. She grew up learning about magic, but she also grew up in the human world. She grew up with friends that believed magic was make-believe. How did she comprehend the fact that her father had an unrecognisable power? And on top of that, he had cruelly and deplorably taken a life.

"Does it hurt?" Asira continued to gaze down at the wooden floor.

His bottom lip quivered. "Today was the first time that I... I turned in years." He uncurled his fingers and clenched his fists. "I had forgotten the pain that comes with it. I'm not a werewolf so the transformation has always felt unnatural. When I was younger, I stopped thinking about my own body and just let the energy rush through every vein and enter every limb. You lose yourself in the rage. The power becomes so overwhelming. Sometimes..." Kai took a moment to try to read his daughter, but she was still sitting poised and staring at the wooden floor. "Sometimes it's like watching a movie. You have no control of yourself."

"Back in Topaz Castle I knew you were keeping something from me." She pinched the skin around her knees. "I knew you weren't telling me the whole truth." She took a moment trying to take in the information he was feeding her. "At home, I never once thought you were keeping things from me. I never pushed you for information about my mother. I knew you didn't like to talk about her much, but I just assumed that was because the pain was still so fresh, even after all these years." She inhaled and turned to face him. "But I need to know now. I need to know everything." Her voice was so stern. She was so stubborn. "I am petrified. I just feel so alone."

"Asira," his voice was so tender. "No matter what happens in this world, nothing will change the fact that I am still your dad and I will protect you no matter what. You are my world, and I will do whatever it takes to protect you. I promise."

"Dad..." her voice was lost in her tears. "I am so afraid."

"I'm frightened too. Your mother was taken from me. I can't lose you too."

There was a tap on the door. Kai glanced up at James as he held out a large glass of whiskey. "I'm sorry for spoiling such a loving moment but I thought you could use a drink, Andrew."

Asira turned to Kai with a questioning look.

"I'll explain later, I promise," Kai murmured.

James walked into the room and handed the glass over. This man with messy wine-coloured hair stood in front of her. "Hello Asira, it is lovely to finally meet you. You look so very much like your mother."

"James, it's good to see you're alive," Kai put the glass on the locker.

"You didn't just think I would curl into a ball and die without making your life a misery first?" James swung his hand and pulled Kai in for a hug. "Eighteen years is a long time to hold a grudge."

"If anyone can do it, I think it would be you," said Kai as he picked up the glass of whiskey and tilted his head back. "Asira, why don't you go downstairs? I'll follow shortly."

James pushed the door closed behind her. "The resemblance is scary." He looked a little distraught as he slugged his own whiskey back.

"You ruin every moment. Call me Kai as well. There are a lot of things Asira doesn't know."

James nodded understandingly. "Keeping secrets, I see."

He rolled his eyes. "She is every bit like Crystal. She talks like her. She is adventurous. She loves hanging out with her friends. She is so stubborn. She loves ice skating. She is exceptionally good at her studies. She loves gazing out at the sea but hates that she is a terrible swimmer. She stays up all night at sleepover's watching movies with her friends, gossiping and giggling about silly girl stuff."

"I visit the grave sometimes." James sat down on the chair across from him.

Kai was thankful to hear he was thinking of her. "We go up as well. I know she is gone almost twenty years, but it is like we buried her yesterday. James, I'll not stop until Draskule is dead."

CHAPTER TWENTY-NINE

The Past

"Volknor was filling me in. Draskule has caused a lot of trouble. Venus was attacked."

Kai glanced up as dread filled his eyes. "Is..."

"Queen Shire was killed, and it looks as if the Haven Jewel was stolen. There are reports that those monsters are lurking around the other boarders as well." James took a fleeting glance towards his empty whiskey glass. "Do you think Draskule is following Patrick, or do you think he was manipulating Patrick from the start?"

"What? You knew Patrick, I didn't. What do you think?"

James shrugged his shoulders. "Patrick could have been a puppet, but honestly," he leaned back into the chair, "Patrick was cunning, deceiving and strong. He would have wiped the floor with anyone. We were afraid of him. Not all the time. We were glad to be on his side. But you made sure you did what you were told, and you did it correctly."

"I think Draskule was working with Patrick behind the scenes. That could be the reason we didn't know about his involvement. The same goes for Adams."

James sat forward and took a deep breath. "Is Asira dying?"

Kai didn't respond. He was looking down towards a knot in the wooden floor. There was tension building up in Kai's arms and his muscles locked out. He could feel the anger building back up. He didn't want to change. Not now. Not again. Not ever again.

"Andrew." James' voice was stern but caring. "Is my niece dying?"

Kai took a deep breath in trying to calm the escalating anger. "Can we talk about this downstairs? I will just end up repeating myself."

"Right, let's go and discuss this then." James jumped from his seat.

Kai hesitantly pulled down his sleeves to cover up the fading black in his veins as he slowly stepped out into the hall. "Asira, what are you doing?"

She was sitting on the floor with her knees bent up to her chest and she was gripping the staph tightly with both hands. "I didn't want to leave your side."

"Come here." Kai pulled her into his arms and kissed her forehead. "Let's go downstairs."

As they approached the sitting room, Kai took in a deep breath waiting for the stares and questions. The students did watch nervously as Kai entered the room. He looked tired, frustrated and queasy. However, as soon as they noticed Asira was wrapped in a gentle hug they soon relaxed.

"Feeling any better?" Volknor stared up from the map.

"Excuse me, Master Volknor," Fabia raised her hand again. "Can you continue your story, please?"

Volknor stared across to Kai. "We were filling them in on the battle with Patrick."

"Oh," Kai said walking over to the table. "That is a complicated story. Where did you finish?"

"Patrick wanted power," Volknor remarked. Kai nodded for him to continue. "So, as I was saying, Patrick wanted to use the jewels as a way to dominate this incredible power. We were trained as his elite captains. As you know, SNs specialise in one power. Patrick thought it was worthwhile investing and focusing on a particular skill. We went into the kingdoms and stole the jewels. We knew it was wrong. We knew Patrick was going too far but he was our general, our boss. We had to follow orders. While we infiltrated the kingdoms, Patrick went to talk with The Council. We were then told to evacuate Cora Town. Though, when we arrived in the town, we found a few soldiers standing in our way."

"We thought they went too far," Kai interrupted.

"Wait? You stood against Volknor and the other SNs?" Asira had settled back in Anton's arms resting her head on his shoulder.

"I had a few close friends in the army. Our squad consisted of myself, Jason who was a werewolf, Erika, and her fiancé who was an essence, Derek. We tried to push the SNs out of Cora Town," Kai said.

Volknor resumed. "We fought Kai and *his* squad. It was seven SN elites against four soldiers."

Kai smirked. "We held our ground."

"Who were the SN elites?" Chloe fluttered her wings excitedly as she settled herself on the back of the couch.

"Myself, Airies, Inferno, Rowan, Zale, Clay and Cipher." The images of his fallen colleagues came into his head. "Zale was the SN of water. Clay was the SN of earth, and Cipher of the SN of shadows."

"Volknor was our group leader." Airies stepped across the room and sat down next to him. Her fingers intertwined with his as she laid her head against his shoulder.

James spoke next. "Patrick knew about my friends and family, and he had advised me to escort Crystal to the Topaz Castle for safe keeping. Believing in Patrick and thinking it was in her best interests, I went searching for Crystal. It had been a year or so since I had last seen her."

"The regular army had already started to go against Patrick's orders. One after another, the units started to hinder his efforts. But looking back on it, it was the first time in years that the borders were quiet." Volknor sat back rubbing his hands through his hair.

"My squad had split from the army. I heard about Crystal's pregnancy and did whatever I could to get back to her," Kai stated. "We defended Cora Town. The citizens were terrified and fled into the forest as the town became a battlefield."

"That was the first time we saw Kai transform," Volknor added. "I was against Kai in a head-on battle. It was the scariest thing I had ever witnessed. He had pure raw strength. Nothing was able to stop him."

"As soon as I was able to escape, I took Crystal to the castle. Patrick came yelling and there was this burning hatred in his eyes. He tried to grab Crystal, I got between them. We scrambled until he threw a punch, knocking me out. I fell down to the ground. When I came around, Volknor and Kai had returned to the castle and Crystal was already dying." James' gripped tightened around his whiskey glass.

"Patrick used Crystal as bait," Volknor murmured.

"All this time he wanted you?" Asira gazed at her dad. "My mother was collateral damage?" She stared across at James who kept his head down. "My mother was killed for some cursed power? So Draskule assumed I had the same power? He thought I was easy pickings?"

"I've tried my best to understand what this power is," Kai's voice was low as the raw memories caused real aches along his tightening muscles and a sickening knot in his stomach.

"I'm a little confused," said Eoin clearing his throat. "Are you Kai or Andrew?"

Kai finally looked up from the wooden floor. "We were advised when joining the war to have an alias. Not all of us had one but some people did. Kai, Inferno, Volknor and Airies are all aliases. James is the name of my twin," Kai said pointing over to the man with wine coloured hair. "Andrew is my real name."

"There is not one day that goes by that I don't regret my actions in the war. Everything is in hindsight. None of us can go back and undo the past." Volknor's tone was solemn.

"Do we have a plan?" Aaron asked catching Volknor's stare. "Do we have a plan to stop Draskule?"

CHAPTER THIRTY

Ember Jewel

The night progressed swiftly as a hint of light began tainting the darkness. Fabia rested in between Peter and Thomas on the couch. Her sleepy head leaning ever so lightly on Thomas' shoulder. Chloe and Blake sat on the floor with their bodies pressed against the back of the couch. Since the opening of the academy, the two fairies had slowly warmed up to one another and since the attack on the castle, they had become inseparable. In the corner of the sitting room, Eoin, Bobby and Zayne stood by a well-polished cabinet admiring the old, new, exotic and well-known brands of whiskey. Mandy and Britanie curled comfortably together in front of the fire. Angelica sat next to them stroking their coarse fur while she discussed many fashion trends back at home and in Velosia with Cara and Katie.

A half full glass of whiskey sat on one corner of the map, while Volknor held down another. "We can safely assume Draskule has the Haven Jewel." He placed a blue pin over the Bonum Kingdom. "We heard on the news other kingdoms were also being surrounded. We know there are only four other places he can target."

Kai picked up a red pin for the Kalis Republic, a yellow pin for the Luce Caelo Kingdom, a purple pin for the Dusk

Kingdom, and finally, he placed down a white pin for the Essence Kingdom.

"How do you know how many jewels there are?" Aaron stood next to Volknor with his arms folded.

"Like a true leader knows nothing," James retorted.

Aaron scowled in response. "I thought there were twelve jewels, one for each power."

"And what are the powers, little wolf-boy?" James snorted, settling himself in his recliner.

Aaron nervously cleared his throat. "There are the earthly elements earth, fire, water and air. Then there are the heavenly elements of light and shadows. Followed by the transitional elements of lightning, sand, vegetation, and ice. And finally, there are the ethereal elements of sun and venom."

Volknor nodded. "Correct. However, the rest of the jewels have been missing for centuries. The only ones left currently are the Haven, Ember, Onyx, Frosted and Glint Jewels."

"The Glint Jewel is in a secured location on Granite Isle," Thomas called from the couch.

Volknor hummed. "All of them are locked away in vaults for protection."

"That means my mother is in danger!" Anton moved from behind Asira and gently propped her sleepy head against the wall.

"I know, Anton," Kai repeated softly, "I know."

"I have to go protect her!" Anton's eyes fixed on the red pin.

"We can't. We're not even sure where Draskule has been already and we don't know where he will strike next," Kai continued.

"We could split up," Airies spoke up.

Volknor's eyes widened in dread. 'What is she saying!' he thought in trepidation as his gaze moved from the map to her narrow frame. 'Split up? Has she finally gone crazy?'

But despite his disapproving looks, she continued. "James can go to Kalis Republic. I can go to the Luce Caelo Kingdom. You can go to the Dusk Kingdom and Kai can go to the Essence Kingdom."

"And each of us fights off a hoard of mindless drones. No! We are not splitting up," Volknor responded irately, the blood quickly boiling under his skin and his nostrils flaring.

"Well, I don't know of another option!" She folded her arms in frustration.

A nerve twitched in his temple. "There is no way I am letting you out of my sight!" He let out a yell and smashed his fist onto the table as a furious flash of blue electricity sparked through his iris causing Airies to jump in her own skin.

"Airies is right. We have to do something. We need to get help. We need to make contact with the kingdoms," Kai said calmly.

"Master Kai, the kingdoms are probably in lockdown already," Cara spoke up. "The army is probably surrounding the Maria Empire as we speak. Daddy probably has men searching the oceans for me."

"History repeats itself." Kai took a deep breath and leaned across the table. "That's true. We weren't able to contact them in the past. How would we be able to contact anyone now?"

"Do you think someone has tried to contact the school?" Airies asked in an anxious tone.

Volknor lowered his head against the map. "So much for trying to keep this quiet and ending it as quickly as possible."

"Ending what? I don't even know what is happening?" Katie said in a panicked voice. "We were attacked at school. Our home has been attacked. We don't even know if our families are okay!" Her voice was trembling.

"Katie dear, it will be okay." Airies rushed to her side, cradling her protectively.

"Master Airies," Katie whimpered, "how can we do anything if Queen Shire was..." Her voice trailed off.

Volknor pulled himself up. "You know, eighteen years ago, we were in your position. We had no clue what was happening. We were pawns in a useless war." He picked up a multi-coloured pin and gazed at the needle. "We lost people we cared about. We were told lies. It seems history is repeating itself. But this time we are going to end it properly." He stuck the pin next to Velosian Academy.

"Where are you going?" Kai asked watching Asira walk to the front door with Cara.

She held onto the staph with both hands. "I just need some fresh air." She gazed across at him with a gentle smile, receiving a somewhat anxious smile from Kai.

Cara closed the door softly behind them as they stepped out of the house. "How do you feel?"

"I feel okay."

"Hey, do you have a plan?" Eoin asked in a hushed voice as he walked from the side of the house with Anton and Aaron.

Anton stepped over to Asira, taking her by the hand. "We're going to Kalis Island."

Asira took a breath, held the staph in front of her with both hands and concentrated. She had realised within the last few hours it had become increasingly difficult to cast any sort of spell. The purple portal appeared before them and immediately became infected with blue pulsating veins. Then her vision began to fog with the might of the spell. She took Anton's hand once again and clutched it weakly.

"I've got you, promise," Anton whispered softly into her ear. He raised her hand to his lips and gently kissed her. "Thank you. I really appreciate this."

"Asira! STOP!" Kai rushed from the house.

"Anton..." she spun on her heels.

Anton raised his arm as flames spiralled from his elbow down, shooting forward, momentarily creating a barrier. By the time Kai cleared the flames and embers, they had all vanished.

"Kai, why did you let them go?" Volknor walked up next to him.

"It's just something she has to do. We know where they are going."

"I was meaning to ask you – do you think she has the same power? When did you first notice the beast?"

Kai turned back around. "I actually don't know. I've seen nothing strange except the fact she is an exemplary sorceress, like I was when I was her age. I was in my early twenties when I found out about it."

"What do you think brought it about?"

"My life being in danger."

***

"It looks like no one has been here yet," Eoin said approaching the mansion steadily.

"It's strangely quiet." Anton stood back, gazing at his home. Kalis Mansion stood silently in the midst of the night. The sea was calm, the moon was high and there was a slight summer breeze.

"I don't smell anything strange," Aaron said glancing over at the perturbed vampire.

"Do you sense anything?" Eoin looked around to Asira who was still clinging onto Anton's arm.

She rubbed her tired eyes before shaking her head. "Nothing." She glanced behind her. "Dad hasn't even followed." Asira swiped her hand over the handle of the door unlocking it.

"Do you have guards?" Cara glanced down the hushed halls. "It's so creepy here."

"Yes." Anton stared around at every ornament and piece of furniture. Nothing was out of place. "Usually, you don't see the guards. They mainly use the hidden cameras to watch the mansion. Mother wanted to make this a friendly home."

"Maybe we should split up?" Eoin suggested, shoving his hands into his jeans' pockets.

"Where would we even start?" Cara asked sticking close to the group and continuously glancing over her shoulders.

"We should stay quiet. I don't want to alarm my mother."

"Anton, if you have hidden cameras then the guards should already know we're here," Aaron said thinking aloud.

Anton contemplated for a moment. "There is something wrong. Maybe we should split up?" He glanced to Aaron for an opinion. At that moment, a strange feeling crossed Anton's mind. Though vampires and werewolves were considered enemies, Anton felt strangely comfortable around Aaron. He considered Aaron an easy-going, kind and strong leader. He considered Aaron his friend. Regardless of any initial animosity, he quickly found himself trusting Aaron. He had confidence in his skills, and he had faith in him as a person.

"I'll go with Asira," Aaron proposed straight away.

Anton gazed back at Asira, slowly releasing his grip as she walked away. "Okay." It was in this moment he realised that he relied on Aaron for more than just friendship but also to protect the woman he was in love with.

Asira glanced back over her shoulder one last time before pulling the wooden staph close to her chest. She was nervous leaving Anton's side, maybe because his warm hugs kept her feeling safe. Maybe it was because she was terrified. Or maybe she was falling in love herself.

Aaron walked with his hands in his jeans' pockets, his eyes were fixed on the hallway ahead. "I don't know why I couldn't smell it before – the werewolf in Master Kai. I wasn't expecting it. I'm sorry I didn't see it earlier. I just don't understand how I missed it."

They walked for a few moments in silence. The halls were decorated with tables, photos and baskets of fruit. An old portrait of a young man and a young woman in regal clothing hung at the end of the hall next to the stairs. Chandeliers hung from the high ceilings. Asira waved her hands across the sconces lighting the wicks of the white candles.

"I don't think you should be using your powers."

"Do I smell like a werewolf?"

Aaron turned his head and sniffed the air around her. "No, you don't."

"I don't think there is any werewolf in my family. I wouldn't worry about it. I didn't see it coming either. I had no clue about that side of dad's past." Asira gripped the banister with one hand. "Aaron, I'm scared." She stopped on the corner step and gripped her chest. "I'm exhausted all the time. I find it hard to catch my breath. I know it's freaking everyone out. It's freaking me out. I don't know if I'm going to live. Aaron," she glanced at her feet, "I... I've never been this frightened before."

"Asira, I... we're all afraid... but just know we will do everything we can..." Suddenly his nose twitched, and he snarled as his bones shifted. Three Scarabs' stood at the end of the stairs. Aaron's howl was loud enough to wake the house. He moved down one step and crouched in a defensive position, snarling aggressively at the black cloaks.

"Asira." The snake-like tone caused chills to run down her spine. "Come back with me. We will live happily. I promise. You will be happy in my head – as a memory." Saria appeared between the Scarabs.

"There's a spell on this house!" Asira exclaimed.

"Very good, sister," Saria giggled as she pulled a red jewel from her bag.

"She has the Ember Jewel." She took a step closer to Aaron.

"Tick tock, tick tock. The clock is ticking. Tick tock, tick tock. Your time is almost up, Asira."

Aaron snapped his fangs and snarled belligerently.

"Calm down, puppy. Everyone is asleep. I didn't hurt anyone."

"Goodbye!" A sarcastic voice called, controlling the vines breaking through the floorboards which wrapped around each of the Scarabs' heads, twisting and yanking rigidly. Their necks cracked with an unsettling splintering sound and the bodies dropped. "You're next."

A vine jutted from the floorboards chasing Saria. She ducked and dodged, running down the hall where she suddenly slipped on a patch of water.

"Eoin!" Asira exclaimed. "I've never been so happy to see you."

"Am I your hero then, Bluebird?"

"Ha! Very clever." Saria dusted off her clothes. "Where is everyone else? Did you leave poor daddy alone?"

"What do you really want, Saria? Do you want to see people suffer?" Anton roared.

"You think I'm a heartless witch. You think I am some sort of monster. I know what you're feeling, I feel the same way. I am a person. I feel everything you do, Asira. I don't want to die!" She gripped her blue shirt. "I ache all over. I'm frightened too! But you have to remember, I'm not you anymore. I'm me. I am my own person and I want to be free." A blue portal opened behind her infected with purple veins. "We have the Ember Jewel. Two down, three more to go." She turned, glancing over her shoulder one last time. "I won't hurt your family Anton, but everyone else is in trouble." And then she vanished into the portal.

The candles on the tables burst into flame, melting across the wooden surface. Anton stared into space. He wanted to chase after her, but he knew he couldn't harm her. "Can you take the spell off this house?"

Asira gazed back into his eyes studying the fear and distress before nodding. Squeezing her eyes shut, she focused on the energy in the house. A pain shot through her chest, but she bit down on her tongue, focusing as hard as she could on the spell. A purple and blue dust rose from the furniture and curtains, ascending through the ceiling and up through the roof as it dispersed into the night sky.

Eoin observed her sickly skin. "I don't really think you should be using your magic, Bluebird." He pushed the vines back down through the floorboards.

"He's right. No more magic." Anton leaned in and kissed Asira's forehead. "Thank you."

She leaned into his shoulder as the throbbing sting became overwhelming. Her body went limp.

***

James blocked the entrance. "You let her go to die?"

A cold angry breath escaped Kai's sealed lips. "There was a reason I never went searching for you after her funeral."

"Because you are a coward and always have been."

"You are the one that went into hiding!" Kai clenched his fists.

"Brothers should not be fighting. No wonder Asira won't sit down and talk to me," a voice echoed.

"Oh... She really does look like Asira." James stared up at the roof as his jaw dropped.

"Uh, I'm sick of that name! It took a lot of energy to find you. I just left Asira behind. I wasn't supposed to find you but what Draskule doesn't know, won't hurt him. Stay out of our way!" The black staph spun between her hands. "Time to divide and conquer." Scarabs rose from the shadows.

"AAAAHHHH! Get off me!" Fabia squealed in terror as she was dragged by the neck screaming and kicking violently while the students rushed from the house.

In her white werewolf form, Britanie yelped in agony as a Scarab tossed her across the ground and another stomped on her ruffled white neck. "Britanie!" Mandy shifted her stance and her brown fur surged across her sallow skin. She snarled and bit down on the arm of the Scarab.

"Avio!" The dirt next to Kai began to crumble, break apart and formed a slithery creature.

Electricity sparked between Volknor's fingers and an electric serpent formed in front of him. He glanced over at Kai and nodded with a mischievous smile. "I've actually kind of missed this."

Both serpents dashed forward. The Avio circled around the students and whipped its massive stony tail across the ground. The electric serpent defended against the Scarabs snapping its electrified fangs into the foes' torsos.

Kai pressed his palm against the earth. A black shadow stretched across the length of the garden, dodging the swinging blows from the Avio serpent. It slithered like a snake as it rose from its flattened shape. Large spiny wings emerged from the soil. A black serpent drifted from the shadows with a red feathery crown. It passed through Fabia and appeared behind the Scarab, wrapping its scaly tail around its legs and dragging the monster back into the shadows.

Volknor swung his leg with all his force, breaking the jaw of a Scarab. It was knocked off its feet and crashed onto its back. Volknor crouched a little and raised his fists as the Scarab rose to its feet once again. It roared an unsettling scream as its broken jaw began swinging. Lightning coursed through his veins and overflowed in an electrified punch, burning the face of the cloaked Scarab.

Airies leapt from the safety of the Avio's tail. She landed on her hands and with all her strength she twisted herself on her palms, spreading her legs wide. The force of her propelling body caused a gust of wind. She spun even faster on her shoulder blades and the wind became sharp, slicing anything in her circumference.

James clicked his fingers and flames burst from the ground around him. A serpent formed from the fiery ring. Its body completely composed of flames and slender in build. It wrapped itself loosely around him and following the direction in which James' arm was stretched, consuming one Scarab after another in its fiery torso.

The students of Velosian Academy remained safe in the rocky enclosure. Britanie was still in her werewolf form, whimpering in Mandy's arms. Fabia's wand was shaking in her grip, but she was adamant to protect Peter at any cost. In a matter of minutes, the Scarabs were eradicated by their teachers.

"Get off my house." The fiery serpent retreated to James legs.

Saria gritted her teeth. "I can feel the pull. She will be able to feel it as well." She tiptoed across the spine of the house. "We're like magnets. We're attracted to each other." She vanished and reappeared behind Kai whispering into his ear. "Daddy."

He swung his fist into the air, but she had vanished from sight.

Fifty more Scarabs rose from the shadows and surrounded the Avio serpent climbing, pulling and tugging at its rocky body. The students rushed from the rampaging rocky tail as the Avio screeched and trashed around.

Fabia flicked her wrist. Sparkles shimmered from the wand and the earth opened beneath the three Scarabs chasing her and swallowed them whole. "Bobby?" From the corner of her eye, she saw the young hexite being pursued into the woods.

Five Scarabs bounded through the woods and dodging around trees. Fabia darted from the safety of the group and trailed after them. She pulled out her wand and flicked her wrist. The dirt and leaves exploded into the air, like a land mine but she just missed them.

"Bobby? Bobby, where are you?" The air suddenly became cold and crisp. "Bobby?" She was lost. "BOBBY!" She followed the shadow in the distance with coarse fur and sharp fangs. It was a large monster standing on its hind legs, tall and wide, standing over the three Scarabs. "Bobby?" She stepped back closing her eyes tight as soon as the creature crunched down on bone. A cold and scaly hand grabbed her elbow. She glanced up and screamed in terror as a large, grey skinned, bald monster lurked over her.

"Fabia!" Bobby ran through the forest. He grabbed her arm and pulled her away. "Are you okay?" There was another growl and out of nowhere another creature emerged from the woods, quickly biting down on the shoulder of a Scarab throwing it into the air. "It's okay. It's only a bear." He patted her back as she sobbed. "He is a friend, I promise." He wrapped his arms around her shaking frame. "That's my power. Animals listen to me." She was sobbing loudly. "Ssshh! It's going to be okay. I promise."

CHAPTER THIRTY-ONE

Patrick Gervais

"She doesn't look good." Eoin gazed down at Asira, limp in Anton's arms. Her cheeks were pale and no matter how much heat he exerted, Anton could not get rid of the goosebumps. "We need to get her back to Master Kai and Master Volknor." Eoin firmly closed the doors to Kalis Mansion.

"What about my home?" Anton looked back at the mansion.

"Asira did take the spell off the house. They will see the video footage when they all wake up. I'm sure they will take the necessary precautions. And after stealing the gemstone, I don't think Saria will be back." Aaron tried to reassure him.

"She didn't hurt anyone here. Why?" Anton pondered.

"With Asira out of commission, how are we actually going to get back to the others?" Eoin looked around at the grassy fields and sparse trees. "There is nothing nearby. You don't even have a car."

"Guys," Cara caught their attention. "I think she is coming down with a fever."

"Asira, wake up." Anton shook her gently.

"We can travel through the channel," Cara suggested.

"What's the channel?" Eoin asked completely confused.

"The channel is the way we mermaids travel. It is protected by the knights of the Maria Empire. It should be secure and quick."

"Do you mean the mer-sharks?" Anton asked still trying to wake Asira up.

"How do we get to it then?" Eoin asked.

Cara gestured to the cliff edge. She knelt down overlooking the calm waves and whispered, "Mer-sharks of old, I beg for your assistance."

"Anton?" Asira squinted.

He knelt down and cradled her in his lap. "How are you feeling?"

"I need to go to her," she murmured.

"What? What do you mean go to her? Go to Saria?"

"You are going nowhere near that witch." Aaron crouched down next to her.

"She is calling me. I can feel her..."

"And do what? Let her kill you?" Aaron jumped to his feet and snarled.

"Princess Cara, why do you call me from the vampires' realm?" A cylindrical watery vortex rose to the edge of the cliff, two hundred feet above sea level. A strange being, with a rounded skull and a beautiful scaly shark's tail lowered the trident as it bowed to her.

"My Knight," Cara bowed in respect, "we are in trouble. We need passage to our friends."

"The kingdoms are in lockdown, Princess. Does your father know you are out here?"

"My Knight, we were separated. My friend is injured. Can you please grant us passage to our friends?"

"Of course, Your Highness. Where would you like to go?"

Asira called out. "Velosian Academy. We need to go to the Velosian Academy!"

"What? That is not where Volknor or Kai are!" Cara turned back in confusion.

"Please Cara. I need to go there." Asira tried to push herself up from Anton's arms. "I will just take myself if you don't."

Cara turned back to the strange sea creature. "Can you please provide us safe passage to the Velosian Academy?"

The mer-shark stepped to one side.

Cara nodded in gratitude.

"Asira, you are not walking." Eoin knelt down in front of her. "Hop on."

Anton reluctantly helped Asira over to Eoin. He knew Eoin was physically stronger than him. He clamped his jaw shut in resentment.

"The gate will not stay open forever." Cara hurried her friends through the channel.

Eoin hesitantly stepped onto what looked like unsteady flooring. The waves were a crisp blue and swirled like a circular tunnel, beautiful and hypnotising. He gripped onto Asira's legs securing her to his back.

The mer-shark led the way through the channel. His tail bobbled up and down in the watery floor. However, Eoin, Aaron, Anton and Cara were able to walk on the water with little effort. It rippled with each footstep.

"Your Highness, why do you stay in human form?" The mer-shark stared forward.

"I remain in my human form when I am with human friends. It is refreshing."

"Comfortable there?" Eoin glanced back at Asira's pale complexion.

"You're too good." She giggled. "I hope I'm not too heavy."

"Touching a bit on the heavy side. A diet wouldn't hurt," he said jokingly.

Aaron kept his hands in his jacket pockets. His eyes were focused on one spot, the end of the channel.

"Nervous?" Anton asked.

"I am a land creature. I don't like the water."

"Thought you werewolves had no fear?" Anton laughed to himself.

"You shouldn't be comfortable here either. You're a vampire, a fire-wielding vampire."

"Ah, it's not too bad. Reminds me of my coffin." Anton laughed as Aaron stared at him in horror. "No, I don't even own a coffin."

Aaron nervously laughed back, his eyes still anxiously drifting to the swirling walls. Then he nodded towards Asira in front and whispered. "I can smell it."

"Smell what?" Anton asked gloomily.

Aaron glared morbidly from the corner of his eye. "Death."

Asira spoke softly. "Eoin, let me down."

"Why what's wrong?"

"I'm going to get..." She gagged. Eoin lowered her down and she crawled to the edge of the channel. She retched, coughed and gagged harshly.

"Asira?" Anton grabbed her shoulders. "You're freezing!" He stared up at Aaron frightened and unsure what to do next.

"What's wrong with her eyes?" Cara cried out.

Anton pulled her back. Her green eyes became infected with a blood red colour. "We need Kai. We need to get her help!" Anton scooped her up in his arms. "Aaron, she's freezing."

"Well, warm her up then!" Aaron called back as they hurried to reach the far end of the channel.

"I am, what do you think I'm doing?! It doesn't seem to be working."

"This way, Princess, only a few more feet until we reach the Agápe River," the mer-shark uttered.

***

"Zayne, I have a plan." Angelica ran over to him.

"Will you be okay for a moment, Peter?"

Britanie and Mandy stood next to him. "Don't worry, Zayne, we'll watch him," Mandy said pumping her fist.

Zayne picked Angelica up under the arms and soared high. From this height, Angelica could see Chloe and Blake fighting off a Scarab mid-air near a tree. Zayne swung her high allowing her to fall through the sky, her black fur pulsating across her limbs.

Her snarl alerted Chloe. "Blake!"

Blake looked up and pulled the Scarab away from Chloe. Angelica pounded on top of the Scarab and ripped into its neck. The Scarab hit the ground hard, and Angelica rolled to a sudden halt.

"Angelica, are you okay?" Chloe fluttered to her side.

She sat up and held onto her wrist. "It's just a sprain. I think I'm good."

"That was absolutely incredible, Angelica! I didn't think you had it in you."

"Thank you, Chloe." She clutched her wrist. "I wonder when Aaron and the others are coming back."

The last thirty Scarabs banded together. Volknor, James, Kai and Airies stood arms' width apart from each other. In front of them were four serpents, one of fire, earth, shadows and electricity.

"Oooh Daddy!" Saria tiptoed like a ballerina along the slates of the roof. She vanished and reappeared beside the Scarabs. "You are so protective of my sister." She examined the cloak of a Scarab, playing with the sleeve. "Do you think I look like her?" She glanced up at him. "Do I sound like her? Act like her?" She took a step forward and twirled around her drones as elegant as an ice skater. "Do I remind you of Mommy?"

Without a doubt, Saria was a doppelgänger for Asira, and as such she looked remarkably like Crystal. She even moved like her. Elegant. Graceful. Even more so than Asira did. Kai watched her graceful actions. He let his guard down. For an instant he remembered a moment when he was a young man. He was taking Crystal out to the local ice rink. She was so nimble and poised in her twirls and dances. Saria got so close – face-to-face, that she managed to rub her hand across his cheek.

"I think that's enough teasing." A dreaded familiar voice came from behind.

Without hesitation, the electric serpent leapt over their heads. Volknor swung around, anger burning in his cheeks, electricity flaring through his hair. The Aviul serpent opened its viper jaws, its fangs large and curved as it swung for a tree closing its mouth around the trunk snapping it in half and causing the tree to come crashing down.

"That wasn't very nice. Is that the best you can do? I was under the impression I trained you better than that." There he stood. He looked the same as he had eighteen years ago. His skin was just a little greyer. His hair was as dark as ever. He wore the same gold bracelet on his left arm which he called his lucky charm.

"Patrick!" Airies hands began to quiver. "I saw you die."

"We buried you! The SNs did it personally. We chained your coffin. We buried you so deep the devil wouldn't be able to find you." Volknor's serpent slithered back to his side.

"Well, guess what? The devil found me! I must say, she really resembles that icy SN. I was flabbergasted when I saw her. What was her name again?" Patrick pinched Saria's cheek then pulled her face to his. "She is currently under my training." He peered at Kai from the corner of his eye and smiled. "I can only assume you are personally training Asira too? I hear you're the greatest sorcerer around and you have been since the war." He smiled wickedly. "I can't have that. I was always the greatest. I am the greatest. I am more powerful than any sorcerer or wizard around." He studied the four individuals carefully. "What no reactions? Too shocked to say anything? Look, I know it has been eighteen years but to be honest I thought there would be a bit more vocabulary thrown at me." He glanced over at the fiery serpent. "I'm not surprised that you've mastered the fiery serpent by now, Inferno. Hiding behind your power again?" He glanced over at Airies. "Still following Sparky?"

Saria leaned into Patrick, her eyes momentarily fuzzy.

"She's dying," Kai responded solemnly.

"Well to be honest, I really thought we would have Asira by now." He lowered his head to hear her whispers. "I suppose it's time to find Draskule. I assume he is almost done."

"Done? What is he doing?" Kai asked.

"I suppose you have already figured out that Draskule was involved in my shenanigans during the war. I was happy with him being a silent partner. It meant he wasn't getting in my way. It was his idea to use Crystal as leverage against you. I have a very vivid imagination. I remember the blade piercing her skin, cutting through flesh. I remember Crystal begging for her life. I killed Crystal and I loved it."

Kai's eyes widened. A strong gust started brewing around them. It was building up like a terrible wrath. Kai heard the dreaded words repeat in his head, 'I killed Crystal.'

"Airies, are you doing that?" Volknor motioned to the sudden storm.

"I think it's Kai," she shouted back.

"You don't even understand who you are, do you?" Patrick hollered over the gale force winds. "Draskule has known for years what you are and what you can do. He knows the power you are hiding. He has spent years planning this. He'll get what he wants because you're too afraid to explore it, to understand it and to control the incredible power you possess. You passed this power onto Asira and it will be her demise. Did you even notice her getting ill? Was she constantly getting headaches and feeling queasy?" There was an evil glint in his eyes.

"You're a manipulative monster," Volknor grimaced.

"I am ambitious." He stared down to the bottom of the garden. "How did I not notice them before? You brought your students into a war zone? Shall I bring them with us? Or shall I put them out of their misery now?"

"Don't you dare touch them!" The electric serpent hissed over Volknor's shoulder.

"I will bring them with us so. Time to return to school children." The scenery morphed, blended and melted into a familiar background.

"The Velosian Academy?" Volknor peered around.

"Shall I teach a lesson? Hmm..." Patrick sat Saria down against the steps. "I'll be the special guest speaker. You know I have been in rehabilitation for eighteen years. I spent months trying to move my arms and legs. I spent longer trying to learn how to walk again. Once I was able to do that, the magic came back naturally. Coming back to life is not an easy task." A dagger appeared in his hand and dangled between his fingers. He flicked it left, the black serpent with a red feathery crown melted into the shadows.

Volknor and the Aviul serpent dashed to the left. He snatched Airies in his arms and tumbled across the ground. The serpent snapped its viper head forward.

"You are all frozen with fear. This will be so much easier than I expected. I was anticipating a bit of a challenge." He pointed his dagger to the right and smothered the fiery serpent. Thick black smoke rose around its struggling body. "Is this what you taught your students?" The blade continued to swing around his finger. "This is a bit of a hoot."

"Enough!" The Avio serpent darted forward swinging its stony tail at high velocity.

Patrick held his palm out and the stone serpent crumbled to pieces in seconds. "Do you remember your classes? The hours we sent training and studying combat?" He stared across at Airies, Volknor and James. "You were my greatest students. Masters of the sky, voltage and combustion."

"Welcome back to school." Draskule stepped from the castle wearing his usual attire. "Patrick, the outside night light suits you."

"Your face looks awful. Maybe you should have a paper bag over your head," Patrick chuckled.

A cold icy breath escaped Kai's gritted teeth.

"I felt that chill," Patrick smirked pretending to rub his arms for warmth. "Can you control the power now? SNs, are you standing up against me again?"

"We are not the same kids you messed with eighteen years ago." Volknor's serpent coiled its body.

"Oh, I know. You are even stupider than I last remember." Patrick gripped his dagger. "Remember, I taught you everything you know." The Aviul serpent pounded forward. Patrick ran from the castle into the courtyard. "I love a good chase." The Aviul tackled him to the ground snapping its large fangs down at him. He struggled to keep the serpents jaws away from his face with only a dagger to defend himself.

Hundreds of black Scarabs rose from the shadows and merged around them.

"Oh, I have been dying to let off some steam." Flames extended from James' arm. The fiery serpent burst back into life and in a magnificent display, splintered in five different directions scorching a group of Scarabs to the ground.

CHAPTER THIRTY-TWO

Battle at Topaz Castle

Kai and Draskule sparred on the steps of the Velosian Academy. Metal on metal clashed as sweat poured down their faces. The perspiration poured along the contours of Draskule's disfigured face. His left eyebrow sloped at an awkward angle. His skin was still raw and red from their previous encounter. Before leaving the safe confines of his basement, Draskule had ingested another lethal dose of pixie dust, just enough to keep him high on stamina, fury, rage, fear and much more.

"Where is your darling daughter?" An evil grin curled Draskule's lips as he pushed his weight against the sword. "Did you lose her? Did she run away from you? Tell me something, has she been feeling sick for the last few weeks? Like a cold or a headache that doesn't seem to go away." He shoved all his weight forward, knocking Kai off balance and back down a step. "Well, bring it on, boy!"

Kai swung his blade again and again. He had spent years teaching himself through self-help books on different calming methods such as meditation. He had learned to suppress the beast when he became irritated. For years he believed the war was the cause of the unique transformation, but he eventually discovered it was only a contributing factor.

The anger, the resentment, all the built-up bitterness finally began to seep back out of every pore. His family were the trigger to his transformation, and he had realised a long time ago he was unable to control his emotions when it came to the people he cared about. With every blink, his eyes faded from green to a bright yellow colour and fangs grew inside his mouth. He was losing himself to everything he hated.

"You're struggling to control yourself." Draskule snorted. "Why don't you just let go." He forced his weight forward once again. "I wish I was there to hear Asira scream." He spoke clearly and slowly as the evil grin returned to his face. "Patrick told me in minute detail how he crept up on her in the kitchen. How he was able to force his hand through her ribs, physically snatching and ripping her soul from her very chest."

With a blow, Draskule's blade was knocked from his hand. Kai tossed his sword to one side. Hand-to-hand, they pushed against one another.

"She's probably dead by now," Draskule tormented.

The transformation was rapid. The black fur exploded across his skin. His body tripled in size as his bones cracked into shape. Draskule struggled to keep the snapping jaw from his disfigured face. The large black beast threw back its head to the early morning sky and howled.

Saria had crawled down the steps and hid behind the railings, peeking through the bars at the monstrous being before her. She was only new to this world, but she knew this wasn't the world she was comfortable in and wondered were these Asira's emotions or her own.

Volknor glanced over his shoulder gawking at the bald figure pinned under massive claws. "Shit!" All around him the students were fighting side by side, protecting themselves and each other.

He pulled the invisible strings, coaching his serpent back to his side but severing the tie. "Guard the students." The Aviul did not question its master's decision.

"One-on-one? Man-to-man!" Patrick jumped to face him and threw his jacket to the ground. Volknor charged his fists and threw the first punch which Patrick evaded. "No powers." Patrick's swing missed too.

The electricity disappeared and with one lethal swoop, Volknor punched Patrick directly in the jaw. "Fist fighting was never your strong suit!"

"You are underestimating me. I was your teacher." Patrick swung his fist again and knocked Volknor to the ground.

Airies sprinted and ran up a Scarab's back, jumping from its shoulders and wrapping her legs around the neck of another one. She constricted her thighs and twisted her body, snapping its vertebrae. She turned, kicked her leg straight up, thrusting her heel through a Scarab's face. Pulling a whip from her belt, she flicked her wrist loosening the leather piece. Swinging her arm, the whip cracked with an echo. With each swing, the hollow smack sent trembling vibrations through the air.

A fiery barricade then suddenly separated Airies from the rest of the mob. "James, there are too many of them. I can't get to the kids!"

"I'll make a path to the kids." James created a blazing wall either side of them as he moved down the narrowing corridor. The fiery wall quickly surrounded the students.

"Are you guys okay?" Airies rushed to examine everyone carefully.

"What the hell?" Zayne pulled his wings close to his body and stroked the smoke from his feathers.

"We're trapped!" Mandy squealed burying her face into Britanie's shoulders.

"Sir, you don't look so hot." Thomas examined the sweat dripping from James' forehead.

"Just tired, kid," grunted James.

Airies glanced back at James taking a moment to assess her friend. She took in a slow breath. "Okay, this looks bad." She peeked over the fiery wall at the zombie mob desperately trying to crawl through the roaring flames. "Our aim right now is to keep you kids safe and get you out of here. However, it doesn't seem like anywhere is safe right now." She stared across at James hoping he would step in. She was usually a positive person but right now she was afraid for her students. She was tense, and she was terrified for everyone's life.

"Master Airies, we want to fight," Peter declared staring directly at her.

"Yes, let us fight. We have each other's back." Bobby pumped his fists into the air.

"So, what's the plan?" Blake fluttered on his tiptoes.

Airies gave a hopeless glance to James and then smiled, defeated by her students. "I'm delighted I have such brave pupils!" Her carefree and heart-warming smile reappeared on her face.

Patrick took a few wobbly steps back and smudged the blood across his chin. "That's..." he stared at the blood stain on his thumb, "that was a good smack. You..." and took another deep breath, "you look a little worse for wear." He bent across his knees. "I just need a minute."

Volknor wheezed a few times. It had been a long time since he sparred so viciously. He hesitated for a moment but finally lowered his fists and looked around for the others.

"They seem a little overwhelmed," Patrick propped himself up.

Volknor glanced over to the fiery wall with the mob of zombies along the outer perimeter. "Airies, Inferno!" He shouted over the roars of the black cloaks. "FIRESTORM!"

The fiery barrier discharged outwards, widening the circle. Airies pushed everyone into one corner as she hopped onto her hands, kicked her legs out and spun as fast as she could before dropping onto her shoulder blades. A strong gust of wind blew across the courtyard. She hopped back onto her palms before elegantly spinning onto her tiptoes. An amber hurricane swept across the courtyard. The students huddled together shielding their eyes from any debris.

Lightning surged through Volknor's veins. It sparked around his limbs from head to toe like an aura veil. Thunder clashed. Lightning struck the ground once, twice. "I hope you remember this one." He glanced up from his arms, momentarily watching the yellow and blue energy surge under and over his skin.

Airies controlled the direction of the wind in a tight circular motion and in a matter of minutes a twister formed. James clicked his fingers. A flame burst around his fist and he watched as the twister combusted, transforming into a blazing tornado swallowing the Scarabs that stood in its path. Lightning darted once, twice and a third time, striking several Scarabs at once and a fourth time less than ten feet from Patrick.

***

The channel opened up at River Agápe in the forest next to the Topaz Castle.

"Thank you for your help." Cara curtsied.

"I am glad to have been of service, Your Majesty." The mershark bowed before disappearing back in the channel.

"Asira?" Anton knelt down. Her skin was as white as snow and her eyes were still blood red.

"Anton, she's close," Asira panted a cold breath.

"We can run faster if I carry her." Eoin crouched down next to them and shrugged his shoulders.

Anton was panicked and frightened. He didn't want to let go of Asira, but he knew he would not be able to carry her for long. Eoin was taller and physically stronger. In desperation, Anton guided her to him.

Aaron morphed shape and led the way through the forest, but it wasn't long until he picked up the distressing sounds nearby and they were soon standing at the edge of the forest overlooking the courtyard.

"What the fudge is that?" Eoin gestured towards the fiery tornado.

"Dad?" Asira glanced up from his shoulder. At the steps of Topaz Castle was a large black monster swiping and charging at another figure. She slid to her feet as Eoin took her by the arm until she found her balance.

"Here you go, Asira." Cara handed her back the staph.

"Aaron!" Angelica ran from the battle and leapt into his arms, wrapping her legs around his waist.

"Are you hurt?" He pushed her hair back and examined all the scrapes on her cheeks and arms.

"I was so worried about you!" Her lips pressed against his. "Never leave me again." She kissed him again. "Next time you have to take me with you."

Blake landed next to them. "Where did you guys go?"

"What's going on?" Anton was staring across at the fiery tornado shrinking in size.

Blake grimaced as he glanced back over his shoulder. "Saria attacked us at James' house. We were teleported here a short while ago."

"Asira?" Cara caught a glimpse from the corner of her eye of a purple figure running across the courtyard. "Where are you going?"

Anton didn't say anything but before his brain had time to register what Cara had said, he was already sprinting after her.

"Dad!" Asira reached the castle steps.

The coal black werewolf, the height of a grizzly bear, turned slowly. As soon as it gazed upon her, the black fur moulted, and bones cracked back into shape. "Asira?"

She rushed up the three steps and bounded into waiting arms. "Dad!"

"You're okay?" He quickly examined her face before pulling her back into a warm embrace. "How are you feeling? Your eyes are red."

"My eyes? Your eyes are yellow." She leaned back into his chest. "I just want all this to be over."

"I promise, it will all be over soon."

"Enough nonsense." Draskule swung his blade.

Suddenly Kai let out a howl over her shoulder as the cold metal pierced his soft flesh. He pushed Asira back and the green colour reclaimed his irises.

"Dad...?" Her hands trembled as his sweaty fingers slipped from her grip and fell to the ground with a thump. "NOOO!" Her scream bellowed across the courtyard.

Volknor turned his head swiftly. Airies and James glanced over at the same time as the tornado died promptly.

"DAD! Dad, nooo!" She tried to press down on the open wound, but the blood continued to pump from his cavity. "Dad, stay awake. Please don't close your eyes." Her eyes swelled with tears streaming down her face. "Dad..."

"That's enough." Saria came from behind and dragged Asira by the shoulders walking her back down a step.

"Dad..." Her eyes were locked onto the blood rushing from the open wound. "He needs me."

"Stop this sister. You're upsetting me now." Saria gazed up with sorrowful eyes as Draskule wiped his blade along his sleeve. "We have to go."

"Get off me, you weirdo!" Asira swung around slapping Saria across the face before crumpling to her knees.

"Andrew..." Volknor released his hold on the stormy clouds and stepped across the scorched bodies of Scarabs.

Airies gasped in terror. "Volknor, please tell me this isn't happening."

Chilling howls beckoned across the courtyard and a strange white mist tersely descended around them. "What's this?" Volknor waved his hand through the frosty mist. "Step back." And he pushed Airies back from the encroaching substance before freezing in one place.

"I can't move," Thomas whispered in a semi crouched position.

"What's happening?" Peter had fallen back onto his good arm. "Are we paralysed? Bobby?" He called over barely even able to glance in his direction.

"I'm here. I'm stuck though." Bobby stood with his back pressed against Fabia. "We're in a particular pickle."

"What do you mean?" Peter called back out.

"Well, there is a Scarab in front of me." Bobby responded staring face to face with a grunting grey head. The small blade he was holding was stuck halfway into the Scarab's chest.

"Me too," Fabia squealed staring back at a Scarab no more than two feet from her.

A few tiny sparkles flickered between Volknor's fingers "Uh! I can't do anything."

"Is it the wolves?" Airies spoke softly.

"Uh?" He stared to his left. A white wolf with red eyes emerged from the fog. "It's white."

"Have you seen anything like this before?" Airies said in a low tone watching the movements of the canine carefully. "It doesn't seem aggressive."

"Volknor, what's happening?" James groaned as he tried wrenching his arms. "Why can't I move? Ugh!" He focused all his energy but to no effect. "I can't even use my powers. You know more about this stuff. Does this mean Kai is still alive?"

Volknor studied every feature of the wolf before him. Its fur was as white as snow. Its eyes were a shade of blood red. It had four muscular paws and a large snout, but the wolf had an inoffensive and innocuous look about it. "This isn't Kai's power." The wolf's red eyes gazed back at him with an innocent stare. "This belongs to Asira."

"Asira? What type of power is this?" Airies struggled to move her fingers desperately stretching for her whip.

"How are we going to get out of here if our teachers can't even escape?" Fabia squealed in terror.

"We will find a way," Thomas said calmly trying his best to reassure her. "My legs are killing me."

Bobby whistled subtly. "Hey guys, I'm going to try talking to them."

"Can you? I thought this was a spell?" Fabia asked trying to turn her head.

"Ssshh!" Bobby stared at a few wolves trying to grab their attention. Then one wandered over to him and lay by his feet. "Hey there," he cooed affectionately as it rolled on its back. "You're a friendly puppy, aren't you? What's happening? Can you help us break free?"

"What are they saying?" Thomas threw his eyes back over his shoulder.

"Nothing," Bobby said in a monotone voice. "They're not talking. It's like they're waiting for an order."

"An order? Who's controlling them?" Thomas called back. "Good job, Bobby, but keep trying."

"Asira," Anton spoke softly. He had tried desperately to reach her when he suddenly became frozen. "Asira, listen to me. I don't understand what's going on, but whatever it is, please don't let this take control. Kai told you not to let fear win. If you lose to fear, you lose the fight." His fingers were outstretched, mere inches from her back. He wanted so urgently to pull her into his embrace where he knew he could keep her safe. He had promised to keep her safe. "Asira," Anton swallowed the lump forming in the back of his throat.

As a vampire, he believed in soul mates and destiny. He had felt the spark his mother had told him about and that he had read about. All he wanted was to keep her happy and safe, even if it meant taking things slow.

"Asira," Anton took another slow deep breath. He was afraid, deeply afraid of losing her. "We only know each other a few weeks but that doesn't matter. I know you, Asira. I know who you are, what you like to do on the weekends, what you like to read, and I know how you like your cup of tea in the morning."

More white wolves stepped out from the surrounding icy mist and encircled the staircase.

"Asira, I love you more than anything else in this world. I love you more than life itself. Please, I'm begging, don't let this control you." He remembered back to the moment he first saw her walking through the ballroom. Her flawless skin was glowing in the candlelight. She was nervously following behind her father, watching everyone who passed by. She had told him she wasn't afraid of vampires, but it was obvious it was her first time around so many of them. She soon relaxed though when he held her hand and whisked her onto the dance floor.

For years, Kai had told Lady Pearse stories of his daughter. As an only child, Anton was usually not too far from his mother's side. He had grown up hearing wonderful tales of a young sorceress who was living with humans and living like a human herself. He had fallen in love with her before he had even met her.

He was not willing to lose her.

"Asira, take a deep breath. Don't lose yourself to this..." Anton said, his voice ragged with worry. He struggled frantically to break free from the invisible restraints.

Draskule struggled to move his head as his eyes were swinging back and forth in his field of vision. With a glance over his shoulder, he glimpsed at Asira unexpectedly appearing behind him. Like a prowling tigress she moved back around in front of him. Embers stained the ground with every step she took. She raised her arm and flames spiralled along her staph.

Saria jumped in, blocking Draskule from the oncoming blaze with an iridescent shield but it soon crumbled apart. Just like Asira, Saria was particularly talented at ice and fire spells. With a swing of her black staph, she created solid chunks of ice and sent them hurtling forward.

Asira tried to evade the best she could with her arms crossed. The icy chunks pelted her arms and face leaving her bruised, scraped and bleeding. She quickly collapsed back to her hands and knees, giving Saria just enough time to flee.

Silence descended on the courtyard.

Her legs wobbled as she stood back up. Her cardigan and dress were tattered and ripped. Her arms were frail. Blood mixed with sweat as it dripped down her temple. "Amer-ula tec-ika raela."

Anton watched her vanish from his sight and at that moment the wolves retreated, the mist vanished, and he fell hard against the concrete steps.

Volknor ran up past Anton and the electric Aviul began winding around the banisters hissing at everything that moved. "Andrew!" He fell to his knees, his hands hovering over the bloody mess. "Andrew, can you hear me?" He lifted Kai's shirt squinting at the sight. The open wound was gushing. It had already drenched his clothes and the ground around him.

Anton watched from his fallen position. The sickly-sweet smell of blood wafted through the air. Anton watched in repugnance as Volknor hastily wiped some of the blood from Kai's abdomen.

He charged his fist. "On the count of one, two, three…" He pressed against the gash. Kai let out a bellowing roar as the electricity seared his flesh. "There, almost as good as new." He stared at the cauterised wound. It would probably leave a nasty scar but if it saved his life, it wouldn't matter.

CHAPTER THIRTY-THREE

Monster

"You didn't see her eyes. She was like a demon. They were blood red." Saria followed Draskule down the stone path. "That mist came out of nowhere!" Her voice was shaky and panicked as she threw her arms into the air. "What was that? Like... those were wolves with white fur and their eyes..." She bit her bottom lip as she stared up at Draskule. "Her eyes were just like theirs."

Draskule placed the Haven Jewel and Ember Jewel on the stone column table. "That is the power I am looking for."

Saria fixed her eyes on the stone arches before turning back to him. "That is the power? I thought you said they were meant to be black wolves, not white."

"There are two wolves. Folklore aptly describes them as the *white phantom wolf* and the *black ghostly wolf*. They are yin and yang. They are opposites. The power of the black wolf lies with Kai. While it seems that the white wolf exists alongside, in his daughter. I am hoping that by killing Kai, the control of the black wolves will fall to you. You would be the next heir to both powerful forces."

She swallowed a lump in her throat. "Draskule, I don't think you can control this power. You didn't feel the energy radiating off Asira. It was like nothing I have ever felt before. When I approached her in Kalis Mansion, she was weak. She was dying. But this was something different. This was like she was not even there. Something else was controlling her."

He grimaced. "I felt the power. It was oozing from her. I also fought her father." His eyes were set on the large gemstones. "All that raw power, and they don't know what to do with it. It is wasted in their hands."

Saria held the black staph close to her chest. "How much longer?" She clutched her blue shirt as pain throbbed in her chest. "Master Draskule, how much longer until this pain will go away?"

"You monster!" Asira stood at the gates and gritted her teeth.

"Ah, finally we can begin." Draskule looked up at her. "Wind, fire," he said nudging the Haven and Ember Jewels on the stone column table and spread his arms wide. "The Great Arches are your connection to home."

"My home?" Asira scowled. A dribble of blood was seeping from her bitten lip.

"I wasn't talking to you specifically. I meant the wolves. The power you possess. These Great Arches are their way home. This is where I will capture that power for myself."

"Over my dead body." As Asira stepped through the gate her knees suddenly buckled.

"You are nearing the end of your journey. You and Saria are now on the same wavelength."

Saria was on her hands and knees, trembling.

"You are both going to die."

Asira gritted her teeth. "You're going to die." She forced herself back onto her feet leaning on her staph for support.

He let out a sadistic laugh. "You can barely stand. You won't be able to stop me."

Every breath was heavy, like a harsh stab through her oesophagus. The sweat was pouring down her face. Her hands were weak, and her legs were shaking. She glanced across at Saria, and for a moment their eyes locked onto each other. For a moment she was gazing at her own reflection.

"Lie down." Draskule flicked his wrist and Asira was flung against the rocky plinth of an arch.

She tried to cry out in pain, but the breath had been knocked from her lungs and her vision was blurred. She frantically tried to push herself up off the ground. She couldn't. She was barely able to move her arms. The energy was draining from her body with each passing second.

Saria's hazy eyes searched in the distance for a purple blur. "I thought you were going to make me stronger." She dropped her head hiding her face behind a curtain of messy brunette hair. "You promised!"

"You were always Patrick's pet project. I never needed you, but he convinced me things would go smoother. Just remember, if you're afraid, you'll lose."

Saria's hand slipped from the edge of the table as she doubled over in pain on the cold stone.

Asira dragged her fingers across the ground. Her vision blurred. She summoned all her strength, whatever was left, and pushed her arms underneath her body, raising herself off the ground a few inches.

"You're wasting your time, Asira." Draskule glanced at her before returning his attention to the red and silvery blue gemstones. "Haven Jewel and Ember Jewel are mortal appellations. The gods called them the elemental gemstones. To be precise, these are part of the earthly elements. They are so small in comparison to the amount of raw power they possess."

"What are you waiting for?" Asira whispered as she tried to hold herself steady.

"I'm waiting on Kai to die so his power is passed to Saria. Then we can move on to the final plan."

"What is the final plan?" Asira's feeble arms finally crumbled beneath her weight.

"The wolves have an incomprehensible divine power. I need it. The gemstones will help me contain it." Draskule held the silvery blue gemstone towards the stone arch with a swirl engraved on it.

"I still don't understand," Asira grumbled under her breath as she tried once again to push herself off the ground.

Saria pushed herself onto her knees. "Master Draskule, everyone was right… You are a monster."

***

"This is sweet. I bet you're worried about your niece. Poor Asira, poor little sorceress. Draskule said she was always part of his plan. He said emotional manipulation was an interesting subject to study. Though, the doppelgänger spell was all my idea." Patrick stepped around the charred black cloaks.

"Stay where you are." James stood in front of the students arms outstretched.

Patrick held his arms in the air. "You know it was Adams' idea to set up Velosian Academy. He felt remorse for his involvement in the war. He wanted to atone for his sins. Draskule and I felt it was the best time to attack. Once Adams realised this, he was going to scrap the school idea altogether. Draskule's plan isn't really going to work. He thinks he can cheat the gods by skipping a few rules.

He needs more than just the Haven and Ember Jewel to accomplish his plan. But I have what I want. I'm alive. I'm not willing to go down with a sinking ship." He stared across at Volknor, who was intently glaring from the steps of the castle, electricity sparking around his fists. "Everyone is exhausted. Let me leave and you are free to follow Draskule." He placed his hand over his heart. "You have my word as a sorcerer."

James' fists were coated in embers. He was exhausted. The fiery serpent had even been reduced to smoke from his lack of energy. He glanced back over to Volknor who gave a slight nod.

Patrick turned. "I will leave you with one parting piece of advice – never believe your enemy." He vanished into the smoke as quickly as he could.

Volknor marched past the students. "Airies, watch the kids." He kissed her tenderly on the forehead. "James, you're with me." Together they sprinted towards the path to the Great Arches, jumping over the scorched zombies.

"Master Airies!" Cara shrieked as several Scarabs' rose from the ashes of their fallen brethren.

The students were being corralled to the edge of the forest. Mandy and Eoin were backed up next to each other. She snarled but her limbs were shaking. Eoin pressed his hand against the tree. The branches came to life and swung with a mighty force against the Scarabs.

"Mandy, we have to run." He gritted his teeth seeing no way out of this situation. Having chosen to stay in her werewolf form, Mandy howled next to him as she turned her attention back to the approaching enemies.

"Eoin!" Peter ran behind the Scarabs. As he crouched, one arm still in a sling, the earth rumbled as the roots of the trees began to creep from the cracking earth. "Run!"

Eoin's eyes widened as he saw the ground erupt before them. He snatched Mandy by the scruff of the neck and ran as fast as he could. The roots broke through the earth and slammed the Scarabs against the ground.

Katie followed Zayne into the air but was quickly pulled back down. "Let go!" She screamed as a Scarab snatched her by the wings. "Zayne, help!" she cried as she struggled to escape their dagger like nails.

Zayne swooped down through the swarm, kicking his leg out and knocking the Scarab away. "Katie, come on let's get out of here." He took her wrist but soon realised she was getting heavier.

"I can't fly. My wings!" she shrieked curling her right wing back.

He pulled her up into his strong grip. "No problem. I'll get you out of here." He flew high evading all the demonic hands reaching for them.

"Leave me by the steps. I can help Master Airies protect Master Kai." Zayne reluctantly nodded before swooping down towards the castle.

"What happened?" Airies swung her leg up. A gust of wind violently sliced down the charging Scarabs.

Zayne landed on the steps quickly examining his sister's wings. "Her wings are damaged. She can't fly."

"Not permanently?" Airies ran to her and gently pulled out her right wing. "Oh," she let out a sigh of relief. "Your feathers will grow back." She handed her whip to Katie. "Like in the movies, swing this. Don't cut yourself. You can stay next to Kai."

Katie cautiously received the whip.

Fabia gripped her wand walking backwards towards the woods. "What do we do? No matter the spell, they just keep coming back."

Bobby backed up next to her pulling a dagger from his pocket.

"Where did you get that?" Fabia inspected the gold-plated hilt.

"James gave it to me back at his house."

"Can you not do that thing from earlier?" Fabia screamed as she ducked avoiding the arms of a Scarab.

"Do what thing?"

"The bear thing!" She flicked her wand and the Scarab exploded into multicolour confetti.

Bobby ran around the trees. "Bear? There are no bears around at the moment. I can't make one appear!"

"Why not? We need a bear right now!"

A much larger black Scarab came charging towards them. Fabia suddenly found herself cowering against the tree. The fear had taken over and she was frozen in one place.

In a blink of an eye Bobby sprang between them and drove his dagger into the Scarab's chest. With all his force he pushed the Scarab back as far as he could. "Run Fabia!" he hollered pulling her from her trance.

She tucked her shoulder next to him, wand clutched in her sweaty palm, the black tornado swirling from the tip drove the hefty Scarabs back down the courtyard. Then gold dust drifted into the tornado strangling the Scarab until it was utterly motionless. Her eyes immediately lit up. "Thomas!"

"Chloe!" Blake scrambled to rescue her from the clutches of a black Scarab.

"Blake!" she screamed for help as the Scarab covered her mouth and tossed her to the ground slamming her head against a rock.

Angelica and Aaron snarled sizing up the Scarab. A gold powder floated through the air. Thomas closed his eyes and concentrated all his energy. He calmed his heart, calmed his breathing as the gold dust radiated off his skin. It was like poison. It leeched onto the Scarab and was absorbed into its pores, causing its flesh to bubble and blister. The Scarab dropped to the ground in violent seizures, trembling before finally lying completely still. Thomas turned his attention back to the werewolves. Three more Scarabs appeared behind them.

A Scarab took Blake by the shoulders and slammed him to the ground. He focused all his thoughts as a black and purple light emitted from his hands. The dark light on his hands discharged, vibrated into the skin of the looming figure. In seconds, the Scarab dropped to the ground.

"Chloe?" Blake leapt to his feet and skidded to his knees. He hesitated barely poking her shoulders. "Chloe, can you hear me?" This time he shook her briskly and she suddenly jumped into his arms.

"I can't believe you saved me. Thank you, Blake," she cried into his ear.

He gripped her tightly, taking the moment to appreciate her closeness. "Let's get out of here."

Eoin turned and skidded to a halt. Vines grew from the ground. Thorns thickened on each strand before shooting through the air and grabbing the Scarabs by the leg.

"Do we just kill them?" Cara watched them dangle helplessly.

"Don't look," Eoin said creating another narrower vine to wrap around their necks and twisted. Mandy pulled her paws over her eyes and whimpered.

"There are too many of them!" Cara screamed. "How are we going to get rid of them all?"

Mandy shot to her feet. "Britanie!" She bellowed. "Where are you?"

"I've got her!" Anton yelled from across the courtyard. A meek-looking white werewolf whimpered behind his legs. Britanie was too shocked to change from her werewolf form. "She's injured." Flames shot from his hands at the approaching zombie herd.

"Drop the flames!" A voice came from behind. Anton flicked his head around and saw Airies running from the castle steps. She landed on her tiptoes before leaping onto her hands and cartwheeling across the courtyard. Her legs wrapped around an individual Scarab, twisting hard and snapping bones. One by one, the black cloaks dropped to the ground. "Burn the bodies, Anton," Airies called.

He watched as the bodies quickly caught fire. The smell of crisping flesh was enough to turn his stomach. He may be a vampire but the smell of burning carcasses was still repulsive. Covering his mouth, he moved around the courtyard and ensured that every black cloak was burned. Finally, he stood next to Eoin.

"I think you got them all," Eoin panted as he bent down for a second. "I think the next priority is to find Asira, don't you think?"

"You're right." Anton glanced towards the path for the Great Arches.

"I don't think so," Airies called out as she took down the last standing Scarab. "Those things were more of a nuisance than actual trouble." She patted down her leggings. A gust of wind blew across the courtyard sweeping the black smoke into the air. "We need to assess the injuries. We need to regroup." A gentle breeze coached them towards the castle.

"Master Airies, I think we need to find Asira," Anton argued.

"I would not get in the way of Volknor or Inferno. Trust me if they can't bring her home then no one can."

"I don't care. I'm going!" Anton turned his direction towards the path of the Great Arches.

"No, you are not." With a high kick to the back of the head, Anton landed flat on his face. "If you don't listen to reason, then you will listen to violence." Airies stood over him. "I'm telling you now in order to survive, sometimes you must follow orders."

CHAPTER THIRTY-FOUR

Heartbroken

"I hope the world crumbles beneath your feet." Asira finally managed to prop herself against the arch. "You creep!" She was so exhausted that her body was numb.

"You don't deserve the powers that were bestowed upon your family. They are wasted on you."

"You are just jealous." Asira's head limply fell against her shoulder. "You're a sad and lonely man."

A blade slid down from his sleeve and into his hand. "I need you alive but that doesn't mean I can't hurt you."

"Don't you dare touch her!" Lightning glinted across the stone path.

"Volknor?" Her blurry vision flickered to a blond figure running through the picket fence. "I can't believe you made it."

James knelt down beside her. "Hey kid, are you doing okay?"

"James?" Her dull emerald eyes drifted to his face. "You kind of look like dad. I can't believe you are twins."

He smirked. "Can you move?"

She shook her head a tiny bit. "I don't think so. I'm so glad you're here."

"Always kid." He smiled back. "I'll carry you out of here. All you need to do is stay awake. Can you do that for me?" He rubbed her cheek. His smile quickly fading as her head slid towards him. "Asira?"

"James, I'm so tired."

"Asira, keep your eyes open. Please kid, stay awake for me."

"How is she?" Volknor glanced over his shoulder. "Asira? James, wake her up!"

"I'm trying." He vigorously shook her shoulders. "Kid, come on. Andrew would never forgive me." James snatched her hand trying desperately to heat up her icy skin. He allowed the energy flow around his body, heating up his veins like a geothermal spring. "Come on, kid, stay awake for me."

"James, did you know my mother?" she whispered softly.

"Of course I knew your mother. We were like the three amigos as children. Your mother kept your dad and me in check. She was one my best friends." He jostled her slightly to get her attention. She slid towards him. A sickening sensation churned in the pit of his stomach. "Volknor," his voice was grim as his fingers pressed down on her wrist, "I don't feel a pulse."

"I... I... we can't go back without her. Andrew won't be able for it." Volknor stumbled back a few steps. A strange sense of blame, remorse, fright, and fear overwhelmed him all at once. He knelt down and allowing a small source of electricity, he carefully and cautiously placed his hand on her chest. With slow breaths he controlled the delicate blue stimulating fibres and allowed them to sink through her skin. After a moment he pulled his arm away and stared regrettably at her.

"Asira..." Saria used all her strength to crawl back to her feet, using the column table for support. A white eerie mist slowly crept in around the Great Arches.

Draskule followed a pair of red eyes as it stalked beneath the cover of the mist. "So, you have received the power of the white wolves."

"What does that mean? What have you done?" Volknor yelled as the electricity sparked wildly across his limbs.

"Asira's dead." Draskule's voice was dour. "The wolves pass onto the next master. I was hoping Saria would take control of the black wolves as well. But it seems Kai is still alive."

Saria struggled to hold her balance. With her last ounce of strength, she raised her head slowly revealing blood red eyes. "You're a monster. You'll never get these powers."

Draskule swung his blade towards her. "Hold your tongue doppelgänger. You know nothing of power."

She glared at the perplexed warlock. "No Draskule, I think it's you that knows nothing about this power. This overwhelming force is frightening. Your plan was doomed to fail from the start and you'll never understand why."

A white wolf stepped out from the mist and pounced, snapping its jaw around Draskule's arm. He flailed, frantically trying to defend himself.

Volknor abruptly swept Asira into his arms. "Let's get out of here, Inferno."

James nodded but took one final glance around at Saria.

She struggled to stand, clutching onto the column for dear life. The white wolf bravely defended the best it could but Draskule finally tossed the wolf to one side. "You disrespectful bitch!" He made his way behind Saria, taking her by the hair and kicking her down to her knees. "Without me there would not even be a you." The long blade sliced along her pale skin and red liquid pumped from her neck. The white mist vanished instantaneously.

Flames erupted across the stone pavement.

Volknor had rushed to the safety of the gate just in time with Asira cradled in his arms. He glimpsed back at the intense flames racing along the pathway.

"You monster!" Footprints were scorched into the stone. "You think I will let you hurt my family without paying the consequences?" Flames whisked up like a vortex surrounding Draskule.

"You think some flames will defeat me?" Draskule stood defiantly. "If three people containing the power of the black and white wolves couldn't stop me, how do you think you have any sort of a chance?"

James picked up the Ember Jewel, watching as the cinders glimmered inside. "You seem to have a bad memory." Rising back to his feet he tossed the gemstone a few inches into the air catching it again and again. "Patrick is a manipulative and brilliant monster. I am very certain Patrick has been using you this whole time."

Draskule swung his sword in a failed attempt to keep the flames at bay as they began nipping at him and scorching his clothes. "You don't know what you're talking about!"

"You forgot something else." James held out the gemstone gazing through it attentively. "This can intensify my power." Bright red flames engulfed James entirely, dramatically intensifying into a bright blue. Horrifically, the flesh began melting from his bones. His eyes liquefied and black holes stared back at Draskule soullessly. His clothes remained undamaged and hung on the bony structure. His trousers hung loosely from his pelvis. His jaw swung open like a broken hinge.

"Stop this!" Draskule frantically swung his sword repeatedly at the whisking blaze. "Do you want power?" The flames encased Draskule's limbs binding him in one place. Panic and fear took over. "Inferno, stop this!" Black swirling magic tried desperately to combat the red flames only to be snuffed out straight away.

Bony fingers passed through the fiery vortex and pinched Draskule's chin. "If I wanted power, I would have looked for it years ago." The blue flames flickered around his bones and latched onto the fiery vortex like a parasite causing it to burst with incredible velocity and power.

"Patrick! HELP ME!" The blue flames became overwhelming. The intensity ripped through Draskule's flesh. "STOP!" The horrific screams were fleeting, followed by silence.

Volknor kept a safe distance as the blue hue spread across the entire pavement. The heat was unbearable. His hold on Asira grew a little tighter as he dodged a few loose embers. He had forgotten the power possessed by his comrade. It was hard to believe one person could control so much raw energy. It made him wonder what sort of power Kai and Asira possessed.

James gazed down at his skeletal fingers, dropping the Ember Jewel. He watched the blue flames flicker like a current, alive in its own strange way. He shrugged his shoulders feeling the muscles and tendons reforming and encapsulating his bones. He stretched out his arms and fingers concentrating on the flames and trying his best to expel the excess energy stored up inside.

"Inferno?" Volknor called out hesitantly.

James gazed back through black sockets. The majority of his body had returned to normal. However, his skull and outer extremities were the last to form. He clenched his bony fingers and stretched out his arms again before shaking out his body one last time.

***

Eoin stared around the courtyard, taking a second to scan the surrounding area again before retracting the vines next to him.

Fabia panted heavily beside him searching frantically before dashing to the castle steps. "Thomas!" she yelled wrapping her arms around his neck pulling him down to the ground.

"Fabia, are you hurt?" He leaned back from her restraining arms to get a better look at her face. She shook her head nuzzling her nose into his chest. He let out a sigh of relief before encircling her in his arms. "I'm so glad you're okay."

"Aaron!" Angelica slipped from Zayne's protective wings. She ran as fast as she could on two legs before leaping into his arms, wrapping her arms around his neck and her legs locking around his waist. "Are you hurt?"

Without a word, his arms fastened around her body and he kissed her firmly, not wanting to let her go. Aaron was a man of few words when it came to emotions. He much preferred to allow his actions speak for him. "I love you, Angelica." She was left stunned, unable to find the words to respond she merely nodded before melting into him, safe in his secure hold.

"Katie, how are your wings?" Zayne landed quietly next to her.

"Don't mind my wings, look at your arms." She took his hands and inspected his skin. "You have cuts and bruises all over."

"It doesn't even hurt," he responded, watching her finger trace the emerging purple and grey bruises.

"That's because your body is still being pumped with adrenaline." She threw her arms around him. "I'm so glad you're okay."

"You okay?" Eoin knelt down and held out his hand. Anton glanced up from the castle steps. His eyes quickly met the face of the Irish voice. "Come on, man." Reluctantly Anton took his arm and let himself be pulled up. He nursed the back of his head before turning his attention towards the castle.

Airies had propped Kai against the banister where she was already examining the cauterised wound. "Volknor is getting a little sloppy. Don't try to move." Her fingers grazed his abdomen. "The wound is going to be sore for a while, but I think Volknor just saved your life."

Kai grunted. "What about everyone else?"

"Everyone else is alive. I'm going to check out any and all injuries now. But I think you should be proud of your students. They fought well."

"Master Airies, is Master Kai going to be okay?" Cara glanced up the steps.

Airies smiled. "With a lot of rest, he will pull through." Glancing in the direction of the Great Arches she spotted familiar figures and without hesitation she ran across the courtyard. "Volknor?" She touched Asira's cold skin. "Don't say it. Please don't say it."

Volknor continued to carry Asira in bridal fashion. Her legs were draped over one arm while her head leaned against his chest. Tears were welling in his eyes as he gazed softly down at her peaceful face. "I tried to save her, Airies. We were just too late."

"This is going to kill Andrew." Airies glanced back over to the castle.

James fists were clenched tight. His eyes were locked on the still frame of his niece. "We won't let it," he whispered.

"She is heavier than she looks," Volknor chuckled a bit as his smile pushed the tears to one side. He adjusted his grasp on Asira before resuming the ceremonial walk across the courtyard, passing the scorched and fragmented remains of the black cloaks that had attacked them.

Eoin stumbled to his feet. "Bluebird..." His words were stricken with pure anguish and sorrow. His eyes caught Volknor's remorseful gaze. "Bluebird... she's not..." His shaky voice trailed off. "Please don't say she's dead!" he roared.

Angelica covered her mouth in horror and curled into Aaron's arms. His limbs were limp from exhaustion, but his stomach was sick from shock.

"Asira..." Anton walked up in front of Volknor. He gazed at her pale face. Her arm dangled away from her body. Her legs were limp. She was cold to the touch. His fear had come true. His soul mate had run straight into death's arms. In that instant, Anton felt his heart splinter into pieces. Without a word, a nod or a signal, he stepped back next to Eoin.

Anton glanced at Eoin who was crying into his arm. Across from him, Angelica was whimpering into Aaron's shoulder. Britanie and Mandy were sniffling into each other's arms. The sorrow seeped down his throat like a sour sweet and the tears poured uncontrollably down his cheeks. None of it seemed real.

Volknor's steps were slow and steady. He was gentle, almost afraid to cause her any more discomfort. Kai was lying against the banister, eyes shut, his hand resting over his stomach. "Kai?" He waited for a moment. "Andrew?" Kai glanced up. Airies and James stood behind Volknor like soldiers. "Andrew... I am so sorry." Volknor knelt down slowly next to Kai and laid Asira carefully beside him.

Kai gazed at her serene face for a few moments before he caressed her pale cold skin. "Hey, Asira?" His fingers pressed against her neck. "Asira, don't do this to me. Please."

"Andrew, it has been a few minutes. I don't think she is going to wake up."

"We can defibrillate her heart. We can still try." He leaned down compressing her chest. "We have to try!"

Electricity charged around the centre of Volknor's palm. He prayed for this to work as he leaned down on her chest. There was no movement. His palm charged again, and he leaned down over her heart. Her body jolted but there was no further movement. "Andrew, it's not working."

Electricity surged around Kai's hands. He pressed down hard. She jolted again. "If we can just get her heart started." He pressed down again and again and again.

"Andrew, stop!" Volknor snatched his wrist. "Let the girl rest in peace."

"Shut up!" Kai banged down on her chest vehemently. "She's my baby!" He pulled Asira's limp body into his own and used whatever strength he had left to cradle her. "She's all I have left." Her cold skin sent chills down his spine. His little girl who had only recently turned eighteen was taken from him so cruelly. "I promised Crystal I would protect her. I promised I would watch over our daughter. Why her? Why not me?"

A warm thin breath skimmed his neck.

Kai lowered his arms and examined her pale complexion.

Volknor watched Kai's face and his eyes darted back to Asira. He snatched her wrist desperately searching for a pulse. In the middle of his prayer, he saw the slight elevation of her chest. "She has a pulse."

"What?" James bolted up the steps and dropped to his knees.

"We need to get her to a hospital, Kai." Volknor smiled up at him. "Seriously, we better move."

"I can carry her and keep her warm," James voice was heartfelt. He shrugged his tense shoulders before taking her ever so carefully into his arms.

"Kai," Volknor put his arm around his shoulder and stood up slowly. "We need to get you to a hospital as well. I don't suppose you can get us there?"

"I might." Fabia pulled out her wand. "Asira was showing me how to open portals."

"Good," Volknor nodded with a smile. "Let's get going."

CHAPTER THIRTY-FIVE

Tensions

Volknor and James stepped into Council Chambers.

"Your Highnesses," James strode down the steps and nodded respectfully towards Prince Manolito of the Essence Kingdom, Princess Amelia of the Luce Caelo Kingdom and Airies.

"We searched everywhere. There is no sign of the gemstones, Saria or Draskule." Volknor approached Kai at the top of the chamber where he was standing.

"I don't know how they just vanished." Kai leaned against the wooden desk.

"No doubt about it. It was Patrick," Volknor added in a sinister tone.

"General Gervais?" Prince Manolito gasped in horror. "How? Why?"

"Master Soniar, is Patrick Gervais not deceased?" Princess Amelia asked, her transparent wings fluttering as she momentarily rose into the air in panic.

Kai inhaled deeply, keeping one hand across his waist at all times. "We are not certain, but it looks like Draskule brought Patrick back to life." Every movement sent a stinging sensation across his abdomen. "Our concern now is keeping The Council together, keeping the kingdoms informed and at peace." He took another slow deep breath. "Patrick Gervais is still on the loose and it is our job to stop him."

"Kai, my dear *amigo*," Prince Manolito began, "I assume our first order of business would be to elect a new Head of Council?"

"A new Head? What has happened to Master Adams?" Princess Amelia turned towards Prince Manolito.

"Master Adams was working in the shadows with Master Draskule and General Gervais," Prince Manolito spoke uneasily.

"It's true. This is something we have only very recently discovered. But please, our concern is keeping the peace. I understand the fear and I understand the trauma this has caused." Kai tried to reassure everyone.

"Master Soniar," Prince Manolito began, "I suggest you take over the mantle as Head of Council. I am sure Princess Amelia will also vouch for you. I would trust no one else, Kai. You are the greatest *hechicero*." He addressed Kai's power in his native tongue, with respect.

Princess Amelia rose to her feet and gripped the banisters next to her. "I believe this would be the right course to take. Master Soniar, we were never able to choose the Head of Council before. I agree with Prince Manolito, there is no one I would rather have represent The Council but the greatest and most modest sorcerer."

Kai glanced over at Volknor, who nodded in agreement. "I..." Kai took another deep breath in. "I would be honoured to represent The Council, Your Highnesses. We can arrange a formal meeting with the other leaders later in the week." He pushed away from the table and regained his balance. "Please excuse me." He tilted his head in a respectful nod towards Prince Manolito and Princess Amelia.

"Kai?" Volknor called slipping into the hall after him. "We have arranged a proper ceremony in the cemetery tomorrow evening for Erika."

Kai nodded. "I'll be there."

"Are you heading to the hospital?"

"Yes, I haven't been there since this morning and it is already six o'clock," he said glancing at his watch.

"I'll go with you."

"No need. I'll be fine on my own Volknor."

Volknor laughed. "You can barely stand. I'm going to make sure you get to the hospital in one piece."

An orange portal opened in the hallway. "Okay, you can keep me company," Kai smirked.

"I have been meaning to ask you what you intend to do? We weren't sure if Asira would gain the same powers as you and as it turns out, it is slightly different. I don't even think she realised it, but she was commanding the white phantom wolves."

"I don't know what I can tell her. You have the most knowledge on it. Maybe it's better if we..."

"Suppress it? Like you've been trying. It's worked for eighteen years but things are different now, Kai."

"I know. You're right. I think it means another journey to Enveronica Island." Kai led the way through the multiple orange colours of the portal, and they appeared in the hospital corridor.

"Master Soniar, you are late for your appointment." A nurse with a pixie hairstyle and pointy ears giddily leapt from reception. "How have you been?"

"Hello Merida, I've been better." Kai walked up to the desk and gripped his side. "I know I'm late. Sorry about that. Could I please see Asira first?"

She nodded gracefully. "Of course you can, sir."

Volknor leaned across the desk. "Is it just me or are there a lot of people here?"

"Well, Sir Costello, there were a few more casualties than first anticipated. We have actually been receiving calls from other kingdoms reporting similar injuries."

Volknor clenched his fist and lightly banged it against the countertop. "Okay, thank you for that."

The nurse nodded. "If you would follow me, Mr Soniar." The nurse gestured to the double doors leading them to the intensive care unit. "We have moved Asira into an isolated corridor of the ICU. We have also placed several guards from the Velosian Police Force along the corridor and hospital grounds."

Volknor glanced around at the police standing guard.

The nurse showed the guards her badge. "She's been in a stable condition since lunchtime. Her operation went well yesterday, and the doctors are impressed with her recovery. Doctor Barton has insisted he remains her physician." She walked into the room and immediately checked Asira's vitals. "Master Soniar, the doctor will be with you in a while to check you over." She nodded before leaving the room.

Both Kai and Volknor stood at the end of the bed. Asira looked so small and fragile in the bed. A drip hung from a metal stand and a blood pressure cuff circled her upper arm. A clear oxygen mask rested over her mouth. The sound of her heartbeat was like a piercing reminder of the constant death that followed them wherever they went.

Volknor examined her chart that hung at the end of the bed. "Has she woken up?"

"No. She hasn't woken up. Volknor, she is still missing the piece of her soul."

"Do you think she can..." Volknor thought for a second about rephrasing his sentence. "Do you think she can live without it?"

Kai sat down in the chair next to the bed. "I don't know. If she wakes up, then there is a good chance."

"I promise you," Volknor began, his voice harsh, "we will find Patrick and the gemstones. We will finish this and take revenge."

There was a knock on the door. "Ah, Master Soniar, I hope you are ready for your check-up. If you would follow me." The doctor held the door open. Kai followed him.

Volknor's eyes trailed away from the door and followed the sound of the steady rhythm of a distressed and weak heart. There was a part of him that ached. He had no children of his own, but he was very fond of his students. If there was anything he could do, he would do it. He wanted to see Asira sitting up in the bed smiling. He wanted to see her laugh again.

***

Kai left the doctor's office over an hour later. As he strolled down the corridor, he adjusted his shirt and buttoned his sleeves. "What's going on?" He stared at the fourteen teenagers. Volknor stood next to them with a huge grin across his face.

"Master Kai," Cara spoke up, "we wanted to see how Asira was doing. We are all very concerned."

"How did you get here?"

"Oh, me again!" Fabia jumped with excitement. "Asira has been showing me the portal spell and..." She stopped dead in her tracks. "Are you mad?"

"No, I am not mad," Kai said curling his arm around his own waist.

"He is actually very proud," Volknor smirked.

"Your parents, The Council – they are going to be very mad. Take out your phones and text your parents. Tell them where you are and tell them I will bring you all back as soon as I have enough energy." He took a deep breath. "Wait, where is Anton?"

"He is in the ward with Asira," Aaron replied.

Kai stepped into the room and stood by the end of the bed.

Anton's fingers grazed her wrist and circled her palm. He could feel the blood pump slowly through her veins. "She is so brave. She kept up a smile, a facade even though she was hurting inside. I never knew she was in pain. She's still fighting." He glanced over his shoulder in a desperate plea. "I could try to save her."

"The doctors are doing that as we speak." Kai took a step closer. "Anton, I think it's time to leave."

Anton watched her and examined every feature of her face before abruptly taking his leave.

CHAPTER THIRTY-SIX

Aftermath

Volknor, Airies, James and Kai stood over a headstone. A priest, in a white shirt, jacket and black pants stood across from them. He sprinkled some holy water over the coffin and read from a heavy old book.

"Isn't it sick? A wooden box will house our forever slumber. After all she's done, all the lives she has saved, all the good she has done and she's the one being buried beneath the soil." Kai placed a white rose on the coffin as it began to lower into the ground.

"She would like it here," Airies spoke softly. "She is close to Crystal." She tossed another white rose onto the mahogany lid.

Kai glanced over his shoulder. "Yes, that is true. She's only about seventy feet away."

"She wouldn't like us to fuss over her. She wouldn't want anything too fancy. I think this is the best way to honour Erika's memory," Volknor said. "She was very brave and dedicated."

"She was so brave. She loved people," James laughed. "That was brave."

"She was so elegant," Airies continued.

"She was a great friend," Kai added, "in every way. She was a great teacher, colleague, friend and comrade. She will be deeply missed."

***

Eoin walked down the busy street. Daily life continued around him. Strangers smiled and laughed, cars passed by on the road. He stood by the traffic lights and gazed over at a coffee shop. He had no intention of going inside but then it started to drizzle.

He glanced at the menu. Inside he was taken aback by the special dessert. "Erm... can I have an apple turnover please and... and a chocolate milkshake, please."

He found a seat in the corner of the coffee shop by the window. Eoin wasn't a religious man. Yes, he believed in some power greater than himself, but he wasn't a churchgoer. However, he took the events of today as a sign.

His mind wandered to her perfect smile. Her eyes always sparkled with life. Her dark hair contrasted with her pale complexion. When he had gone back with the other students to see Asira, he was not the first at her bedside, but he was definitely the next. He had waited for Anton to leave the room before he gazed on her troubled face.

The rain was pelting against the windowpane. He had returned home about three weeks ago. Life was continuing around him as normal. No one in Ireland had any clue of his ordeal in the past few weeks. There was no one he could really talk to. His family were against him ever returning to Velosia. It had been three weeks since he had heard anything of Asira. There had been no update of her health or even whether she was awake. Maybe they wouldn't contact him? Should he try to reach out to her?

***

"Father, Mother, it was a series of unfortunate circumstances. That is no reason to go against the school. The primary foundation of the school is solid. It achieved its initial goal."

The king and queen of Atlantis sat at one end of the table. Three large eels sat in the corner of the room like guard dogs.

"We were all able to stay in close vicinity of each other, study and play. Yes, there were a few quarrels, but that was to be expected when placing a substantial number of teenagers into a room together." Cara took a breath, a few air bubbles escaped her lips. "Even when it came to defending ourselves, we helped and protected one another. The primary aim of the school is to bring the races together and forget the wars of the past. This is evident in the group of students currently attending Velosian Academy." Cara inhaled and exhaled as politely and as discreetly as possible.

***

"Aaron," said Chief Connelly as he entered the tent, "in three months' time we are hosting Angelica and her family here."

Aaron nodded respectfully to his father. "Father, before you go…"

Chief Connelly turned back to his son.

"I have been meaning to ask you, the next time you attend a meeting at The Council, could I accompany you please?"

He smiled. "I would be delighted to have you attend with me. It only makes sense to have the next in line be seen more frequently." The Chief took off a ring and handed it to Aaron. "This shows the other werewolf clans where you belong on the hierarchy scale. Wear it proudly."

"I will, Father." He placed the ring on his finger but realised it was too large.

"We will actually be attending a meeting in a few days' time. I hear Master Soniar wants to put himself in for Head of Council."

Aaron looked up in surprise. "Are you going to vote for him?"

"Only makes sense to. He is a good man. I have known him for a very long time. My nose has never been wrong."

"Father, have you heard anything?"

"Like what?" He gazed at his son, pondered for a moment and then he remembered. "News on the little sorceress? Unfortunately, I have heard nothing."

"It's just, it has been three months since everything, and I don't know how she is."

"I know how upsetting this is and how concerned you are for your friend. We will find out at the meeting. I will make sure we get an update."

"Father, how are Britanie and Mandy?"

"Mandy is doing fine. Her mother is delighted to have her home. Britanie has suffered minor cracks along her ribs and vertebrae. Her shoulders are bruised but she will live. Chieftain Razor has always been the overprotective father, so of course he has blown her injuries out of proportion."

"I'm glad they're okay. Father, they both fought well."

***

Anton gazed down at the pictures of when he was young. His mother was in a lot of them. She had cared for him when he was sick, scraped his knees and she put up with all his temper tantrums.

"Anton, what are you doing?"

He clenched his fists. "Mother, I am so sorry I was unable to protect you or the gemstone. I have let down the vampire race."

"Don't be so silly." She took his hand with her frail and shaking fingers. "You do more for the pride of the vampire race than your father or I could have ever imagined. You attended Velosian Academy and proved that you were the stronger member of your society. You were there alone with four werewolves from different clans. That was bravery." She smiled gently. "Will you attend the next meeting of The Council with me? It is in a few days. Master Soniar wishes to be Head of Council and the more votes he gets, the better. He might even reopen the school."

"Of course I will come with you. Have you heard anything about Asira?"

She shook her head. "I am afraid not, my dear. We can ask Kai at the meeting. I am sure he will have a few developments for us."

***

There was a light knock on the door. Katie turned from her vanity table. "Come in."

The door creaked open as Zayne strolled in. "How are you feeling?" His wings were curled behind his back.

Katie turned back to her mirror and continued to braid her hair. "I'm feeling much better. How about you?"

Zayne lifted his arms over his head in a cross shape so Katie would see his bandaged arms in the mirror. "New bandages."

She giggled swinging her legs over the bench. She stretched out her right wing. "The feathers are growing back nicely."

Zayne bent over and studied the new feathers. "Have you tried to fly yet?"

She shook her head. "I think I will give it a few more weeks."

"Nonsense. The longer you wait, the scarier it will be." He took his sisters hand leading her to the open window. He crawled out and hunkered on the roof tiles. "Do you trust me?"

She knelt on the windowsill. "You know I trust you with my life."

"Good." He coaxed her outside and she immediately crawled into his arms and stood firmly on his feet. "Hold on tight." His feet slipped off the edge of the roof.

She gripped onto his shoulders nervously. "Am I not too heavy for you?"

"You forget I work out on a daily basis, sister. Now, try to flap your wings." She shrugged her shoulders loosening her muscles as her wings followed the motion. "It's like teaching a baby to fly," Zayne teased as he slowly and carefully released his grip around her waist.

She pushed herself from his grip, concentrating on the movement of her own wings. "I've missed this, just the feel of the open breeze across your wings. Thank you, Zayne."

"I am proud of you, sis."

***

"Thomas!" Prince Manolito entered the throne room where he was waiting patiently. "I am glad you were able to take time to meet me. I am sure it took a lot of convincing to pry yourself from the arms of my sister, *mi hermana*."

Thomas laughed. "Mother has been a bit smothering since I've come home."

Prince Manolito sat on the step next to the throne and patted a spot next to him. "Sit and tell me all about it."

Thomas sat down. "Well, where would you like me to begin?"

"Did you make any friends?"

He nodded. "Yes. Bobby, Eoin and Peter were my close friends there. But honestly, we all got on very well."

"That is good, very good. Do you know there is tension between the nations again? They fear Patrick."

"That monster. Master Volknor filled us in on him."

"The fairies are securing their boarders again."

"And us? What are you doing?" Thomas glanced up questioningly.

"I am doing what I normally do. I am going to try to impress the gorgeous Princess Sylvia."

"Actually, Chloe and Blake have grown close. Chloe is the niece of Princess Amelia and Blake is the nephew of Princess Sylvia."

Prince Manolito leaned back into a comfortable position. "Princess Sylvia is a creature of great beauty."

"Well, to be honest, I think they like each other."

"Like?" Prince Manolito glanced over at him.

"Yes," Thomas chuckled. "It looked like the beginning of a teenage romance."

He threw back his head laughing. "That is a good thing." He hummed to himself, "Hmm, that is a very good thing."

CHAPTER THIRTY-SEVEN

New Council

Anton sat waiting anxiously on the cushioned red velvet seat as he gazed around Council Chambers. Every leader from the different races and kingdoms had arrived. They were all waiting patiently for Kai and Volknor to show up. The room was designed like an auditorium in that the seating arrangement was curved and surrounded the elegant desk and grand chair at the centre of the room on three sides. This was the table where the Head of Council would sit and address the other council members.

Anton and his mother were sitting in the middle section of the front row. Five seats to their right and two rows back were Chief Connelly, Aaron, Priestess Alora and Chieftain Razor. Aaron gave him a little nod and a smile. Priestess Alora and Chieftain Razor were not Council members, so it was unusual for them to make an appearance.

To Anton's left and at the back of the room were Prince Manolito, Princess Sylvia and Princess Amelia. A new person sat in the front row on the far left. Master Airies sat next to her along with James. King Griffith sat three seats down from Lady Pearse. As usual in meetings such as this, there were no guards present. It was simply a meeting between the leaders of the kingdoms.

The door creaked open and Volknor stepped into the room. "Good evening Your Highnesses. I am delighted that you were all able to come at such short notice." He nervously walked down the steps, nodding respectfully to the royal figures before he stopped at the desk. "Master Soniar will address The Council, the new members and esteemed guests to discuss recent events."

The door opened and closed again. Anton turned expecting to see only Kai but immediately jumped from his chair astonished. "Asira!"

Aaron leapt from his seat as soon as he heard her name. His father pulled him by the arm to sit back down.

Asira followed Kai down the steps to the desk where Volknor was waiting. She gave a little wave over to both Anton and Aaron.

"Your Highnesses, thank you very much for coming on such short notice." The wooden staph materialised in Kai's hand and he passed it back to Asira. "First things first," he cleared his throat, "I would like to elect myself as Head of Council."

Prince Manolito rose from his seat. "Señor, I will gladly vote for you, *mi amigo*. Raise your hands to vote in favour of Señor Soniar." His Spanish accent travelled through the room. In a matter of seconds, everyone in the room raised their hand. "Unanimous. It is to be." He sat back down.

Volknor rustled through the drawers of the table and placed a feather pen and parchment in front of Kai. Kai turned to face him. "Andrew Soniar, sorcerer by blood, I do declare you elected Head of Council and as such, you will take on the responsibilities of the Velosian Kingdom. Do you agree to serve the office with respect and majesty?"

"Yes, as Head of Council, I agree to serve the office with respect and majesty."

"Please sign the parchment with your signature and the other council members will sign beneath yours."

Kai took the feather pen and signed his name without hesitation, Master Andrew Kai Soniar. He turned to the room. "Thank you for this amazing opportunity. I promise you all I will do better than my predecessor." He gazed at each council member. "As Head of Council, I would like to welcome Queen Celine of the Bonum Kingdom. I am delighted to greet you in the Velosia Kingdom and welcome you to The Council. That said, I am deeply sorry it is under these circumstances. I think we should take a moment of silence for the late Queen Shire who bravely and with astounding courage, protected her kingdom with her life."

After the minute of silence, Queen Celine stood up. "Thank you, Master Soniar. The moment of silence was very thoughtful. I would like to congratulate you on your new position. I would also like to state that I will honour the late Queen, my beautiful aunt, and respect The Council and the Bonum Kingdom."

Kai nodded. "You are very welcome, Your Highness." He inhaled a steady breath. "I would like to introduce my daughter, Asira, to those of you that do not know her. She is also a young sorceress." Asira glanced up at the crowd and gave a little wave. "I suppose it is time to discuss the events of the last three months or so. I suspect rumours have been travelling the various towns in each kingdom regarding what exactly happened. People are frightened. They are looking to you for answers but up until now you were not able to provide solace to those who have lost loved ones." Kai glanced over at Volknor. "To get straight to the point, council member Master Draskule and my predecessor Master Adams betrayed not only The Council, but Velosia."

"Betrayed The Council? From what I have heard, they stole the Haven Jewel and the Ember Jewel and wreaked havoc across Velosia!" Chief Connelly scoffed.

The atmosphere darkened in the room and a cloud of dread descended. Kai straightened his spine and crossed his arms behind his back. "We have recently discovered that both Draskule and Adams had been working closely with Patrick during the Great War. Between them, they experimented on cadavers. The monsters you have seen on the news, those are called Scarabs. They are mindless drones, zombies. The sick thing is they were once people." A chill echoed around the room.

"Those things came into the palace. My guards never stood a chance. A beautiful *señorita* was leading the troop of monsters. I had to double take. I had seen this young *señorita* before," Prince Manolito said in disgust.

"I was unable to comprehend that they stole the Glint Jewel. I thought they just managed to steal the Ember Jewel and Haven Jewel." Princess Sylvia turned to Prince Manolito in disbelief.

"That young sorceress was Saria. She is Asira's doppelgänger. Another pawn in Draskule's plan. But it gets worse." Kai grimaced. "They brought Patrick Gervais back from the dead."

"What?!" King Griffith smashed his fist on the table. "Patrick Gervais is alive? It has been eighteen years since his death. How could anyone come back from the grave?"

"I do not understand!" Princess Sylvia declared in a despairing tone. Prince Manolito took her hand and shushed her.

Kai spoke with authority. "I know how concerning this is for everyone. I know security has been tightened across many of your kingdoms. I don't blame you. I wish to do the same. I would like to rebuild the Velosian Army. I thought it was wrong to disband it after the Great War, but I understand why it was done." Kai turned to Asira and gestured to her. "The reason this meeting was not held until today was because Asira was still recuperating in hospital. She was beaten to within an inch of her life. An unspeakable curse was placed upon her and she is still struggling with the consequences." She unbuttoned her blouse and revealed a scar along her chest. "She underwent emergency surgery the day she was admitted to hospital."

"Will this segregate the kingdoms again?" Chieftain Razor spoke up. His arms were folded across his short-sleeved top with its jagged edges. His hair was as white as snow. His eyes were golden.

"Master Soniar, I am a Priestess. My job is to understand the soul and the spiritual world. What I do not understand is a soul being split in two and this girl still standing before us." Alora was the Priestess of the Amazon Forest Clan werewolves. Her skin was a beautiful tan colour. Her hair was as black as the night sky, plaited elegantly and wrapped neatly in a bun.

"Master Erika Roberts discovered the origins and was promptly murdered in cold blood by Draskule."

"What was the purpose of the spell?" Priestess Alora asked in shock. Goosebumps crawled across her skin.

"There was no purpose. It was a fanatical sorcerer with too much time on his hands that created the spell."

Anton anxiously waited in his seat. His fingers were digging deeper into his trouser legs.

"I am sorry for interrupting, Master Soniar," said Queen Celine rising from her seat, "my aunt died to save the Haven Jewel. Where is it?"

"Patrick escaped with the gemstones. He also left with the bodies of Draskule and the doppelgänger. We managed to burn Adams body to a crisp and the Scarabs' that attacked us. We have been searching everywhere for him and we do not intend to stop searching."

"This is revolting behaviour," said Priestess Alora crossing her legs.

"Master Soniar, I have tripled security around my kingdom and my children's kingdoms. I assure you the seas are secure," announced King Roland.

"The lands on earth should be safe," Chief Demarco added.

"I have reinforced the security within the Bonum Kingdom," Queen Celine raised her hand.

"I will pass a law for the Velosian Army to be reinstated." Kai leaned against the table. "Just to make this clear, this will in no way isolate the kingdoms. I am a firm believer of keeping people connected. I believe it is better for everyone if we keep the gates of communication open and work together to soothe any threat." He stepped back to the left next to Asira. "Before we break for refreshments, could I kindly ask you all to sign the parchment? Thank you."

One by one, the leaders present signed their names under Kai's. The parchment read:

The Council of Velosia:
Master Andrew 'Kai' Soniar   Master of Sorcery, Head of Council
Lady Catherine Pearse   Lady of the Kalis Republic
Prince Manolito of the Granite Isle   Prince of the Essence Kingdom
Princess Amelia Aetós   Princess of Luce Caelo Kingdom
Princess Sylvia Selinofoto   Princess of Dusk Kingdom
King Roland Griffith   King of the Maria Empire
Queen Celine Aingeal   Queen of the Bonum Kingdom
Sir Christopher 'Volknor' Costello   Master of Lightning

Dame Amber 'Airies' Kennedy	*Master of Wind*
Sir James 'Inferno' Soniar	*Master of Fire*
Chief Noah Connelly	*Chief of the Australian Werewolf Sand Clan*
Priestess Alora Carvalho	*Priestess of the Amazon Werewolf Forest Clan*
Chieftain Razor North	*Chieftain of the Arctic Werewolf Snow Clan*
Chief Demarco Orie	*Chief of the African Werewolf Savannah Clan*

Aaron and Anton leapt from their seats and rushed over to Kai and Asira.

"Sir," Anton greeted Kai and swiftly turned to Asira. "Asira, I thought you were dying. There has been no update on your condition. I have never been so frightened in my life."

"I'm so sorry, Anton. I know everyone must have been so worried. But I'm actually feeling so much better." She smiled gently.

"What about your scar, what..."

"Anton, compose yourself." Asira giggled. "I have never seen you lost for words." She took his hand. "Apparently my lungs were filling up with fluid and my heart was failing. So, they drained my lungs. Then my heart went into cardiac arrest and my artery ruptured." Asira gazed at the floor as she spoke.

"I can't believe you are walking around." Aaron carefully examined her.

"I am actually on extremely strong painkillers right now." She glanced up and giggled.

"Why did you not call?" Anton asked, his tone a little wretched.

"Anton, I am so sorry, I... I just have not been myself the last few weeks. I'm still finding it hard. You can understand. I'm still frightened."

"I thought you needed Saria?" Aaron enquired.

"So far, so good. Looks like I don't need her at the moment."

Anton took her hand pulling her into a hug. He tightened his arms around her back. "I am just so glad you are okay."

"That is so sweet." Lady Pearse commented as she joined Kai. "How are you doing, Kai?"

"I am doing much better, Catherine, thank you. How are you feeling? How is Kalis?"

"Master Volknor," Priestess Alora approached Volknor across the room, "I am impressed. If I may be frank, I did not think the school would work but since my daughter has come home, she has spoken nothing but amazing things about the subjects, teachers and the friends she has made. I was also sceptical that werewolves and vampires could get on. I am overjoyed. I never thought I would see the day."

"It is charming to see. I am immensely proud of every student," Volknor responded as they watched Aaron, Anton and Asira laughing and chatting casually together.

CHAPTER THIRTY-EIGHT

Reunited

It had been a strangely blissful few months. Asira had spent three months in the hospital recuperating and undertook Wiccan therapeutic sessions every few days.

Kai had been overprotective and never left her alone. She was never left alone in the house and whenever they travelled, Kai either brought her along or James was left in charge. It was shortly after Asira left the hospital that James moved into the house for a few days every week. Asira soon realised that James was a much different person than she had first imagined.

James spent all his free time with Asira. He took Asira out to the shops, down to the beach and they even went sightseeing in London. After a few weeks of resting, Asira even attempted the portal spell to finally return James home to Spain.

Though she was recovering quite rapidly, she maintained radio silence for a total of six months after her operation. She spent a lot of her time in the hospital. The only other person she had spent time with was Anton, especially when James and Kai were working.

On one cold afternoon in February, Asira found herself waiting anxiously in Kai's office, the same office which had once been occupied by Master Adams. She paced up and down the length of the desk and rummaged through the books lined neatly in the adjacent bookcases. The last time she had seen her friends was months ago in a devastating situation. She was excited and nervous.

The last few months had been strange, and she had gladly locked herself away from the outside world. She had learned to distract herself in an attempt to evade the pain and the nightmares that had been keeping her awake.

Her eyes flickered across Kai's neat desk. It was lined with pens and books on the history of each kingdom. On one corner of the desk sat several photographs. She gazed fondly at them, at the people her father held dear to him. The first photo was of herself and Kai, when they had travelled to Venice the year before. The second was of Erika and Kai at the beach a few years ago. The final frame was well polished. It was a photo of her parents together. They were so young, in their early twenties skating in the centre of Cora Town.

***

Kai stepped through an orange portal into the dining room at Topaz Castle.

"It would be nice to know why you've gathered us together after six months." Eoin was irate as he stared around at the other fourteen faces.

"I will be back with answers shortly." Kai stepped out into the hall.

"Eoin! I wasn't expecting to see everyone again." Bobby ran from the other side of the dining room with Peter next to him. Bobby held out his hand, high-fived Eoin and pulled him in for a slight hug. "Nice to see you again, man. Have you heard anything?"

"Not a thing. And it's really annoying me," Eoin replied. "Peter, how's your arm?"

"I had to have an operation, some internal fixings. It still stings but it's getting better." Peter's arm rested in a cloth sling.

Angelica, Britanie and Mandy were chatting away in one corner of the room. Cara, Fabia, Thomas, Chloe, Zayne, Blake and Katie were sitting around the dining table. Anton and Aaron stood on the other side of the room.

"Do you think this is news about Asira?" Peter queried. "Or do you think they are just going to close the school?"

"I don't expect the school to stay open," Eoin remarked. "They should tell us something about Asira. Anything! It has been months since we've seen her. We don't even know if she is alive. We don't know if she is on life support, or if she has ever woken up!"

Bobby gave a sympathetic look. "Do you think Anton would know something? Isn't he dating her?"

"Maybe he was sworn to secrecy?" Peter added.

"I don't know. It's very wrong to keep us in the dark though," Eoin mumbled for a moment while listening to the chit-chat in the background. "I just want to know she is okay." Suddenly the room became silent, and the only sound was the dining room door shutting. Eoin hesitantly turned around and in a split second his heart stopped.

Asira stood in front of them, wearing dark skinny jeans, a white blouse and a purple cardigan. Her skin was pale as always, but her cheeks were blushing pink. Her eyes were a bright emerald green. Her brunette hair was neatly pushed behind her ears. "Hi, it's good to see everyone again."

Cara rose from her seat and squealed at the top of her voice. "Asira!" She crawled across the table as swiftly as she could, stumbled off the other side, falling flat on her face. But she leapt with all her might into Asira's arms. "Oh my goodness! Asira, you are okay!"

"Hey Cara, I have missed you too!"

Eoin steadily walked across the room. "Bluebird?"

Asira glanced up over Cara's shoulder and smiled. "Hi Eoin, it's good to see you. I'm so glad you're okay." As soon as Cara moved back, Eoin took his chance. His feet moved faster than lightning as he snatched her into a mighty bearhug. He just wanted to hold onto her for as long as he could.

"Me? Bluebird, I thought you were dead. No one told me anything. I was left in the dark. I really thought I had lost you."

An arm slipped around her waist and tugged her from his grip. Asira giggled and glanced back at Anton.

"Well, to be honest, I thought I was a goner as well. Look, I'm really sorry I haven't arranged this meet-up sooner, but I've been undergoing a lot of medical check-ups and therapeutic sessions and I still am. I really hope you guys understand."

"I can't believe you were so selfish, Asira." Angelica pushed herself in next to Eoin. "Like, you ran off and fought a warlock by yourself. We could have protected you and fought by your side." Angelica folded her arms in disgust and closed her eyes, peeking very slightly.

"Thanks Angelica!" Asira wrapped her arms around her neck. "You are so brave, and I am sorry. You're right. I should have waited for you guys."

"If you have faced death…" Katie began.

"You should have no problem flying with me again!" Zayne continued.

"Oh Asira, I've been working really hard on that portal spell. But it's actually really exhausting," Fabia squealed.

"Tell me about it!" Asira giggled.

"What is going to happen with the school?" Peter asked fixing the soft material around his arm.

Asira glanced over at him. "Peter! You're not wearing your hat. I love the new look!"

"It is a pleasure to see everyone again looking alive and healthy," Volknor said with a big smile as he and Kai stepped into the dining room. "I hope you have enjoyed the well-deserved rest at home?"

"Master Volknor, Master Kai, is the school closing?" Peter asked again.

"Well, that is an interesting question." Volknor took a step back and glanced at Kai.

"As Head of Council," Kai began, "I feel it is in everyone's best interests, in terms of safety and continued progress, if the school remains open on a permanent basis."

"WHAT! Really?" Mandy squealed with excitement grabbing Britanie by the wrists and jumping up and down.

"Of course, it would be up to each individual if they would like to return as the senior class of Velosian Academy. No one would hold it against any of you, especially after what has transpired, if you did not want to return," Kai stated.

The room was silent for a few moments. A strange tension began to build between the young teens as they recalled the events which injured all of them but also killed many.

"Myself, Anton and Aaron have already signed up for the new term," Asira finally broke the silence.

Eoin gazed up in shock. From the corner of his eye, he caught Anton glaring across at him again. "I would like to return."

"I will have to check with mummy, but I would like to return." Fabia raised her hand.

"Actually, my uncle was encouraging me to come back," Thomas added. "He said it would be a good way to learn about controlling my powers and training to rule in the future."

Kai cleared his throat. "Of course, you will all have time to think this through. The Academy will not be re-opening until later on in the year. In the meantime, I have organised a dinner for you all." As Kai finished speaking, five butlers stepped out of the adjoining kitchen doors and began setting the table.

The table was quickly set. Large trolleys were wheeled from the kitchen. Bottles of pink and red lemonade were poured into wine glasses.

Cara picked up a fork. "Asira, do not worry, I will talk you through the use of the forks and knives." Cara sat next to Anton and he was to Asira's left.

Eoin managed to get the only other seat next to Asira. He happily watched and listened to Asira laugh and joke. She chatted away to everyone around the table describing her therapeutic sessions and medical check-ups.

"It was weird at first being back at home." Britanie sat next to Mandy in the seats across from Asira.

"Yes Asira, once we were all checked over, they sent us home. In the space of seven hours after leaving Topaz Castle I was back at home in the Amazon." Mandy stretched across the table and grabbed the plate of garlic bread.

"Daddy has been very protective. If it was not for the recent council meeting, I do not think I would have been allowed to come back. My parents are very frightened. Our people in the Maria Empire are very frightened," Cara spoke glumly.

"Hey Eoin," Asira turned around, "I think you owe me a milk-shake."

"Anytime, Bluebird." He gazed fondly at her, mesmerised by her inspiring spirit and her intoxicating laugh. She was perfect.

"Eoin," Bobby stretched across Peter and whispered, "I know that look." He nodded covertly towards Asira. "Just be careful. I would hate to see you get hurt."

Eoin stared down at his plate and played with the leftover food. He knew Bobby was right. Asira was with Anton and Anton had made that very clear. There would be no point in pursuing her. But he could not turn off his feelings. He knew what he felt, and he had felt this way for a long while. Was she worth pursuing? If he felt so strongly, was it worth mentioning? Would it ease the tightness in his chest?

Her intoxicating laugh gripped his attention once again. She had been through so much and now she actually looked genuinely happy and healthy. For now, he was content with that. But he still pondered the thought, 'If I told Asira how I feel, would she – could she feel the same?'

Please Review

Dear Reader,

If you enjoyed this book, would you kindly post a short review on Amazon or Goodreads? Your feedback will make all the difference to getting the word out about this book.

Thank you in advance.

Author Biography

Ila Quinn, author of the debut novel
Cinders & Rime from *The Eternal series*

Website: www.ilaquinnauthor.com

Instagram & Facebook: @ila.quinn.
author

Goodreads: www.goodreads.com/
user/show/129198933-ila-quinn

I la Quinn was born in Dublin and now lives in Wexford with
her family and beloved corgi. She has a love for rich cultures
and chose to study history and web design in college.

Ila is an avid reader of YA fiction, fantasy and romance and is
an admirer of all types of literature and adaptations from novels
to manga's – both have distinctive art-styles with well-designed
and interesting characters and allow for a variety of important
and relevant worldly topics from love, war, history and social
constructs. Fiction is central for development, growth and imag-

ination, while fantasy only enhances our creative thinking. Ila has a vivid imagination and this is evident in her writing. Her adoration for writing began with fan fiction and grew immensely until she decided to take the next step by composing and publishing her debut novel.

9 781914 225239